JONATHAN JANZ

WOLF LAND

This is a **FLAME TREE PRESS** book

FLAME TREE PRESS
6 Melbray Mews, London, SW6 3NS, UK
flametreepress.com

Distribution and warehouse:
Marston Book Services Ltd
160 Eastern Avenue, Milton Park, Abingdon, Oxon, OX14 4SB
www.marston.co.uk

Thanks to the Flame Tree Press team, including:
Taylor Bentley, Frances Bodiam, Federica Ciaravella, Don D'Auria,
Chris Herbert, Matteo Middlemiss, Josie Mitchell, Mike Spender,
Cat Taylor, Maria Tissot, Nick Wells, Gillian Whitaker.

The cover is created by Flame Tree Studio with
thanks to Nik Keevil and Shutterstock.com.
The font families in this book are Avenir and Bembo.

Flame Tree Press is an imprint of Flame Tree Publishing Ltd
flametreepublishing.com

A copy of the CIP data for this book is available from the British Library.

HB ISBN: 978-1-78758-152-4
PB ISBN: 978-1-78758-151-7
ebook ISBN: 978-1-78758-153-1
Also available in FLAME TREE AUDIO

Printed in the UK at Clays, Suffolk

JONATHAN JANZ

WOLF LAND

FLAME TREE PRESS
London & New York

This is for the late Jack Ketchum (Dallas Mayr). You were always there for me, and you showed me and so many others what true kindness looks like. You were the main influence on this novel, and your work continues to influence me. Thank you, Dallas, for everything.

First off, a warning. This novel started out as one thing and turned into something quite different. I don't apologize for the graphic content in this book, but I do like readers to know what they're getting into. This one, friends, is dark – probably darker than anything I've ever written.

…One legend, dismissed for centuries as apocryphal, was deemed veracious by several important folklorists of the medieval and Renaissance eras. Though the accounts differ in some respects, they dovetail with regard to the following particulars:

There lived a trio of sisters in a remote, densely wooded region of what is now known as Belarus. Predictably, the small village of Berstuk was brutally patriarchal and treated women despicably – especially attractive young women like the Antonov sisters. One sister had flowing golden hair, the other two black and red. Since very little is known of thirteenth-century Berstuk, folklorists differ regarding the sisters' motivations for what would follow. One source claims that all three sisters were serially abused – sexually or otherwise – by their male family members. Another source hypothesises that it was Divna, the eldest sister, who sought retribution for a rape at the hands of a village elder, and who coerced her two younger sisters into joining her quest for revenge.

Whatever the case, the entire village of Berstuk was thriving in the spring of the year 1202. By the summer of the same year every last man, woman and child had been slaughtered by what were at the time called *vucari*, or what are now referred to as werewolves.

Were this account isolated to a wildly superstitious peasantry, the tale of the Antonov sisters would warrant little further investigation.

Yet for the next half millennium there exist accounts of three voluptuous sisters – blond, black, and red-haired – wreaking havoc throughout the forests of Russia, Eastern Europe, even mid-eighteenth century France. In each account there are three young women of extraordinary physical beauty, and each account ends with startling violence. If indeed the Antonov sisters were lycanthropes, they were lycanthropes of the sort that did not age, that feared no authority, and that killed without remorse.

The last trace of Divna and her sisters might be found in the tale of an 1883 transatlantic voyage that ended with a nightmarish vision: a British steamer – the *Prosperity* – running aground in Boston Harbour with its entire passenger list of ninety-two travellers and crew members decapitated. In many cases, the bodies had been devoured by what the perplexed American authorities deemed 'wild animals'.

If the murders were indeed committed by the Antonov sisters, it is the last known record of their horrific exploits. There have been no accounts of them since…

Dr. Clark Lombardo Coulter PhD
Lycanthropology

PART ONE
MARKED

CHAPTER ONE

A few hours before she witnessed the slaughter of her former classmates, Savannah was shovelling down her second bowl of spaghetti. "Maybe I'll just stay here," she said.

From the other side of the kitchen, Barb Callahan eyed her without sympathy. "You always eat this much when you're nervous?"

"I hate wearing lipstick anyway. This'll motivate me to wipe it off before I go."

"That was supposed to be a half-hour ago."

Savannah eyed Barb, who stood across the sleek quartz island from her nursing a glass of Riesling. The vision was slightly incongruous. In her mid-fifties, her brown hair showing some grey, Barb was six-foot-two and broad all over. If she hadn't known the woman better, Savannah would've pegged her for a beer drinker. Or maybe tequila.

"Jake will be fine," Barb said.

Savannah dropped her fork with a clatter and crossed her arms. "I didn't say anything about Jake."

"I'm just taking away the excuse before it occurs to you."

Savannah arched an eyebrow. "Do you always have to be so ruthless?"

"I'm babysitting, aren't I?"

"Yeah, but that's because you enjoy it."

Barb sipped her wine but didn't otherwise answer.

Savannah glanced toward the living room, where Jake was playing with Barb's considerable collection of Lincoln Logs.

Barb said, "You've already said goodbye to him. Twice."

Savannah spread her arms. "Maybe I want to again. Is there something wrong with that?"

"When you're being chickenshit, yes."

"Hey!"

"You told Joyce you'd be there tonight, right?"

Savannah looked away, shrugged. "Maybe."

"And she hardly knows anybody else at this shindig."

"She knows Short Pump a little."

"That's one of the worst goddamned nicknames I've ever heard."

"It's what we've called him since high school."

"Most people are idiots in high school."

Savannah fished her compact out of her purse, studied her reflection and frowned. "Some don't get much smarter afterward."

"Can't argue with that."

Savannah made a face, shook her head. "But that's the problem. It'll be just like high school." She reached out, fiddled with the strap of her purse, but made no move to pick it up. "The reunion's next week. I don't see why we have to hang out the week before too. Isn't once painful enough?"

"Why don't you quit bullshitting and admit you're afraid of seeing Mike again?"

Savannah compressed her lips. "That's not what I need."

And it wasn't. Not remotely.

Yes, she and Mike had been a thing back in high school, and yes, she'd assumed they'd get married after graduation. But what irked her – no, what wounded her deeply – was how wrapped up Mike was with everything that had gone wrong in her life. The disappointment at being abandoned by him after high school. The muddled college years. The return to Lakeview. Then the pregnancy and her parents' nightmarish ostracising of her and Jake, like they were in seventeenth century New England or something.

Now here she was, ten years out of high school, working a thankless job, with only three real friends in the world – Joyce, Barb, and Short Pump – though Short Pump hardly counted since he wanted in her pants.

Barb was staring at her.

"What?" Savannah asked. "More criticism?"

Barb's eyes narrowed. "This isn't just about Mike, is it?"

Savannah heaved a shuddering sigh, marched over to the wine bottle, and poured herself a glass. She downed a third of it in a swallow.

"Easy on that stuff," Barb said.

"I'm not going to wrap my car around a telephone pole. I just need to calm my nerves."

"What do you have to be nervous about?"

"Not being a good role model for Jake."

"What, drinking?"

Savannah rolled her eyes. "It's just...I should be doing more with my life. I'm tired of working for a misogynistic lawyer who thinks I'm too stupid to alphabetise files."

"Are you?"

Savannah saluted her with a middle finger.

"So find another job," Barb said.

"Where?" Savannah gestured toward town. "At McDonald's? The Super-Walmart?"

"You've got a degree."

"In graphic design," Savannah snapped. "How many graphic design jobs are there in Lakeview?"

"I wouldn't think very many."

"Exactly."

"So move."

Instead of answering, Savannah took another sip of wine.

Barb said, "Your folks have long since moved away, and they were assholes to begin with. You've only got a few friends. What's keeping you here?"

Savannah crossed her arms, stared at the older woman. "What do you want me to say? Fear? Cowardice? Being a slave to routine?"

"Can I choose all of the above?"

"This isn't helping."

"Who says I'm trying to help?"

"Barb, you don't understand—"

"I understand your life didn't turn out like you wanted it to. You hitched your wagon to the wrong horse."

"That's a lousy way to put it."

"You're only what, twenty-eight? Your boy's young. He hasn't even started kindergarten yet. Why not move now?"

Savannah's mouth worked mutely for a moment. She blew a lock of blond hair out of her eyes. "Okay, where?"

"Somewhere with more opportunity than Lakeview."

"And where is that?"

"Throw a dart at the map."

Savannah slouched on the island, exhaled wearily. "I'm late."

"Then get your ass in gear. Poor Joyce is probably having to fend off advances from that Weiner guy."

Savannah chuckled. "His name's Weezer. And he's not that bad."

"Unctuous little creep is what he is."

Savannah left the half-empty wine glass on the counter and grabbed her purse. At the doorway she looked back over her shoulder. "You ever thought of being a trifle more sympathetic?"

"You mean enable you to wallow in self-pity? Nope. Not in my nature."

Savannah strode over and crouched beside Jake. He'd erected a knee-high tower of Lincoln Logs, the structure impressive but alarmingly bowed in the middle. He had the blue plastic roof poised over the tower, his tongue poking out the corner of his mouth in concentration.

Savannah knew where this was going.

"Jakers?" she said. "Can Mommy put the roof on for you?"

"I can do it," Jake said, his eyes never wavering from his task.

He dropped the roof from a distance of perhaps three inches, but the impact was forceful enough to collapse the tower to ruins. Jake made a fist, punched his leg. His lower lip quivered.

"It's okay," she said, removing the roof from the rubble. "Can Mommy help you rebuild your tower?"

"It's a haunted house," Jake said. "The one at Beach Land."

"Ah," she said, clearing the foundation and beginning the job of restacking the logs. "Is it a scary one?"

He nodded. "The scariest place in the world." He joined her in rebuilding the structure. After they'd worked for a minute or two, he said, "Mommy?"

"Yes?"

"Thanks."

She kissed his forehead and continued to stack the logs. The bonfire could wait a little while longer.

★   ★   ★

Duane hated being designated driver. Especially for Weezer. Glenn was never too rowdy when he drank, but Weezer...there was no predicting what kind of behaviour Weezer would exhibit when he got blitzed.

Glenn braced an elbow in the passenger window of Duane's royal blue Chevy Silverado. "You talked to Savannah lately?"

Duane glanced at him. Glenn's tone had been too casual, too inflectionless. *You're not going to start that again, are you?* he wanted to ask.

But instead, Duane said, "She said she'd come if she could find a sitter."

From the backseat, Weezer said, "Tell her to drop her kid off at that dyke's house."

Duane winced. Jesus. He asked himself for perhaps the thousandth time why he still hung out with Weezer. The guy made racial jokes, discriminated against all kinds of people. On many occasions, Duane had suspected him of having impure thoughts about girls who were far too young to be daydreamed about.

As if to confirm this misgiving, Weezer said, "Any high school chicks gonna be there tonight?"

Glenn shook his head. "For Christ's sakes, Weezer."

"What?" Weezer asked. "I didn't say I was gonna do anything with 'em."

"Right," Duane said. "You just want their opinions on the current state of music."

"Shit, I don't need opinions on that. Music today sucks ass."

Duane fell silent, deciding he couldn't argue with that.

But Weezer was not to be put off. "You had sex with girls back in high school, Glenn. What makes it so different now?"

Glenn half-turned in his seat. "Do I really need to explain it to you?"

"I'm asking, aren't I?"

"The difference," Glenn said, an edge to his voice, "is that I'm not in high school anymore. Am, in fact, a decade removed from high school. Which is why you need to stop talking about this shit." He shook his head. "You keep it up, we're going to have to register you as a sex offender."

Duane laughed.

"Don't see what's so funny, *Short Pump*," Weezer said. Duane stiffened at the utterance of his nickname. "You know you'd go for some young hottie if she showed an interest in you."

Duane's fingers tightened on the wheel as he took a left onto County Road 250. "I wouldn't if she was underage. That's just sick."

"Shit," Weezer said. "With a belly as big as yours, you can't be too choosy. Am I right, Glenn?"

Glenn's face was expressionless. "I think you need to stop drinking, Weezer. You're already being an asshole."

"That's the problem with the world," Weezer said meditatively. "Not enough honesty. I say what's on my mind, and you two get all high and mighty on me."

Duane glanced at him in the rearview mirror. "That's because you're being disgusting."

Weezer glugged from the beer can, wiped his mouth. "'*Disgusting*'? Man, you know how prissy you sound?"

Duane focused on the road, resolved not to let Weezer put him in a bad mood.

But Weezer wouldn't shut up. "You know, Short Pump, if you worked out a little more, lost some of that weight you're carrying, you might get some pussy now and then. You're what, six-four? Think how good you'd look if you were built like me and Glenn."

Glenn grunted. "Weezer, you're built like a scarecrow."

Weezer chugged more beer. "Least I'm not obese."

Duane felt sweat beads forming on his upper lip. *One of these days*, he thought. *One of these days I'm really going to snap.*

And like a stubborn turd that refused to be flushed, a memory of Duane's parents arose. The day he'd gotten cut from the junior high basketball team, the coach having told him he was too passive to contribute. Duane had made the mistake of relaying the coach's words to his parents. He'd hoped his mom and dad would – for once – support him, but when he saw the looks on their faces he knew they were only going to make him feel worse.

His dad: "I told you he wouldn't make it."

"There's still football," his mom said.

His dad scoffed. "Hell. If he's too passive to play basketball, he'll get his dome ripped off on the football field."

Duane dared not say a word. He no more wanted to play football than he wanted to masturbate with sandpaper.

From across the dinner table, his dad's bloodshot eyes squinted at him. "Did you do any of the things I taught you? Did you play a lick of defence? Get a single goddamned rebound?"

His mom put a hand on his dad's arm but didn't otherwise intervene.

Duane stared down at his bowl of chilli. For once he wasn't hungry.

"I tried to," Duane said, "but the other boys were quicker. I...I couldn't jump as high."

"Couldn't *jump* as high?" his dad said, his rheumy eyes widening. "Jesus Christ, son, with an ass that big, all you had to do was block out and wait for the ball to come to you."

Duane studied his chilli.

His mom said, "Maybe you can ask the coach for another chance. He always did such a great job with your brothers."

His father grunted. "That's because his brothers knew how to work for something. Not a one of them as big as Duane, and they all ended up starting varsity."

Duane withdrew, knowing all of this by heart. The varsity letters. The sectional championships. His oldest brother getting hurt his senior year and going no further athletically, but his next two brothers getting partial scholarships to play ball at Division II schools.

His father was still rambling. "...does is play video games and watch those damned slasher movies. It's no wonder he's so goddamned flabby."

"Honey," his mom said.

"Well, dammit, it's the truth!"

And Duane just sat there and took it like always. While he tried and failed not to cry. It made him wish there were no such thing as sports, or maybe just wish that he'd been born smaller. Then there'd be no pressure, no expectation. Most of all, no disappointment when he—

"Hey!" a voice shouted. "You missed the goddamned turn!"

Duane jolted back to himself, saw he'd indeed motored right by the lane leading to the Marvins' land.

"What the hell is wrong with you, Short Pump?" Weezer demanded. "It's like you're dreaming about eating a chocolate cake up there."

Duane glanced askance, noticed Glenn was scanning the row of cars along the country road.

"He's not here," Glenn said in an undertone.

Duane shifted in his seat. He thought for a second that Weezer wouldn't pick up on Glenn's train of thought, but then Weezer said, "If Freehafer does show up, you're gonna kick his ass, right?"

Hell, Duane thought.

He'd been best friends with Glenn and Weezer for a long time, but he'd also been close to Savannah forever, and because of that, he'd naturally been friends with Mike Freehafer back in high school. Glenn and Weezer had always given Duane shit about it, as though by treating Mike decently Duane had been betraying them. Duane didn't particularly fancy the notion of dredging up those old animosities tonight. Or ever.

"Maybe he won't show up," Glenn said.

"If Savannah's here, he sure as hell will," Weezer said. "Hell, I would if I was Mike."

This time Glenn turned all the way around in his seat. The look he gave Weezer made Duane's balls shrink.

"What, man? What'd I say?" Weezer asked.

Glenn stared hard at Weezer for a good ten seconds. Then he faced the road again, his expression stony.

Duane decelerated and prayed Glenn wouldn't go apeshit on Weezer.

Glenn glowered straight ahead and said nothing.

A half-mile beyond the lane, Duane checked the rearview mirror, executed the U-turn, and headed back toward their destination.

No one spoke again until they reached the bonfire.

CHAPTER TWO

Mike Freehafer parked his rusty white Yukon and studied the gleaming chain of thirty vehicles strung along the sloping, grassy shoulder. It was still twilight, but the orange western glow was rapidly giving way to violet. In another hour or so, full night would descend upon the countryside.

Stepping out of the Yukon, Mike inspected the line of cars unspooling before him, trying to spot one or two that were maybe familiar.

Who was he kidding? He was looking for Savannah's yellow MG convertible.

He smiled ruefully and slammed shut the door.

Making his way down the blacktop toward the metal gate, Mike decided she'd probably given up the MG since he'd seen her last. That was how long ago? *Man*, he thought. More than five years.

His throat tightened up, a dark throb of guilt starting in his chest. He questioned the logic of showing up here tonight. Granted, he'd been invited. Hunter and Brian Marvin, twins he'd known since elementary school, had made it a point to stop by Mike's dad's house when they heard Mike was in town, to invite him to their bonfire. Their parents owned a hell of a lot of land, and they'd partied here all through high school. The way the Marvins had made it sound, returning to the old forest would be a blast: tons of girls and more booze than anyone could handle.

But as Mike approached the pasture gate, he felt foolish, like a over-the-hill actor playing a sports star in some dreary straight-to-video movie.

Hell, he thought, stepping over the waist-high gate. He wished he hadn't thought of sports. Because it brought back the tide of memories that had ultimately forced him to seek professional help, to begin medication for depression. Zoloft, the drug was called, though Mike was taking some generic crap because it was cheaper, and his insurance sucked.

He started toward the forest, keeping to one of the wheel ruts that threaded through the weedy lane. He should be feeling giddy about this, about seeing the old gang and catching up. Instead he felt like he was marching to his execution. But rather than a climb to the gallows and a snapped neck, he'd be tortured slowly, the last decade of his life vivisected by everyone who'd thought he'd make it big.

Who were no doubt delighted he'd failed.

Mike faltered and stared at the forest's rim.

He shouldn't be here.

If life were fair, he'd be playing for the Cubs, who were in San Diego tonight. Were, in fact, starting in half an hour.

But instead he was here. Standing in a pasture on a Sunday night, the smell of cow flops overwhelming his cheap cologne. He heard the music. Predictably, Steve Miller's 'The Joker'. The kind of shit they listened to in high school.

Then he'd been drafted. The fourteenth pick of the first round. The Chicago Cubs. His favourite team. His *dad's* favourite team. They'd been to how many games over the years? Fifty? A hundred? Going to Wrigley Field was like going home, and when he heard his name called – his parents had thrown a party that day – the whole house had erupted. The whole *town* had erupted. Hell, it was the biggest thing in Lakeview since...well, since maybe ever, unless you counted the tornado of 1973, and that was only famous because it had been so destructive. In comparison, Mike's being drafted should have been a good thing, the town's favourite son going off to deliver the Cubs from their century-long misery.

He'd barely made it past Single-A.

Actually wouldn't have made it past Single-A had the Cubs not been so bullish about his potential. They were disappointed in his first month's batting average, sure. How could they not be disappointed when he was sitting at .219? But they'd drafted him for his raw power, for his lightning swing, and had promoted him to Double-A Tennessee not for his performance, but for his potential. And as a result, the players at Tennessee had treated him like a spoiled kid who'd been handed everything he had, who no more deserved to play professional ball than the fucking mascot.

Then Mike hit like the fucking mascot.

.130 in June.

.112 in July.

He'd actually strung together a fairly respectable string of games in early August, which earned him a call from the team president. *You're really putting it together, Mike. This is precisely why we drafted you. Just keep raking and you'll sniff Triple-A soon. Then it'll be the fast track to the big leagues, slugger, and you'll be holding down third base for the next decade at Wrigley Field.*

Except he didn't hold down anything. Could barely hold down his lunch the next day because all he kept thinking about was the team president having all that faith in him.

If Mike hated anything, it was people having faith in him.

Why? he wanted to cry out. *Why the hell would you have faith in me? Even worse, why would you squander the fourteenth pick on me?*

If the team president had just left him alone, he might have made something of himself. Instead, he went out that day and struck out four times.

Four. Fucking. Times.

And it wasn't like the opposing pitcher was a juggernaut either. He was a minor league lifer, just roster filler. A guy whose rubber arm was lucky to break eighty-five miles an hour.

Yet he made Mike look like a goddamned moron.

The first at-bat, he swung at and missed all three pitches. But at least they were close pitches and they were good swings.

The second time, that had been worse. Disconcertingly worse. He'd taken two good pitches and then told himself the dickhead pitcher – who looked older than Mike's father – would certainly not throw another one right down the middle.

The dickhead threw one right down the middle.

Mike plopped down on the bench. His teammates eyed him with open disdain.

Third time up, Mike damn near screwed himself into the ground, he swung so hard. Too bad the pitcher's control was off and the ball was spraying all over the place like Uzi fire. Had Mike gotten hold of one, he would have sent it over the state line. As it was, he only succeeded in embarrassing himself, on one swing actually blundering into the umpire and landing at the obese man's feet.

"You're out," the umpire said.

The fourth time, that wasn't quite as bad. At least he didn't fall at the umpire's feet like some uncoordinated penitent. But the at-bat still wasn't good. Four pitches. Two called strikes. One swinging strike.

You're guessing, the Tennessee manager told him when he slunk back to the dugout.

I guess I don't have it tonight, Mike said and ventured a grin. It was a grin that had won the hearts of many people over his first eighteen years.

The manager didn't return the grin.

You need to learn how to hit, he told Mike.

Mike glared at him.

I know how to hit, he'd answered.

The manager gave him a dour look. *Sure doesn't look like it.*

Mike's confidence, already meagre, had dwindled.

He struggled through the rest of August.

The team president was ominously silent. No phone calls offering encouragement. No pep talks from the manager, who seemed to think Mike had the skill of a mentally challenged otter. The year ended as miserably as it had begun, and Mike was thrust into a primeval training regimen designed to, in the team president's words, "reboot his approach at the plate by restructuring his mental, emotional and physical makeup".

Translation: *Start hitting or we'll void your fucking contract.*

The experience was gruelling, humiliating. The team president was a progressive thinker, or so he liked to proclaim. He employed a New Age mystic to help Mike align his priorities with the franchise's. A former Olympic silver medalist wrestler to alter Mike's body.

That first week, Mike thought he would die. By the end of the first month, he'd learned that his physical being wasn't actually real. He was simply vapour being directed by his spiritual core.

Then why do my legs hurt so much? he asked the mystic.

You are shackled by material matter, the mystic answered.

But despite being utterly befuddled by the mystic – who told him his aura needed cleansing, and promptly changed his entire diet to one bereft of grains, milk and fibre – Mike didn't hit the ball any better than he had before. Now, he was not only terrible at recognising breaking pitches, he was paranoid, hungry and constipated.

He was finished with minor league ball after three catastrophic years.

He refused to go back to Lakeview.

The friends he'd considered losers were still there, but rather than attending high school during the day and hanging out in the Burger King parking lot at night, they were working shitty jobs during the day and hanging out in the Burger King parking lot at night.

Mike refused to work a shitty job. And he sure as hell didn't want to hang out in a parking lot, comparing engine sizes.

But by that time the friends Mike considered intelligent were already most of the way through college. If Mike had started his college education at twenty-one, he'd have been twenty-five by the time he finished. Problem was, he didn't have a clue what he wanted to be because he'd always thought he'd be a major league baseball player. Getting drafted in the first round had seemed to cement that fate.

Turned out, the only thing being the fourteenth pick had cemented was the precipitousness of his fall.

Mike grew depressed.

At first he didn't think he needed medication. *It's not a chemical issue*, he'd told one girlfriend, a woman eight years his senior, *it's my situation. I'm really goddamned tired of disappointing everyone, and it makes me screw up even worse. I'm buckling under the pressure.*

Maybe you were just overdrafted, the woman had said.

Mike had stared at her, appalled. How the hell had she even *known* such a word, much less understood how aptly it applied to Mike?

So at twenty-one, Mike had tried to hedge his bets by joining a semipro team, thinking to work out his contact issues there.

This had proven one of the most disastrous decisions of his life.

Because the guys in semipro were even more toxic than the guys in Double-A. They were okay to him at first because they didn't know who he was. He'd moved to Pennsylvania thinking he could eventually try out for one of the East Coast major league teams.

But someone had googled his name and informed the entire league of his story. How he'd been drafted fourteenth, how he'd crashed and burned.

They found out about his signing bonus.

It was this fact that damned him. The guys he played against were mostly in their late twenties and thirties, and they knew they'd never make more than ten or fifteen grand playing ball. But the fact that he, a guy whose only success had come against high school pitching, had been gifted a seven-figure signing bonus was too much for them.

They set out to destroy him.

Oh, no one tried to kill him or anything – unless you counted leading the league in hit-by-pitches as attempted murder – but they insulted him mercilessly, conspired to exclude him from team functions, batted him eighth in the order and generally did all they could to force him out of the league.

It worked.

But he still couldn't return to Lakeview. He especially couldn't face his high school sweetheart.

Savannah Summers was, if the reports he'd gotten from his few remaining Lakeview friends were true, even hotter than she'd been in high school. He and Savannah had been prom king and queen, and had been considered a sure thing to get married. But Mike had developed an inflated sense of worth after being selected by the Cubs, and he'd pretty much shunned Savannah after leaving town.

He figured she'd spit in his face if he ever showed up again.

What he did do was finally swallow his pride enough to go to Dayton University. His thinking was simple. He'd already alienated the people he knew in Indiana, Tennessee, and Pennsylvania. Ohio wasn't tainted yet.

It was by the end of his freshman year.

The thing Mike hated most about technology was how easy it was for people to find out about you. He'd met a girl he really liked and dated her for most of the year. He'd left out the story of his failed baseball career because he didn't know how she'd react. And sure enough, when she found out about his past, she lost all trust in him and branded him a predator.

This was because he'd claimed to be eighteen, like her, rather than twenty-two, which he was. At eighteen, he figured, there weren't four years to account for. So he lied. And got busted.

And dropped out of college.

He saw Savannah once, but he couldn't think about that now. Too painful. He proceeded to knock around at a series of crappy jobs in Ohio and southern Indiana for a few years. One night when he was twenty-five, he was boozing at a local dive in Jasper, Indiana, when on a whim, he decided to tell a hot Hispanic chick about his baseball career, such as it was. She had just turned twenty-one, and as a result was even drunker than he was. Mike had gotten pretty good at getting laid, and since he figured he'd be able to seduce the Hispanic girl no matter what he said to her, he told her the truth.

The problem was, the more he said to her, the more he felt he should give the story a more interesting ending. Being cut by the Cubs just wasn't a good climax. It wasn't happy, obviously, but it didn't even have the sexiness of tragedy. It just…ended. So Mike told her he'd been hit in the face by a fastball.

She'd practically straddled him on the barstool.

Yeah, he'd continued, rubbing the scar beside his left eye. *Right here.*

Bastard had a hundred-mile-per-hour heater, and he pegged me right in the temple. It took four reconstructive surgeries and years of rehab just to be able to drive a car again.

Poor baby, the Hispanic girl had said.

Then they'd rutted like animals.

Mike took his tragic pitch on the road. Working construction now, he was able to move around a lot, live the life of a womanising nomad. He retold his tragic tale to hundreds of women over the next several years, and astonishingly, very few of them failed to put out. They'd never know the truth about his baseball career, never know the real cause of his scar: jumping on and falling off a bed when he was four years old.

The sex had been grand.

But over the past year, something unsettling had taken place.

It happened, fittingly enough, when Mike was leaving the apartment of some skank he'd picked up. He was driving the same Chevy Yukon he'd purchased with his signing bonus – the money was almost gone by this time – and had pulled into traffic thinking the road was clear.

He got sideswiped by a Honda Civic.

Had it been any other vehicle, he would have been killed. As it was, he was left with a massive deductible and a disturbing question.

How had he not seen the Civic?

He'd looked twice before turning. As irresponsible as Mike was in his private life, he'd never been a reckless driver. The roadway had been clear before he'd turned. He was sure of it.

So he dismissed it as bad luck and went on with his life.

And had another crash.

This one had been scarier, a lane change screwup on Highway 65. He'd checked to make sure no one was in his blind spot, even craning his head around the way they taught you in driver's ed, but when he moved into the left lane, his back bumper had clipped a black Mustang, and then he was skidding sideways and flipping three times in the grassy median.

You're fortunate to be alive, the doctor told him that night in intensive care.

Mike had stared at him. *How did it happen?*

You were at fault, the doctor said. *The police will need to talk to you.*

Black dread lapped at Mike like polluted seawater. *Is the other driver all right?*

The driver is in stable condition, the doctor said.

Mike swallowed. *Were there other...*

There was a teenage girl.

Mike had stared at the white-haired doctor and tried to make sense of the verb tense. *There was a teenage girl. There was a teenage girl. Was. Was. Was...*

Not only was the girl dead, but the girl's father was rich. Able to afford good lawyers. Which they promptly sicced on Mike.

Bonus money, gone.

Future gone too.

He only just avoided jail.

It turned out he had a degenerative eye condition that had robbed him of most of his vision in his left eye. The main eye he'd used to identify pitches. The eye he'd claimed to have had injured by the mythical hundred-mile-per-hour fastball.

The irony was so thick it smothered him.

He had returned home a couple weeks ago. It had been a few weeks shy of a decade.

His parents knew all about his failed career, knew all about his accident. He'd written them letters, but he'd never called them and had certainly never seen them. They'd gotten divorced, it turned out. His mom had decided that sleeping around beat monogamy.

Mike decided he didn't want to see his mom anymore.

He didn't enjoy seeing his dad either. Because everything was about baseball. *You see who the Cubs called up the other day?* Or, *The Cubbies need a third baseman.*

Trying to find ways to broach the subject with Mike.

Mike asked, *Is Savannah Summers still in town?*

Yep. Has a kid, his dad said. Dropping it on him just like that.

Then his dad said, much too casually, *You ever go to the batting cages? You know, like the ones they have at that go-cart place in town?*

The thing was, Mike didn't want to talk about baseball with his dad. Didn't want to talk about baseball with *anybody.* He'd rather have his penis snagged by a rusty fishhook than talk about how he'd failed with the Cubs.

After a time, Mike reached the bonfire. The groups of people clustered around the kegs, the grill. Several pairs and trios dotted the clearing, guys telling stories with raised voices, pairs who were clearly on the verge of hooking up.

Christ, he thought. *Just like high school.*

He'd made a mistake coming out here so late, everybody already buzzed or drunk.

Was Savannah here? If she was, he hoped she was good and liquored up. Not so he could have sex with her, but because he was terrified of facing her, terrified of what she'd say.

Thanks a lot for leaving me.

How dare you come back? You've got some nerve.

I just happened to bring this rusty fishhook.

But he knew if he stood here in the shadows, he'd lose his nerve, and then he'd spend the rest of the evening listening to his dad cook up new and increasingly more transparent ways of asking him what went wrong with his baseball career. And it was this prospect that galvanised him, that got him moving forward into the clearing, where he saw Savannah Summers for the first time in five years.

CHAPTER THREE

When Weezer spotted Mike Freehafer, he knew there'd be trouble, but not the kind of trouble Weezer enjoyed. Not the kind where a pretty boy like Mike got his ass kicked. First off, Mike wouldn't fight Glenn because he knew he'd get trounced. Secondly, Glenn wouldn't do anything Savannah didn't want him to. Such was her hold on him.

Weezer's lip curled into an unconscious snarl. Savannah was a stuck-up bitch. She'd never given Weezer the time of day.

Now Melody Bridwell...

She'd never encouraged Weezer, but she'd never *discouraged* him either. And unlike Savannah, Melody had a reputation for loving dick.

Weezer crossed the clearing, met Melody at the keg.

"Hey, Mel," he said.

"Hey, Weezer," she said. And looked away.

Weezer felt his smile slip. "You craving another beer?"

She raised her cup. "Just got one."

He hesitated, considering this new development.

"So I'm good," she added.

Weezer turned away before she could see his expression change. The whore. It wasn't like her standards were so high that she couldn't consider having sex with him.

Weezer waited until she wasn't looking; then he allowed his eyes to crawl over her body.

Hot damn. *That* was why he was willing to put up with her haughty attitude.

That ass.

The jean shorts were perfectly snug, a dark strip of midriff visible between the waistband and the bloodred tank top. He leaned to his left so he could better see her tummy, and what a tummy it was.

He bet it was a better stomach than Savannah's, which had already spat out a kid. No matter how hot Savannah looked, under those clothes he suspected her body was wrecked beyond repair.

He had a sudden, unwelcome memory of the one and only time he'd had sex with a girl who'd had a kid. Disgusting. Shrivelled belly, the damned thing looked like overripe fruit collapsing on itself, like it would split open at any moment and belch flies.

And the tits? As limp as deflated windsocks. Sure, she'd probably had big knockers while she nursed, but the moment her screeching urchin was weaned, those things flattened out like elongated pancakes. Staring at those dead, dangling dugs was like examining the pages of a *National Geographic*, those native African ladies with bones through their lips and tits so long they dragged in the sand.

With a jolt he realised Melody had caught him staring. "You're making me uncomfortable," she said.

Weezer's mouth drooped open.

"Here's what's going to happen," she said slowly. "You're going to walk away and not talk to me again tonight." Her eyes swept him up and down. "Preferably not ever. I'm not interested in you. At all. Does that make sense?"

Weezer blinked three or four times, as though there were a stiff breeze blowing his way. Then the hurt began to seep in.

And the anger.

The flaming *bitch*.

Goddammit, Weezer hated her right now. Most of the time he had no feelings for Melody either way, other than harbouring a long-standing affinity for her ass, but he sure despised her now.

Weezer eased down on a five-gallon bucket and stared into the bonfire.

It had to be the 'Vette, he decided. That's why women liked Glenn so much. The 'Vette and the hair. Glenn had hair like one of those TV cops in the seventies. Like the dudes from *CHiPs* or what was that other one…?

Starsky and Hutch. Yeah, that's how Glenn looked. When you combined the hair with the cherry-red 'Vette, the muscular frame and the confident way Glenn carried himself, how could a guy like Weezer compete?

For the millionth time, Weezer made a secret wish his best friend would be disfigured in a construction accident. Not killed, but definitely messed up good. Like having his bottom jaw dislocated by an errant wrecking ball, or maybe suffering a deep gash from a snapped wire or something. But the scar would have to be a hideous one, not an embellishing one.

Weezer adjusted his position on the bucket and glanced askance at Freehafer. He and Glenn had driven by Freehafer's dad's house a couple days ago and had seen Mike's beat-up Yukon parked in the driveway. The damn thing looked like it hadn't been washed since that communist bastard Obama was in office, and it probably had about two hundred thousand miles on it.

Weezer sighed. The Yukon still beat his shitbox of a truck, a rusting Ford Ranger. Goddamn thing barely got up to seventy these days, and Weezer had to get out and push to reach that speed.

And that was another thing that pissed him off.

Weezer. The hell kind of nickname was that?

With Short Pump, at least you knew where the name came from. There was a story with it, even if the tale itself was pretty dull.

But with *Weezer* there wasn't even that. He'd have killed for a boring story. Because no one, not even Glenn – the first guy Weezer could remember calling him Weezer – remembered where the nickname came from.

Weezer had once asked his friends if it had something to do with the rock band. They had some decent songs.

No, it wasn't from the band.

Did he wheeze while he talked? Or when he ran?

No, they'd never known him to wheeze.

Was it because he had an Aunt Louise? You know, sometimes Louises were called "Weezie". Like that old show with the rich black people? *The Johnsons* or *The Jacksons*?

Nope. Had nothing to do with his aunt or that old show.

Then where in the fuck did the name come from? he'd shouted at them.

Shut up and drink your beer, Glenn had answered.

Shut up. The words echoed in Weezer's overmedicated brain. *Shut up.*

Were there any two words in the English language he hated more than *shut up*?

He couldn't think of any.

Except for Weezer. If that was a word. Weezer didn't think it was, which made him even madder, because if it were an honest-to-goodness word, it would have an honest-to-goodness meaning. Like,

weezer (*wee-zuhr*) – noun:

1. the metal cylinder that houses a pencil eraser
2. slang for a breathing mechanism used by sufferers of chronic emphysema
3. a rare type of rectal polyp

No such luck. Weezer sipped his beer, scowled. He glanced over at a couple of girls he'd never seen before. They looked young, nubile.

Maybe he'd hit on one of them later.

★   ★   ★

Glenn introduced Duane to a couple of out-of-town women, and of course Glenn had to call him Short Pump. Everybody laughed like usual, and like usual, Duane stood there wanting to explain to everyone that his dick wasn't actually small. But that wasn't the kind of thing you could easily fit into a conversation.

Hey, my name's Duane McKidd, but they call me Short Pump. I got the name from something completely unrelated to my penis size, but that's where everyone's mind goes when they hear it. How can I tell? Oh, that nasty smile some guys get, all teeth and barely restrained laughter. They hold back for a few seconds and invariably end up making some stupid joke. They laugh about it like we've known each other forever, and it's usually a great icebreaker for everyone. You know, mock the tall fat guy with the little penis. But the thing is, my penis isn't that little. That's the point. At least I don't think it is. I'm not hung or anything – I mean, I've seen porn before; who hasn't, right? – but I seriously doubt my dick's any smaller than any other guy. I mean, any normal *guy. Not those shaved, overtanned dudes in the movies who look like their moms crossbred with an Appaloosa stallion. But not tiny either. You know?*

Duane sighed. At some point, the two out-of-town women had wandered away, and Duane had gotten stuck with a group of idiots. Of course, most of the people here tonight were idiots, but this was an especially annoying group of idiots.

Led by Billy Kramer, who said, "...then the guy turns to me and yells, 'What the hell are you lookin' at, man?'

"I tell him," Billy Kramer went on, flipping his light brown ponytail aside for emphasis, "'why don't you put the brass knuckles away, bitch?'"

Duane let the story fade into a slurry drone. He'd heard it perhaps fifteen or twenty times over the years and found it uncanny how the tale diverged further from reality with each retelling. This version sounded like a Jackie Chan movie, back when Chan moved like a cartoon superhero. Billy Kramer not only made himself the star of the fight, but he gave his best friends, Randy Murray and Colton Crane, cameos as well.

Duane let his gaze drift around the clearing, the sounds of Billy Kramer's tall tale actually a bit soothing. He saw Weezer moving away from Melody Bridwell, a defeated cast to his downturned face. Duane hoped Melody hadn't been too vicious with him. She had a bad reputation, but Duane had long been intrigued by her. He sensed a depth in Melody, something haunted and perhaps anguished beneath the tight clothes and the hard body. Truth be told, if he weren't so in love with Savannah, he'd ask Melody out on a date.

Not that she'd say yes.

A few feet away, Billy Kramer was still regaling his audience – a trio of women Duane had never seen before, likely more tourists visiting from Illinois – with his fantastical tale of bravery and martial arts. Billy's ponytail was flipping wildly, his buddies nodding their encouragement. Duane couldn't take it anymore, so he moved away and ambled toward another group of people. The bonfire smoke was blowing in his direction, and for a moment he had no idea what was going on around him. It was a phenomenon Duane had never understood: wherever he went, the smoke seemed to follow.

But when he emerged from the whitish, acrid cloud, he realised what he'd walked into.

Glenn. Savannah. Mike.

The lovers' triangle from hell.

He was about to turn away when Savannah spotted him and smiled, the dimples in her cheeks showing. "Hey, Short Pump!" she called. "Come over here and talk to me."

Duane couldn't refuse. "Hey, Savannah." He nodded. "Mike."

Mike nodded stiffly. "Hey, Short Pump."

Glenn just glowered at Mike.

This wasn't going to be easy, Duane decided. He glanced at Savannah, noticed how her smile didn't reach her eyes. She needed Duane to save her.

He would save her.

"You look just like you did last time I saw you," Duane said and clapped a hand on Mike's shoulder. The shoulder felt bony, which jived with the rest of what Duane was seeing. Mike Freehafer looked very bad indeed. Accidentally killing somebody tended to have a negative effect on a person, if he had any conscience at all. Mike apparently did. "How's your dad doing?" Duane asked.

Something flitted across Mike's features, and Duane knew it had been the wrong thing to ask. "He insists on talking baseball."

Duane nodded. So Mike was putting it out there, the failed baseball career. It made him respect Mike a little more. Despite their high school friendship, Duane had actively disliked Mike for a good while – any guy who abandoned Savannah deserved to be disliked – but now Mike was making himself vulnerable, and in front of Savannah of all people. It thawed Duane a little.

Unless Mike was using the sad sack story as an angle.

This would bear watching, he decided.

Savannah shrugged. "Well, your dad always loved baseball. It's probably hard for him to let go."

Glenn grinned viciously. "Especially when his son forgot how to hit."

Savannah frowned. "Be nice, Glenn."

"It's fine," Mike said, but judging from the look on his face, it wasn't fine.

Glenn's sharkish grin never wavered. "Sure, it's fine, Savannah. It's all fine. Tell me, Mike, have you met Savannah's son?"

Jesus, Duane thought.

"No," Mike said in a low voice.

"I guess you wouldn't have," Glenn said, "being gone so long."

Duane turned to Savannah, said, "I ran into Mrs. Dooley the other day."

"Oh yeah?" Savannah asked, but her voice was faraway and small. Like she was resigned to the fisticuffs about to explode in front of her.

"Uh-huh," Duane said. "Mrs. Dooley said she was hoping she'd have your boy in a few years. Unless she's retired by then, of course."

When no one said anything to that, Duane went on, "I remember I had the biggest crush on Savannah back then. When was that..." He pretended to think. "...fourth grade, Savannah?"

"Third," she supplied.

"That's right," he said. "I was so smitten with Savannah that I'd cut in the lunch line to stand next to her."

Glenn cocked an eyebrow at him. "You sound like a stalker, Short Pump."

Duane nodded, playing the good sport. As always. "If I could've, I'd have followed Savannah around all day."

"It sounds like you did," Mike said.

"Not really," Duane said, and when everybody looked at him, he amended, "Okay, maybe I did."

And everybody laughed. Not a cathartic, tension-eliminating belly laugh, but it was something. Savannah grasped his hand and said, "We really should see each other more often, Short Pump. You only live a mile from me, yet we haven't hung out in, how long? Six months?"

Duane shrugged like it was no big deal. The distance between their homes was actually 1.2 miles, and they hadn't seen each other in eight months, three weeks, and six days. And he did sort of stalk her, but he sure as hell wasn't going to say that now. What he did say was, "It'd be fun to get together. Maybe we can go to the Roof."

Savannah favoured him with a weary smile. The Roof was a bar overlooking the lake at Beach Land. Once it had hosted such well-known acts as Jefferson Airplane and Janis Joplin. Now, like the amusement park itself, it was just sort of sad.

"Isn't that where the reunion's going to be?" Mike said.

Duane opened his mouth to tell him it was, but Glenn jumped in first. "Don't tell me you're sticking around that long?"

Mike shrugged. "I was considering it."

Glenn grinned mirthlessly. "You getting a job here? Or is it Savannah you're after?"

Savannah gave Glenn a pained look. "Please, Glenn. Don't."

"Don't what?" Glenn snapped. "Don't point out the obvious? That Mike here treated you like garbage?"

Duane shifted uneasily. "Maybe it's not really our business, you know? I mean, Mike probably has his reasons—"

"Reasons for *what*?" Glenn barked. Duane realised with dawning apprehension that Glenn's eyes had taken on a glazed look, that cruel hardness that infected them whenever he'd drunk too much whiskey.

"It's my business," Mike said.

Glenn stepped closer. "And coming here makes it *my* business. I've been here all along, Mike. Where the hell've you been? Crashing cars? Killing teenagers?"

The first flickers of rage banked in Mike's eyes.

"Please, Glenn," Savannah said.

"Please what?" he asked.

"Please don't be an asshole."

Glenn's smile this time was genuine. "Now that's what I like to hear. I know you've got guts, Savannah. Why not tell this prick off?"

"You're telling me what to do," Savannah said. "And if you keep it up, I'm going to punch you in the teeth."

Duane laughed. He couldn't help it.

"I shouldn't have come," Mike said, glancing at his shoes, which Duane now noticed were ill-chosen loafers that were spattered with either mud or cow shit.

Glenn smacked Mike in the back. "Well, you're here now, pal. How about a drink?"

Mike looked like he'd just tasted something bitter. "Might as well, *pal.* Thanks for the warm welcome."

Together, they made their way toward the kegs.

Duane turned and looked down at Savannah, who exhaled trembling breath.

"What are the odds of those two making it through the night without beating each other up?" she asked.

About the same as my odds of making love to you, Duane thought.

"Not too good," he said.

"Thanks for intervening," she said.

"Thanks for saying we should hang out more often."

She looked at him thoughtfully. "I meant it, Short Pump. We should."

Duane ignored the nervous flutter in his belly. "How's that boy of yours?"

"He tried to eat a Matchbox car today."

He laughed. After a beat, he said, "You can go talk to Mike if you want."

She frowned. "Why would you say that?"

He pretended to study the bonfire. "I just figured, you know...it's been a while since you two talked, and..." He shrugged, offered her a lame smile.

Savannah glared at him. His smile curdled.

"Everybody would be better off," she said, "if they stayed out of my business. Don't tell me who to talk to."

"Hey, Savannah, I didn't mean to—"

"I know you didn't mean to," she snapped. "But if I want to hang out with you, say yes or no and leave it at that. Don't tell me to go talk to someone else. Got it?"

Duane nodded. "Got it."

"Now let's get another drink," she said. "I need one to make it through this shit."

CHAPTER FOUR

Joyce was drinking water, but she drank it from one of the red plastic cups so it would look as though she were drinking beer. She detested beer, detested most forms of alcohol. Occasionally, wine tasted good to her, but she seldom indulged in it because even two glasses gave her an insidious headache the next morning. She'd experienced a couple of hangovers in college, but she realised early on how much she loathed that cottony taste in her mouth, the boiling tang of bile in her throat and the dogged headaches that shadowed her movements the rest of those miserable, hungover days.

Joyce blamed it on her mother.

No, it wasn't her mom's fault she got hangovers when she drank, but that feeling of guilt, that sense of having transgressed and deserving punishment...yes, that certainly *was* because of her mother.

You let a boy touch you, her mother would caution, *and pretty soon you'll grow too enamoured of the sensation.*

She later learned that her mother – who while a teaching assistant at Western Indiana University had been impregnated by a philosophy professor – was speaking from experience.

The ones you have to beware of are the nonconformists. The bad boys, the rebels. The James Deans and the Marlon Brandos.

All this while reading Joyce bedtime stories when she was six years old.

Joyce had nodded, despite having no idea what a rebel was or who James Dean or Marlon Brando were. Maybe authors? Or sausage makers. Didn't they eat James Dean sausages for breakfast?

Alcohol, her mother would continue, *leads to relaxed morals, and relaxed morals lead to stolen passion.*

Joyce didn't know what passion was, but she knew stealing was bad.

Her mom's owlish gaze loomed over her. *How do you think I came to have you? A nip of red wine, some James Taylor music. And then a moment of weakness.*

Joyce just wanted to get back to her Dr. Seuss book.

She shivered and let her eyes rove over the partygoers.

Her gaze fell on Glenn Kershaw. And lingered.

Look away, she could hear Mother demanding. *He's exactly the type of lothario a discerning woman should avoid.*

Joyce watched him move. And felt a pleasant tingling in her belly.

She'd only spoken to Glenn a handful of times, but that had been more than enough to supply two years' worth of sordid fantasies. If she could only get him to *notice* her.

"Hey, Jane," a voice said.

She turned, thankful for the darkness that obscured the flush on her cheeks.

It was Glenn's friend, the one who looked like he'd own a Confederate flag.

She flailed mentally for the man's name, but he saved her by chuckling and saying, "It's Weezer. How you been, Jane?"

And though now would have been the perfect time to correct him, Joyce said, "I'm just people-watching. Are you having fun?"

Weezer grunted and plopped down on the felled tree from which she observed the proceedings. He leaned back a trifle unsteadily and gazed up at the canopy of trees, through which glinted scraps of the star-littered sky. "I don't have fun at these things," he said. "Mostly I just get hammered."

Joyce took a moment to appraise him more carefully. Honesty was rare. Not that she'd been to many of these events, but the handful she'd attended had been riots of duplicity.

People drank. And talked. And screwed.

Or tried to screw. From her experience, Weezer was one of those who typically ended up alone.

He glanced at her. "I smell bad or somethin'?"

"Not at all," she answered and continued to study him. Red baseball cap worn backward. Dark hair stringing down to his shoulders. Thin, scraggly facial hair. Red T-shirt with cutoff sleeves, his body scrawny but veined, suggesting he worked some job requiring manual labour. Blue jeans with torn knees and frayed cuffs.

"You're making me feel like a bug or something," he said. "If you're plannin' on making fun of me, I'd just as soon skip it. Already had enough of that for one night."

Referring to Melody Bridwell, of course. Joyce had watched the whole depressing rejection take place and beheld the bleak dismay in Weezer's face when Melody had unleashed her wrath on him. It wouldn't help to mention this, would only embarrass him to know his shame had been witnessed. Nor would it help to point out that Melody was a walking petri dish who was probably carrying about thirty strands of venereal disease.

Joyce put her hand over Weezer's. "I'm not cruel."

Weezer gave her a look that told her she'd gone too far. Which was the danger with men. They were, for the most part, akin to dogs. She knew that was a cliché, but after owning a dog – which had disappeared less than a year after she'd adopted it from the no-kill shelter – Joyce realised just how apt the threadbare analogy was. Her dog, a black-and-white mutt she'd named Weasley because of her affinity for the Harry Potter books, had lived for two things: food and humping blankets. The first part hadn't surprised her, though she found it uncanny how persistent he was in his quest for things to devour.

It was the blanket-humping that really took her aback. Whenever she curled up with her grandmother's quilt, Weasley would leap onto the couch next to her and begin thrusting away on the quilt like a canine rapist. She'd indulged him that first time with momentary bemusement until she began to fear he'd climax all over the quilt, at which point she'd abruptly wrenched away his patched paramour and reprimanded him for being so disgusting.

The look in Weezer's eyes reminded her a lot of the horny gleam Weasley had once worn. Their names were even similar, she now realised. Only Weezer wanted to hump her instead of a quilt.

You see? her mother said. *All men are slaves to their libidos.*

Lips compressed, Joyce shook herself free of the voice.

Weezer said, "You in the mood for some tube steak?"

For a time, she could only gape at him. Then she cleared her throat. "Look, Weezer, I don't want to give you the wrong idea—"

"Of course you don't!" he snapped with such force that she recoiled. He motioned toward the bonfire. "None of you bitches wanna give me the wrong idea. But you flaunt those tight little asses and flap those titties in my face, and then you have a hissy fit the moment I show any interest. What am I supposed to do? Wait for a written invitation? Send you flowers first so you won't be rude to me?"

Joyce took a shuddering breath. "I'm not being rude to you. I merely—"

"*Bullshit!*" he snapped, loudly enough to draw the attention of several partygoers.

Joyce's cheeks burned. But what had she to feel embarrassed about? This...*person* had jumped to a conclusion – an insulting and incorrect conclusion – and she'd gently corrected him. She was about to say something to this effect when Short Pump intervened.

"Hey, man, let's go get a refill," Short Pump said to Weezer.

Weezer sprang to his feet, jabbed an index finger into Short Pump's chest. "Don't fucking talk to me like that! Don't act like I'm some moron who needs looking after!"

Short Pump brought up his hands, palms outward. "I just thought you'd like a beer."

Weezer shoved Short Pump in the chest, the movement so quick and violent that the larger man stumbled back a couple paces, his beer sloshing over his forearm.

"What you *thought*," Weezer growled, "was that you'd get in good with this bitch by being her hero. Can't get any pussy on your own, you gotta screw your friends over to have a chance. Hoping she'll throw you a mercy fuck?"

Weezer shouldered past Short Pump and stalked off into the woods.

She looked at Short Pump. "You okay?"

He was wiping himself off, though all he was really accomplishing was soaking different parts of his black T-shirt with beer. "Sorry about him," he muttered.

She studied him. "How long have you been friends?"

"Since we were kids."

"Is that why you put up with it?"

"What are you talking about?"

"I've seen you with Glenn and Weezer," she explained. "They treat you like the court jester even though you're smarter than they are."

"That supposed to be a compliment?"

"I'm only trying to be truthful."

"Truthful's overrated."

"Is self-respect?"

He tilted his head, eyeing her with real asperity now. "I came here for beer, not psychoanalysis."

He went off without another word. Joyce watched after him.

She saw Savannah coming toward her, probably to make sure she was okay.

It would be another two minutes before the world was drenched in blood.

CHAPTER FIVE

Glenn watched Weezer disappear into the forest with a sharp twinge of concern.

Mike was grinning, the plastic cup hovering before his lips. "What the hell's his problem? He gets shot down all the time. I've never known Weezer to get that worked up."

"You haven't been around either," Glenn pointed out. "People change over time."

Mike cocked an eyebrow. "You don't believe that. Just look at this scene." He swept an arm around to take in the clearing. "Except for the age on some of us, this looks exactly like it did when we were in high school. People drinking, bullshitting. Guys trying to get laid. Even the cow manure smell is the same."

Glenn glanced at Mike. "Is that what you're counting on? The notion that no one has changed?"

Mike gave him a pained look. "Man, don't tell me we're back on that. Savannah's cool with me being here. The Marvins invited me. Why can't you just chill out and have a good time?"

Glenn wanted to feel the strobing rage that had gripped him only a few minutes earlier, that seething red tide of emotion that had crashed over him when he first spied Mike Freehafer at the rim of the woods. But his mind was still on Weezer, still on the way he'd blown up at that librarian, whatever the hell her name was.

Like he'd read Glenn's thoughts, Mike said, "Weezer ordinarily get that irate?"

Glenn shook his head. "If he does, I never see it."

"Probably just drank too much."

Glenn said nothing.

Mike said, "Or maybe he's tired of being rejected by every girl he talks to."

"We all get rejected, Mike."

Mike grunted. "Some of us more than others."

Glenn turned and scrutinised him. Mike's expression was bland, but there'd been something in his tone...something gloating. Or had that been Glenn's imagination?

"How long are you in town?" Glenn asked.

"I thought I might stay."

The same bland expression. The same undercurrent of gloating.

"You mean, find a job here?"

Mike shrugged. "Why not?"

Because you turned your back on everyone. Because you consider this place rock bottom. Because even though you don't deserve Savannah, she just might take you back.

Glenn sighed. "No reason."

Mike nodded. "Who's that?"

Glenn didn't even bother to look. Maybe it was the beer, maybe it was the long hours at the machine shop today. But for whatever reason, he felt unutterably weary.

"Seriously, man," Mike said. "Who the hell is that?"

Glenn swivelled his head to look, and as he did he noticed that several other partygoers had spotted the newcomer as well.

The man stood maybe thirty yards away from where Glenn and Mike were standing, and perhaps twenty feet away from the nearest partygoers, whom Glenn now identified as Dan and Jessica Clinton. Dan had impregnated Jessica in high school, and they'd gotten married. Now they had six kids and lived on the lake.

The man remained where he was, the shadows veiling his face. He was dressed curiously. He wore all black, but the clothes were too formal – dress slacks, a button-down shirt. The clothes hung off the man as though he'd lost a great deal of weight recently. Glenn was reminded of a scarecrow. Or an itinerant preacher with parishioners too cheap to tithe.

"You know the dude?" Mike asked.

Glenn shook his head. He didn't know the man, and he wasn't sure he wanted to. Maybe it was the Jack and Coke, or maybe it was the heat from the bonfire, which danced and licked the air with rabid orange tongues, but there was definitely something unnatural about the figure. The man hadn't moved at all, for one thing. For another, Glenn was pretty sure he could see the man's eyes, even from this distance. They were chips of blue ice, piercing and not at all friendly.

Hunter and Brian Marvin had also noticed the interloper. Maybe, Glenn reasoned, one of the brothers had invited the guy. But that didn't seem right either. There was something about the way the man stood that suggested experience. Glenn couldn't shake the idea that one of their former teachers had shown up. Or some other hostile authority figure from their pasts.

"Come have a beer," Brian Marvin called. Brian was the easier-going of the two brothers, and no doubt wanted to defuse the weird tension that had permeated the gathering.

The man in the shadows didn't answer. Didn't move. Glenn was sure he could see the man's eyes glowing now.

"Ah, to hell with this," Hunter Marvin said and began to stalk forward.

Glenn felt a chill. Hunter was a state champion wrestler and didn't possess the peacemaking tendencies of his brother. If Hunter decided to attack the man, things might get very ugly indeed. Probably sensing the danger here, Brian moved up alongside his brother and barred him with an outstretched arm.

"*You are wayward lambs,*" the man said.

The rest of Glenn's lethargy burned away in a white-hot blast of fear. The man's voice had been resonant, erudite. Yet there had been a croaking, disused quality to it, as if the man's lungs were a pair of ancient bellows, the vocal chords leeched of moisture. Had he been alone, Glenn would have taken off running.

But Mike was chuckling. "'Wayward *lambs*'? What the hell is he talking about?"

Both Marvin brothers were laughing too. In fact, it seemed that most of the partygoers found this newcomer an innocuous novelty someone had hired to enliven the proceedings.

But there were also those who weren't laughing.

Savannah and her friend, the librarian whose name Glenn couldn't recall…they were watching the newcomer with real trepidation. As was Short Pump, who was standing by himself about fifteen feet behind Glenn and Mike. Short Pump had a beer clutched in one hand, but his other hand was resting on his thigh, the fingers there tap-tapping against his jeans.

"You gonna have a beer or not?" Brian Marvin said. "I can't prevent my brother from kicking your ass much longer."

Jessica Clinton said, "What the hell's up your ass, man?"

Without moving, the man looked at Dan Clinton and said, "*Tell your woman to be still.*"

A few partygoers chuckled, but no one else saw much humour in the comment, least of all Jessica Clinton. She was sassy, Glenn knew. A woman pretty much had to be sassy to manage six kids.

Jessica flipped her long, auburn hair aside and strode toward the figure. "You better start apologising right now."

The man laughed softly. "*Helpless, wayward lambs.*"

Glenn's chill deepened.

But Jessica's husband had evidently had enough. So had Hunter Marvin. Together, they stalked toward the figure, who Glenn realised was bigger and stronger than he'd initially estimated. The black clothes remained a bit roomy, but the figure inside them was far from emaciated. To the contrary, the arms and legs seemed muscular now. Even if he was older, the man looked stout enough to put up a fight.

"*This is your only warning,*" the man said, his voice deepening.

Hunter Marvin spread his arms. "You're warning *us*?"

"*If you run now,*" the man continued, "*you might escape retribution.*"

Now the laughter was more pronounced.

"You believe this shit?" Billy Kramer said to Colton Crane. "This douchebag thinks he's gonna take us all on."

One person who apparently took the man's threats seriously was

Josh Roller. A couple years older than Glenn, Roller was a known gun enthusiast. Brushing past Glenn and Mike, Roller said, "Fellas, I'm gonna put a stop to this bullshit, pronto."

Which meant, Glenn knew, that Roller was trudging to his beat-up Ford pickup in order to retrieve whatever weaponry he stored there. Roller had driven through one of the fields and was parked only about fifty yards away.

Time to go, a voice whispered.

But that was impossible, Glenn knew. Not only were the odds in their favour – hell, there were how many people here tonight? Fifty? – but he would appear gutless if he turned tail now. Not to mention Savannah. What would she think of him?

Don't you want to protect Savannah?

Sure, he thought uneasily. *Of course I do.*

"Last warning, asshole," Hunter Marvin said. "Either leave or tell us who the hell you are."

"And apologise to my wife," Dan Clinton added. Dan was ordinarily a pretty reasonable guy, but he looked pissed off enough to make the interloper pay for his rudeness.

"*You want to know who I am?*" the interloper asked.

Hunter Marvin grinned, glanced back at the other partygoers in exasperation. "That's what I said, didn't I? You hard of hearing or something?"

"*Hard of hearing is one thing I am not,*" the interloper said. "*I hear everything. I hear the wind and what it conceals. I hear the language of the night, the music of the ancient world. I hear the leaves. I hear the worms, eager to writhe in your carcass.*"

Hunter hesitated. "You're a real freak, aren't you?"

The figure turned his face this way and that, sampling the air.

"*I smell your fear,*" the interloper said. "*It is the scent of impending death.*"

And now, for the first time since they'd met back in junior high, Glenn saw Hunter Marvin take a backward step. Hunter had always seemed eager for a confrontation, but several factors were conspiring to undo his courage now.

The interloper's body no longer looked bony at all, but instead packed the voluminous clothes with brawn and sinew. Though there was still something in the voice and bearing that bespoke experience, Glenn now wondered just how agile this man might be. His whole frame seemed to thrum with caged energy. And something else. If hatred was a tangible thing, this man was broadcasting it. The contempt in his voice was real, the desire to inflict pain.

"Hey, guys?" a voice behind them said.

Glenn turned and saw Short Pump, whose apologetic expression only partially masked his terror.

"What?" Mike asked.

"Think we should maybe, I don't know, get the hell out of here?" Short Pump asked.

Glenn was about to agree with him, his reputation as a badass be damned, when the figure said, "*You were wrong to return.*"

Next to him, he sensed Mike stiffen.

Glenn swallowed. "Hey, I think Duane's got a point. Maybe we should get Savannah and—"

"*See what your deeds have wrought,*" the figure interrupted.

Glenn tried to swallow but couldn't. The voice seemed to fill the clearing, to absorb the flames of the bonfire and swirl about them until the air was no longer breathable, was a superheated cauldron in which they would all boil.

Dan Clinton stepped closer to the figure. "Look, I've asked you to apologise to my wife, and if you're not going to—"

"*Come,*" the figure said.

Dan faltered, a stricken look on his face. He glanced about uncertainly, then said, "You mean me?"

"*I mean anyone with a modicum of courage. Even one who has failed an entire town.*"

And this time there was absolutely no doubt to whom the figure was speaking.

CHAPTER SIX

Mike thought, *I didn't mean to let anyone down.*

The figure was gazing stonily at him. At first Mike assumed it was a joke. Like those people who dressed up like zombies and shambled around big cities, trying to scare people. But this was no zombie. This was – he tried but could not escape the word – a werewolf.

Only not the kind he'd seen in films. Mike wasn't big on horror movies. Could take them or leave them actually, and most of the time he preferred to leave them. Yet that's what this figure reminded him of, at least in its appearance. The eyes were the most prominent, of course. Blue, at first, but now a glowing yellow. Lit by some inner hellfire, their insidious gleam bereft of pity, without remorse. But the face wasn't right either. The cheekbones, for one thing, protruded too far, and the brow reminded him of a battering ram. The face was hairy in a way that struck Mike as unnatural. It wasn't just the wild, untended nature of the man's facial hair that so unnerved him, it was the fact that it seemed to be spreading.

Werewolf, his mind insisted. *Werewolf.*

But werewolves were kid stuff, right? The conjurations of overactive imaginations, the kinds of creatures dreamed up by superstitious peasants and frightened villagers? A lamb got eaten? Blame it on a werewolf. A child went missing? It must be some supernatural beast roaming the forest.

Wayward lambs. The figure's words echoed in his mind like a death knell. *Wayward lambs.*

And the beast had targeted Mike.

(*Run*)

But there must be some explanation, he reasoned, some cause for the man's—

(*creature's*)

Man's! Man's! It's only a man!

(*Run!*)

Mike couldn't flee, no way, not now. Not after fleeing for the past ten years, not after casting off Savannah like a used condom and treating his parents like they had the plague. Holy crap, he thought, maybe that was why they'd gotten divorced. Maybe that was why his mother had cheated. Searching for male attention, her son gone MIA and her husband obsessed with a dead dream. God, what a mess he'd made of things, what a hideous, unholy, fucking mess. He was a runner, a fleer, a jilter of good-hearted girls and a betrayer of caring parents.

So stop running, he told himself. *Now. Right here.*

(Mistake)

Fuck you! he screamed at the hectoring voice. *I know about mistakes, all right? I know about screwing up and losing your chances, but goddammit, I'm only twenty-eight. I can still take control of my life. Still show Savannah I'm not a runner. If this guy is challenging me*

(It's not a guy)

I can face him and show everyone I'm better than I ever was. I'm more than my failures, more than a baseball player. I'm—

The man darted toward him.

Mike's bladder let go.

★   ★   ★

Duane would replay the scene many times in his head:

The gigantic figure whose hairy muscles writhed and jumped like severed power lines.

The shocked faces of the crowd as the beast stormed past.

Glenn stepping in front of Mike, Glenn moving toward the hurtling figure rather than away from it, Glenn jerking up an arm to shield himself as the figure crashed into him and over him, despite the fact that Glenn had done nothing but badmouth Mike for as long as Duane could remember.

But there Glenn was, getting tackled by the marauding figure, being slammed to the sparse grass of the clearing, and then flopping onto his back, knocked senseless by the collision, his forearm striped with glistening slash marks.

The figure, creature, beast, whatever the hell it was, tumbled end over end, swept past them with the incredible momentum it had built up. Then it was splaying out its limbs, reminding him of a dog regaining its balance.

No, Duane thought, *not a dog.*

A wolf.

But the figure was still more man than any other species. When it peered up at Mike, there was a sinister intelligence glinting in its eyes.

Then it turned its gaze on Duane.

He didn't cry out or piss his pants or abandon himself to paroxysms of panic. The only physiological reactions that took place when the beast looked at him were a painful puckering of the sphincter and a sudden retraction of his balls.

The beast grinned at Duane. As though marking him.

Then it sprang for Mike.

CHAPTER SEVEN

Savannah was sure Mike wouldn't do anything at all, would just acquiesce to his fate. She had been locked in place by fear ever since the creature's first appearance. Next to her she'd sensed Joyce's interest in the creature, watched in disbelief as Joyce had even taken a couple of steps toward the beast. Then things had taken that ghastly, surreal turn, the man changing in front of their eyes, and before Savannah could do anything, the beast had loped across the clearing toward Mike.

And then Glenn had jumped in front of the creature.

She was sure the beast would kill Glenn, but then Mike's trance broke and he was stepping over to the fire, bending, grasping a stout branch, and facing down the creature. In the sparking heat shimmer, Savannah could see what was happening.

Mike was settling into his batting stance.

She didn't feel the thrill she once had when watching Mike play baseball – those feelings were dead. But despite this fact, watching Mike turn away from her, the firelight dancing on his back, was like stepping into her eighteen-year-old self at the high school baseball field. The tree branch he'd selected was longer than a normal bat and maybe twice as thick. She assumed the thing weighed a ton, but Mike handled it like it was any other piece of lumber. A full half of the branch was blackened from the fire, and perhaps six inches of its tip glowed a brilliant red.

Mike crouched, twisted that front foot of his, and dug into the batter's box. He cocked the long bough, bringing his hands way back, and wiggled his butt the way he did when preparing for the pitcher's delivery.

Reliving his former glory. Realising his promise.

Becoming the hero everyone had assumed he'd become.

The beast charged at him.

Mike rocked onto his back foot – the part of the swing called the load, she remembered – and began to unleash his fury.

In that moment, in those glorious milliseconds when the broad, bludgeoning branch began to knife through the strike zone, Savannah was certain the beast would have its neck broken by the blow. The scorched cylinder of the makeshift bat and the fiery orange brand at its tip came howling toward the beast, Mike's body a powder keg of coiled power.

But Mike missed. The bough scraped over the ducking body of the beast, and Mike lost control of his weapon. The branch went skittering through the air like a dying dervish and landed somewhere in the underbrush. The beast, having cleared the swinging cudgel, slammed into Mike, snarling and scratching. The beast lifted Savannah's long-ago boyfriend like a weightless mannequin and braced him above its head with one massive hand. The skin of the beast, Savannah saw with little surprise, was an unwholesome tawny hue, though most of it was furred with wiry black hair. The creature's back was broad and muscled, the arms attenuating the fabric of its shirt.

At some point the beast had either scratched or bitten Mike, Savannah now saw, for in the firelight Mike's whole front, from the stomach of his shirt all the way down to his thighs, was slathered in blood. Mike was gaping down at the creature, perhaps still dumbfounded at his inability to hit yet another moving target, but Mike didn't gape for long. The creature reached up with its free hand and slowly, almost sensuously, buried its claws in Mike's stomach. Blood poured from Mike's belly in soupy rills, more blood coughing out of his twitching lips. Mike was still alive at that point, though he'd already begun to pale, so when the creature brought Mike's face lower, Savannah was pretty sure Mike knew what was happening.

The beast's face looked vaguely human. But in the firelight painting it, she could clearly make out the differences. The elongated ears. The oversize jaws. The wrinkled forehead. The extra hair.

The leering golden eyes.

As though he were toiling to speak, Mike opened his mouth, closed it, opened it again, the lips working like a dying trout.

The creature opened its mouth as if to kiss Mike's lips. Then its teeth vised down on Mike's chin. A gurgling, high-pitched yowl sounded from the pit of Mike's throat. The creature's teeth hinged together, the bones of Mike's jaw splintering like balsa wood. Blood gushed around the beast's writhing lips, Mike's eyes starey and horrorstruck.

The creature began to shake Mike's head in its mouth, a stomach-churning growl issuing from its lethal maw.

"Somebody do something!" a shrill voice screamed.

Savannah turned, saw Jessica Clinton waving her arms at the rest of the partygoers, as if they all hadn't just witnessed the same thing she had.

Then Savannah realised that Jessica had a point. No one was *doing* anything. Despite the fact that they had the beast outnumbered, despite the fact that some of these men had guns in their vehicles. Despite all this, a man was being devoured before their very eyes.

No. Not just a man.

Mike Freehafer. The boy she'd been certain she would one day marry. They were going to live in a big city. Boston, or maybe even New York. She'd travel with the team, shop at the fancy stores. Then, when he'd struck it big in free agency, they'd settle down, raise a family.

That dream had been brain-dead and on life support for a long time, but now it was officially over. The beast had reduced Mike to a gore-streaked rag doll.

Jessica Clinton's words were still ringing in Savannah's ears when the creature hurled Mike's lifeless body into the woods and raised its arms to the group. *"Will you watch while I use you for food? Won't you flee so I can experience the pleasure of running you down?"*

Savannah scanned the faces of her fellow partygoers. Most were still staring at Mike's twisted body with sick expressions. A few were glancing around, maybe seeking for the one brave soul who would challenge this monster.

Then two figures broke loose from the crowd. One was Dan Clinton.

The other was Joyce.

★　★　★

"What are you *doing*?" Savannah asked, but Joyce barely heard her.

Joyce had been watching the beast with a growing sense of déjà vu, and for reasons she couldn't explain, Jessica Clinton's plea had given her the jolt she needed.

Joyce had no plan, had no idea at all what she would do when she reached the beast; she certainly had no delusions of vanquishing it. Yet something told her this was the moment she'd been waiting for her entire life, the destiny she'd suspected would one day materialise if only she had the courage to embrace it.

She wasn't a muscular woman, nor was she especially physically fit. She walked a lot, and she ate healthily, but if Mike Freehafer – a former stud athlete in the prime of his life – had been ripped to pieces by the beast, what chance had she?

Little, if she was being objective about this, but objectivity had been her ruler for far too long. In the books she read – and lately, the stories she'd tried to write – anything was possible. They were all about characters stepping outside themselves, confronting deep-seated fears and then living or dying on the basis of their own wiles and fortitude.

At the very least, Joyce had to try.

Why? she heard her mother's shrill voice demand. *Because it's dangerous? Because it makes you feel rebellious?*

Yes, she decided, striding closer. That was precisely why she was doing this. Her mother would have run shrieking in the other direction by now, or perhaps taken refuge in a hollow log.

But Joyce was doing something she'd never done before, something she'd dreamed of doing her entire life.

She was taking a chance.

She was risking something.

She was *transgressing*.

God, it felt amazing!

But when Dan Clinton reached the creature, the stocky man moving in an ungainly sprint, Joyce realised she'd made a mistake.

The beast snatched up Dan Clinton as though he were an irritating insect and hurled him into the flames.

CHAPTER EIGHT

Duane threw up in his mouth. He'd seen stuff like this in movies, but he'd sure as hell never witnessed anything like it in real life. One moment Dan Clinton was barreling toward the beast like a Viking in cargo shorts, his face frozen in a fierce, unyielding grin; the next, the beast was plucking Clinton by the shirt and tossing him like a Frisbee into the jetting flames. The bonfire had been blazing too high as it was – Duane wondered earlier if the Marvin brothers were trying to summon some pagan god – but when Dan Clinton hit the mounded stack of logs, the bonfire erupted in a starburst of sparks and yellow sheets of flame so brilliant that Duane had to shield his eyes to keep them from being scorched.

Had the fates been on Dan Clinton's side, he might have entered the fire headfirst, perished quickly, and been spared the agony of burning alive. But fate was obviously not with Dan tonight. He'd twisted as he'd flown through the air, his arms windmilling like a hapless extra in an action film, and he'd landed on the seething stack in a belly flop. Duane actually saw Dan push himself up off the swirling flames before the bier beneath him gave way. Then his whole burning body descended into the fiery maelstrom. The sight of it made Duane want to cry, but the worst part was the way Dan's scream continued for a full five or six seconds after he'd been devoured by the bonfire like a sacrificed virgin.

The beast stalked toward Joyce, who held her ground.

Duane held his breath.

The beast towered over Joyce. "*Give me your hand,*" it demanded.

Joyce said, "No."

In a motion so quick Duane barely saw it, the beast seized Joyce's wrist and wrenched it sideways. There was a sick crunch as her wrist bones snapped. Moaning, Joyce fell against the beast. It sank its other clawed hand into the meat of her shoulder, blood bubbling around its sabre-like fingernails.

The beast's body jolted and the crack of a rifle shot tore through the clearing.

"Get away from her, you ugly son of a bitch!" Josh Roller snarled. He raised the rifle again.

Three or four partygoers cheered.

Yee-hah, Duane thought.

Then the clearing devolved into chaos.

The sight of the creature staggering sideways, knocked off balance by the rifle shot, must have emboldened the crowd, because several partygoers grabbed what was nearest them and made to hurl the objects at the beast. Hunter Marvin, who'd been one of the few to approach the beast earlier, went one better. Ignoring the potential danger of being sniped by Roller, Hunter bolted straight at the beast, looking every bit as agile as he had the day he'd been crowned champion at the state wrestling meet ten years ago.

Duane hadn't been there that day, but watching Hunter's nimble movements, it wasn't difficult to imagine him dominating an opponent, countering every manoeuvre, pinning him to the mat in a flurry of limbs.

Hunter hit the creature before it had fully recovered. Josh Roller shouted at Hunter to "Move! Move!" so he could get off another clear shot, but Hunter was too busy proving his valour. Hunter made a move to take the beast down, and Duane felt a cheer rising in his throat. The beast pumped a taloned hand into Hunter's belly and straight through the small of his back. Hunter's body went rigid, his arms and legs straightening spasmodically. Then the creature stood erect, Hunter hanging impaled on the crook of its arm, and flicked Hunter's body aside like a booger.

The beast turned toward Roller, growled.

Roller took aim.

The beast broke into a series of wolflike bounds. Josh Roller was an experienced hunter, but the defenceless does and bucks he'd bagged, Duane knew, moved nothing like this beast did. Zigzagging with an appalling blend of speed and unpredictability, the beast reached Roller's left flank in less than three seconds. Roller fired just as the beast thrust a forearm against the rifle's barrel. The shot cracked, but zinged harmlessly into the overhanging foliage, and then the rifle was in the creature's grip. Like a jealous child, Roller actually reached for the gun. The creature raised the rifle above Roller's head, barrel down, and plunged its tip straight into Roller's upturned left eye. The barrel ploughed through Roller's brain and split the long hair at the base of his skull, the hunter already jittering in his death throes.

Brian Marvin, compelled into action by the slaying of his brother, rammed the creature in its side. Though not a decorated wrestler like his twin, Brian was nevertheless an imposing guy.

But he never stood a chance. The beast was driven sideways perhaps three or four feet, but then it gained traction, reached down, and sank its talons into the base of Brian's back, just under the rib cage. With an upward tug, it splintered Brian's ribs and flayed open his back. Brian toppled, pawing at his exposed lung and gasping for air.

Numbly, Duane turned to Savannah, who had rushed forward to save Joyce before the beast could finish her too. Joyce was kneeling and apparently disoriented. Duane took off toward them. There were still dozens of people in the clearing, though a good many had run off screaming into the forest, and just when Duane thought the beast would turn and make him its next victim, it disappeared into the forest after a group of partygoers.

The sounds of shrieking soon followed.

"Help me," Savannah said. She'd hooked her wrists under Joyce's armpits and was attempting to haul her to her feet.

"I'll get her," Duane said. His only experience with saving lives had come vicariously from war movies. The fireman's carry, Duane remembered, was the position of choice in those films, whether it was John Wayne doing the carrying or Robert DeNiro. He bent down to scoop Joyce up and promptly felt his jeans give way with a farty *brrrrrrip!*

Nice job, hero! he told himself, but Duane ignored the taunting voice, concentrated on hoisting Joyce onto his shoulders. Once he'd gotten her good and balanced up there, he turned to face Savannah. From that angle she wouldn't be able to see his tighty-whities through the gaping hole in his jeans.

"Lead the way," he said.

Savannah nodded and set off toward the main trail.

As Duane made to follow, he identified several problems. The first was the fact that he was a pretty slow runner to begin with. In PE he'd usually get lapped by the speedsters when they ran the mile. Now, with a full-grown woman weighing him down, he was worse than slow – his progress was damn near glacial. Savannah, by contrast, had been a good athlete in high school, sectional champion in the long jump and the hundred-metre dash. And watching her pull ahead of him, he decided she hadn't lost a step.

Another complication was the darkness of the night and the narrowness of the dirt trail they were on. He couldn't see a thing, which meant he kept stumbling over rocks and exposed tree roots, and several times he only avoided pitching face-first onto the trail by the grace of God. Not only that, but the woman on his shoulders made navigating the slender trail a dicey proposition. He kept knocking her feet into the trees, and once he almost brained her on the trunk of a big sycamore.

There was also the fact that the screams were currently coming from directly ahead of them.

"Think we should take another route?" he called ahead.

"And end up the middle of nowhere?" Savannah answered over her shoulder.

Duane panted. "But it sounds like that thing is ahead of us."

Savannah didn't respond.

Duane continued to chug forward grimly, a sharp pain corkscrewing into his side. It wasn't as though Joyce was a heavy girl. No more than average, he figured. But as a physically unfit director of technology for the Lakeview school system, he rarely found himself performing tasks that required stamina. Unless staying awake at his desk qualified as an act of stamina.

"Can't you go faster?" Savannah called back.

Of course I can, he thought angrily. *I was just taking it easy on you. You know, since you've got the body of a Greek goddess and aren't fucking carrying anyone.*

"I'll...try," Duane grunted.

They continued on, the woods growing darker and darker the farther they strayed from the clearing.

"I think we could make better time if you put me down," Joyce said.

"You sure?" Duane panted.

"Yes," she answered.

Thank Christ, Duane thought.

Setting her down and feeling that weight leave his aching lower back was such a wonderful sensation that Duane was tempted to moan in pleasure. But he figured that might hurt Joyce's feelings and kept his jubilation to himself.

"How much farther to the road?" Joyce asked. She sounded a little groggy, and she winced as she spoke, but as far as Duane could tell, she looked spry enough to run on her own. He sure as hell hoped she was. He didn't relish the prospect of lugging her down the trail again.

Savannah shook her head. "Doesn't matter. We have to go."

Duane couldn't argue with that. They took off again with Savannah leading the way. He was alarmed to note how easily she pulled away from him even without the burden of another human on his shoulders. Even worse, Joyce ran apace with Savannah, so that Duane was soon left far in the rear, which made his pulse race even faster. Because now it was pitch-black. Now he was alone.

Now—

He gasped as he slammed into Joyce's stopped form. Joyce went blundering forward and landed on her injured wrist. She hissed in pain, teeth bared, and thrashed her head about, obviously attempting to keep silent.

"I'm really sorry," Duane whispered.

But neither of the women was listening to him. Savannah stood on the trail beyond where Joyce lay clutching her wrist. He figured Savannah was merely listening for the beast, but when he pulled up next to her, he discovered what had made her stop.

On the trail before them lay a severed human leg. A few feet farther on, there was another leg.

The worst part was, they'd come from two different people.

"Should we turn back?" he asked her.

Savannah licked her lips, continued to gape at the legs. Both of them were right legs, one slender and swathed in blue jeans, the other one bare and obviously male. Unless some woman did a hell of a lot of squats and hadn't shaved in years.

"Watch out for the barbed wire," a voice said.

He turned and saw Joyce, who was still rubbing her injured wrist. Then, with a glance toward where Joyce was looking, Duane discerned a mangled barbed-wire fence, the posts having come loose from the ground and lying in a bed of weeds.

"Hey," he said to Joyce, "I really am—"

"Thank you for saving me," she said and smiled wanly up at him.

Duane almost managed to smile back.

Then two figures darted toward them, and Duane's smile vanished.

Duane recognised the pair right away. Dalton and Carrie Green. They'd been two of the biggest partyers in Duane's class ever since junior high. Duane remembered the way Dalton used to brag about how far he'd gotten with Carrie back in seventh grade, a fact that Duane now considered pretty creepy. Dalton had always been regarded as one of the coolest kids in school, a dope smoker and hardcore barefoot skier. Hell, he still barefooted during the summers in the Beach Land ski show, the epitome of the suntanned stud.

But now he was shrieking like a toddler fleeing a tarantula.

Dalton was easily outpacing Carrie, who was shouting for him to "Wait for me, goddammit! Wait!" But Dalton had no such inclinations. It was obvious his plan was to save himself so he could live to ski another day.

As Dalton swept past, Duane and Savannah parted to let him through. A moment later Carrie blasted through the same gap, still bellowing outrage at her husband.

Dalton disappeared around a bend and Carrie was about to follow when an enormous shape pounced on the trail ahead of her. How the beast had gotten ahead of the Greens or how it had moved so stealthily through the woods, Duane had no idea. But now it rose up, the remains of its black clothes in blood-drenched tatters, its hairy face dripping with viscera.

"Dalton!" Carrie screamed. She backpedalled slowly away from the creature. "Dalton, goddammit, you come back here and help me!"

Dalton had evidently decided on a different course of action.

Carrie pulled even with them, and Duane had time to think, *Why aren't we running away too?* before the creature strode forward, smiling ferociously, and pushed Carrie onto her back. Ignoring everyone else, the beast climbed on top of her and pinned her wrists down on either side of her face.

Do something! Duane told himself.

It was Savannah who acted first. She leaped atop the creature's broad back and began digging at the base of its neck with her fingernails. She shouted curses at the beast, used language Duane had never heard her use before. Snarling, the creature pivoted, the force of its twisting torso launching Savannah into the weeds. The beast climbed off Carrie Green – who had lost most of her throat – and clambered toward the place where Savannah lay, stunned, on the ground.

The only thing he could think to use for a weapon was one of the fence posts still partially attached to the barbed wire. As the beast climbed atop Savannah's supine form, Duane dragged the muddy post toward it.

He feared the barbed wire still attached to the topmost section of the post would prevent it stretching far enough to do any good. But by digging the heels of his sneakers into the soft earth and straining with all his might, he was just able to make it reach.

As Duane raised the post, which was tapered at one end, visions of the many cinematic Van Helsings he'd seen over the years flitted through his mind:

Edward Van Sloan.

Peter Cushing.

Herbert Lom.

Anthony Hopkins.

Hugh Jackman.

And now, Duane McKidd.

Aka Short Pump, Werewolf Slayer.

He thrust the post toward the beast's back.

With a blur of movement, the beast whirled, seized the post.

Hurled Duane to the ground.

The creature's bestial face loomed closer, its noxious stench clogging Duane's nostrils. He shoved against it, attempted to buck it off, but it was like trying to dislodge a collapsed overpass from atop a crushed car. The barbed wire from his failed weapon had gotten trapped between them, the jagged, rusty spikes puncturing Duane's chest, tearing him open. Blood trickled down his rib cage. He realised he was going to die.

The creature opened its jaws.

Its eyes shot wide.

Duane felt the barbed wire embedded in his chest tug, then grind sideways. The pain was excruciating, but the effect on the beast was somehow more pronounced, the creature now roaring in fury. Then its roar abated, its eyes filling with panic. Its talons dug at its neck, and Duane finally understood why. Someone had wrapped a section of the barbed wire around the beast's throat, was tightening it. The creature tumbled off, a deep, anguished rumble issuing from its wide-open maw.

In disbelief, Duane pushed onto his elbows and looked at his saviour.

Savannah gripped the barbed wire like the reins of a horse, straining backward, the beast's muscular body bowing dramatically. Duane hoped the beast would give in then, but with a desperate jerk, it detached the barbed wire garrote with a meaty *shlick*. The barbed wire tore free of Savannah's fingers and, judging from the way she cried out and clutched her hands to her stomach, also removed a good deal skin from her palms. Duane knew the beast wasn't fatally injured, knew it was only a matter of time before the son of a bitch continued with its onslaught.

So he strode over to it.

The beast rose to its full height. Duane positioned himself between the beast and Savannah.

"Run," he muttered to Savannah.

"Fuck you," she said.

Then I guess we'll die together, he thought.

The beast extended its enormous arms, bellowed at them in triumph.

Duane steeled himself for the impact.

And watched in shock as the creature went dancing backward, the forest around them erupting in a fusillade of gunshots. He and Savannah stumbled away and burrowed into the weeds as five, eight, ten more shots sounded, the reports deafening in the peaceful country air. The beast roared, twisted, its eyes vast with outrage. Then it scrambled into the shadows.

"Let's go," a voice said to them.

Duane looked up, saw Joyce hauling Savannah to her feet, and just had time to think, *Where the hell have you been?* when another surge of gunfire shattered the night.

"Over there!" someone shouted.

"It's heading for the creek," someone else called.

No fewer than seven hunters scampered away in pursuit of the beast.

"We've got to go," Joyce urged.

Duane looked at her. "You okay?"

"Fine," she said. "Savannah, we have to—"

Savannah nodded. "I want to see my son again."

Duane started down the trail behind Savannah and Joyce. As they picked up speed, he considered Savannah's little boy and wondered for perhaps the thousandth time if Savannah might someday view Duane as a potential husband and stepfather.

Then Duane's thoughts dried up like a sunblasted lake bed.

Jesus Christ, he thought.

Glenn.

But still he ran, knowing there was little he could do now.

Coward.

No! he thought. He had to protect the women.

More like them protecting you.

Duane set his lips in a grim line, told himself he'd done what he could do. He hadn't acted cowardly.

Had he?

Glenn sacrificed himself for Mike, and they were long-time enemies. Glenn's your best friend, and you're just going to leave him back there to die?

Duane skidded to a halt. Savannah, who was perhaps twenty yards ahead, threw a glance at him. Then she too stopped. "What in the hell are you doing, Duane?"

"I've gotta get Glenn," he said.

"Are you completely insane?" she demanded.

Joyce stood watching them. Duane felt a rekindling of dread, though of a different sort this time. It was almost like Joyce no longer possessed a healthy fear of the beast. She could have been out stargazing for all the concern she was showing.

"Hey!" Savannah said, grasping him by the shoulders and giving him a rough shake. "Do you have a brain or not? Because if you do, you'll get your ass up that trail with us and get back to town."

Duane wanted to be persuaded. But the image of Glenn stepping between the beast and Mike Freehafer dominated all. For all his faults, for all his womanising and selfishness, Glenn had come through when it mattered most. And while Duane had done better than, say, Dalton Green, who'd abandoned his wife to have her throat ripped out by the monster, Duane still reckoned he ranked pretty low on the heroism scale.

He had to go back.

Duane looked deep into Savannah's blue eyes, noticed the lighting out here was just strong enough to reveal the tiny freckles on her nose and her cheeks. Her strawberry-blond hair swayed fractionally in the midnight breeze. Duane studied her full lips, which were slightly open now, her concern for him plainly written in her expression. He reached out, slid his arms around her, leaned forward…

"Duane?" she asked.

He closed his eyes, brought his lips—

"*What the hell's wrong with you?*" she snapped. She shoved him away, glowering.

Duane smiled lamely but could think of no good answer. Kissing her had seemed the natural thing to do. He might be going toward his death, after all.

She sighed. "Well, good luck. I still think you're being a dumbass."

And with that, she took off down the trail.

Duane turned back toward the woods where he heard shots being fired, raised voices. Hopefully the hunters would keep the beast away from him.

With a shuddering inhalation, Duane set off to rescue his friend.

CHAPTER NINE

The distance to the clearing didn't seem as vast this time, but his body still felt taxed, the stitch in his side like a blade some Spanish inquisitor was slowly twisting. The sounds of the hunters and the occasional howl of the beast were now somewhere to his right, either at the farthest reaches of the forest or the cornfields beyond. Once he'd heard screaming of the sort he'd heard earlier, that high-pitched caterwaul that bespoke of mortal terror and incalculable pain.

He hoped Savannah and Joyce had made it out alive.

Duane was maybe fifty yards from the clearing when he heard a soft whimpering to his immediate left. It sounded like a small animal, the really pitiful sort of sound a puppy made when it was first taken from its mommy.

He ducked below the bough of a maple tree, shouldered his way between a couple saplings, and discovered the figure curled up on the ground. It was a woman, and there was blood on her right side. It looked oily and black, and it glistened in what little starlight filtered through the overhanging trees.

"Hey," he whispered, bending closer to the figure. "You okay?"

He knew it was a stupid question, but making conversation was difficult with a bloodthirsty monster roaming about.

The girl uttered another one of those pitiful whimpers. Duane knelt and placed a hand on her arm.

She gasped and scuttled away. He got a brief glimpse of her face this time – it was Melody Bridwell – but she didn't seem to recognise him. She was gaining her feet, stumbling toward a thicket of spruce trees.

He chased after her. "Wait a second," he hissed. "It's me, Duane!"

She kept going, blundering through the brush and exhibiting a serious limp.

Duane stopped, sighed. "It's Short Pump."

Melody froze. She looked back at him with mascara-streaked eyes. "Short Pump? You promise it's you?"

"Keep your voice down," he hissed.

With a moan she launched herself toward him. Duane caught her and almost stumbled backward. She let loose a gush of words into his chest. She really was a tiny thing.

"It hurts, Duane."

He frowned at her, then remembered the blood on her shirt, her hip, her upper leg.

"Let me see it," he said. He had no medical training, hadn't even taken a course on first aid since college. If she needed a Band-Aid, he supposed he could stick one on her, but if any measures were required beyond that, she'd better look elsewhere.

Duane saw her wounds and felt his stomach lurch.

They weren't fatal. At least he didn't think so. But they were extremely gross, and there was a hell of a lot of blood. Duane prided himself on never squirming during a gory movie scene, but in real life he was pretty squeamish. The sight of Melody's leg wounds, which were deep enough to reveal gristle and the pale gleam of bone, made him want to toss his cookies.

He unbuckled his belt.

"What the fuck are you doing?" she gasped.

He stared at her. "Stopping the bleeding."

She blew out trembling breath.

He slid out his belt, cocked an eyebrow at her. "What'd you think I was doing?"

A tear gathered in the corner of one eye, dripped down her cheek. "I'm not used to chivalry."

Duane cinched his belt around her thigh hard enough for her to yelp.

"Does it have to be this tight?" she moaned.

"I'm afraid so," he said. "It looks to me like you've lost a lot of blood."

She made a pitiful humming sound and tottered on her feet. Duane put a steadying arm around her. "I've got one more thing to do, and then I'll get you out of here."

She seized a handful of his shirt. "Don't leave, Short Pump! What if that thing—"

"It's not going to come back," he said. *Not unless you bring it back with your screaming.* "Now just sit over here," he said, half-carrying her to a spruce tree with a slender vertical gap near the ground, "and wait for me."

"You can't go!"

"I'm coming back, Melody, I promise."

"But—"

"Glenn's still in the clearing," he explained. "I've got to get him out of there."

"But Glenn is an asshole."

He nodded. "Be that as it may, he's still my friend. Now,"—he forcibly detached her fingers from his shirt—"I'm hiding you here so that thing won't find you."

She peered at him from the shadowy place in which he'd stashed her. "What if it does come back?"

Then you'll be ripped to shreds?

"I'll only be gone a minute."

She stared up at him hopefully and even ventured a smile, and in that moment Duane felt bad for all the things people had ever said about her. It was common knowledge she'd known a lot of guys.

Not that Duane had ever enjoyed the privilege.

His eyes travelled to her blood-soaked clothes, her meaty leg wound. She was in wretched shape. He hoped the doctors wouldn't have to amputate. Of course, that assumed Duane would get her back to a hospital.

With a nod of encouragement, he set off down the trail. It occurred to him he hadn't heard any gunshots since finding Melody. He tried not to attach too much significance to this, but it sure as hell brought back his fear of being eaten. He remembered Carrie Green's anguished screams, recalled the way the monster had eviscerated Mike Freehafer.

Pushing the images away, Duane hurried along the trail, hunched over and listening for any sound. Why he was hunched over he wasn't quite sure; he was too damned huge to be overlooked should the beast come prowling. But it did make him feel better to create a lower profile, the way soldiers did in movies.

He spotted Glenn.

His friend was on his hands and knees, crawling out of the clearing like an inquisitive infant testing his boundaries. As Duane hustled over and squatted beside Glenn, he glimpsed his friend's arm wounds, which were bloody but perhaps not quite as deep as Duane had first assumed.

"Looks like you're gonna make it," Duane said.

"I've been better," Glenn grunted. "Arm hurts like hell."

There were four stripes on the meat of Glenn's forearm, which reminded Duane of the creature's wicked talons, which reminded him the thing was still out here somewhere, and it was no longer revealing its whereabouts to him or anyone else. The hunters weren't firing either, not even intermittently.

So they killed it, he thought.

Or it killed them.

The little hairs on the back of Duane's neck prickled.

"Hey, buddy," he said. "You think you can walk? I'm a little antsy to get out of this forest."

Glenn winced. "That thing rang my bell pretty hard, but I think I can get up. Here..." he said, and Duane took his good arm. Together, they hoisted Glenn to his feet. He stood there swaying a moment, then leaned against Duane for support.

"Ready?" Duane asked.

"Just about," Glenn said. "But there's one more thing you gotta do."

"What's that?" he asked and cast a fearful look into the forest.

"Weezer's over there," Glenn said, nodding back over his shoulder.

Duane stared at Glenn for a moment, amazed he'd forgotten about Weezer. Then again, things had been so insane that Duane felt he could be forgiven this oversight.

He nodded, his hackles absolutely tingling now. "Okay. There are already two of you I've got to get out of here. Melody's hidden in a tree up there a ways."

Glenn squinted at him. "She's in a tree?"

Duane gestured impatiently. "No, not literally in a tree, but sort of tucked beneath – ah, to hell with it. You wait here and don't get eaten. I'll get Weezer."

He left Glenn and hunched down again, his movements quicker than ever. Because now he wasn't just being compelled along by pants-shitting terror, he was being spurred by the growing notion that he'd pushed his luck as far as it would go. He hadn't heard a howl or a gunshot for so long now he was growing certain that the beast had picked off the hunters one by one and was now circling back to continue his rampage on the unarmed partygoers. If the hunters had killed the beast, Duane reasoned, they would be celebrating their triumph, perhaps even trying to parlay it into some sort of notoriety – an article in the paper or even some conquering-hero sex. But the forest was silent, save for the crackle of the bonfire.

Duane scanned the clearing for Weezer.

Duane spotted Mike Freehafer, or what was left of him. He looked away before the sight could nauseate him. He saw several other carcasses lying about, but none of them was Weezer.

He whirled, heart pounding.

No sign of the beast.

Duane clenched his fists, made his legs move forward.

"Weezer?" he said in a hushed voice. "Weezer, you there?"

Maybe the beast took him.

Duane shook his head, crept around the bonfire. He performed a slow, trembling revolution, his eyes scouring the woods. But there was nothing.

He was about to scamper away when he spotted them, the black soles of two work boots. Even though he could only discern a fraction of them through the weeds, he knew they belonged to Weezer. Duane stepped that way, and as he did, he distinguished the denim cuffs of Weezer's jeans, the faded red fabric of his friend's shirt.

"*Weezer*," he breathed, reaching his friend and kneeling beside him. Weezer was lying in the weeds, his face buried in the crook of an arm. His head was bobbing and jerking on the ground, giving Duane the impression that Weezer was eating the dirt and the dead leaves under his face.

"Hey, buddy," Duane said, putting a hand on Weezer's back. "We gotta go."

Weezer's head continued to bounce in that bizarre sewing machine way.

What the hell?

He reached down, jostled Weezer's shoulder. "Hey, get up, man. That thing's gonna..."

Duane trailed off as he noticed something he hadn't before, a reddish streak on the top of Weezer's head. The brown hair there was matted and sticky.

Nervously, Duane reached down, rolled his friend over.

And sucked in breath.

The slash marks ran the length of Weezer's face and didn't stop until his jawline. He'd been disfigured, one of his eyes gone entirely, his lips cleaved into wormlike segments.

Jesus, Duane thought. *Jesus God.*

Weezer was thrashing his head about, whimpering and uttering garbled words and phrases, almost none of which Duane could make out. Something about a teacher and staying after class and the word *sorry* at least two dozen times.

Duane reached out to stabilise his friend's thrashing head, but a gout of syrupy blood slapped over his fingers. Duane pulled back, grimacing.

You have to do this, he told himself. *So stop being a wuss.*

Mastering his gorge and his revulsion, Duane grasped Weezer by the shoulders, whispered "Shhhh" over and over until his friend's head stopped whipping. Speaking directly into Weezer's face, he said, "We have to get you out of here, buddy. You're going to make it, but you're really—" He swallowed. "—really banged up." Duane looked around, licked his lips. Had there been a sound in the forest?

"Look," he continued, then realised that was a poor choice of words. "Listen," he said, "I'm going to get you on your feet, but you're going to have to walk out of here. Melody's got a bum leg."

He hoped Melody was still alive. He had no idea if his tourniquet had done any good; she might very well have bled out under that spruce tree.

Weezer was weeping silently, his tears and blood mixing into a translucent gruel.

"Okay," Duane urged. "Here we go."

He lifted Weezer off the ground and stood him on his feet. His friend was short and wiry, but he still weighed more than Joyce had. He supposed he could carry Weezer if he had to, but moving that way, they'd get out of this godforsaken forest sometime next week.

"Come on, buddy," he said, and slung Weezer's arm around his neck. The height disparity made it awkward going, but at last he was able to transport Weezer out of the clearing back to where Glenn stood waiting for them.

A minute after that, he, Glenn, Weezer, and Melody were staggering down the lane like the survivors of some gruesome scientific experiment.

CHAPTER TEN

The sounds of something scraping. A pencil scratching on paper. Someone was writing something down near him.

Glenn opened his eyes, and though his vision was very blurry, he discovered he'd been right. There was a nurse scribbling on a clipboard.

Glenn waited until the nurse was gone. Then he set about disconnecting the many wires they'd taped to him. The most painful one was the blood drip. He figured he could just slide out the needle, but in his foggy state he didn't realise the needle was held in place by approximately seventy strips of tape. At that point he stopped jerking on the needle and examined the thing. He realised he could detach it higher up, and though this caused him to leak blood, he was able to stanch the bleeding by packing a wad of cotton into the tip.

He heard the trickle of water, frowned, and glanced down. The narrow tube connected to the drip sack was pissing liquid all over the floor. Glenn grasped the tube, kinked it, and clumsily tied it off.

He was halfway to his feet when a wave of dizziness bowled him over, sent him slumping on the edge of the hospital bed. He had no idea what time it was, nor did he have any clue which hospital he was in. Lakeview Memorial, he assumed, though it was possible he'd been airlifted somewhere else after they'd sedated him. For all the fuss they'd made, you'd have thought he'd lost all his limbs and a couple vital organs.

Glenn's dizziness started to pass. His eyes drifted down to his arm, the one without a hundred holes and tape marks on it. There was a thick white dressing over his forearm and dammit, more tape.

A surge of superstitious dread flowed through him at the sight of the bandage. But why, he wondered, did the prospect of examining his wounds scare him so much?

You know why, Professor. You're frightened because when you see the wounds, everything that happened tonight will be confirmed as real, and you'll no longer be able to cling to the desperate hope that it was all some monstrous nightmare.

But that wasn't quite true, he realised. For one thing, the arm barely hurt at all. He wanted to attribute that to the painkillers they'd no doubt pumped into him, but why then did his head feel like it was being prised apart from within? Why did his ribs ache from being taken down by the beast? If he was feeling this much pain, shouldn't his mutilated arm be aching too?

Now you're getting it, a voice murmured. *Deep down, you know what you'll see under that bandage, and you have a good idea what it'll mean. Wounds don't heal like that, Glenn. Unless something unnatural is happening to you.*

Glenn raised the bandage, hoping against hope that the wound would be as ragged and ugly as it had been when the beast first attacked him.

But it wasn't. The angry red lines had already begun to knit, almost as if the stitches themselves were nuisances hindering the healing process.

Glenn stared at his forearm. *Well, shit.*

Nauseated, he rose from the bed and shuffled toward the door. He figured once he reached the hallway, there'd be a nurse there to shout him back to his bed. He had a vague recollection of a woman built like a defensive lineman asking him questions he was too dazed to answer. If that behemoth was his nurse, he had even more incentive not to get caught.

Glenn peered right and left, saw no one. Only the elongated shadow of someone at the nurses' station down the hallway.

But where was Savannah? According to Short Pump she was just fine. Her friend, the librarian, was *not* fine, however, so she would be in intensive care just like Glenn.

So find the librarian. Savannah might be with her.

Glenn shuffled forward, aware for the first time of his lack of clothing. Was it really necessary, he wondered, for hospital gowns to flutter open in back? As if an exposed butt helped facilitate the healing process?

He reached the first door, the one next to his. He opened the door and poked his head inside on the off chance it was the right room.

It was.

The librarian was sitting up in bed, watching him.

"She's with her son," the librarian said.

Of course she is, Glenn thought. He'd been foolish to think she'd be anywhere but with Jake. Sure, she cared about this peculiar friend of hers, but to think the librarian would supersede Savannah's desire to protect her child? Man, he really was addled from the drugs.

"Sorry," he muttered, "I'll just—"

"It's better, isn't it?" the librarian said.

He stared at her. "I don't know what—"

"Your arm," she said. "It's healing already."

Glenn opened his mouth, closed it. Then, with a glance down the hallway at the nurses' station – still no one coming – he stepped inside and pulled shut the door.

"I'm sorry," he said. "But..."

"Joyce," she supplied. "Joyce Pertwee."

"That's an odd name. What is it, French?"

"Huguenot," she said. "How did you know that?"

He gave a little shrug. "Other people read, you know."

"Let me guess. Historical fiction?"

"I'm not in the mood to talk books. Have you heard from Savannah?"

"She called a few minutes ago. I wouldn't let them take my cell phone."

She flourished it. "It has my e-reader."

"Wouldn't want to lose that." He moved closer to where she sat, noticing as he did she looked more like a spa patron than a woman who'd been badly injured. At her bedside, he said, "What you said earlier about..."

"Healing," she said.

"Yeah, healing. Why did you say that?"

She brought up her arm, which was bandaged about the wrist. She made a fist, rotated it back and forth. "There are a couple of shoulder lacerations that haven't quite healed, but my wrist bones are already beginning to bind. The doctor scheduled surgery to insert pins, but after the last X-ray, he says that might not be necessary."

Glenn realised he'd begun to rub his forearm. He forced himself to stop.

Joyce noticed it. "So the question is, what does it mean?"

"It means we got lucky," Glenn answered. "And a whole lot of our friends didn't."

"I didn't know any of them."

Glenn stiffened. "You don't care that they're dead?"

Joyce didn't wilt beneath the heat of his glare. "I didn't say that."

"You didn't have to," he said. "Which room is Weezer in?"

"I don't—" Joyce started to say, then her eyes darted over his shoulder.

"What are you doing out of your room?" a stern female voice demanded.

Glenn turned and beheld his nurse, a broad-shouldered woman with black hair so shellacked with hairspray that it looked like Darth Vader's helmet.

"I needed to see Joyce," he explained.

The nurse strode over to him, her lips going thin when she spotted the needle jutting out of his skin. "This was giving you medication, Mr. Kershaw."

"I don't need it."

"Yes, you do," she said. "Dr. Morris says you were attacked by a wild animal, and you need antibiotics to prevent infection."

Glenn glanced at his arm. *Yes*, he decided. *Definitely healing.*

"You can keep your antibiotics."

The nurse followed his gaze, and her expression clouded. Then she seemed to fight off whatever uneasiness the sight of his nearly healed arm had engendered. "You need bed rest. I'm not going to say it again – get back to your room."

"It wasn't an animal," Joyce said.

The nurse glowered at her, placed her hands on her considerable hips. "Now don't you start in on that again. I wasn't even supposed to be working tonight, but after what happened..." Her brow knitted, and when she spoke again, her tone was softer. "You both need sleep. Will you please cooperate?"

Glenn asked, "Which room is Weezer's?"

The nurse's scowl returned. "Now don't go thinking you're—"

"Two down from mine," Joyce said.

Glenn frowned. "Who's next door?"

"It doesn't *matter* who's next door," the nurse snapped. "What matters is that you two—"

"The Bridwell girl," Joyce said.

Glenn's mouth went dry at the memory of her mutilated leg. *Poor Melody*, he thought.

The nurse abruptly grabbed him by the flap of his white gown. "To bed, Mr. Kershaw. You won't do your friends any good by barging into their rooms. They're both heavily sedated, and both in very serious condition."

Glenn felt a lump forming in his throat.

The nurse's hand moved to his lower back, and this time her voice was gentler. "I know you're worried about him, but Mr. Talbot will only get better if he's kept in a controlled environment. That means constant supervision and no visitors. We need to minimise the chances of infection."

Glenn looked at her.

"His wounds were very deep, Mr. Kershaw," she explained.

Glenn frowned, but he had to admit what she was saying made sense. He allowed her to lead him out. The truth was, he did feel utterly exhausted. The nurse helped him onto the stiff hospital bed, reclined the upper half a bit, and drew up the sheet. It took a few minutes to reattach all the tubes and wires to his arms – more tape – but at last she succeeded. Then she extinguished the lights and went out.

Glenn closed his eyes, settled back into his nest of pillows.

It's better, isn't it? Joyce had asked. She'd known he was healing. How had she known it?

Because her wounds are healing too.

The human body was a resilient thing, he knew, but to recover with such startling rapidity from such hideous wounds...

It wasn't possible.

Yet it was happening. Could Weezer and Melody Bridwell also be healing as quickly?

With a sick jolt, Glenn remembered Weezer's ruptured eye, popped like an overripe pimple. A wound that grievous would surely never heal.

God. He couldn't imagine how Weezer must be feeling, couldn't imagine how Weezer would feel once the medication wore off and the true state of things revealed itself.

I'm sorry, Weezer, he thought. *I'm sorry.*

Glenn was brooding about his friend's missing eye when sleep finally took him.

★   ★   ★

Bobby Wayne Talbot, otherwise known as Weezer, heard the nurse close the door, and he was left with the horrible, stultifying silence of the intensive care ward. He could make out the beeps and blips of the monitors, the occasional click of some machine, but predominant among all sounds was the absence of sound. And that was the worst thing of all.

Because into it flooded a parade of voices and images that refused to be displaced. And they weren't good memories – what few he had – they were the embarrassing ones, the remorseful ones, the gut-wrenching ones.

They'd strapped his fucking hands to the bed because he kept trying to claw off his bandages. But he couldn't help it. There were live things crawling over his face, or at least that's how it felt. Centipedes and ants and pill bugs, he imagined them all worming inside the trenches carved into his flesh, licking the coagulated blood, scooping out more of the scarified meat until they teemed through his skull, transforming it into a network of dripping tunnels and scar tissue.

Jesus, Weezer thought. *Jesus, just kill me now. I can't take this, can't take the agony of the bugs and the worms and the eggs they're laying under my skin.*

He bucked on the bed, strained against the leather straps. He remembered the nurse saying something about pain medicine. What a crock of shit. They kept pumping more and more of that stuff into his bloodstream, and all it did was make him itch more severely.

And maybe the constant, deepening itch wouldn't be so bad if the movie in his mind weren't so unbearable. At Duane's urging he'd once watched a movie called *Eraserhead*. They all dug horror flicks, and Duane kept claiming *Eraserhead* was a real trip. *Surreal*, Duane had called it. Well, it had been surreal, Weezer supposed, if surreal meant really goddamned confusing and completely fucked-up.

What Weezer was seeing in his mind right now was worse than *Eraserhead*, but the disconnected, grainy quality of the images came closer to *Eraserhead* than anything.

He saw his dad – lazy fuckup that he was – allowing Weezer and his younger sister, born only a year apart, to run loose at the town dump, to climb all over immense mounds of sand that had turned out not to be sand mounds at all, but piles of dangerous trash concealed by shallow membranes of sand. So Weezer and his little sister Callie had come away with shards of glass embedded in their feet and their palms, Callie with one gash so deep in her heel it got infected and made her limp ever after, though that hadn't been long since she'd died when she was eight.

Which was the next thing he saw, Callie's funeral, such as it was, conducted in the Talbot home and limited to friends and family. Callie had been placed in an open casket but hadn't been embalmed or anything, so that the late August heat had baked her corpse in the Talbots' living room, their house not air-conditioned. And Weezer had kept leaving the house on some pretence until his mom collared him and informed him it was disrespectful to ignore his sister like that. If he'd watched her in the first place, she might still be alive. He supposed that was the truth and he supposed he owed it to Callie to remain in the cramped living room with the crowd and the casket and the putrid fish smell, but try as he might, he couldn't take it. He imagined every eye was on him, assessing him, deciding it was his fault Callie had been run over like a fucking mongrel, the teenage girl who hit her insisting Callie would be okay, she'd be just fine, the teenager fluttering around Weezer while he touched Callie's face and whispered to her and begged her not to die. But her neck was all wrong, her hip poking out of her shorts in an unnatural way, and the teenager said, *It's okay, she'll be okay in a minute*, and Weezer thought, *It's my fault this happened. I was looking for cigarette butts with some tobacco in them.* It felt grownup to do that, to cough and splutter and make the smoke, and his parents didn't care, they must not, because they were visiting friends somewhere and had left Weezer to watch Callie for the day. And at the funeral that wasn't really a funeral because there was no preacher and no real ceremony, the fish smell kept getting worse and worse, and at one point his cousin Ervin had sat down on the couch beside him and asked him what it had sounded like.

What did what sound like? Weezer asked.

You know, Ervin said.

Weezer stared at him.

It, Ervin said.

I gotta go, Weezer said, beginning to rise.

But Ervin, older and stronger than he was, clamped a hand over his leg, pinning him to the couch.

Her body, Ervin said.

Weezer shook his head, the tears coming.

When the car hit her body, Ervin explained.

Weezer hung his head and shook with sobs.

Bet it thudded really loud, Ervin said. *Hey, did she fly through the air or anything?*

I don't know, Weezer moaned.

Shhh, Ervin said, the hand on his leg squeezing. *You don't want to hurt your mama any more than you have already, do you?*

Weezer felt hot acid boiling in his gullet.

What I was wondering, Ervin whispered, leaning closer. *Do you think she coulda got away from that car if she didn't have such a limp?*

And Weezer had strained against the imprisoning hand hard enough to draw attention, and he'd been dragged into the bathroom and given a hiding with his father's belt, the buckle and all. So he had bloody trousers the rest of the day and they still made him sit in the living room with the flimsy pine box and the deteriorating body and the fish smell getting more and more revolting.

In the hospital bed, Weezer thrashed against the smell, strained against the imprisoning straps, and under his flesh the maggots wriggled and wriggled. He could see them in there, squirming their way deeper. Jesus Christ, why couldn't it have been him that had gotten run down that sweltering August day? Why couldn't he have died and not Callie, Callie who went along with whatever dumb scheme he cooked up? Jumping out of trees, sneaking nips of their parents' cheap liquor, smoking the rank butts of discarded cigarettes.

"You don't have to grieve for her anymore, Bobby," a voice said.

Weezer froze. The voice had been in his head. More surreal shit.

He exhaled shuddering breath. Maybe if the nurse gave him one more dose of the drugs, he'd actually go under, rather than perpetually dwelling in this fever dream of memories.

"Now that you're an initiate, you share a telepathic link with our species."

Weezer began to moan.

"Accept it, Bobby."

This time Weezer lifted his head, opened the eye that didn't feel like a glass-choked garbage dump. It took several moments for his eye to adjust, and even when it did, the room was so dim he could scarcely make out the figure seated in the corner.

Weezer opened his mouth to cry out, but no sound escaped.

"I made a mistake," the man said. "I let passion govern me."

Weezer squinted into the gloom, but only the man's icy blue eyes were visible.

"You a doctor?" Weezer heard himself croak.

The man laughed, but it was a bitter, haunted sound. "I'd only planned on killing one, but I lost control. The hunger mastered me. And now the master must control the population."

Weezer didn't like the sound of that.

"Will the master kill me too?" he asked.

The man glanced at him. "Almost certainly. But even if you were spared, the suicide rate is very high. Many never adjust."

"Who is the—"

"*Silence!*" the man shouted.

Weezer recoiled.

"When you become something beyond the pale of the natural world, you attract attention. We don't want attention. We survive by lurking in the shadows."

Weezer swallowed. "Why'd you come to the party then?"

"I abandoned myself to bloodlust, it is true," the man said. "With much luck I shall be permitted to live." The man smiled. "But you...the others who were wounded...the master will come for you by week's end. In the past, they would have waited a fortnight, but not this time."

"What's a fortnight?"

"Gilles Garnier, they once called me," the man said. "Then David Gilles. I have survived longer than most. Until my unconscionable lapse in judgement."

Weezer's eye must have indicated his puzzlement, because the man went on. "I must go. But I will tell you this..."

The man rose, strode forward through the murk. Weezer began trembling.

The man leaned forward, his rough-hewn, animalistic features totally bereft of mercy.

"If you feel the urge to resist."

Weezer stared helplessly up at him.

"Give in," the man said.

And before Weezer could comprehend the meaning of these words, the man turned and exited.

PART TWO
CHANGES

CHAPTER ELEVEN

The next morning Joyce opened the library, stepped inside, and inhaled deeply. She'd suspected it before, but the transformation of her olfactory sense was now so obvious that she couldn't ignore it.

For the past six years she'd been entering this old building at 7:00 a.m., a full hour before the library officially opened. And for six years she'd been locking the door behind her, stepping a few feet to the left so anyone passing on the street wouldn't catch a glimpse of her, and drawing in a long, luxuriant breath of the more than fifty thousand books that populated the three storeys of the Lakeview Public Library. It gave her great pride to note – privately, of course; she'd never brag to anyone about her exploits, not even Savannah – that she'd increased the number of books by more than 30 percent since taking the job. And she hadn't done it by dumping a lot of crappy promotional copies or tattered old math textbooks into circulation; she'd been patient, strategic. Every new addition to the LPL was a worthwhile book. The library now boasted an impressive speculative fiction section, a more thorough representation of the classics. Even a strong foreign language area for those who wanted to improve themselves.

But now…but now…

Now it wasn't just books she smelled. Now the undercurrent of mildew that never seemed to go away, no matter how many dehumidifiers she ran, was a full-blown riot. The aroma of aged wood, pleasant in small doses, now carried with it the stench of rot, of disease, of termites. She'd have to call an exterminator, though she couldn't imagine how offensive the poisons would be to her hypersensitive nostrils.

Joyce strode over to the circulation counter, dropped her bagged lunch and her current novel – Brian Keene's *The Lost Level* – next to her monitor. She'd turn on the computer later. She needed to spend the next fifty minutes or so in research.

On the way to the speculative fiction section, Joyce mulled the facts of her situation.

Four of the people at the bonfire had been bitten or scratched. She, Bobby Talbot – otherwise known as Weezer – Melody Bridwell, and Glenn Kershaw.

It was now…she mentally calculated the time…thirty-two hours since the attacks.

Her wounds were almost healed. Her wrist fracture ached, but there was no explanation for how briskly the bones had knitted. She suspected that if an X-ray had been taken of her bones immediately after the attack, the findings would have revealed a break far more severe than the images she was shown at the hospital. That quickly, from the attack at the bonfire to the hospital, her bones had reformed into a fracture that wouldn't require surgery. While at the time of the injury she'd been sure the bones within her flesh had been ground into splinters.

Joyce climbed the spiral staircase, her wrist protesting only a trifle as she gripped the handrail.

What else do you know? she asked herself.

You're changing, she answered. *You can say it any way you'd like, but it boils down to the same thing: you're changing.*

Though only thirty, Joyce prided herself on accepting facts as they were, not as she wished them to be. It was this attitude that gave her a stronger-than-average self-knowledge.

She was not ugly, but she wasn't a stunner. To the right man, her looks were intriguing enough that, when combined with her intellect and her personality, she could become very attractive. But it would take the right man. And so far, she hadn't come close to finding him.

Despite the fact that she wanted to get married someday, she believed herself to be reasonably happy alone. She had her library. She had her books. And she had her small house on Bluff Street.

For now, that was enough.

At least, it *had* been until the attack.

Because now she found the longings that had been latent within her blossoming into full-fledged yearnings. Since childhood she'd been a vegetarian, not out of any ideological stance, but simply because she preferred the taste of fruits and vegetables. Occasionally, she'd experienced a craving for meat, but those moments were infrequent.

Until the attack.

The morning after the bonfire, she'd relished the taste of bacon strips, while grimacing at the staleness of her cornflakes.

Her other senses had grown keener as well. Her eyesight, twenty-twenty to begin with, now possessed a crystalline clarity that convinced her to eschew her reading glasses.

Her skin was more sensitive. The little hairs on her forearms prickled whenever someone approached. This morning she'd felt, by a tightening of the skin at the base of her neck, her neighbour Mr. Turpin eyeballing her from his kitchen window. No doubt he and everyone else in town had read or seen something about the bonfire murders, and like everyone else, Mr.

Turpin was no doubt curious about Joyce's story. But to feel his hungry eyes on her through a window at a distance of more than forty feet?

And her sense of hearing, she thought, making her way past the science fiction bookcases, had grown startlingly acute. This morning Joyce had stopped at a red light and heard a talk radio personality yammering on about the current crisis in health care. Yet Joyce's radio had been off, and there was no one in the lane next to her.

But across the intersection from Joyce's little Honda CR-V there was an elderly man nodding whenever the talk radio host made an emphatic point.

Her sense of hearing was uncanny.

So what, she asked herself as she neared the horror section, did it all mean?

Joyce stopped in front of a cherrywood bookcase and selected the book she'd been thinking about since the attack.

Lycanthropology, by Clark Lombardo Coulter PhD.

Joyce flipped the book over and scanned the back cover synopsis:

Repudiated by the academic establishment, reviled by the medical and psychiatric communities, the furor over the 1937 release of *Lycanthropology* ended Professor Clark Coulter's tenure at Columbia University and led to a tragic downward spiral of drinking, depression and suicide. Yet in 1963 – over two decades after Coulter's death – Hardscrabble Publishing's rerelease of Coulter's bizarre meditations spawned widespread critical acclaim and a devoted cult following. Now considered an underground classic, this notorious book is regarded as a masterful work of fiction, one that stands with Guy Endore's *The Werewolf of Paris* and Robert McCammon's *The Wolf's Hour* as one of the preeminent works of lycanthropic storytelling in the horror canon.

Smiling, she clutched *Lycanthropology* to her chest and moved down the aisle. From the folklore section, Joyce selected three relevant volumes from *Man, Myth & Magic*, two more books that dealt with shape-shifting, and tomes about Native American, Irish and Scottish folklore.

Stacking the books before her on a shelf, she frowned at their bulk. Better to make two trips down the stairs rather than attempt to lug them all at once. Especially with a bum wrist. Joyce was about to balance a cluster of five books in her hands when an inexplicable whim seized her, and she gathered all nine books to her stomach.

Though the stack reached all the way from the zipper of her shorts to her breasts, the weight felt like nothing at all.

With a mixture of elation and misgiving, she made her way down the loft aisle, then tromped down the spiral staircase, her feet moving with an excess of vitality that she hadn't experienced in years. She felt, God help her, like dancing.

But first she needed to learn what was happening to her.

Rather than sitting at the circulation desk, Joyce selected a spot near the back window, which overlooked the small hollow that abutted the library. As she read about the history of werewolves in ancient Europe, her thoughts drifted to Glenn. Was he healing as well?

She suspected he was.

Was he changing in other ways too?

Joyce tapped the pages of her book, found her eyes sliding out of focus.

She might as well admit it.

She wanted to go to him, ask him how he was doing. She even had an excuse to do so. An in. They'd endured a tragedy and for the first time shared common ground.

Would he be annoyed if she stopped by his house? If he was, she could simply return to her hermetic existence, no worse off than she'd been before.

But if he welcomed her inside…

Joyce's flesh tingled at the prospect of his touch.

Beware the rebel, her mother's voice reminded her.

Joyce pushed the thought away with little trouble.

Perhaps, she decided, Glenn was the one who needed to be wary of *her*.

A playful smile curling her lips, Joyce returned to her book.

★　　★　　★

Late that afternoon, six hours after being allowed to return home, Melody Bridwell worked up the courage to unwrap the tape with which the doctors at Lakeview Memorial had mummified her and peek under the discoloured gauze. The stain was a rusty brown, and it had begun to stink, but so great was Melody's dread of what she'd find under the gauze that she'd refrained from changing it like she was supposed to.

Through the bathroom door, she heard her father call, "Where'd you put my remote?"

It's where it always is, Melody thought. *If you weren't so lazy, you'd reach down and find it in the crevices of your recliner.*

"Be out in a minute," she called.

Melody bared her teeth as she pinched an edge of the gauze and peeled it back. The rank odours of unwashed skin and coagulated blood overwhelmed her.

She peeled the gauze back a bit farther and gasped at the way the large scab tore away from the new flesh. A wave of nausea lapped over her as she studied the lumpy brown scab. Like a hunk of beef jerky, the kind her brothers chewed when they were out of tobacco.

An armada of terrible images assaulted her. The cloying apple cider smell of Red Man tobacco. Brown teeth with a string of jerky fat dangling between them. Rank breath huffing over her averted face. Feverish grunting. A tearing pain. Then the unwanted lubricant of semen.

Melody caught sight of herself in the mirror, clapped a hand over her mouth. Yes, she was crying, but that was no big deal. She'd wept plenty of times over the past sixteen years of her life, ever since she'd developed the first alarming bumps on her chest and caught one of her brothers watching her while she played shirtless in the sprinkler.

What scared her was the way her teeth seemed to be elongating. It had only been a fleeting moment, and when she'd opened her mouth again a few seconds later, her teeth looked like they always did. White. Straight. The only member of her family who didn't look like she'd just pigged out on mud and barbecued pork.

Shivering, Melody thrust away the image of her distorted freak teeth and returned to the gauze pad, which was now halfway off.

"Melody Ann Bridwell, what the hell you doin'?"

Her muscles tensed, but she concentrated on removing the rest of the gauze. Biting her lower lip, she tore the last of the pad from her skin, discarded it in the overflowing trash can – she'd have to empty it soon even if it was her brother Robbie's only chore around the house. Well, that and porking his girlfriend Adriana Carlino.

Melody shivered. She could detect a dozen odours emanating from the dingy plastic receptacle, none of them pleasant. There were Adriana's wet wipes, which she prided herself on never flushing. That was probably better for the plumbing, but when the damn things smelled like old period blood, diarrhoea and unwashed cooter, Melody considered the trade-off a poor one. Add to those odours the smells of crusty tissues – her brother Donny still jerked off several times a day, despite being thirty-six this past April – banana peels, half-full spit cups, and several other withering stenches, and the bathroom was a horror show for her newly sharpened sense of smell.

Melody didn't linger long on this phenomenon because it made her uneasy. She'd decided the morning after the attack that her senses were more acute not because of anything unnatural, but rather because she'd adopted a new appreciation for life due to her near-death experience.

Sure, she told herself. *That has to be it.*

Biting her lower lip, Melody began to work her fingernails under the remaining scab, the one that began at her hipbone and crept all the way down to the back of her knee. There was some blood, some yellowish pus, and a whole lot of discomfort, but in the end she was able to scratch away the chunky layer of scab.

Leaving her with a large span of bright pink skin. She was certain there'd be no scar.

So why did this scare her so badly?

Melody turned, drew up the short sleeve of her shirt and suppressed a moan. The scab was flaking away on her shoulder as well, and like her leg, the flesh here was shiny and unblemished, like that of a newborn.

Yet on Sunday night the wound in her shoulder had been ragged and deep. Like a divot chunked from soft sod.

Melody remembered the beast thundering toward her, the eyes like hellfire, the heaving chest muscles as broad as a bodybuilder's, the hair so thick she could scarcely make out the rippling striations. She remembered the beast's gloating snarl, the steam-shovel talons. She remembered shrieking for help, screaming in pain, the droplets of blood flying like water from a summertime sprinkler, like—

"*Goddammit, girl, get your ass out here!*"

Melody jumped and leaned on the sink for support. Her father's voice battered the outside of the bathroom door again. Then his fists made the wood dance in the jamb.

Automatically, Melody went over, twisted open the lock. The door flew inward, sprawling her against the commode.

"What the hell is wrong with you, girl?" her father demanded. "My shows come on at six!"

Melody nodded, made to move past him, then remembered the gauze pad, the tape. Fragments of her scabs lay all over the floor and speckled the sink like flecks of red pepper.

She turned, hoping she could blot out her father's view of the mess. "I'm sorry I took so long, Dad. I'll be out in a second."

She thought her father would go, but peripherally, she saw him freeze.

His voice tight with suspicion, he asked, "What's that crap on the floor?"

Melody looked down and saw that the crap was her leg dressing, the unspooled strands of tape, the stained gauze pad.

"It's nothing, Dad. I just need to pick up—"

"Lemme see," he growled, and before she knew it, he'd yanked up on the leg of her shorts.

She could feel his eyes crawling over her flesh. And what was more, his beer breath was fouler than usual, because mingling with the Old Style scent were the onions she'd chopped for his hamburger earlier that day. As his knobby, loathsome frame drew closer, she smelled his body odour, like maggoty beef soaked in sour sweat, and the stench of his shit-streaked underwear. And underneath that, she could smell his need. His spoor, percolating in his vas deferens.

He began fondling her leg.

His voice husky, he said, "Looks like you're healin' up good, girl."

Closing her eyes, she nodded. "I think so."

"I think so, *Father Bridwell*," he corrected and slapped her on the butt.

She compressed her lips, nodded. "Father Bridwell."

"Say it, *bitch*," he ordered, crowding her now, his sex granite-hard against the flesh of her hip.

Melody said it and began to weep.

Like always, her tears were silent.

CHAPTER TWELVE

It was Tuesday, early evening. Since leaving the hospital, Glenn had slept a total of forty minutes.

Actually, he reflected as he slathered some butter on a burned slice of toast, forty minutes was a pretty generous estimate. The true number was somewhere closer to twenty, but hell, it was difficult to keep track of time when you were mired in a surreal fever dream.

Glenn bit down on the crunchy toast and frowned, his gorge rising. He was going to puke again unless he rid his mouth of the repulsive charred taste, the slimy patina of artificial butter slicking his tongue. He even tasted the knife he'd used to spread the butter, metallic and not entirely clean from its last use. His face crumpling in revulsion, he realised he could taste peanut butter on the knife, and when was the last time he'd eaten peanut butter? Two weeks ago? Three?

Glenn lunged to the kitchen sink, his chair overturning with a skull-piercing clatter, and geysered a jet of partially digested food into the basin. When his body unclenched, he made the mistake of looking down at what he'd regurgitated.

Hot dog chunks.

Barely-chewed bits of porterhouse steak.

Salami.

Glenn yarked again, this time only producing a reddish broth.

It didn't make a damned bit of sense. He could gobble any kind of meat he craved – and he was craving it all the time now – but if he so much as touched certain foods his gorge revolted violently.

This wasn't alarming by itself. Didn't most people's palates change as they grew older? That Glenn's change had come so rapidly on the heels of the bonfire incident was disquieting, yes, but perhaps that contained its own logic as well. Didn't traumatic events leave an imprint on their victims? Glenn had not only been attacked, he'd seen people torn to *shreds*. Or at least had heard about it afterward. Was it so far-fetched that an event like that could alter a person, including his diet?

Glenn moved to the back door, opened it. The outside air smelled exhilarating, though the sunlight was harsh on his eyes. Shielding them from the glare, he stared into the forest behind his house and remembered yesterday taking a twilight walk in the woods. Then a run. He'd been invigorated, alive. He had no idea how far he'd ended up running, but it had to have been more than five or six miles. And when he'd returned to his backyard, dusk having given way to darkness, he'd masturbated in the moonlight. He'd never done such a thing before, but it had felt liberating and perfectly natural.

Glenn frowned.

He moved through his backyard, noticed that the grass was in dire need of a trim. But a part of him enjoyed the primitiveness of the overgrown lawn, savoured the perfumes of the wildflowers and the weeds.

Glenn had motored to town last night, expecting the drive to do him some good. He figured the fragrant night air might even lull him into a state weary enough to sleep when he returned home.

But the air was anything but fragrant.

Glenn prided himself on taking great care of the 'Vette. He changed the oil himself, a function he performed twice as often as necessary. He only fed the girl premium gasoline, and he made adjustments to her several times each month. He doubted there was a better-loved car anywhere; Glenn was intimate with every inch of her.

But last night she'd made him sick.

In fact, by the time he'd reached Weezer's apartment building, he had felt so lousy that he'd needed to walk for a few minutes before rapping on Weezer's door. But if Weezer had been there, he'd decided not to answer Glenn's knock.

Yet the crazy thing was, Glenn was certain Weezer *had* been there. For one, there was Weezer's gamy body odour. He'd never been much bothered by it before, but he'd always been aware of it. It was an incisive, acrid odour that reminded him of old sweat and battery acid. Many times Short Pump had confided about how smelly Weezer was and should they maybe stage an intervention to persuade him to bathe more frequently? But while Glenn had always found the stench mildly unpleasant, he'd never been sickened by it.

But he was last night.

He was also sure he'd *heard* Weezer last night. Not his voice, but the sound of his breathing through the closed door. On top of that there'd been another sound, a subtler sound, and once Glenn had honed in on it, there'd been no mistaking it. The problem was, he knew it couldn't be what he thought it was.

It wasn't possible to hear someone's heartbeat, was it? Through a closed door? If it hadn't spooked Glenn so much, he would have chuckled at how much it was like that old Edgar Allan Poe tale.

But Glenn wasn't laughing. Not at Weezer's apartment, and certainly not on the way home. He judged he'd been about a mile outside town when the 'Vette ran down a possum. He had been imagining Savannah, naked. But rather than Savannah as she really was, this had been an alternate version of Savannah. A bushy-haired, long-toothed Savannah. Like a Savannah from the left side of the evolution chart. But in his vision, the musk emanating from her crotch had been so intoxicating that he'd run down the possum without even realising what he'd hit. It was only on performing a U-turn that he identified the animal.

By that time it was dead.

Furthermore, it was split wide open, its intestines strung out all over County Road 400. Glenn knew he should have been appalled by this gruesome sight, but for reasons beyond his understanding, the glistening entrails made him salivate with hunger. Impulsively, he'd scooped up the intestine string and bitten into it. There was shit inside it, but there was blood too, which drove him crazy. Before Glenn knew what was happening, he was ripping open the possum's belly and burying his face in the pinkish-red innards.

It had been incredible, the thrill even more sexual than his autoerotic behaviour in the backyard.

Yet when he'd returned to the 'Vette, slathered in possum blood and chunks of fur, and beheld his face in the mirror, he had looked like...

Himself. Whatever the internal changes were, he looked the same as he always had. He wasn't changing into *anything*.

So he could eliminate all the full moon horror movie bullshit from the list of possibilities. Yes, he was acting like a wild animal, but he was decidedly *not* a wild animal. He might be a carnivorous, masturbating possum eater, but he was still Glenn Kershaw.

But he sure as hell would not be going into the machine shop tonight. Let his coworkers pull their weight for a change. Glenn needed to get some sleep. He needed to get his head on straight. He also needed to see Weezer. Whatever was wrong with Glenn, he had the unshakable feeling that something much more troubling was occurring in that squalid second-storey apartment.

CHAPTER THIRTEEN

After two days of being interviewed by the police, and after making the difficult decision to avoid the funerals of their classmates later that week, Duane decided that what he and Savannah needed was a diversion. Though it was Wednesday morning and the wounded survivors had all been released from Lakeview Memorial, neither Glenn nor Weezer would respond to Duane's texts. It nagged at him, but he figured they were also trying to put the experience behind them and dealing with the trauma in their own ways.

Duane was sure as hell traumatised.

But very few towns this size, Duane reasoned, contained their own amusement parks, so they might as well use it. Though Beach Land was closer to a travelling carnival than a major theme park, it was nonetheless a diverting way to spend a day. The boardwalk, which fronted the lake, was maybe three hundred yards long and crammed with shops, food stands, and games engineered to steal your money. Inland, the park encroached another hundred-and-fifty yards, with a deep bay eating into the southern end. Beach Land had five decent roller coasters, another dozen rides, and one of the best haunted houses Duane had ever seen. The northern end of Beach Land boasted a respectable water park, with four tortuous water slides, the Lazy River, a kiddie area, and, of course, a sandy beach. Adjacent to the water park were the arcade, numerous food stands and restaurants, and an open-air bar called The Roof where famous rock bands used to play.

Not bad, Duane thought, for a town of only ten thousand people.

So when he'd asked Savannah to spend the day at Beach Land, Duane had counted on it being the three of them – him, Savannah and her boy. But when Savannah had invited Joyce along, he found it difficult not to let on how disappointed he was, how psyched up he'd been to show her the way things could be.

See, Savannah? he'd been thinking. *Just because you're not married yet, that doesn't mean you and Jake can't enjoy all the benefits and security of a loving nuclear family. I might not look like the traditional leading man, but I'm smart and I'm steady and I care a lot about both of you. Granted, Jake doesn't know me that well, but when he does, he'll take a shine to me. I can just about guarantee it.*

Except Jake scarcely made eye contact with him. From the moment they entered the park, Jake had been grafted to Savannah like a full-leg tattoo, the boy so clingy with his mom that Duane and Joyce might as well not have been present.

Which left Duane to make small talk to Joyce.

Not that he disliked her, of course, and not that he held her presence against her. How could she know the whole day was part of Duane's elaborate plot to marry Savannah? But not only was Joyce not the woman around whom his plans revolved, she was also far less engaged than she ordinarily was.

At the merry-go-round in Turtle Cove, the area for younger children:

"Hey, you look great, Joyce. You must be a quick healer."

Joyce going pale.

Duane shifting from foot to foot. "Not that you looked bad before."

In line for the Ferris wheel:

"How are things at the library? People checking out more werewolf books this week?"

Joyce arching an eyebrow at him.

"Yeah," he said, scuffing the pavement. "It's probably too soon to joke about it."

While they dropped popcorn into the teeming swarms of giant carp that congregated around a bend in the boardwalk, a foul, stagnant area so crammed with the giant brown fish that Duane felt as though he were watching a nature show about the Amazon River basin:

"Jeez. I'd hate to be the guy that slipped and fell into that."

Joyce eating her popcorn, her eyes glazed and unseeing.

Duane glancing at Savannah and Jake about ten feet down the boardwalk, Savannah holding the bag of popcorn, Jake tossing individual puffs into the water. Jake leaning out between the rails a bit too far for Duane's liking. "I hope Savannah's got quick reflexes," he murmured.

Joyce still saying nothing.

Duane, testing her: "I think I'll strip naked and dangle my private parts for the carp to nibble."

Joyce, without looking up: "The popcorn would probably make more of a meal."

Duane thinking, *At least she still has a sense of humour.*

After they'd grabbed lunch, Jake wanted to ride the merry-go-round again. Duane couldn't blame him; the carousel was surprisingly large and ornate, given the relatively pitiful scale and drabness of the rest of the park.

Savannah started to nod and take Jake's hand, but Duane said, "Maybe Joyce can go with him, and you and I can check out the Devil's Lair."

Savannah eyed him. "You joking?"

Duane smiled. "Why not? I haven't been inside since we were teenagers."

Jake had wandered over to inspect a blown-glass display in one of the many shop windows.

Savannah turned and eyed the upper reaches of the Devil's Lair. "Haunted houses creep me out."

Duane shrugged. "I'll be with you."

He knew he was in danger of overplaying his hand. Savannah might take his desire to split up the wrong way – *Why are you trying to get rid of Jake?* Worse, the kid might look at Duane as the guy attempting to steal his mom. Duane knew Jake was perceptive, and he knew the bond between a single mother and her child could be fierce. What if his Devil's Lair request had alienated both mother and child in one fell swoop?

He glanced at Joyce, hoping she'd help him out a little, but she still appeared lost in her own world.

"…not sure," Savannah was saying. She turned to Joyce. "What do you think? Do you mind looking after Jake for a little while?"

Joyce gave a faint nod. "Be happy to." She extended a hand, moved toward Jake. "Come on, pal."

His eyes still on a glass swan, Jake nodded and permitted Joyce to lead him away.

Watching them go, Savannah said, "You think they'll be okay? She's a zombie today."

"Glad you noticed it too," Duane said. "I assumed I'd offended her."

Savannah ambled toward the Devil's Lair. "You *have* said some pretty dumb things today."

"It's her silence," he said, struggling to keep the plaintive note out of his voice. "I get nervous when people don't talk."

"What's wrong with silence?" Savannah said. "It's not a bad thing to be content sometimes."

He shot her a look as they drifted into the shadows beneath the overhang. To their left was an Old West shooting gallery inset on the eastern side of the Devil's Lair. To their right was the ticket booth.

"I'm not content," he heard himself saying.

She glanced up at him. "Meaning?"

He coloured, grateful for the shadows enshrouding them. Because, though he knew exactly what he meant, he wasn't remotely comfortable verbalising the rest to her.

See, Savannah, I used to be content – no, that's not the right word. I used to be resigned. Yes, resigned to my lot in life: An overqualified assistant technology director for a rural school system. Overweight. Single. Definitely on the geeky side when it comes to my taste in movies and books. Clothes not very stylish. I was resigned to remaining single.

But I'm not resigned anymore. Not since the bonfire. Not since both of us almost died.

"Duane?" Savannah said, an edge to her voice.

He started, realised she'd said his name a couple times already.

"Sorry?" he said.

She smiled, nodded at an older lady with grey hair and a puckered mouth who eyed them from the ticket booth. "She needs ten dollars. I spent my last cash on popcorn."

Duane extricated his wallet from his back pocket. "Isn't this covered by our wristbands?"

"The Devil's Lair is not a pay-one-price attraction," the grey-haired lady said in a brittle monotone.

Duane opened his wallet. "Can you break a fifty?"

"No," the lady answered.

He sighed, began counting out bills. "I hope you don't mind a bunch of ones."

The lady didn't answer.

When he'd counted out enough bills and exchanged them for a pair of hand stamps, he said, "I guess I won't be going to the strip clubs tonight."

Walking toward the holding area, a space about twenty feet by fifteen, Savannah said, "You don't have to do that, you know."

"Do what?"

"Make bad jokes to impress me."

Stung, he stopped next to her and glanced about the semidarkness of the holding area. There was fluorescent yellow paint scrawled on the black walls. The messages ranged from the hokey – *Abandon hope all ye who enter here* – to the disquieting – *Guests with pacemakers and/or heart conditions should exit immediately.* The exit was marked with glowing red letters.

Loud voices sounded from their left, more people entering the Devil's Lair. Duane sighed.

"Disappointed?" Savannah asked.

"It's scarier when there's no one else around."

"I figured you wanted to put the moves on me."

Duane's throat went dry. In truth, the idea hadn't occurred to him.

He glanced beyond her and saw the group of college-age kids headed their way. And since Savannah was looking that way too, Duane decided to study the part of her face he could see. The skin of her neck. The hint of cleavage showing above her blue shirt.

What if I do put the moves on you? he wondered. *What if I show you just how much the bonfire changed me? Because I'm tired of being resigned. The bonfire was a wake-up call. A smack in the face reminding me that life is short and I'm wasting mine. So maybe I will put the moves on you, Savannah. Maybe I'll even do it with these giggling idiots right beside us. And if you slap me, you slap me. At least I'll know I tried.*

There were four guys and two young women. All the guys – even the one with his arm around a girl's waist – had noticed Savannah. But one in particular was leering at her.

"Hey, sweetie," he said to Savannah. Like Duane wasn't standing there.

"She's with me," Duane said.

The guy squinted at him. "You her uncle?"

Duane rummaged through a dozen withering retorts. The guy was probably twenty-two or twenty-three and was attired in a yellow Stephen Curry basketball jersey and jeans hanging so low that a good bit of his plaid boxer shorts showed over the waistband. The guy's head was blond and close-shaved, and his arms were banded with muscle.

"I'm her friend," was the only thing Duane could think to say.

The blond guy grinned. "Friend."

"*Boy*friend," Savannah corrected.

Without ceremony, she threaded her fingers through Duane's and stared at the closed elevator doors. The jerk subsided, muttering something unintelligible.

Without turning, she whispered, "Bet you didn't think I'd be putting the moves on you, did you?"

Duane tried not to fall to his knees and give praise.

The elevator doors opened. She gave his hand a squeeze, and they went inside. The college-age kids crowded in after them.

Duane barely noticed the middle-aged man who entered the elevator last.

★   ★   ★

The top floor was more about the buildup than the payoff. Kind of like Duane's sex life.

He'd experienced an electrifying thrill at the touch of Savannah's hand in the holding room, but he'd begun to worry about his palms sweating as the elevator made its slow climb to the fifth floor. Savannah spared him the worry after they exited the elevator, perhaps figuring it was unnecessary to keep up the boyfriend ruse in the lightless corridor.

Because they'd entered the elevator first, they exited last, which meant they should have been the rear members of their group. But somehow, the middle-aged guy had ended up behind them.

And that totally screwed up Duane's plan.

Of course, he didn't really believe he'd be able to do anything meaningful with Savannah in the haunted house, not with her son in the same amusement park, not with people constantly passing through. And, of course, there was the small fact that she'd demonstrated zero physical attraction to him.

But he thought maybe, if the conditions were perfect, and if she found herself in a magnanimous mood, and if her earlier show of good will had involved something more than a desire to tell off the blond-haired jerk, he'd thought *maybe* he could steal a kiss.

But not with the bespectacled man behind them.

How the guy had ended up back there, Duane had no idea. One moment the elevator doors were opening into darkness, the next the group of college-age kids were spilling out and making enough racket to disturb even the old hag down in the ticket booth. Duane hadn't noticed the other man at all, but he must have slipped sideways out the elevator doors, waited for Duane and Savannah to pass, then emerged from his hiding place to follow them. From overhead speakers Duane heard spooky organ music, the occasional chortle of some fiendish madman.

Duane glanced back and beheld the figure moving slowly through the weak greenish light.

Goose bumps rose on Duane's arms.

He couldn't help thinking of the bonfire.

"Look," Savannah said, crowding closer to him. He glanced ahead and saw, illuminated by a flickering orange sconce, a pair of hands protruding from the wall. The sextet ahead of them had just reached the protruding hands. The blond guy said something to a shaggy-haired friend, apparently egging him on. The shaggy-haired guy took one of the hands as if to shake it, but at that moment both arms shot toward him, driving him back against the women.

"What the hell?" the shaggy-haired guy shouted, and his companions all laughed uproariously. All except the girl he'd slammed into. She was slapping him on the arm and muttering curses.

Duane and Savannah waited until the group was far ahead of them, then sidled around the groping arms, which had begun to recede into the wall. Ahead, the hallway angled left, and just before they made the turn, Duane glanced back to see if the groping hands had claimed the middle-aged man.

But there was no sign of him.

"He still back there?" Savannah asked.

Duane shook his head. "No clue."

She chewed her bottom lip. "He didn't look dangerous."

"Looked like a serial killer."

She smacked him on the chest. "Short Pump!"

"Well, that's how they all look, isn't it? Gacy? The BTK Killer? Ted Bundy? They looked like regular guys. Like insurance salesmen or English teachers."

"Bundy was handsome."

"That's a weird thing to say."

"It's true," she said. "Just because he killed people—"

"And ate them."

"—doesn't mean he wasn't good-looking."

They were quiet a moment, staring into the pooled darkness behind them.

Duane whispered, "Where the hell did he go?"

"To get his silverware?"

He grunted breathless laughter. "Jesus, Savannah."

"You love it," she said.

Their faces were eighteen inches apart, the dim orange glow glinting in her blue eyes. There was no movement in the corridor. He could smell her perfume, though he had no idea what the scent was called.

Duane found it difficult to breathe.

She searched his face, smiled – a little sadly? – and said, "Let's get moving."

Duane gritted his teeth. *Coward!* he thought.

"I wouldn't mind letting those jerks get a little farther ahead of us," he said.

"Me either," she answered. "Except that means we'll be alone with Ted Bundy."

★　★　★

Glenn switched off the 'Vette's engine, and with the wad of paper towel shoved against his nose, he stumbled into the parking lot. This was getting absurd, he thought as he wheezed and coughed. He'd never heard of an allergy coming on so suddenly.

His coughing finally under control, he made his way toward the stairwell. This time, he decided, he'd break the damned door down if Weezer refused to answer. Glenn had begun to worry that his friend might be dead in there. Who would be the wiser? The guy's parents never checked on him. They were too busy losing money on the riverboats near Chicago to worry about their only living child. And other than Short Pump and Glenn, Weezer didn't have any friends. So where did that leave him?

Flyblown and putrefying, he thought.

"Hell with that," Glenn muttered and took the steps two at a time. He'd never felt better. At least with regard to physical fitness. The other changes were borderline terrifying – he still couldn't think about what he'd done to that possum – but he'd never felt stronger, more agile. As if to test this belief, he paused halfway up the final flight of stairs, crouched, and leaped.

And made it easily.

Glenn glanced behind him, unwilling for the moment to accept what had just happened. He estimated the distance at about six feet. But it was six feet of *vertical* movement as well as horizontal. Surely that wasn't possible.

But he'd done it.

He stood there grinning for a time. Then he remembered why he'd come.

Turning, he moved down the dreary hallway and stopped outside Weezer's door, 2F. He'd often kidded that Weezer should change the number to 7F so it could match his high school report cards.

Which was really goddamn funny, wasn't it? a caustic voice asked.

Glenn's fist paused a few inches from the door. *I was just teasing him. Lighten up.*

Easy for you to say, the voice answered. *Talk shit, make him feel even worse about himself, then claim you were kidding. No harm done, right?*

I didn't say that.

The hell you didn't. Weezer looks up to you, asshole. All you ever do is belittle him.

Glenn stared down at his feet a moment, trying and failing to fend off the tide of guilt. Surely he hadn't been that bad to Weezer, had he? Hell, he'd hung out with him since they were in junior high, and that kind of longevity was worth something, wasn't it?

Evidently, it's not enough to warrant decent treatment.

Glenn sighed. He'd always been in his head a lot, but now the voices were so unrelenting – and ruthless – that he felt as if a team of quality control monitors were following him around and critiquing his every move.

He knocked on Weezer's door.

No answer. Of course.

"Dammit, Weezer," he called. "You better be dead in there, or..." The words congealed in his mouth. What if Weezer really was dead? He'd been well enough to leave the hospital on Monday afternoon, but this was Wednesday. Had anybody heard from him since then? Thinking about his friend's pathetic, solitary life, Glenn began to rattle the knob. Then he hammered on the door, surprised at how violently it tremored in its jamb. He was stronger than he'd been since...well, *ever*. Had he possessed these physical tools back in high school, it would have been he, and not Mike Freehafer, who would have been drafted by the Cubs. And had Glenn been drafted, he sure as hell wouldn't have abandoned Savannah. He would've taken her with him, would have—

"Glenn?"

Glenn recoiled from the voice on the other side of the door.

"That you, Weezer?" Glenn asked.

A long pause. Then, "I just got up."

Glenn frowned. It was two in the afternoon. A hypothesis began to form in Glenn's mind...

"Hey, buddy. You been drinking these past couple days?"

Another pause. "Yeah. That's what I've been doing."

Glenn scowled at the door. Not only had Weezer's voice sounded unhealthy – it was too low, for one thing – he'd detected a strong note of mockery in the words. Was Weezer messing with him?

Glenn said, "You wanna do something tonight?"

Again came the voice, oily with derision. "Sure, Glenn. I'd love to hang out with you."

Glenn took a step back from the door. What the hell?

"Where would you like to go, Glenn?" the new Weezer asked.

What was up with all this "Glenn" crap? Weezer either called him Kershaw or nothing at all. The way Weezer said his name now reminded him of a teacher who had something on him. Or an ex-girlfriend about to bust him for cheating.

Glenn scratched the nape of his neck. "I don't know. We could try the Roof, see who's there."

Weezer didn't answer, but Glenn could hear him breathing. And smiling, he realised.

What a crock of shit, he thought. *How the hell can you sense a smile through a door?*

Glenn had no idea, but he was surer of it than he was of anything. Weezer was grinning at him. And not in a kind way.

Like a predator getting ready to pounce.

Glenn blew out weary breath. The notion of Weezer as some lethal killing machine proved what Glenn had suspected since the changes began. He'd gone online and done some reading about sensory hypersensitivity and found that in many brain trauma cases, patients underwent transformations a lot like the one he'd been experiencing. In the case of brain lesions, even the appetite could be affected.

Glenn thought it entirely possible that he'd incurred a lesion when the beast had attacked him. The creature had rammed into him with the force of a runaway train, after all, so it was likely he'd suffered some sort of brain injury. That the doctors hadn't found anything during his stay at Lakeview Memorial meant nothing. This was advanced stuff. Far beyond the pale of their limited expertise.

"How have you been eating lately, Glenn?" Weezer asked.

Glenn's heart began to gallop. Dry-mouthed, he stared at the door. "Why?"

"No reason," Weezer answered, the knowing taint in his voice thicker than ever.

Unaccountably, Glenn decided he needed to get out of here. He wasn't scared exactly — what was there to be frightened of? — but Weezer's behaviour was flat-out bizarre, and...okay, the guttural voice *did* give him a slight case of the willies.

Glenn had taken a step toward the stairwell when Weezer said, "How about the drive-in?"

Glenn paused. "What's playing?"

"Does it matter? It's the experience that counts, isn't it?"

Glenn couldn't argue with that. They'd practically lived there during high school and in their early adulthood. They only went once or twice a summer now, and they hadn't been yet this year.

But the more Glenn thought about it, the more he thought the drive-in might be exactly what he needed to inject a sense of normalcy into his life.

He nodded. "What time you want me to pick you up?"

Another one of those pauses. "Let's meet in the back."

Weezer didn't need to explain what this meant. They always staked out an area near the rear of the drive-in, where the ivy crept up the weathered fencing and no little kids ran around shrieking.

It was the best place to take a girl.

Not that Weezer had experienced much success in that arena. Glenn could count on two fingers the times Weezer had scored at the drive-in, and in both of those cases it was a matter of some dog-faced friend of a girl Glenn had picked up being bored or desperate enough to hook up with anybody.

More belittling, the voice in Glenn's head lamented. *Won't you ever learn?*

"All right," Glenn said. "I'll meet you there." He turned to go, paused. "Hey, Weezer?"

"Yes, Glenn?"

Glenn's triceps tightened. He was about to tell his friend to knock the

Glenn crap off, but bit back his angry words at the last moment. "Why haven't you been answering your phone?"

Fittingly, Weezer didn't answer.

"Or your door," Glenn continued. "I was here yesterday." He tried to smile. "You too good for me now?"

All the humour drained from Weezer's voice. "I've never been too good for you."

Ice water trickled down Glenn's back.

"Well," he said, retreating, "I better get going. I haven't been to work yet, and I figure the place has gone to hell."

"To hell," Weezer said, and this time the voice was so soft Glenn could barely hear it.

Without another word, he turned and hurried down the stairs.

CHAPTER FOURTEEN

Dusk, the pole barn. On Wednesdays it was a standing date. Melody wished she could steal away to the attic, but if she did that, they might learn her secret, and if they learned her secret, the one decent thing in her life would be wrested from her. Father Bridwell would never stand for a secret under his own roof. And Father Bridwell's sons would go along with whatever Father Bridwell decreed.

So Melody remained in the kitchen and kept on scrubbing the soup pot. It had been clean twenty minutes ago, but the longer she stayed inside, the longer she'd avoid the pole barn. Experience told her this was unwise, that they'd get pissed off being made to wait, but the thought of going out there tonight was unfathomable.

Yet she knew she'd go. She always did. Because the alternative was worse. The handful of times she'd thrown a fuss about their Wednesday nights had ended in injuries that had taken weeks, even months to heal.

Stop it, she told herself. She inhaled quaveringly, concentrated on scrubbing a stain from the base of the soup pot. The stain was russet-coloured, like a splotch of blood, and had been there for as long as she could remember. But now it seemed very important to remove it. She nudged the water hotter, thinking that would loosen the stain, but when that didn't help, she bumped it all the way to the left, where the water began to steam. She filled the soup pot, the soapsuds popping from the heat, just a scrim of milky fizz now. Her fingers were entombed in the superheated water, the heat blistering, so hot it almost felt icy, and still Melody worked the scrubber, the tendons of her forearms standing out. The pain in her fingers was exquisite. She couldn't see the stain anymore, but still she dug at it, scratching and scraping the steel, wincing at the pain but relishing it because it was better than what awaited her. She shot a look through the window and saw, sure enough, Donny flinging open the door of the once-yellow pole barn and stalking through the driveway toward the house.

It wouldn't do to let him see her like this, the air of the kitchen hazy with steam, like a sauna now, swirling around and coating her skin and moistening her upper lip. She drew her fingers from the scalding pot of water and was about to turn off the tap when she caught sight of her hands. It wouldn't have surprised her a bit had the flesh been dotted with blisters, or if the skin had begun to peel off. What she didn't expect was the coarse black strands of hair sprouting from her fingers and palms as well.

Now that's interesting, she thought.

The back door banged open. Hissing, Melody thrust her aching hands into the front of her blue apron, turned to face Donny.

Who looked back at her, his expression baffled. "Just what in the hell is keeping you?"

She manufactured a close-mouthed smile, knowing her skin was darkly blushed.

Donny took a step closer. "What're you doin' there, diddlin' yourself?"

Melody nodded over her shoulder. "Dishes."

Donny's eyes flicked to her apron. "Why you hidin' your hands?"

"I'm just finishing up."

An ugly sheen of sweat peppered Donny's forehead, his eyes glazed with lust. "You been finishin' up for going on an hour now. We're waitin'."

"Just a few more minutes," Melody said and made to turn back to the sink, but Donny was on her then, across the room like vengeance and spinning her around to face him in one fluid motion. He wrenched her wrists away from her apron, jerked them into the air so the overhead light glared down at them, and for a terrible instant Melody was sure he'd see the black strands stringing over her flesh like she'd had some sort of experimental implants, the world's first female hair plugs engineered especially for the hands.

Donny stared at her hands. So did Melody.

They were normal. Except they were bright red, like baby's hands.

"The hell's goin' on with you?" Donny asked. His breath was as rank as ever, but now Melody noted how untamed his beard had become, the reddish-brown curls matted in places and straggly in others. There was food collected here and there, and not just the beef stroganoff and mashed potatoes she'd made tonight. There was older food there too, and that disturbed her. He'd always been sloppy, indolent, and rattlesnake mean, but like their father and brothers, there'd also coursed through him that preserving streak of vanity that prevented the Bridwell men from stooping over and accepting their true nature as cruel, libidinous apes.

Donny squeezed her wrists. "I asked you a question, *Mel-o-dee*."

Melody grimaced, as much at the teasing pronunciation of her name as at the grinding pain in her wrist bones.

"I'm washing dishes," Melody said, doing her damnedest to keep the moan out of her voice. She almost managed to.

But Donny'd heard how much he was hurting her. He showed large, discoloured teeth. God, he looked like their father. And like their father, he was violent, more violent than John, which was saying something, and far more violent than Robbie, which wasn't saying much since Robbie mostly watched, and just did what his dad and brothers did so they'd give him their approval. Robbie was the only one she ever slept with willingly, and he'd only ever raped her in front of the others. Some nights she'd even begged Robbie to sleep in her bed to keep the other three off her, and sometimes the ploy worked.

Sometimes it didn't. Sometimes her father or Donny or John would bust the door in and find them together and smack Robbie around before taking her and doing it in front of Robbie on general principle. *See, you stupid little baby? See how she deserves to be treated?*

And Robbie smacked her some, but that was only on Wednesday nights, and she was pretty sure that was for show. At least she hoped it was for show.

Now, gazing into her oldest brother's muddy brown eyes, Melody was thankful Robbie was out there in the barn. He'd slap her, sure, he'd rape her and she'd struggle against him, but with him present, she was certain it wouldn't go too far. Robbie would never let them kill her.

This is what she told herself.

"You pulled the same stunt last week," Donny said.

She blinked up at him. He was almost six feet tall. And strong.

"And the week before," he added.

"What stunt?" she asked.

"Stalling," he said, his voice strained and hoarse.

"I told you, I wasn't—"

"*I know what you told me,*" he growled. "And I don't believe a word of it."

She opened her mouth to protest but spotted the wheedling grin on his lips, realised he was goading her, giving himself an excuse to really unload on her, to have at her before the others could.

Then he let go of her wrists. But not gently. The Bridwell men were never gentle.

"Two minutes," he told her in a flat voice, and went out. She listened to his work boots crunch the driveway.

Two minutes, he'd said.

Melody thought, *Okay, Donny. Two minutes. I'll be there in two minutes. So you can do your thing, all four of you. And I'll go along. Because I don't know any different. Or because I'm chickenshit. I would've slit my wrists sixteen years ago if I'd had the guts.*

My God, Melody thought. *Has it been that long?*

Yes. The pole barn nights had begun sixteen years ago, because that's when the pole barn had been built. And she often wondered if Wednesday nights had been the real reason behind the construction. Her father stored equipment out there, her brothers their old junkers they bought and tried to fix up. But the biggest part of the pole barn, the part that was kept clean, the dust there soft and feathery, almost like someone had hauled in several truckloads of beige talcum powder, that was made for Wednesday nights.

Melody glanced at the digital stove clock. A minute had already gone by. At least a minute. Donny would be waiting. Father would be waiting. They'd all of them be livid. Best not to let that anger whip into a fury. With a convulsive movement, Melody started toward the back door.

She'd seen what they could do when they got furious.

★ ★ ★

Jake thawed eventually. Maybe, Duane decided, it was the fact that he'd returned Savannah intact after their excursion to the Devil's Lair. Or maybe it was the greasy elephant ear and the cone of pink-and-blue cotton candy he'd purchased for Jake on the way out of the park. Whatever it was, after they'd eaten supper at the Pizza Hut buffet and dropped Joyce off at her house, Jake had consented to allow Duane to read him bedtime stories.

"You mind?" Duane asked Savannah before he followed Jake into his bedroom.

"Do I *mind*?" she asked. "I'm dead tired. I'd love a break from reading."

"So how many books do you and your mom read?" Duane asked after closing the door behind him. "Three? Four?"

"Fifty hundred," Jake answered.

"Fifty hundred? That'd take us awhile."

"I don't mind," Jake said.

Duane nodded and hunkered down before a cheap white bookcase on the brink of collapsing. "What do we have here? Curious George...Thomas the Train...*Frog and Toad Are Friends. The Lorax*." Fingering the spines, he turned to Jake. "Which ones sound good to you?"

"All of them."

Duane gathered an armload and made his way to the bed, where Jake had assumed official reading position. The boy had propped himself up on four fluffy pillows, the pillowcases white with the exception of one, which featured brown cowboys on a light blue background. Jake had also placed an enormous chunk of slanted foam next to him.

Jake nodded at the stiff foam pillow. "Mommy leans back on the wedge."

"Ah. The wedge." Duane climbed onto the bed, leaned back. The wedge wasn't particularly comfortable and was about as soft as a hunk of plywood. Additionally, there was no head support, so Duane had to worm around until he found a position that didn't make his back ache.

"Curious George first," Jake said.

Duane nodded, opened the book – a bright yellow anthology – and said, "'Curious George and the Ice Cream Shop'."

"Not that one," Jake said immediately.

Duane looked at his resolute little face. The boy had Savannah's freckles, but his hair was already darker. He also had his mom's blue eyes, dimples and obstinate expression. Her nose too.

Jake certainly looked nothing like Mike Freehafer.

"I don't like the ice cream one," Jake explained. "The guy gets too mad at George."

Duane flipped a couple pages, studied the irate ice cream shop proprietor. "Doesn't someone get mad at George in every story?"

"Yeah, but not *that* mad."

Duane turned the page and saw Jake's point. The ice cream shop owner looked like he was about to have George drawn and quartered.

"Go to the table of contents," Jake said.

Duane drew back a little. "How do you know what a table of contents is?"

Jake shrugged. "Mommy told me."

"You sure you're only five?"

Jake wrested the book from his hands and flipped to the table of contents. "This one," he said, tapping a finger on "Curious George Visits the Aquarium."

"That one's better, huh?"

Jake nodded earnestly. "There are penguins in it."

"Yeah?"

"And a beluga whale."

"Cool," Duane said. He turned the page and cleared his throat. "'This is George. He was a good little monkey and always very cur—'"

"Hey!" Jake snapped.

"What now?"

"Mommy lets me say 'curious'."

"You mean—"

Jake rolled his eyes. "You read the first part and I say 'curious' at the end."

Duane went on, glancing quickly at Jake's Spiderman wall clock. They'd been at it nearly five minutes and they'd read a grand total of two sentences.

But they soon settled in, and Duane found his groove. They read three stories from the Curious George anthology, then switched over to Clifford the Big Red Dog. Duane tried to read *The Berenstain Bears and the Green-Eyed Monster*, but halfway through Jake seized Duane's wrist.

"I just remembered," Jake said.

"What's wrong?"

"I don't like the monster."

"The green-eyed monster?"

Jake nodded, his face the colour of ash.

Duane flipped a couple pages, careful to keep the images concealed from Jake. He found the green-eyed monster and decided Jake was right. Not that he would've forced the kid to hear the rest of the story anyway, but seeing that ghostly green skin, the blazing yellow eyes, the arched black eyebrows, he wondered why adults had to make kids' stories so scary. The green-eyed monster looked creepy as fuck.

He tossed that book aside and went on to Thomas the Train. They read a couple stories about cheeky engines, then segued into Frog and Toad. It was going on forty minutes, but Duane found he didn't mind. The kid was solemn much of the time, but when Jake cracked a smile, Duane found it difficult not to smile too.

At around the fifty-minute mark, his throat started to feel scratchy, and it reminded him just how seldom he talked in his day-to-day life. He had coworkers at the school, of course, and he shared an office with the other two tech guys, but most of the time they were immersed in their own work, content to exist in a virtual world rather than the real one. By the time Jake's eyelids started to droop, Duane's voice felt downright lousy, and he was coughing every half page. He asked Jake if they were done, and the boy nodded, already drifting toward sleep. Not wanting to freak the kid out by hugging him, Duane caressed Jake's forehead once and whispered "Good night."

When Duane left Jake's room, he smelled popcorn, hot and buttery and maddening. Not like movie theatre popcorn and especially not the way it was at the drive-in, but still damned good. Duane's stomach rumbled.

Savannah was washing dishes.

"Want some help?" he asked.

Without looking up, she said, "Took you long enough."

"Mind if I steal a beer?"

Savannah didn't answer.

He retrieved a bottle of Budweiser from the fridge, said, "I'm detecting a stormy mood over there."

She flipped a pot over and let it clank on the counter. There were still soapsuds on the bottom of the pot. "I'm tired, all right? I've been dealing with a lot of stress."

"I understand."

She grunted. "I doubt it. Unless you know what it's like to be a single mom."

"I wouldn't know anything about that."

She was quiet a moment, moving dishes around.

He said, "You feel bad we're gonna miss Mike's funeral?"

She turned on him. "Do you?"

"Yes."

She scowled, went back to her dishes. "That's the wrong answer."

"Sorry."

"After all the crap we've had to deal with…talking to the state cops, being asked the same questions by two different sets of people, I figure I've earned a little time away from it."

He nodded. "You've got a point. You ready for the movie?"

"Is it all blood-and-guts?"

"Not at all," he said, plucking the DVD off the kitchen table and holding it up for her to see. "I picked out a classic tonight."

She cocked an eyebrow. "What is that?"

He inspected the DVD. "*Bubba Ho-Tep*. It's about Elvis fighting an ancient Egyptian mummy in a nursing home."

She stared at him.

"Elvis's friend," he went on, "is this black guy who thinks he's JFK."

"Elvis and JFK are both dead."

"Well," he said and gestured vaguely, "not in the world of the movie."

"Sounds lame."

Duane frowned at the DVD cover. "I'm not really doing it justice."

"Who's in it?" she asked as she made her way past him to the living room.

"Bruce Campbell," he said.

"Who?"

"Bite your tongue."

She sighed. "Put it in then. I don't have anything else to do. Might as well watch Elvis fight some mummies."

★   ★   ★

Melody stood in the centre of the cavernous pole barn. To her right was a sheet metal wall and her baby brother Robbie. Behind her was an automatic door tall enough to accommodate a full-size RV. John, her second-oldest sibling, was stationed there. To her left was the largest open space, which led to where the cars were worked on. Her oldest brother Donny manned this area because he was the strongest and the meanest, even worse than John, who had a temper like a switch.

Before her, barring the illuminated storage area and the back door of the pole barn, stood her father. Robbie had once started out there, and she'd made the mistake of darting past him, had even managed to make it out the door and most of the way to her Chevy Beretta, but Donny had brought her down, and despite the fact it hadn't been full dark yet, he'd taken her right there in the driveway. A car or two had whooshed by, but if the drivers glimpsed the incestuous rape occurring in the deep bed of gravel, they hadn't cared enough to stop. More likely they hadn't even noticed the cluster of Bridwells in the drive. Folks went way too fast down their road, often topping out over eighty.

"You've been acting inconsiderate of late," her father said. When she didn't respond, he added, "Making us wait so much."

"Lotta bullshit," John put in.

Donny snickered, but Father Bridwell held up a hand. "It's not funny, Donny. Not a bit."

A chill went through Melody. Father Bridwell looked severely pissed off. And, she realised, even drunker than usual. Which was why it was dangerous to delay the festivities. The later they started, the drunker they got. And the drunker they were, the worse the treatment.

She glanced over at Robbie, who stared back at her expressionlessly. If there was any emotion in him, it wasn't showing tonight. He looked bored by all of it. Or maybe he was resigned to it. She hoped that was it. Because if Robbie stopped caring…

"Dad spoke to you, girl," Donny snapped. "What have you got to say for yourself?"

Again she looked at Robbie, who was now, she realised with a jolt, glaring at her in much the same way as Donny was. "Answer the question," he demanded.

The desolate sense of betrayal his words brought on was worse than anything he could have done to her.

"Something wrong with you?" a voice asked, and Melody turned in time to see John closing on her, his strong arms shooting out and sending her sprawling onto her side.

"Look at her," Donny said, standing over her now. He toed the seat of her jean shorts with a work boot. "Been shakin' that tush all over town. Now she's too uppity to do right by her own kin."

"Dumb cunt," John muttered.

Another shadow fell over her. She looked up.

Robbie.

His lips were twisted with disdain.

Donny crowed laughter. "Woo-hoo! Look at poor Robbie. I do believe he's jealous."

John's eyes were hooded, impersonal. "Got no more claim to her than any one of us."

"Course he don't," Donny said. "But you know how Robbie is. Always actin' like him and Melody's different. Like they're married or something."

Melody eyed Robbie, scoured his wintry expression for some sign of tenderness. Even a slight one, something so subtle only she could pick it up.

Robbie's eyes flashed. He reared back, kicked her in the stomach.

Melody was caught off guard. She collapsed around his shoe, coughing and wheezing and wondering what she'd done wrong. Thinking it was how they treated the dogs, the ones they penned behind the pole barn. Often Father Bridwell or her brothers would give one a kick for no other reason than boredom or maybe sport. And the dogs would look up at them with those sad, uncomprehending eyes, and Melody knew if she looked up now she'd resemble one of those dogs, and she'd be damned if she'd sink that low.

So she got control of herself. "Let's get on with this."

And John, who seemed the horniest tonight, had begun to take her up on the offer when her father spoke up. "Never thought I'd hear it."

John, who'd been fiddling with the apron in an attempt to get at Melody's shorts, hesitated. "Hear what, Dad?"

Father Bridwell produced a pack of cigarettes, shook one out. Lit it. Slid the red Bic lighter back inside his hip pocket. He smoked soundlessly for what felt like forever. Everyone waited.

Father Bridwell said, "I never thought I'd hear my daughter talk like that. 'Let's get on with this.'" He made a scornful sound. "Sound like some kind of streetwalker."

And so subdued were his tones that they all turned to stare at him, even John, who hadn't risen but seemed to have forgotten about sex for now.

"What do you mean, Dad?" Donny asked. Donny was a disturbed cretin, but where their father was concerned, he was as worshipful as any zealot.

Father Bridwell looked strangely formal back there in the lower-ceilinged storage area. The lighting there was muted, umber-coloured. Good enough to see but with a shadowy quality that seemed appropriate for their Wednesday night horror shows. But behind her father the down-hanging fluorescents shone so brightly that the man seemed rimmed with a heavenly corona, as if he were bathed in the glow of righteousness.

He spoke righteously too, though if he'd ever set foot in a church, Melody wasn't aware of it. "We're family, and family's supposed to have fun together. When your mama passed on, you had to take on more than your normal share, and for that I've always been proud of you, even if I might not have said so."

He'd never said so, had never complimented Melody in any way, but she kept quiet, listened.

"You've changed, daughter, and not for the better. You've become acid-tongued. Sarcastic. And sarcasm is something I won't abide from any of my children, least of all my only girl."

Is that so? Melody thought. *Never mind that Donny's the most sarcastic jackass in the county. Never mind that you, Father Bridwell, could cleave granite with your biting words.*

He was going on. "But you've been getting worse. And don't pretend you've been behaving yourself in town either. I know the kind of shenanigans you've been up to. I talk to plenty of the old-timers, and they know which girls are giving it up too easily."

A boot nailed her forehead without warning. Melody's head snapped back. So unexpected was the blow and so severe that she lay dazed on her back for several moments without a clue as to what had happened or who had attacked her. Then, through the blanket of grogginess, she heard the scuffle to her right, glanced that way and saw both Donny and John subduing her little brother, who looked nothing at all like Robbie now and more like an enraged beast, with spittle frothing from his mouth and his red-rimmed eyes shimmering with tears. Robbie was incensed, she now realised, because he was jealous.

"Just calm it down, Rob," Donny was soothing. "Just take 'er easy."

Her father's voice was meditative. "See what you've done to this family, girl? See what kind of pain and torment you're putting your kid brother through?"

Robbie lunged toward her, but John and Donny were too strong for him. They drove him back toward the sheet metal wall, their combined force denting it, Robbie's kicking heel bowing it out at the bottom, so that a delicate crescent of twilight peeked through. From her place on the ground, Melody fancied she could scent the influx of outside air. The atmosphere in here was dank, chalky, like an old schoolhouse. But out there it was crisp and exhilarating and perfumed with the fields and the forests and beyond that the lakes, with their fish and their cooling brown waters.

God, how she longed to be outside.

"I'm gonna give you a chance to atone for your mistakes, Mel. I'm gonna let you plead for my forgiveness. Your brothers, I can't speak for. What they decide is up to them."

"Forgiveness for what?" she asked.

Robbie darted at her, but John and Donny reined him in. Barely.

Her father nodded. "I don't blame you for being agitated, Robbie. But maybe that's just the kind of person she is. Leadin' everybody on. Making every man who lies down between those legs of hers think he's special." He tilted his head back, chuckled mirthlessly and blew out smoky air. "You know what old Fred Kershaw called you?" He glanced at her, his eyes twinkling. "You remember old Fred?"

Of course she remembered him. Fred was Glenn's father, and Glenn was one of the many guys she'd dated, though *dated* wasn't really the right word for it. *Hooked up* was more like it.

Melody thought of Fred Kershaw, who wasn't evil or anything. Just typical. Blue collar. Misogynistic. Always watching her with that lascivious glint in his rheumy eyes. Always undressing her mentally, creating scenarios. And passing that on to Glenn, a shitty example like so many men of that generation.

"What did he call me?" Melody asked, her voice as dry as dust.

She knew the answer before her father said, "The village bicycle. You know what that—"

"Of course I know what it means," she interrupted. "Everyone's had a ride. It's older than you, that saying."

Her father sucked on his cigarette, breathed out a ghostly puff of smoke. He was holding the cigarette like a joint, something she doubted he'd ever tried. In fact, he didn't smoke a lot either, preferred chewing tobacco instead. Unless he was stressed about something, in which case he smoked several packs a day.

"You know the saying," her father said, "but you don't seem bothered by it. Am I to understand that's correct?"

She closed her eyes. "Sure, Dad."

Even with her eyes closed, Melody sensed a drastic change in the room. It wasn't until the hackles on the back of her neck had begun to stir and her skin had tightened into goose pimples that she realised that everything smelled different too. Her little brother smelled like anguish. Donny and John, they smelled like fear. When Father Bridwell got mad, he got wildly unpredictable, and the way he was talking, bad things were afoot.

And speaking of her father, he smelled of violence. So she wasn't surprised at all when he said, "Donny, go fetch me that branch from the office."

Donny blinked at Father Bridwell. "Branch?"

Father turned his flinty gaze on Donny. "The fir branch," he explained. "The only goddamned branch in the office?"

Donny hesitated. "What about Robbie?"

She noticed that Robbie was still straining against his captors.

But Father Bridwell said, "Robbie'll behave himself or Robbie will get the same treatment that Melody here's gonna get."

Donny's eyes glittered, a small, horrid smile appearing on his wet lips. "What kinda treatment?"

"You know how you like to do it to her," Father Bridwell said softly.

Donny's grin broadened. Melody felt like throwing up. After violating her the traditional way, Donny was fond of penetrating her anally. She'd once needed medical attention, it had been so bad. Amid the bleeding and the crying she'd had to repeat the lie over and over again to the nurses, *I don't know the guys who did it. They just grabbed me in the parking lot and took me into a field.* But the nurses, they'd known. She'd been sure of it. They'd known, and even worse, they'd been disgusted by her silence, disgusted by her cowardice, her unwillingness to divulge the truth.

Melody's fingers bunched into fists.

"Get the branch," her father said to Donny. "Fir's good for giving splinters."

Melody was shaking.

Her dad's eyes narrowed. "Why're you growling, girl?"

Melody realised she *was* growling, but it wasn't her, didn't sound like her one bit. She glanced down and discovered her forearms were sprouting hair.

"What the hell are you doing, Mel?" Donny asked.

And glancing up at her brothers, even John looked scared. Melody felt like something was twisting inside her, ripping her bones and organs apart. She crawled forward, the sweat pattering on the dust, and moving in that fashion was good because it kept her hairy arms concealed by the dust clouds, and even better, it kept her face down. Because her face felt strange.

Yet moving on all fours was oddly natural. She clambered faster. She reached her brothers, who parted for her, and she crashed into the sheet metal wall down at the bent part, and the base of the wall split, and she shoved through, the flesh of her shoulders sheared by the split metal, and then they were calling after her, but she was accelerating, nearing the bean field, and it was dark enough now she could move faster, and then she was hurrying away from the voices.

CHAPTER FIFTEEN

Savannah bent over, retrieved the remote control. As she did, the neck of her blue tank top drooped open, and Duane caught a glimpse of the breasts beneath. No bra that he could see. He forced his eyes back to the screen, where the mummy was trying to suck out someone's soul.

"You could make it less obvious," Savannah said.

Duane glanced at her, face blank. "Huh?"

"You know what I'm talking about."

Duane blushed, fearing he did know what she was talking about. "You don't like the movie?"

"At least I'm *watching* the movie."

"Uh…"

"Yeah," she snapped. "*Uh*."

He set his beer on the stand beside him. "Hey, Savannah, I didn't mean to—"

"The hell you didn't," she said, loud enough he worried she might wake her son.

Duane felt very small all of a sudden, as though his mother had caught him looking at *Playboy*. "I didn't mean to…" he trailed off, the force of Savannah's withering stare robbing him of speech.

"Didn't mean to what? Ogle me?"

"That's a harsh choice of words."

"All you see is tits and ass."

"That's not true."

"It *is* true. You, Glenn, my boss. You're all a bunch of pricks."

"Take it easy."

"No, *you* take it easy. I got called into Tom Carroll's office last week and spent twenty minutes with him staring at my hooters."

"That's terrible."

She jabbed an index finger at him. "You just did the same thing!"

He opened his mouth, shut it. Her glare was like a heat lamp. Duane tried to meet it but felt himself shrivelling.

There was a silence.

Finally, Duane said, "Why'd Carroll call you in?"

"He warned me for missing so much work."

"Have you been?"

"What do you care?"

He blinked at her. "I care."

Savannah rolled her eyes. "You're so typical."

"Now listen," he said. "I'm sick and tired of you generalising."

Savannah gave him a challenging look. "Prove I'm wrong."

"I have proven it," he said.

"Tell me you don't want to get in my pants."

"Of course I want to get in your pants!"

"See?" she snapped. "You're—"

"You want generalisations? How about all the women who shoehorn every man in the world into the same unflattering mould? You don't even give a guy a chance."

"Bullshit."

"It's true. I've been good to you, Savannah. I've treated you like an honest-to-goodness person."

"With big tits."

"You know how you've been treating me?"

"This should be good."

"It *isn't* good," he said. "It's horrible and it's unfair. You've been treating me like I'm some sort of wolf who only thinks of sex."

"Do you have to use that animal?"

"As a matter of fact, I do." He rose, began pacing. "A walking libido, that's how you see me. That's how you see all men. Because that's the way you've been treated."

"It's none of your business."

"It *is* my business, Savannah. It's certainly my business because I've been the one who's treated you with respect. When Mike ditched you for the big leagues—"

"I don't want to talk about this."

"—I was the one who stayed behind, the one who held you while you bawled."

Her eyes narrowed. "And you did it all out of the kindness of your heart, didn't you? You didn't have any ulterior motive."

"Yep, I just wanted to screw you. You're just a life-support system for a vagina to me. Because that's all any guy wants. No matter what he does, all guys are evil sex maniacs."

"I didn't say that."

"You don't have to say it, Savannah. You live it. When the truth is you're the superficial one."

Her mouth fell open and she uttered a breathless little laugh.

Duane nodded vigorously. "Blasphemy, isn't it? How dare I imply that a woman might choose a man based on her sexual desires? Because you're above that."

"Who's generalising now?"

"I am, Savannah, and it's to make a goddamned point."

"If there's a point somewhere in all this, I'm not hearing it."

"Because you aren't listening. Because what I'm saying is so foreign to you that considering it would be akin to considering the possibility that witches and goblins exist."

"What in the *fuck* are you talking about?"

"I'm talking about *me*. And you. And just because I also happen to be attracted to you doesn't make me a bad person. Both genders can be assholes, Savannah." At her look, he nodded. "Okay, so women have gotten the short end of the stick."

She arched an eyebrow. "You think?"

"Of course. Men treat women like shit all the time."

"That supposed to be ingratiating?"

"But it's possible," he pressed on, "that guys can be good people too."

"And you're one of the altruistic ones, right?"

"I don't know what I am, but I do know I've been good to you." Duane snatched up his Cubs cap. "And I'll keep being good to you no matter how much you shit on me."

For the first time, some of Savannah's hardness seemed to abate. "That's not fair."

"You're right, it isn't fair. Your bar for me is impossibly high, you realise that? I can be good to you for years, and then the moment my eyes wander a little, you act like I'm a lecherous monster."

"Short Pump—"

"And in case you hadn't noticed it, you happen to be smoking hot."

She folded her arms. "That makes it okay?"

"That makes it hard to not look at you, sure."

"So we're back to that old argument," she said. Her voice went lower, her brow furrowed. "'I can't help it, honey. I'm a guy, and guys just gotta have it.'"

"Oh no," Duane said. "All guys should be monastic and bloodless and never, ever make the mistake of looking at a woman."

"Fine," she said, shivering and pushing her hair back over her ears. "Let's just watch the rest of the movie, okay?"

"As a matter of fact, it's not okay." Duane jerked on his ball cap. "Have a good night." He strode toward the door.

"*Short Pump*," she called.

He let the door slam, moved down the walk toward his pickup.

The door banged open behind him.

"What's the matter with you?" she shouted. "You could have woken Jake."

"That'd be fitting," he said, "since I'm the one who got him to sleep."

He turned at his truck door and saw her expression cloud.

"How'd you do it?" she asked.

"I read him about a dozen stories," he said and got into his Silverado. He started the pick-up.

She frowned. "That's why you took so long?"

"What'd you think," he said, shoving the gearshift into drive, "that I was in there explaining how all women are pieces of meat?"

"Come on, Short Pump. I didn't mean——"

But the rest was lost as he drove away. He told himself not to glance in the rearview mirror as the pickup gained speed, but he did anyway. Savannah was standing by the road, her arms folded. God, she looked beautiful even now, with the moonlight silvering her brown skin and her long hair stirring a little in the breeze.

Duane detached his eyes from the mirror before he could be mesmerised by her.

Too late, a voice in his head murmured. *You're permanently mesmerised by her.*

He wanted to argue, but he couldn't. What he could do was get back some of his self-respect, and if that meant driving away from her, so be it. And anyway, she and Jake would be all right on their own. She'd lock all the doors and make sure the windows were fastened.

That beast is still out there, a voice reminded him. *And it's sure as hell stronger than any doors or windows.*

"They're fine," he muttered, casting another glance in the mirror.

But his nerves had begun to thrum. The farther he got from Savannah's, the tinier her house seemed. In the daytime her street was full of kids on bikes, and cars moving ceaselessly up and down. But now, in the darkness of late evening, the houses seemed vulnerable, insignificant. The cornfields surrounding the subdivision swished and undulated, the stalks abnormally high for early June.

Duane eyed the fields with mounting disquiet. Anything could be hiding in there.

He swallowed. Thought of the man in the Devil's Lair today.

Duane would go home, take a shower and try to read himself to sleep.

But if sleep wouldn't come, maybe, just maybe he'd drive by Savannah's to check on her and Jake.

Just to be on the safe side.

CHAPTER SIXTEEN

God, Glenn loved the drive-in.

He had since he was a kid. First, there were the movies. True, he no longer paid much attention to those, but the mere presence of a film on that big white screen was like occupying the large fenced space with an old friend. Some of Glenn's favourite movies had been drive-in discoveries. Superhero movies. Big adventure flicks. And horror films. With a friend like Short Pump, there were always horror films.

It was sort of a relief not to have Short Pump here tonight. Glenn felt uncomfortable about the prospect of hanging out with him, but it wasn't until today that he'd realised why.

Glenn understood how anomalous his own behaviour had been. The running naked. The masturbating. The episode with the possum. Despite the fact that he knew Short Pump knew nothing of his recent weirdness, that still didn't prevent Glenn from being wary of him.

Because Short Pump was perceptive. Oh, he might grin and laugh at everyone's jokes and generally play the part of the harmless buffoon, but underneath all that was a razor-sharp mind. And if he and Short Pump talked long enough, Glenn was sure his friend would figure out all he'd been up to.

So for now…let the big guy hang out with Savannah. It would give Short Pump something to fantasise about.

On the other hand, if Short Pump were here, Glenn might not feel so edgy about Weezer.

But he did. There was no doubt about that.

Glenn heard Weezer coming before he spotted him. Or his truck rather. He knew Weezer couldn't afford a new truck, but man, that old Ford Ranger was a babe repellant if ever there was one. If Weezer had a lot more on the ball, maybe the truck wouldn't have mattered. But a guy like that, he needed all the advantages he could get. And a rusty beat-up truck that wasn't all that nice to begin with was not helping matters at all.

Glenn glanced uneasily at Mya and Rebecca, the two tourists he'd picked up this evening. He'd met them, fittingly enough, at the liquor store. And he figured it would take a hell of a lot of liquor to coerce either of them into sleeping with Weezer.

Just as he suspected, the bright-eyed, up-for-anything expressions that had been plastered on the women's faces only thirty seconds ago were now shifting into looks of concern and disappointment.

Weezer's red Ranger crept down the thoroughfare, drawing the stares of a good many people standing around talking in the twilight. Most of the people gripped red or blue plastic cups, which were no doubt full of mixed drinks, but a few were taking fewer pains to conceal their alcohol consumption. A guy in a White Sox jersey was sipping from a flask, and one of his crew was guzzling from a beer can inside a black huggie.

"Is that your friend?" Mya asked as Weezer's pickup turned onto their lane.

Glenn maintained a neutral expression. "His car's in the shop. He just keeps the Ranger around for running errands."

Mya nodded. Glenn cursed himself. The lie was simple enough, but it was one that could easily come back to haunt him. He'd need to pull Weezer aside, communicate this vital bit of information, and that would require hurting Weezer's feelings. Shit.

The one named Rebecca took a step past Glenn. "Is he wearing...is that an eye patch?" she asked.

Glenn sighed, wishing he'd thought to prepare the women for this.

"Is he a pirate or something?" Mya asked.

Glenn looked from girl to girl and realised his earlier assessment of them had been flawed. Ever since Mya had told him her favourite drink was Jack and Coke back at the liquor store, he'd been sure she would be the one he'd end up boning. Not that Rebecca was hideous or anything, but she seemed more reserved, the tougher nut to crack.

"Is he?" Mya asked as the Ranger crunched to a stop in the space next to the 'Vette.

"Is he what?" Glenn asked.

"A pirate?"

Glenn sat on the urge to tell her to fuck herself. It wasn't just the repetition of the bad joke that nettled him – it was the self-satisfied smirk Mya wore as she repeated it. Like Glenn and Weezer weren't friends. Like losing an eye was the funniest thing in the world. *Ha ha, you're right, Mya! Let's all swab the poop deck and search for buried treasure!*

Fucking bitch.

"Want another beer?" Rebecca asked.

Glenn glanced over at her. He'd been wrong to focus on Mya so hastily. Sure, she had that hardbody thing going, the short, punky hair and the perky boobs he enjoyed so much. But Mya knew she had a great body, and that could often contaminate what was between the ears.

The brain truly was the largest erogenous zone, and Rebecca was currently stimulating that crucial region. She was cute, for one thing. Not a knockout, but her face was nice, and she had some imperfections he considered quite fetching. One was a tiny gap between her front teeth. He'd always dug women whose teeth didn't look like they'd come straight out of some toothpaste commercial. Those small imperfections...the teeth slightly crowded, or the canines a little too long...

Like Patricia Arquette in *True Romance*. Jesus Christ, she had driven him crazy in that one. The teeth and the cleavage and the wiliness and the vulnerability…man, it made him woozy just thinking about it.

"Glenn?" Rebecca asked.

He blinked, realised he'd never answered her. "Sure, I'll have another."

She gave him a wry smile he really liked. "I'll get it."

A couple more things in her favour, he thought. One, her voice was cool – a kind of breathy huskiness that made it seem like she was recovering from laryngitis. He loved voices like that. The kind of voice his favourite noir writers might call smoky.

Weezer's truck door opened, but Glenn hardly noticed. He was too busy watching Rebecca's butt.

The other thing he liked about her was a small thing, but to Glenn it went a long way: she'd offered him a beer.

Now, he was all for chivalry. He opened doors for women, paid for dinners, all that stuff. But it did aggravate him when a girl acted like it was her right to always take and to never give. That Rebecca had been considerate enough to offer him a beer…any girl like that was all right by him.

"Hello, Glenn," a voice said.

He turned and saw Weezer.

Glenn hardly recognised him.

It wasn't just the eye patch, which would take some getting used to; it was the drastic change in the rest of Weezer's appearance that struck Glenn dumb.

The hair was totally different. Up until now, Weezer had feathered his hair back. Granted, Glenn combed his own hair in a similar style, but that's because it looked cool on Glenn. On Weezer it had always seemed like what it was – a sad attempt to mimic Glenn.

Yet now Weezer's hair was slicked back, the comb marks visible between the glossy ridges. Studying it, Glenn realised where he'd seen the hairstyle before – old movies. Yes, this was how Cary Grant and Jimmy Stewart had worn their hair back in the forties. Where Weezer had gotten the right oil or cream to achieve such a look, Glenn had no idea. And what was even more perplexing was the gnawing suspicion that Weezer had actually pulled the look off.

In a way, Weezer's hair looked sort of cool.

As did the black button-down shirt and the blue jeans.

Holy shit, Glenn marvelled. *Weezer actually looks cool.*

Mya had noticed too. That gleam of mockery had left her face, in its place a curiosity that could bode very well for Weezer tonight. That was, if Weezer didn't start talking about illegal immigrants and Democrats and all the other shit that invariably turned women off.

Weezer clasped his hands before him, right at crotch level. Like they were doing a drug deal or something.

"I'm Bobby Talbot," he said. "But as Glenn no doubt told you, everybody calls me Weezer."

"Hey, *Weezer*," Mya said, leaning on the name a little. She had a playful look in her eyes, obviously digging whatever vibe Weezer was putting out. "I'm Mya. Rebecca and I are visiting from Tinley Park."

Weezer nodded. "I'm really glad you decided to come down."

Mya's smiled brightened.

Keep it going, Glenn thought. *You just might be able to change your luck.*

Weezer looked at Glenn, gestured toward his eye patch. "So what do you think? Do I look like Snake Plissken?"

Glenn appraised him. "Sans the muscles maybe."

"No need to denigrate," Weezer said, smiling at Mya.

Glenn gawked at him. *Denigrate? Are you fucking kidding me?* It was Short Pump who was literate, not Weezer. In fact, whenever Glenn and Short Pump talked books in Weezer's presence, Weezer scowled at them like they were committing some sort of betrayal.

"Here you go," Rebecca said and held out a sweating can of Bud Light to Glenn. She turned to Weezer. "You must be Glenn's friend."

Weezer introduced himself.

Glenn's own smile faded as Rebecca's grew.

"Hey, Weezer," she said, a little too shyly.

Glenn stared at her and thought, *What the hell?*

But if Weezer was amazed at the women's adoration, he made no sign.

Weezer drew in a smiling inhalation, let it out. "So what's on tap for tonight? Something gory?"

"*The Guns of Santa Sangre*," Glenn said. "Didn't you see the marquee on the way in?"

"Must've missed it," Weezer said, without taking his eyes off Rebecca. "Have you gotten popcorn?"

"Let me get my purse," Rebecca said.

"I've got it," Weezer said. And son of a bitch, he actually took Rebecca's arm and led her toward the concession stand.

Leaving Glenn with Mya.

They stood there looking after Weezer and Rebecca, Mya's expression one of competitive fury.

Glenn folded his arms, realised that was exactly what he was feeling too. Weezer, the audacious little prick, was actually challenging him. Never in his life would Glenn have guessed Weezer would possess the sack to do that.

But maybe, Glenn mused, this was just another aspect of life after the bonfire. He himself had already changed a great deal, so why should he be surprised that Weezer had changed too?

Glenn glanced at Mya, feeling considerably better about life. They were only halfway through the first movie trailer, for God's sake. Who cared that Weezer had scored points first? History was on Glenn's side. History and the fact that Glenn had far more game than Weezer could ever hope to have.

"How about a Jack and Coke, Mya?" he said.

She stared at the concession stand. "Not in the mood."

"Then let's have some more of whatever you're drinking."

"Seagram's Blue Hawaiians."

"What are those?"

"Wine coolers."

Glenn suppressed a shudder. "That sounds tasty, Mya. Can I interest you in some popcorn too?"

Her shoulders slumped. "May as well."

Glenn led her toward the concession stand and maintained a smile. With difficulty.

★　　★　　★

Duane had trouble going to sleep on a normal night, so to expect he'd fall asleep on a night he and Savannah had fought – for the first time, *really* fought – was more than folly; it was delusional.

Sighing, Duane tossed the covers aside, pushed out of bed, and dragged on the same T-shirt and blue jeans ensemble he'd worn earlier.

He didn't feel like watching a movie because that would remind him of Savannah, and even worse, it would remind him of his loneliness. He didn't like to articulate it to anyone, but he often felt absurd engaging in certain pastimes because he considered them communal activities rather than solitary ones. Like watching movies. Going for walks. Having sex. It was why he could never sleep after he masturbated. It just felt pathetic for a guy of almost thirty to slap his meat before going to sleep in a pool of his own desperate sweat.

Duane inspected himself in the bathroom mirror, swished some mouthwash around, then spat and inspected himself again. His face still looked too round, the lines in his forehead too pronounced. *You're twenty-eight*, he told himself. *How old will you look at forty?*

He scooted out of the bathroom as though fleeing a brushfire and plopped down on the couch to lace up his boots. He liked how thick the heels were, how dark and sleek the leather looked. He felt the boots gave him an edge he lacked, an air of danger that might, under the right circumstances, turn a woman's eye in his direction.

He sighed, recognising the self-deception. He'd bought the boots because they looked like Glenn's. And since Savannah sometimes seemed interested in Glenn, Duane reasoned the boot similarity might also transfer some of her interest to Duane.

God, he was pathetic.

Duane snatched his wallet and keys from the front table, let himself out into the warm June night, and breathed deeply of the cornfields surrounding his house. Earlier he'd toyed with the idea of patrolling Savannah's house just to make sure there was no danger lurking in the vicinity, but now, the night seemed tranquil rather than threatening, and besides, he'd squandered too much energy – hell, too many *years* – worrying about Savannah.

He'd head to the Roof. It was the only place that didn't totally depress him, maybe because there were usually live bands there rather than a DJ spinning auto-tuned crap for the tourists.

The drive took about five minutes. He noticed with some surprise that Beach Land wasn't too crowded. Not for a Wednesday night in June. After making his way inside the park, he navigated the maze of cottages where the summer employees lived. Soon, Duane ambled by the log flume ride, the Cropduster Express, which was a decent-sized roller coaster made of wood, one of the oldest in the nation. As if that were a good thing.

The Cropduster roared past him, the screams of its riders shrilling as it hung a sharp turn and vanished into a tunnel. Duane scented the oily tinge of corn dogs, the sugary aroma of funnel cake. His stomach growled.

He continued into the alabaster spill of light cast by the game corridor. On his right there was a whack-a-mole game, the football toss. A stand where you hurled a softball at milk bottles that probably weighed ten pounds each. On the left there was a ring toss, skee ball, a game where you aimed quarters onto a sheet of green felt and watched a copper-coloured block steamroll everything toward a drop-off. As a kid Duane must've wasted a hundred dollars on that game, dropping quarter after quarter just for the joy of watching a useless toy tumble over the edge into the winner's slot.

Grinning a little, he moved past the glassblower's shop, an enormous verdigris fountain littered with pennies, and onto the boardwalk. Here the games resumed, the larger ones requiring open air and a lot more space. The basketball shoot. Another football toss, this one with a mechanised moving target. The games gave way to rides, small ones like the Scrambler and the Tilt-a-Whirl on his right, the area of the park that bordered the lake. On his left there were more games, several shops that sold clothes and trinkets. Interspersed with the shops were indoor rides, one a haunted pirate ride, the other the kind where you shot laser guns as the rolling car moved you through a poorly lit array of fluorescent targets. The crowd, though slightly smaller than he would have expected, was raucous. Several teenage boys dribbled basketballs, their shirts tied like rags around their low-hanging belt loops. Girls wore bikini tops beneath saggy tank tops. Duane moved past the bumper cars, also on the lakeside, and then the waterpark, which accounted for half of Beach Land's allure. It was closed this late at night, but the beach area, the teal-coloured snarl of water slides, the meandering Lazy River, and the garish kids' splash park were all illuminated by tall light poles. Beyond the water park, the dark water rippled lazily as boats idled past. Several eateries drifted by on Duane's left, the rock music blasting out of the open-air bar becoming more and more pronounced. He identified the song right away as Wild Cherry's "Play That Funky Music" and suppressed an eye roll. He wondered if Midwestern cover groups were required by law to include the song in their sets.

With a quick glance at the old-school video arcade straight ahead, he mounted the steps leading to the Roof, retrieving his wallet as he climbed. He paid the cover, went in, and discovered the place was even less populated than the amusement park. Rather than the normal three hundred or so people that typically crammed the place on summer nights, this evening there were maybe half that number nursing drinks and nodding their heads listlessly to the music. Duane was encouraged by the presence of several attractive women, though a goodly number of them were with men, or just as frighteningly, with groups of women. Maybe if Glenn were here Duane would have a chance at engaging one of the women in conversation, but on his own he knew he'd never have the guts to separate one of them from the herd.

Duane deflated onto the bar. The whole process seemed unbearably daunting. All that effort, and what would come of it? Whatever came of encounters like these? You either hooked up for a night never to see each other again, or you agreed to meet again and suffered through a painful date. Or, the woman never called you back at all, and you realised she'd just been humouring you at the bar.

Duane ordered a beer and eased down on a stool. Onstage, the band said they'd be back in ten minutes, and blessedly, the bar was filled with conversation rather than the grating sounds of crappy seventies music.

He glanced down the length of the bar, which was maybe fifty feet long and lacquered to a dark, shiny brown, and saw how the lines to the bathrooms beyond had swelled. The bartender brought his beer, carelessly sloshing the foam over Duane's knuckles, but Duane said nothing, paid, and swivelled on his stool to take in the rest of the room. Decent-sized dance floor to the left, tables and booths to the centre and to his right. Ceiling fans blowing the hot air around, the ceiling painted black and made to look like a miniature night sky with a thousand pinpricks of light peering through. Beyond all that, the water park and the lake with its scattering of idling boats, their red and green lights trawling silently through the summer darkness.

Quite a few patrons migrated from the tables around the dance floor and crowded the bar on either side of Duane, and though there were a couple familiar faces in the throng, he didn't know either of them well enough to hope for an invitation to their respective groups. There were several vacant tables, and though he worried he'd choose one that was already claimed, he liked the fact that the tables were nearer the boardwalk, nearer the lake.

He rose and began moving through the crowd. He sipped his beer, nodded at a woman maybe fifteen years his senior who was gazing up at him from a booth. He filed away the eye contact for later, thinking if he got drunk enough she could give him a ride home.

He took a table for two against the railing that overlooked the boardwalk. That way, if fate did happen to smile on him, or he got desperate and decided to try it with the older lady, there'd be a place for someone else to sit.

Duane sipped his beer and frowned at the empty chair.

Who was he kidding?

Not only were the odds of him hooking up dismally low, the fact was Duane didn't really want to hook up anyway. If he couldn't have Savannah, he didn't have a whole lot of interest in the opposite sex. Oh, he found women attractive all right. But he was content to look at them rather than going through the whole excruciating process of luring one back to his house, feigning passion where there was none, and feeling like hell the next day. It wasn't really guilt he experienced the day after a one-night stand. More like a general feeling of grossness. Like he'd compromised himself and the woman. That he was inevitably hungover on those headachy mornings didn't help, nor did the awkwardness of seeing the woman to the door and kissing her goodbye despite the fact that they both had horrible yeasty morning breath. But primarily, it was the unshakeable truth that it wasn't supposed to be this way, wasn't supposed to be faked and quick and soaked in alcohol. Maybe he was old-fashioned, but he could never be like Glenn. No, Duane was too sentimental to pretend he didn't care. And that was the point of a one-night stand. To not care. To rut like dogs and then pretend like it didn't matter.

But for him, it did. Maybe that was a character flaw. Sighing, Duane let his eyes rove over the crowd. Soon, the room would settle and the band would butcher another song. Duane squinted at the bass drum, attempting to discern the name of the group. After leaning forward and narrowing his gaze further, he discovered it was Dance Naked. There'd been a John Mellencamp song of the same name, he thought. Wasn't that a copyright violation or something?

He leaned back, rested an elbow on the railing that overlooked the boardwalk. Breathed in the night air. Even if he was alone, even if he'd never woo Savannah, at least he could appreciate these simple pleasures. The sky, he saw at a glance, had begun to gleam with tiny spangles of light. Maybe he'd take a walk when he got home, just breathe the night air and let the star glow wash over him. He frequently told himself he'd do things like that, but he always ended up doing something pointless instead. Surfing the Internet. Watching a horror movie on Netflix he'd seen a dozen times already. Wasting his life. It was about time he woke up and—

"Mind if I join you?" a voice asked.

Duane looked up at the man who'd addressed him. The same man, he realised, who'd shared their elevator ride in the Devil's Lair. The man looked just shy of fifty. Conservative. Khaki pants and white, short-sleeved, button-down shirt with green and blue pinstripes. Hair parted on the left side and slicked down the way they used to do it in the fifties. Black-rimmed glasses. The guy looked like a CPA or something. Maybe an extra from an old TV show, *Leave it to Beaver* or *The Honeymooners*.

The man watched him politely, seemingly in no hurry. Hands dangling at his sides, standing at a distance of maybe ten inches from Duane's shoulder.

Uncomfortably close.

Was the man gay?

Not that Duane had anything against the guy if he was, but it did make him feel a bit awkward. Duane didn't have much experience in shunning the advances of the opposite sex. How did one go about turning down a homosexual proposition?

The same way, he supposed. Be polite. Don't make a thing of it.

Duane forced a smile. "I'm waiting for somebody, actually. She should be here any minute."

"May I wait with you until she comes?" the man asked.

Duane took a swig of beer. The man was still standing too close, the benign expression on his face somehow disquieting.

"I'll go it solo," Duane said. "But I appreciate your offer to pass the time."

"I'm offering more than that," the man said.

Definitely gay, he decided. *Gay and not taking the hint.*

"Look," Duane said, "my girlfriend won't like me sitting with—"

"I don't want you sexually," the man said with a hint of a smile.

Duane shifted uneasily. "Oh, I knew that, I just figured I'd be better off—"

"What's her name?" the man asked, sliding into the chair opposite.

For a long moment Duane could only stare. The guy's plain features remained carved in that patient, interested look. Was the dude just socially awkward?

"You don't know her," Duane said. He made a point of turning his gaze toward the bar area, as if trying to pick out his nonexistent woman.

"You're probably right," the man said. "I'm new to the area and don't know anyone."

"Huh," Duane answered, but refused to give him more than that.

"I'm just trying to get acclimated."

Duane sipped his beer. He could feel the man's gaze boring into him.

"Don't you want to know where I'm from?" the man asked.

God. The guy was clueless. "Like I said, I'm waiting for someone."

"Mm," the guy said. "It's good to have people who are important to you."

Duane glanced at the man without turning his head, and sure enough, the guy's expression was still maddeningly polite. Duane toyed with the notion that he was part of some hidden-camera reality show. "*Watch how this obese bar patron reacts when one of our actors tries to engage him in conversation!*"

"Yeah," Duane said. "She's very special to me."

The man sat forward. "Tell me about her."

Well, why not? Duane cleared his throat, studied the milling crowd. "She's my age. Blond. I mean, *actual blond*. Farrah Fawcett blond. Blue eyes with these yellowish flecks that make her look sort of feline. She has freckles

WOLF LAND • 101

on her cheeks." Duane smiled, imagining Savannah. "On her nose too. I tease her about them sometimes. Then she scrunches up her nose and says she hates her freckles and why don't I stop talking about them. But I think she secretly likes it. Knows that men find them attractive."

The man's expression was changeless. "How long have you dated her?"

Duane shrugged. "Not long. I mean, we're not officially *dating*, though I was over there earlier tonight."

"Yes?"

Duane nodded. "Watching a movie. *Bubba Ho-Tep*?"

"I'm not familiar with it."

Duane felt himself relax. The guy wasn't trying to pick him up. He was just new to the area and starved for some conversation. Maybe Duane was the one who needed to alter his behaviour.

"So, uh, you're not into movies?" Duane asked.

The man shook his head, glanced down at the table. "Not particularly. Mostly, I read."

Ah, Duane thought. *Some common ground.* "What kind of books are you into?"

"Nonfiction mostly," the man said. Duane tried to conceal his disappointment.

The man added, "I can see why someone might read fiction, though."

"Yeah?" Duane asked, scanning the tables again. About half of them had filled back up. One of the band members had returned to the stage, was messing with an amplifier.

"Absolutely," the man went on. "Real life can be a horrid thing. Take that terrible business a few nights ago, for example."

He shot the man a look. Did the guy know Duane had been there? Despite the fact that Duane had just taken a healthy guzzle of beer, his mouth felt cotton dry.

"Indeed," the man continued, as though Duane had agreed with him. "That Freehafer boy wasn't yet thirty years old."

Duane frowned. Whether the man knew of Duane's association with Mike or not – how could he? – this wasn't the kind of thing to talk about in a bar. Or anywhere, for that matter.

"I suppose his parents are beside themselves with grief," the man said.

Duane pursed his lips, forced his tone to remain level. "I'm sure. Of course, they're not the only ones, right?"

The man went on as though Duane hadn't spoken. "It's a good thing Mr. Freehafer wasn't married."

Duane raised his chin, stared at the man with narrowed eyes. "And why is that?"

The man spread his hands as though it were self-evident. "Why, because his wife would be a widow, of course. And his children would be fatherless."

"Mike didn't have children," Duane said.

"Not even a girlfriend?"

Duane felt a chill. "No."

"Hm. I would've thought a young man with Mr. Freehafer's looks would have plenty of girlfriends. And a great many friends too." The man nodded at Duane. "Other than you, of course."

For the first time, Duane turned to face the man. "How do you know we were friends?"

The man smiled at him, unabashed, and again the chill whispered down Duane's spine. "The men at the gas station. The ones who drink coffee there? They said Mike's friends were named Short Pump and—" He frowned, appeared to consider, "—ah yes, someone named Savannah."

Duane set down his beer.

The man's smile broadened. "Savannah was easy enough to locate – after all, it's a rather uncommon name, isn't it? Particularly in a town this size?"

"Listen, what are you—"

"But Short Pump, that didn't help me at all. I had to get a physical description, ask around town. Finally, one of the girls working at the bakery said she knew you, thought your real name was Duane."

Duane's body had gone numb.

"She was very helpful," the man said, "and the cinnamon rolls were delicious."

Duane scooted back from the table. "I think we're done here."

"If you're certain," the man said.

Duane stood up, fought off a wave of dizziness.

"Are you well, Mr. McKidd?"

Duane glanced at him, swaying a little. He steadied himself, closed his eyes to rid them of the bleariness. For a moment there, he'd been seeing things. He could've sworn the man's face had grown darker, the sideburns thicker, wilder.

"Please sit down," the man said.

Was the voice deeper?

"I'll do what I want," Duane muttered. He pushed away from the table, tottered down the aisle toward the bar.

"I'll see you and Savannah soon," the man said.

Duane hesitated in midstep, but couldn't bring himself to turn and face the man.

A blast of drums made Duane yelp and throw out his arms. On the stage, Dance Naked had begun Aerosmith's "Walk This Way."

And Duane had apparently nailed a guy standing to his left with an errant forearm. The guy – a kid, really – was glaring at him with his arms out. "What's your problem?"

"Sorry," Duane muttered and pushed past a group of older couples ranged around a booth. In moments he passed the stage and was almost to the exit when he threw a glance back at the table where he'd been sitting.

The table was empty, Duane's unfinished beer bottle the only proof anyone had sat there at all.

A chill spreading through his limbs, Duane hurried down the steps toward the boardwalk.

CHAPTER SEVENTEEN

By the time they were halfway through *The Guns of Santa Sangre*, which turned out to be a fucking werewolf movie of all things, neither Rebecca nor Mya were showing the slightest inclination toward switching allegiances to him. Far from it. They were treating Weezer like some sort of rock star, from the sickening way they laughed and leaned against him when he told a joke to the way they seemed to hang on his every word.

And the part that drove Glenn craziest was Weezer's unshakable aplomb. Like he'd been lavished with attention this way his entire life. As if, only three days ago, he hadn't been slinking up to half a dozen women – some of them certified skanks – and being shooed away like a starving mongrel.

Glenn sipped his Jack and Coke and watched the trio. Weezer had let down the tailgate of the Ranger and laid out a blanket for them to sit on. Glenn's view of Mya was impeded, but he could see easily enough how Rebecca had cosied up next to Weezer.

This shit had to end. Pronto.

Glenn moved beside Rebecca. "What do you think of the movie?"

She looked at him with what he interpreted as forced politeness. "I'm not into horror. With so much unhappiness in the world, why create more?"

Shit. This was worse than he'd thought.

He did his best to look unconcerned. "Too bad. The film has great cinematography."

She gave him a close-lipped smile – still with that forced politeness – and turned back to Weezer.

Glenn resisted the urge to knock their heads together. And slap himself in the face. The film has great *cinematography*? What kind of stupid-ass comment was that? A remark like that, that was Short Pump territory. Geek City all the way. The kind of comment guaranteed to *not* get you laid. Why not just ask her about her favourite *Lord of the Rings* character and make sure she thinks you're a complete tool?

Man, he was off his game.

So? a voice in his head spoke up. *The night's still young. Regroup and return with your A-game.*

If I still have it.

Did that beast take your balls as well as your confidence? the voice chided.

Glenn ground his teeth. *Hell no.*

He'd just about resolved to steel himself with another Jack and Coke when he picked up the thread of conversation between Weezer and the women.

"...wasn't sure, so I kept moving toward the clearing," Weezer said.

"Weren't you scared?" Mya asked. She sounded half-soused.

"I was," Weezer admitted. "But my friends were back there. Glenn had been knocked unconscious, and I had to make sure he was safe."

Glenn realised with dawning horror that Weezer was talking about the bonfire. Why this was so surprising to him, he had no idea, but on an instinctive level he felt like Weezer was betraying some sacred trust between them.

"Did you worry about getting hurt?" Rebecca asked. With a hand on Weezer's arm.

Weezer gave a little shrug. "I suppose I did worry, but it was imperative that I did what I could for my friends."

"*Awww,*" Mya said in a voice that made Glenn want to cram the Seagram's Blue Hawaiian down her throat. "That's so sweet of you, Weezer."

"And loyal," Rebecca added.

And inaccurate, Glenn amended. He listened to Weezer's account with growing disbelief.

"When I got to the clearing, I couldn't believe what I saw. The bodies...they were laid out like...like meat at a slaughterhouse."

That was right, Glenn decided. It had looked like that.

"Then I saw it standing there in the clearing."

Weezer went on, his voice hushed, his enunciation crisp. As if, in being mauled by the beast, his IQ had risen fifty points. "It was alone. Its muzzle was glistening from its victims."

"You're kidding me," Mya said.

Rebecca looked at her. "Haven't you read the news? Everybody who was there gave the same account."

"*Most* of them," Weezer corrected. "There were some who were too frightened to talk about it honestly. They claimed it was only a large dog. One woman said it was a bear, even though the last bear in this region was spotted sometime during the 1800s."

Glenn moved closer so he could see Weezer better. The drive-in screen was crammed with bloody images of werewolves shredding victims from the Old West. But what arrested Glenn's attention was the way his friend was holding court, Weezer looking more like some graduate student than a white-trash degenerate.

Maybe he's only white trash because of how he was raised, that new voice muttered.

Of course, Glenn thought distractedly.

And maybe you've kept him that way with your relentless condescension.

Bullshit.

Weezer was going on. "I assumed at first it would rush me the way it did Mike. Or maybe throw me in the fire the way it did to poor Dan Clinton." Weezer shook his head. "Dan left a wife and six children behind…a terrible shame." And made a tutting noise that sounded not the slightest bit like him.

"So what did you do?" Rebecca asked, her voice even smokier than normal.

"I spoke to it," Weezer said.

Glenn frowned. Despite the authority with which Weezer was telling the tale, this sounded to Glenn like a sharp left turn into the Merry Old Land of Bullshit. Weezer claimed he spoke to the beast? That implied Weezer had been brave enough – or foolhardy enough – to attract the beast's attention, and that prospect flew in the face of everything Glenn knew about his friend.

He resolved to let Weezer go on, to shovel more bullshit until the tale became too untenable to support.

"What did you say?" Mya asked. She was sitting cross-legged on the tailgate and leaning toward Weezer, so that her shirt fell open quite a bit at the chest. Her breasts were even better than Glenn had first suspected, and he made a mental note to consider this new development after he'd won back both women and could choose between them.

Weezer's voice hardened. "I said, 'Leave my friends in peace.'"

This was too much. Glenn looked at him dryly. "Come on, man. You're claiming you asked that thing to leave us alone, and it decided you were right?"

Weezer's remaining eye pierced Glenn. "Does it look like it left me alone?"

Glenn winced.

"I didn't ask it to leave," Weezer corrected. "I asked it to leave my friends alone."

Rebecca was hugging herself. "You mentioned them by name?"

"That's right. Short Pump. Jessica Clinton." Again with the piercing Cyclopean stare. "Glenn."

This sounded even less believable than the rest of it, but Glenn decided to play along.

"Then what?" Mya prompted.

"Then it walked toward me."

"Wait a minute," Glenn said. "You say it 'walked'?"

"You don't believe me?" Weezer asked.

Glenn grunted. "I'm sorry, but no, I don't. That thing didn't walk anywhere. It moved like a Bengal tiger on crystal meth."

"It moved like a man."

"Like a really goddamned *agile* man, one that was part…" Glenn broke off, the blood rushing to his cheeks.

They all waited. The corners of Weezer's mouth turned up in an indulgent grin. "Why not say it, Glenn? Does the word frighten you?"

Glenn suppressed an urge to knock the smile off Weezer's face. It felt like the temperature had risen twenty degrees.

Glenn looked from face to face, knowing he couldn't just put them off. Forcing himself to make eyes contact with Weezer, he said, "It looked like a wolf."

"A *werewolf*," Rebecca said. "That's what the *Sun-Times* called it."

"Why didn't I hear about this?" Mya asked.

"Because you get your news from the E! network," Rebecca said.

"So the werewolf was walking toward you," Mya prompted.

"And talking," Glenn added. "Don't forget that. It was going the route of diplomacy."

Weezer seemed unperturbed. "It wasn't speaking at all. I wouldn't have heard it if it was. The men with guns were all around by that point, shooting and yelling."

Glenn mentally calculated. Was that before or after Short Pump had saved him? He couldn't remember. Everything from that night was so muddled in his mind...

"So you ran, right?" Rebecca said. "It had already killed all those people."

"I stood my ground," Weezer said.

Glenn tossed back his head and laughed. He couldn't help it.

When he looked at the three of them ranged along the tailgate, he noticed that Weezer wore the same knowing expression, but Rebecca and Mya were both glaring at him.

"What's so hilarious?" Rebecca asked.

Glenn nodded at Weezer. "Why don't you ask the hero here why he wasn't in the clearing before that?"

Mya scrunched up her eyes. "What are you talking about?"

Glenn indicated Weezer. "This whole wild story began when Weezer entered the clearing."

"So?" Mya said.

"So, he was there when the beast first attacked. Where was he when the thing was killing everyone?"

The woman turned to Weezer, and Glenn thought, *Finally*. It had taken long enough, but he'd finally discovered the necessary angle to shed light on the ludicrousness of Weezer's tale. He crossed his arms, eager to watch his friend squirm.

Weezer nodded. "I was in the woods when the werewolf first appeared. I watched what happened from the forest. When everyone ran, I did too."

Glenn couldn't keep the smugness out of his grin.

Rebecca was eyeing Weezer closely. "But you came back."

"I did," Weezer agreed. "There had been enough death at that point."

Glenn's grin faded a little.

Weezer continued as if his story hadn't been interrupted. "It said to me, 'Your lifeblood will flow.'"

Mya's hands flew to her mouth. "It was threatening to kill you."

Weezer gave her a funny look. "That's what I assumed."

"But you don't now?" Rebecca asked.

Instead of answering, Weezer glanced up at the sky. The glittering stars. The sliver of moon.

Glenn was sweating hard now, his clothes soaked through. God, he needed water in the worst way.

He asked, "Is that when it attacked you?"

"Just about," Weezer said. "I was looking at it one moment. The next I was staring up at the trees."

"And then?" Mya asked.

"And then there was the crack of a rifle report, and the thing fell forward."

Glenn felt faint, both from the smothering heat and the aching thud of his heart.

"It was only there for a moment," Weezer said. "It struck me in the face. I'm certain it could have killed me then, but for whatever reason, it didn't."

Rebecca tilted her head, perhaps searching Weezer's face for a lie. "It just...left you?"

"After the shouts erupted from nearby, yes, it left me. I blacked out, but not before seeing it hurry into the darkness, the hunters giving chase."

Glenn felt his muscles unclench, but the feverish heat remained. He'd go to the restroom, give himself a chance to regroup. He had to take a leak, and though he ordinarily would have done this along the back fence – no one was parked within thirty yards of them anyway – he needed some water, and he needed it right now. And maybe a coney dog. Or whatever else they had at the concession stand that might contain some protein.

"Where are you going, Glenn?" Weezer asked.

"Be right back," Glenn said, moving away.

"Would you like me to accompany you?" Weezer asked.

Piss off, Glenn thought. "I'm fine."

"Don't forget to wipe!" Mya called.

Glenn glowered at the gravel in front of him. What a bimbo. She would definitely be Weezer's tonight. Good for him. Maybe this newfound confidence would make things easier on Glenn. His friendship with Weezer and Short Pump had lost him many a lay over the years. If this new Weezer was actually attractive to women, Glenn could finally relax a little and not have to worry about playing matchmaker.

Nearing the concession stand, he glanced up at the movie screen and beheld the glowing yellow eyes of a werewolf about to kill a screaming woman.

Shivering, he thrust the image away and lumbered toward the bathroom.

Glenn was hoping the bathroom would be empty, but even that good fortune was denied him when he pushed open the door and discovered the big oaf relieving himself at the urinal. There was another urinal open beside the guy, but Glenn wanted privacy. Plus, the oaf might have BO, and that wouldn't agree with Glenn's hypersensitive nose.

He made his way over to one of the two stalls – the one farthest from the fat fuck at the urinal – and flipped it open. The door banged loudly enough to hurt Glenn's sensitive ears.

"Jesus!" the oaf shouted. "Take it easy, would ya? Scared me half to death!"

Glenn said nothing. His fever had grown downright nasty during the short trek to the restroom. He felt lousy. He knew you could get a lot of savage bugs from the hospital. Maybe he'd picked something up while he was there, it had incubated for the past couple days, and now it was really sinking its teeth into him.

Glenn unzipped his fly, leaned forward and braced himself on the cinderblock wall.

"I say you scared me," the oaf repeated.

Glenn didn't trust himself to answer. His bladder was on fire, but the odours of the bathroom distracted him. Christ, he thought. How often was this pigsty cleaned? The concrete surrounding the toilet seemed permanently damp, not only from a hundred dudes' errant urine streams, but also from the leaky plumbing and what he suspected were a great many loogies as well. Yes, he could smell the dried spit beneath the dampness, some of it containing the memories of masticated popcorn and candy, much of it laced with tobacco juice. God, it was horrible.

"I've had kidney stones all spring," the oaf remarked. "Some days it's damn near impossible to push a squirt out, if you know what I mean."

Glenn winced, ground his teeth. His abdomen was smouldering. If he didn't piss soon, he was afraid his penis might explode from the pressure.

"*Oooo*," the man moaned. "I can feel it *burning*."

Glenn felt the muscles of his forearms bunch and hop. He needed water. He'd lurch over to the sink now, but he was afraid if he chanced it, his bladder would finally let go, and he'd be left with a dark blue crotch and a shitload of mockery from Weezer and the women.

"It muggy in here to you?" the oaf asked.

Boy, is it ever, Glenn thought. Unbidden, the image of the big man over there at the urinal filled his mind. The beige T-shirt soaked through with sweat. The too-short black shorts, which probably stank of the guy's swampy ass. The white legs, the black socks. The guy's shoes probably smelled so bad no amount of spray or odour-eating inserts could kill the stench. The kind of feet that clouded a room.

"*Ohhh damn*," the man said, and made a sucking, hissing sound. "*Damnity-damn-damn*."

Glenn closed his eyes, willing the oaf to finish his business and clear the hell out. The sweat was dripping off Glenn's hair, his nose, and spattering the rim of the toilet, which was marred by fine speckles of diarrhoea, several hooks of pubic hair.

"Golly," the oaf groaned, "what I wouldn't give for an air conditioner in this joint."

And sure enough, Glenn smelled it then, the odour wafting over from the oaf at the urinal. It was even worse than he'd anticipated, the smell like bacon grease left to congeal outside some squalid kitchen door, the flies crawling over it and laying eggs in it. He heard the man shifting from foot to foot, and the stench magnified, and in Glenn's mind he saw the ivory maggots with their black-brown faces writhing in the rancid bacon cream.

"*Awww crap*," the oaf moaned. "I told 'em there was another stone in there, and you think they believed me? Now look at that. Blood."

Glenn smelled it, the stench overpowering the half-dissolved pink cake in the urinal drain.

The oaf said, "That ain't good, man. That means more of that laser crap. I gotta go back on that gosh-darned diet. Crud, man."

Glenn's whole body was rimed with sweat now. He was having trouble pissing, but that was because, he noticed with a downward glance, he was half-erect. And here was another surprise: his cock was a good two inches longer. And hairier too. Not just the area around the shaft, the part he kept neatly shaved to make himself appear longer, but the penis itself was now threaded with long black strands of hair.

What in the holy hell?

"Hey, buddy," the oaf called. "You deaf or something? Wouldn't that be just my luck? Talking to a deaf guy all this time?" A pause. "Wouldn't it?"

The fire was blossoming over Glenn's shoulders, was scalding his neck like a superheated yolk. He suppressed a whimper. Yes, this was definitely the flu. Or what did they call that infection people got from hospitals?

Staph.

Shit, he hoped it wasn't a staph infection. That was some serious stuff. People lost limbs from that, even died because of it. If he got a freaking staph infection from his stay at Lakeview Memorial—

The stall door rattled. Glenn gasped, whirled.

"You alive in there, buddy?" the oaf called.

Glenn stared at the sliver of beige shirt in the slender gap between the door and the frame. Glancing higher, Glenn spotted an eye.

The man watching him through the gap.

"You don't look so good, buddy," the man said.

Glenn turned back toward the toilet. The thighs of his jeans were restrictive, the shirt a couple sizes too small.

"You want me to call the manager, have them fetch a doctor?"

Glenn opened his lips to tell the guy to mind his own fucking business, but his mouth was suddenly full of teeth. Hot drool glopped over his bottom lip, his chin. The heat in his body was unbearable, like he would at any moment ignite and melt the blue plastic stall around him.

"Suit yourself," the oaf said. "I need to take something for this pain. You ever had kidney stones?"

Glenn looked down at his hands. *Oh Jesus.*

The oaf said, "Believe me, pal. You never want to know. Worst stuff in the world."

A spasm racked Glenn's body, doubled him up. And like the oaf's words had somehow infected him, he now felt a molten pain spread through his urethra. But it didn't stop there. It burned through his loins, sizzled down his quadriceps. Urine squirted everywhere. There was an immense cracking sound in the middle of his back, and Glenn let out a coughing groan. He felt a burst of wet heat in the seat of his jeans and realised he'd shat himself. He figured the oaf would comment on that, but the guy was washing his hands now, the dull roar of the faucet masking Glenn's bodily functions.

"You're not getting off, are ya?" the man called.

Oh my God, Glenn thought. *Get out now.*

The oaf chuckling. "Sounds like you're doing the hokey-pokey in there, pal." The man began to sing, his voice jolly and high. "*You do the hokey-pokey and you take yourself a dump — that's what it's all a-bout!*"

Glenn's arms were juddering, twitching, the liquid fire spreading through his joints, even his fingernails.

"I oughta call the manager," the oaf said, and from the sound, he was facing the stall again. "Come on out of there, pal. I got kids here tonight. I need to make sure you're not some weirdo, perpetrating some kind of weirdo stuff in there."

Glenn's body was a jitterbugging blur. He bent backward, his face upturned to the cobwebbed ceiling, the ceiling somehow too close, like he was on stilts. The pain swam over him, the heat a metronomic blast on his throat, his shoulders, his—

"That's it, buddy. No fooling. I'm going for the manager."

Glenn whirled and backhanded the door. It flew open and crashed against the wall, the hard plastic splitting, the cinderblock shrapnel spraying the area between them. As the dust settled, he saw that the oaf was indeed staring at him, the man's face going slack with shock. And over the oaf's shoulder, Glenn beheld his own reflection and understood why.

But before Glenn had time to register the shock of what he saw in the mirror, he scented something that made his muscles seize. The dribble of blood soaking the man's underwear. The greater, pulsing network of arteries and veins under the man's pale, blubbery flesh. The oaf backed up and sat on the sink, his ample buttocks actually drooping into the basin.

Glenn realised his vision was clearer, more crystalline than any high-definition footage he'd ever seen. But this was a mere afterthought, his other shrieking senses obscuring what he saw. He scented every fold and crevice in the man's body, the stink between his toes, the gathered filth in his navel. He heard the beat of the man's heart, the guy's malfunctioning plumbing, the backed-up urinary system, the gurgle of his bloated belly. But most maddeningly of all, he could feel the rough chafe of his own stretched clothing, could taste the taint of the alcohol he'd drunk earlier, so impure compared to the flesh that quailed before him.

The oaf's hands were out, the man's face a pathetic, quivering mask. Drool spilled over the sluglike lower lip, the man's sobs inciting something deep within Glenn, some dark crimson urge.

Glenn took a step in the man's direction, ready to rend him to pieces, but as he moved he caught his own reflection again, saw the metamorphosed face, the hairy, satanic mask and the yellow wolf's eyes.

Choking down a growl, Glenn said, "*Go now*," but the man, the stupid fucking slack-faced man, he didn't move at all, if anything showing even greater horror at the rumble of Glenn's voice.

And then Glenn was hurtling forward, his blackened nails sinking into the flesh of the man's torso and shredding down and inward, the deep furrows that bloomed reminding Glenn of gills, ragged, bloody fish gills, and the blood splashed over the basin in brilliant torrents, the man vomiting and gibbering and keening and begging, and maybe this was what flipped another switch in Glenn, the goddamned begging. He punctured the man's womanish breasts, closed and opened his fingers as though kneading dough, only the blood and the tissue and the thrashing removed the thought of bread straightaway and replaced it with the floor of a slaughterhouse, the purple offal and the dripping cutting boards and the heat and the man was wailing for mercy and Glenn needed to cut off that wail, but before he buried his muzzle in the distended puff of throat, he reached down, unzipped the man's fish-white belly with a single swipe. But that was worse because now the shriek rose higher, so loud it chipped away at Glenn's overtaxed eardrums, which would surely burst and spew blood and pus over his shoulders, so he thrust his thumbnails between the man's locked-open lips, punctured the pink roof of the mouth, the blood and saliva swirling over his knuckles, transforming the wail into a machine-gun gargle, and when the spray of bloody spit misted over his face, he could restrain himself no longer. Glenn's jaws unhinged and he buried his tearing, grinding teeth in the fleshy wad of the man's throat, and beneath the blast of scarlet that splattered his face Glenn felt the man's convulsive denial, the twitching of his big head helping Glenn's teeth razor through the fat and sinew. Glenn gulped the spurting blood, his tongue flicking, his teeth shaving off sheets of membranous flesh, the fat melting in the oven of his maw, coating his tongue, the glorious lifeblood spurting—

The outside door opened.

Glenn stopped in midchew and stared in astonishment at the man who entered.

The funny thing about it was the way the guy, a white-haired man in black leather who looked like a hardcore motorcyclist, moved into the room about eight paces before he even looked up at Glenn and his victim. The guy was gripping a cigarette between thumb and middle finger, the narrow spiral of smoke rising lazily up his arm. For an endless moment, the ribbon of smoke was the only thing that moved in the bathroom. The man's squinting, hard-lived eyes betrayed almost no emotion, but Glenn thought he discerned a species of sardonic disbelief in the man's gaze. Like the guy figured he was being put on, a hidden camera situated in the room capturing his reaction to the gruesome tableau at the sink. Glenn was still nestled between the oaf's splayed legs, gripping the big guy like a giant sex doll.

Then the biker frowned. He was listening, Glenn realised, to the rapid drip-drip-drip that pattered onto the floor beneath the basin. The man's eyes traced the downward trajectory of the blood, took in the spreading lake beneath the sink, then slowly crawled back up to behold Glenn's face anew.

The man's squinting, nicotine-ravaged expression didn't change.

The man turned and strode toward the door.

Glenn was on him with a bound, the biker's head cracking the bottom of the door, throwing the whole thing open, both their bodies skidding into the half-enclosed entryway and revealing to them the ghostly spill of images on the screen, the faces of the characters too white, moonlike, the echoes of four hundred car stereos drilling into Glenn's ears. The man's attempts at escape were silent but determined, the biker like a powerful old turtle crawling toward the row of rear bumpers. Glenn knew there would be more men coming any moment now. This was the only restroom. He couldn't devour this biker, couldn't revel in the font of lifeblood as it drenched his lips. He couldn't remain here an instant longer. To do so was suicide. And dammit, Glenn wanted to *live*. He mashed the biker's face into the scabrous concrete, twisting it back and forth like a stubborn cigarette butt, and the man's skin rashed off like a moulting snake, a circle of bloody peels removing the biker's squint, removing the biker's face, and Glenn forced his thrumming muscles down on the head until the skull cracked, split, the exhilarating odour of exposed brain boring into Glenn's nostrils.

But he saw the moonlike faces on the screen, knew similar faces would appear at any moment. Some ancient race memory revealed to him a circle of faces, a killing mob, and when his energy was spent they would converge and immolate, and he would die in a howling blaze, the raging villagers bellowing in triumph, and he would not permit that, he must go, so with a black-nailed flick he opened the biker's jugular, stumbled to his feet and lurched into the darkness. He knew well enough where the Corvette was parked, but he didn't know how he'd drive it, not with the toenails and the barbed heels, and what would the women think, whatever their names were? He heard voices nearby, laughter. A question or two. A figure approached, a man with his arms out, as though he were a preacher and Glenn a lost soul. The hands twitched, beckoning him closer.

Weezer.

Glenn opened his mouth to tell his friend it wouldn't work, there was something wrong, when a chunk of meat the size of a sugar cube slipped off one of his daggerlike canines. Glenn moved to cover his face, but Weezer didn't act abashed at all, only ushered him forward. Weezer slipped an arm around Glenn's enlarged shoulders and shepherded him toward the pickup truck.

Weezer said, "I know you're worried about the 'Vette, but I told Rebecca she could drive it. She's smart and won't hurt your baby, so you don't need to worry."

Glenn shot a look at his car and noticed Rebecca wasn't even looking at him, was fiddling with the stereo. Behind Rebecca was the Ford Focus the women had arrived in, and though Mya appeared to be watching him from the driver's side window, it was so gloomy back here it didn't matter.

"Just lie down," Weezer said, helping Glenn into the Ranger, "and no one will see you."

Glenn climbed in behind the driver's seat and slumped onto his side. He tried to ignore the squishy sound of his sodden clothes on the cracked vinyl seat, but it still made him shiver uncontrollably, the guilt so heavy he would surely suffocate beneath it.

Weezer got in, slammed the pickup door and started the engine, which stuttered like a diseased heartbeat. Glenn was shaking so hard he thought his ribs would splinter.

Weezer's voice was silky smooth. "Don't worry, friend. We'll get you out of here. There's no commotion yet. By the time they find out what you did, we'll be well on our way to your house."

Glenn's voice was an agony of gravel and broken glass. "*Kill me*," he whimpered. "*Please kill me*."

"Here we go," Weezer said, the pickup looping toward the drive-in exit.

Glenn's scrotum tightened as the shouts erupted from the area of the restroom. Beneath the muffled score of the horror flick there were hysterical voices, demands that somebody call somebody.

"As long as the girls follow us," Weezer said, "we'll be just fine."

From the quality of Weezer's voice, Glenn knew he was watching the other two cars in the overhead mirror. Glenn supposed he could turn around and watch too, but he was too distraught to do that.

The streetlights outside the drive-in spilled over the pickup. Glenn shut his eyes. They stopped, waiting for the women to catch up.

"There's Rebecca," Weezer said.

An endless pause. Glenn held his breath, mumbled disjointed prayers to no one in particular. Just let him get through this. Just let him stay undiscovered. He hadn't meant to do any of it.

He realised he was weeping.

"Shhh," Weezer soothed. "Shhhh."

Glenn shivered with revulsion at the blood sliming his chin.

"And here comes Mya," Weezer said. "Good. We'll make for Rangeline Road. It's not as direct as I'd like, but it gets us out of town faster."

Glenn nodded, unable to process anything. The shouts, which had swollen like a polluted cloud from the other side of the drive-in's tall concrete façade, were now diminishing, the voices no longer so accusatory, no longer so reminiscent of torches and burning hair, of writhing death and judgement.

Glenn knew the town well enough to know when they halted at the red blinking light and when they were headed toward Rangeline Road, the pickup gaining speed fast. He could hear the sweet purr of the 'Vette behind them and the graceless chuff of the Ford Focus behind the 'Vette. When they turned onto Rangeline Road, which would take them closer to Glenn's house in the country, Glenn began to think about Weezer, about the way his friend had known how to handle the situation, and though Glenn knew he was stupid for missing all of it before, he now wondered with a sharp stab of fear how Weezer had known what Glenn had done.

Had Weezer been watching?

Of course not, he realised. Weezer had been with the women, prepping them for their escape.

Glenn pushed himself up on an elbow, attempted to speak, but his throat was a white-hot sheet of flame. He coughed, tears streaming down from his eyes, and clutched his burning oesophagus.

"Easy," Weezer soothed. "There's nothing so important right now it can't wait. What matters is we're all just fine, and we'll be at your house within minutes."

Glenn tried to swallow, couldn't. Finally, he was able to manage, "*The women will see me.*"

"I'll park in the garage," Weezer said, "and come out to meet them." Weezer's one-eyed face scowled at Glenn in the overhead mirror. "You haven't installed a security light recently, have you? One of those motion detectors?"

Glenn shook his head.

"Then they won't see you pass from the garage to the house," Weezer said.

Glenn decided this made sense. His garage was detached, which was unfortunate given his current situation. But it was darker than a grizzly bear's asshole out there, and the women would need night-vision goggles to make out anything more than a vague figure when Glenn attempted to get inside.

They turned off Rangeline Road onto County Road 575, off which Glenn's house and its four acres of land were situated.

"Almost there," Weezer said. "When we reach the garage, you bust ass out the side door and go straight to the bathroom by the laundry room."

Glenn nodded, seeing the logic. It wasn't the bathroom he typically used, but it was the most isolated, the one farthest from the front door. There was a shower there too.

Weezer's voice was focused, businesslike. "I'll pick up a little speed. There's no way the girls will lose us when we're the only cars out here. Well, Mya might lose us. She's got a brain like a radish. Anyway, Rebecca's sexier."

Glenn stared at his friend with dawning shock. "You're still planning on..." He licked his lips, made a face at the coppery taste. "...you know, partying with them?"

Weezer's laugh made Glenn's toes curl. "Come on, Glenn. You know better. We're going to do a lot more than party with them."

And as they crunched into Glenn's driveway and made for the stygian gloom of the garage, Glenn tried not to think about what Weezer's sharkish grin might portend.

CHAPTER EIGHTEEN

Joyce strode down the Bluff Street sidewalk, her face upraised. Only since the bonfire had she begun to realise how lovely the night could be, how intoxicating. Like being surrounded by velvet and silk, the quiet houses and the silence like a painting come to life around her. She loved her books, felt an almost orgasmic joy at curling up with a great novel in her flannel sheets and down comforter. Yet this...this was *living*. This was drinking rather than reading about wine, this was tasting rather than imagining the warm, heady merlot.

My, what she wouldn't give to share this with someone.

Someone like Glenn.

The skin of her chest burning, Joyce forced herself to keep the thought of Glenn at arm's length, at least until she climbed under the covers tonight. For now, there was enough beauty to divert her from the body-racking waves of lust that had besieged her the last couple nights. She looked around, breathed deeply of the fragrant air. Bluff Street was dark and deep and very much like she imagined it would have been a hundred years before. All the houses were that old, the library much older.

The library, she thought. *Yes.*

Joyce's steps quickened. Had she known she'd end up at the library tonight? Perhaps on some level she had. Because she knew there was work to do. A part of her, one so shrouded in paranoia and uncertainty she didn't care to examine it, suspected the work would be nasty and unsettling.

But that was madness, of course. *Lycanthropology* was a diverting read, but the author's earnestness and scholarly tone couldn't conceal the underlying luridness of the subject matter, nor could the multitude of Dr. Clark Lombardo Coulter's leaps in logic be ignored. It was no wonder he'd been labelled a lunatic.

Yet she already had proof of his theories, didn't she?

She had been badly bitten, but she had healed within hours.

Irrefutable.

She had grown stronger, healthier, even if her new desires were a bit peculiar.

Incontrovertible proof.

No, this wasn't fiction, wasn't just a wives' tale or a fanciful legend.

This wasn't a horror movie.

This was real.

Joyce was transforming.

And what was more, deep down, she wanted it, wanted the transformation to happen. Had the others turned yet? God, there was so much to think about, so much to learn.

Joyce reached the library and glided up the steps. At the double doors, she paused, the key inches from the lock.

She heard sirens.

Police sirens. An ambulance. Headed north. Odd, but not necessarily abnormal. There were many reasons the sirens could be blaring, most likely some nonagenarian at the retirement village having passed on.

A man in his late fifties appeared under a streetlamp across the street and proceeded down the sidewalk. He was walking a dog so small it would get stuck in a mousetrap, the kind of tufted, shaven creature that yipped and nipped and generally made her wonder what the fun of owning it could possibly be. But the man would dote on it, she was sure.

Even as she watched, dog and man moved into a spotlighted circle of sidewalk and paused, the man kneeling beside the dog and scratching it under the chin. The little dog's eyes watched the man adoringly, and Joyce thought, *That's nice. Now look over here.*

But the man continued to scratch; the dog continued to adore its owner.

Joyce bit her bottom lip. It was true she was relatively obscured by the shadows on this side of Bluff Street, and the man had no reason to suspect the presence of another person at this time of night. After all, who walked alone after ten o'clock? Who but dog owners and the ultralonely?

Warm moisture and the taste of sheared metal brought Joyce's attention to her bottom lip. She swept two fingers over her bleeding lip, and my, had she bitten it! The blood was trickling over her chin, tracing a capillary-thin streak down her neck. She knew it would soak into her green top, knew the bloodstain would be difficult to remove.

And she didn't care. What she wanted was the man to look at her. Was that so much? She wanted him to rise from his worshipful canine genuflecting and to by God notice her. *Look!* Joyce thought angrily. *I'm more interesting than the rat-dog!*

The man rose, but only to slide a hand inside his hip pocket. He produced a smattering of small chunks, a treat for the dog. Of course. The ratlike animal gobbled them lustily from its owner's hand.

Seeing the dog's paddle-shaped tongue reminded her that she was still shredding her lip. The trickle had become a stream. Joyce took a step toward the man, daring him to see her.

But no, it was still too shadowy. So she moved toward the edge of the sidewalk, now on the curb, now on the street. Man and dog continued forward, cocooned in their simple bond, and Joyce's fingers curled, her forearms tensing. *Look at me, damn you! LOOK AT ME!*

Man and dog pulled even with her. They didn't spare her a look.

Joyce fell in step with them, noting as she did the chorus of sirens wailing toward the drive-in and the fast-food places. There must be something serious going on, a reaction like that. This was no dead nursing home resident, no raisin-skinned woman in a wheelchair being defibrillated. This was a house fire or a deadly car accident. This was...this was...

An *opportunity*, she realised. Yes. If the police and the fire department and the ambulances were all indisposed, that meant she could indulge the urge that had been growing in her for the past couple nights. Funny, she thought as she crossed the street, she hadn't even been aware of the desire. She'd noticed changes in her behaviour, alterations in her body chemistry. She'd studied *Lycanthropology* as though it were the third stone tablet Moses toted down from Mount Sinai, but what she hadn't done was examine the need that was building in her.

It was so simple, she realised as she neared the man. Perhaps it had been in her all along, and her near-death experience had merely awakened it.

But no, she thought, to say her brush with death had given her a new perspective on life was too trite, too reductionist. She didn't feel that way at all.

Yet she did feel alive. Alive in a way she never had. She mounted the curb a few feet ahead of the man, who glanced at her, startled. The dog immediately yipped and darted at her, and might have bitten her had the leash not caught it and planted it on its stubby-tailed ass. It scrambled clumsily to its feet, began hopping on its hind legs, the man soothing it with tender strokes. Joyce stood over the pair, barring their way, and waited for the man to speak to her.

"Shhh-shhh, Orson," the man said. "*Shhhh*."

"Is he named after the director or the author?" Joyce asked.

The man stood, adjusted his glasses. "I don't go to the movies."

Joyce had mixed feelings about this answer.

The man frowned at her, adjusted the thick black frame of his spectacles. "Why, you're bleeding."

Joyce watched him impassively.

"You're bleeding," the man repeated.

"Yes," Joyce said. "I am."

The man cleared his throat. He reminded Joyce of someone you'd meet at a church potluck. One of the elders. Not elder*ly*, but over sixty. He looked like someone from her childhood. No one specific, but the kind of faceless, conservative man who'd wear an outdated suit to church.

"Well," he said, "if you're sure you're okay—"

"I'm not."

Behind his spectacles, his owlish eyes blinked at her. "Not what?"

"Not sure I'm okay. You never asked."

He stared at her, bemused. Orson watched her too. Put some glasses on the dog, and its expression would be identical to its owner's.

"You never asked if I was okay," she explained. "You just told me I was bleeding, which I already knew."

The man blinked, his mouth opening and closing. Then, he coughed into a fist. "Hm. Are you okay?"

"No," she said at once.

"No," the man repeated.

"Uh-uh," she said. "I'm very far from okay."

The man turned, glanced in the direction of the distant sirens. "Maybe you should, I don't know…" He gestured feebly toward the noise. "Maybe you should go down…"

She leaned toward him, eyebrows raised. "Go down…"

He cleared his throat, motioned to the north. "You know, investigate what's happening."

"Your advice is for me to investigate the sirens."

He chuckled, a miserable, embarrassed sound. Cleared his throat. "I just thought they, you know, might be able to administer aid to you. If they're not all occupied by…"

"Look at me."

He did, his eyes widening.

Joyce placed her index finger on her bottom lip, massaged the wound until her fingertip was enamelled in blood. Then, her eyes never leaving his, she stuck the finger into her mouth, sucked on it languidly.

The man stared at her, spellbound. Orson didn't so much as growl.

"Did you like that?" she asked.

The man started slightly, his lips trembling on the verge of speech.

"Give me your hand," she said.

The man didn't move. So she reached out, took the hand that wasn't grasping Orson's leash. Brought it toward her.

"You might avoid…" the man said, his voice hollow. "I mean, that's the hand that Orson licked…the dog saliva…"

Looking deep into the man's eyes, Joyce placed his flat palm on the flesh where her throat and chest merged, and began smearing the bloody contrails all over. Her Adam's apple, her shoulders. Her cleavage.

The man jerked his hand away. Orson had begun to yip.

In the absence of his hand, Joyce reached up, dragged her fingers over her bottom lip, which was still leaking, and wetted them. She slid the glistening fingers over her jaw, her neck, let them slide over her breasts, which were covered by the stretchy jade fabric but very much alive and tingling.

The man swallowed, backpedalling. "You have…" he said, licking his lips. "You have problems, I think." And turned in the direction he'd come, speed-walking toward the glow of the streetlamps. Orson watched her over his shoulder, the little feet pattering to keep up.

Joyce smiled, watching him go. She thought of how much her mother would disapprove of her behaviour and felt an almost sexual thrill at the rebellion.

Her body tingling, Joyce recrossed the street and let herself inside the library.

* * *

Glenn let the scalding water from the showerhead assault him.

The music was so damned loud Glenn was sure the speakers would be damaged, if not blown. Under normal circumstances, this would have enraged him, would have led to a severe beat down of the person who inflicted the damage on his speakers – they'd cost him two grand, for chrissakes – but at the moment the monetary loss seemed utterly insignificant.

All that mattered were the two corpses at the drive-in.

His stomach clenched, and Glenn regurgitated more hunks of pink meat. He kept his eyes studiously shut so as not to glimpse what lay on the floor of the beige tub. He knew there was a lot of it, the meat, because the water level had begun to rise, which meant that there was enough collected in the drain to clog the goddamned thing. And the thought of all that meat burbling down there was enough to get him purging again. His throat felt like someone had dragged sadistic fingernails up and down its length, the tender flesh harrowed into pink, blood-tinged curls. Glenn's gorge threatened to rocket upward again, but he focused on the music, the earsplitting, headache-inducing music, and slowly, his stomach muscles began to unclench.

At least Weezer had selected good artists. His tastes were stuck in time, but if he was going to be stuck in any time, Glenn figured, the late eighties were as good as any. Over the last twenty minutes, while Glenn had upchucked in the shower, Weezer's playlist had included Guns 'N' Roses, Aerosmith, Bon Jovi and now Motley Crüe. The album Weezer was currently spinning was one of Glenn's own mixes. The bruising notes of "Primal Scream" shook the tile under Glenn's fingers. His skull felt like it would split.

He knew he couldn't stand here forever, and besides, the water had cooled appreciably. He reached out, twisted off the water. He pushed aside the curtain, was about to step out onto the mat, when he caught a glimpse of the tub drain. Or rather where the tub drain should have been.

Among the chunks of meat lay a human fingertip, sheared neatly off at the top knuckle.

"Oh my Jesus Christ," Glenn moaned and promptly sprayed wine-coloured bile all over the wall. "Oh shit," he muttered, his chest heaving. "Oh shit."

He stumbled out of the bathtub, snagged a towel, and glanced at the mirror. It was too steamed up to reveal his face, so he reached out, wiped it with the towel, and peered into his reflection.

He looked the same. That was the remarkable thing. Sure, there was a strained expression on his face, maybe a slight shadowing below his eyes, but absent that, he looked just the way he always did. Hard and pitiless.

But Glenn didn't feel hard. He didn't feel pitiless. He felt like he deserved punishment for what he'd done.

Who the hell was he kidding? Of *course* he deserved punishment. He deserved death, if the magnitude of his crimes were the only consideration here.

It isn't, he thought.

Oh no? a mocking voice answered. *Tell that to the dead men. Tell that to their families.*

Glenn's stomach clenched, his throat tightening into a sob. He looked like a child working his way toward a good, hard cry. The sight of it was too much to bear, so he lurched away from the mirror, jerked open the bathroom door, and peered into the hallway to make sure he was alone.

He scurried forward, locked himself in his bedroom, and listened to the throb of "Primal Scream" as it blazed toward its climax. He wished he could enjoy the music, wished he could pretend he hadn't transformed into some horror-movie monster and ripped to shreds two innocent human beings.

Female laughter murmured through the wall from the living room, reminding Glenn he had guests.

No, not guests, he reminded himself. *Witnesses.* At least, if he didn't get his ass in gear and play the polite host. The women would no doubt hear about the murders. Under no circumstance could he give them the impression he was the one responsible. And the only means of preventing that was to behave as normally as possible.

Yes, he thought. *Think of it from their perspective.* They hadn't been present in the restroom. They didn't know what had taken place. And Weezer had apparently sold them on the notion that Glenn had merely been sick.

So don't give them anything to be suspicious about, he told himself.

Glenn crossed to his dresser, slid on underwear, a fresh pair of jeans, a clean black T-shirt. He turned and surveyed himself in the bureau mirror. Yes. He looked normal. Maybe a little beleaguered, but that could be explained easily enough. *Yeah, ladies, it's been a rough week. I lost several close friends at that bonfire. Let me tell you about it. Yeah, come sit by me on the couch. Or better yet, have you seen my room?*

Glenn swallowed. No way could he do that. Not tonight. For maybe the first time ever, sex was the only thing not on his mind.

Glenn heaved a deep breath, shook out his arms to relieve some of his nervous energy and headed toward the door. Halfway there he paused and sniffed his hands. A shiver rippled through him. He could still detect the odour of blood on his skin, caked under his fingernails. He strode over to the dresser, selected a bottle of cologne, and spritzed it liberally over his fingers, his chest, even in his hair.

He entered the living room and discovered the three of them, Weezer, Rebecca and Mya, grinding in the middle of the room. The women had Weezer sandwiched, their fingers roving over his body like he was some kind of rock star. Hell, shirtless and sweating, he even looked like a rock star now.

On Glenn's stereo, Motley Crüe's "Wild Side" had begun to blare. The song was ordinarily one of Glenn's favourites, but now it sounded obscene, distasteful, the sinister lyrics a bitter counterpoint to Glenn's remorse.

Weezer spotted him. "Hey, man," Weezer said as the women's hands caressed his sides, his hips, "come party with us."

Mya had her back to Glenn, but Rebecca's eyes flicked toward him, then to the back of Weezer's neck. Had there been a hint of come-hither in Rebecca's gaze? Or was her naughty mood confined to Weezer, the guy who before tonight had never impressed a woman in his life?

Glenn tried to muster what confidence he could, strode casually over to the trio, but they were grouped too tightly, their twining limbs reminding him of the Hindu goddess Durga. The thought rooted him in place. What had Durga stood for? Obviously a feminine deity, she was a mother goddess of sorts…and what else?

Destruction, he now remembered.

He watched with dim revulsion as one of Rebecca's arms snaked around Weezer's waist and cupped his package, the fingers kneading him through his jeans. On the stereo, Vince Neil sang of murder and rape. Mya leaned over Weezer's shoulder, tongued Rebecca, who lapped at Mya's lips greedily. Weezer thrust his midsection against Mya, her tight butt tremoring from the force.

Sickened, Glenn slid past them and into the kitchen. He couldn't bear it anymore. Glenn had taken on two women on several occasions, but the act now taking place in his living room made him want to run screaming from the house.

Jealous, the dark voice teased.

But that wasn't it, Glenn decided. Not entirely. Sure, he'd been jealous earlier. He'd been stung by Rebecca's interest in Weezer. But very little of what he was feeling now boiled down to jealousy.

He went to the fridge, fetched himself a cold bottle of Budweiser. He pressed the bottle to his temple, the icy condensation soothing him. He exhaled. This was what he needed. It was maybe eighty degrees in the house, perhaps more. He'd been sweating without realising it. Glenn twisted off the bottle cap, chucked it onto the counter and took a swig.

And nearly choked on it when he heard the squeal from the living room.

His heart thundering, Glenn hurried in to find Rebecca sitting on the couch and Mya standing a few feet from Weezer, a hand covering her mouth, her eyes stitched with pain.

No, Glenn realised after a moment's study. Mya looked more surprised than injured. And Rebecca wasn't *sitting* on the couch, she was *sprawled* there. Almost liked she'd been thrown.

Frowning, Glenn pushed the Off button and silenced Motley Crüe.

Weezer groaned. "Man, the guitar solo was coming up."

Glenn looked at the women, then at his friend. "Weezer, what the hell is going on?"

"He bit me," Mya said, though her speech was garbled. Half, Glenn thought, because of the blood on her lips, and half because of the alcohol she'd been guzzling. Seven or eight beer bottles were already strewn about the living room.

"You hurt too?" Glenn asked Rebecca.

She gestured at Weezer. "This asshole threw me."

Weezer was staring at Mya, who kept fingering her lips and examining the dollops of blood she found.

"Hey Weezer?" Glenn said. "What exactly is happening here?"

Weezer gazed steadily back at him. "I suppose I should treat others as kindly as you have tonight."

Glenn swallowed. "You need to apologise to—"

"Of course," Weezer said, moving toward Mya. "I wasn't very gentlemanly, was I?"

She eyed him apprehensively. Not buying his contrition exactly, but not opposed to a reconciliation either.

"You fucking hurt me is what you did," Mya said.

Weezer reached out, placed a hand on her waist. "I simply got carried away. The way you were grinding on me, I guess I just lost control."

She allowed him to draw her closer. "Well, it *hurt*."

"I know," he said. "Let me make it better." And he leaned in to kiss her.

Glenn felt a little queasy, watching their lips come together. Rebecca too seemed disgusted that her friend would forgive a guy who'd just bitten her.

Mya's eyes widened.

Glenn heard a low growl.

The growl swelled exponentially, and then Weezer's face wrenched away from Mya's, and in the split second before Mya's hands flew to her mouth, Glenn beheld her exposed bottom teeth, her gums beading with blood.

Weezer turned his head and spat out Mya's bottom lip.

Rebecca screamed, her hands framing her pretty face. Mya staggered toward the hall. As her horrified eyes were swallowed by the shadows, Glenn glimpsed the blood coursing down her knuckles, reddening the throat of her white top like a crimson cravat.

Rebecca shrieked again, and Glenn followed her gaze to Weezer, whose back muscles were expanding, whose jeans were sprouting slits, whose growl was coarsening to something feral. He noted how tall Weezer had grown.

Weezer took a step toward Mya, another. Then he catapulted toward her. She spun and took a couple of shambling strides toward the bedroom. Then Weezer's body crashed down on hers, pinned her to the floor, and Rebecca was trembling at Glenn's side, watching the slaughter from twenty feet away, neither of them saying a word, lifting a finger, and Glenn thought, *This is worse than before. Even though I'm not doing the killing, this is infinitely worse. Because I am in control now, I can do something. I'm just not.*

Blood sprayed everywhere, thick rills of it splashing the walls like a Jackson Pollock painting.

Glenn stared.

Weezer's hands ripped, tore.

Beside him, Rebecca's mouth hinged open in a voiceless scream.

Glenn watched, unable to look away.

Part of Mya's breast plopped down in the middle of the living room.

Rebecca shook her head in mute denial.

Mya's flesh came away in glabrous sheets. Weezer plunged his head into her belly, seized hold of what lay within.

That's you, Glenn thought. *That's what you are now.*

"Please help me," Rebecca whispered.

Glenn nodded. Nodded but didn't do anything. Not until Weezer turned and regarded them with a grin that was more than bloody, that was far worse than cruel.

Weezer's face was accursed.

More human than animal, the wolflike countenance was tufted with hair, the eyes vast and yellow, the eyebrows thick and arched, the teeth grossly elongated and splotched with bloody tissue.

"*Save her, Glenn,*" the Weezer-thing rumbled.

But it was Rebecca who seized Glenn by the arm and towed him toward the kitchen. Once away from the Weezer-thing's malefic stare, Glenn was able to move his legs, was able to trail after Rebecca, who thrust open the side door with enough force for Glenn to slip through before the thing banged shut.

Rebecca swerved toward the driveway, fell, scuttled forward like a blind crab, reminding Glenn how drunk she was.

Rebecca finally gained her feet but again veered off course, reminding him of a participant in one of those silly kids' games, the one where you stood a baseball bat on end, put your forehead on it, and ran in circles until you got good and dizzy. Then you stood up and promptly sprinted into a nearby rosebush, really fucking funny, but this wasn't funny at all. Rebecca was struggling to make it to Mya's car, but her feet got tangled and she went lunging forward, headfirst into the door. Glenn heard a thud as her head dented metal, and Rebecca flopped down, weeping and grasping her bruised forehead.

Glenn hustled over to her, feeling weightless, insubstantial. He shot glances at the glowing windows of the front room, expecting any moment to see Weezer. Or what Weezer had become.

Say it, Glenn.

No, he thought. He bent and reached for Rebecca.

Say it now, you pussy!

No! He hauled Rebecca to her feet, pawed at the door handle, sure the thing would be locked.

Werewolf.

Glenn whimpered, made his hand grip the handle.

Were-wolf, it repeated. *Say it.*

Glenn tugged on the handle. The door swung open.

Say it!

Glenn nudged Rebecca toward the passenger seat, started to shut the door, then stopped when he noticed her right leg was still poking out of the car. He tucked her foot under the dash, slammed the door home, then circled the car, his eyes never leaving the glowing orange windows of his front room.

Icy fingers caressed Glenn's neck. Had he seen something moving within? A shifting of shadows?

Or a shape-shifter? the voice teased. *Admit it, Glenn. You two are werewolves, only Weezer is the bigger and scarier one.*

I'm not a...

The thought died before it could finish.

Glenn opened the driver's door, slid into the seat. He shut his door, groped for the ignition.

Empty.

His eyes flitted to the front windows. Still orange. Still vacant.

Glenn held out his palm to Rebecca. "Keys," he demanded.

She looked at him, horror-stricken. "I don't have them."

He stared at her. "Where are they?"

Rebecca shook her head. "I don't know. Mya's purse?"

Glenn's eyes went to the house again. He could go back in and get the keys. He could also remove his nipples with a hacksaw.

There was Weezer's truck. Would the keys be inside? Or the Corvette? If speed was the main concern, they should take Glenn's car. He shot a look at Rebecca, noticed how she'd leaned forward, doubled up. Weeping. Awaiting death.

Glenn put a comforting hand on her back, let his gaze linger on the side door of the house. Any moment, Weezer would burst through it. But they couldn't just wait here.

He took a steadying breath. He'd get out, check the 'Vette and the Ranger for keys. Whichever one had them, he'd fire up. When he drew even with Mya's car, he'd transfer Rebecca to the running vehicle.

Or you'll keep on driving and leave her here to die.

No! he thought, grinding his teeth. He wouldn't do that.

Glenn took one last look at the house, reached for the handle—

And bellowed in terror as the living room window exploded in a mass of snarling muscle.

Rebecca shrieked, climbed over the console toward him. Glenn huddled against the door, but it was a desperate, futile measure. Weezer had landed on the lawn, the jagged shards of glass twinkling around him like sinister rhinestones. Then the Weezer-thing was barreling toward them, its head down, but not enough to conceal its snarling teeth, its maniacal yellow eyes. Rebecca scrambled over Glenn, shoved open the door, and spilled out onto the gravel like quivering afterbirth. Glenn watched her, saw her gain her feet, take a few shambling strides toward the cornfield that bordered his yard. The growling huff of the beast brought Glenn's gaze around as Weezer bore down on the side of the car. Glenn whimpered, braced himself for the impact, but then the Weezer-thing was launching itself over the roof, rising, disappearing, then reappearing on the opposite side of the car, and Rebecca had fallen, had turned to see the beast sailing toward her. She scuttled backward on her elbows, and she was pleading with Weezer to "Stop it! Stop it!" and then the Weezer-thing was on her, its talons ripping her cheeks like old curtains, the blood black and gushing in the moonlight. The Weezer-thing mauled her, ate her nose, her brow, her face becoming a featureless ruin.

Glenn closed his eyes. Trying to unsee what he had seen. But the images remained vivid, remained just as gruesome, as at the edge of the cornfield the macabre soundtrack of the feast continued to blare.

PART THREE
SHADOW SIDE

CHAPTER NINETEEN

The thunking sound reminded Duane of the big picture window in the front room of his house growing up. The view had been pretty and everything, but at least once a month there'd come a dull, sickening thump from the front room, and it always meant the same thing: another bird had died. Ordinarily the victims were sparrows, but sometimes they were bigger. Robins. Cardinals. The occasional blue jay. But whatever the species, it all boiled down to the same thing.

Death.

They'd usually twitch a lot, their wings broken and folded at unnatural angles. There'd be blood trickling from their beaks, though not a lot of it. Just enough to ram home the indelible fact that these birds were not getting better. They'd rustle and spasm and convulse for a few seconds, but they sure as hell wouldn't get up again.

So Duane had painted the outside of the window white. A big, graceful robin had dive-bombed the window while Duane was sitting there playing Legos. Duane had actually seen the poor thing coming, the bird having just vacated a branch on the oak tree that stood sentry outside their house. The robin fluttered out of the tree in the direction of the road, changed course as if it had forgotten some important item and hurtled right at the window. Duane had watched the robin approach with numb dread, fully aware that even if he did leap to his feet and flap his arms like a madman, the sun glare on the window would prevent the robin from seeing him.

Blood had actually splurted from the robin's beak upon impact, a testament to its speed. Looking back, Duane was amazed the window hadn't shattered, or at least spiderwebbed. But it had held, and the robin had landed in the mulch bed like a plump acorn. When Duane rushed out to examine it, the desperate reassurances already strobing through his mind – *It's only stunned...Its wings will mend...It's just a fractured beak* – he was aghast to find it flopping around in a pile of its own guts, the force of the collision so violent its entrails had blown out of its ass.

And so great had been Duane's sense of injustice that he'd marched down to the basement and found the paint his mom used to touch up the trim around their house. He was only seven at the time, but his thinking was very clear, very pragmatic. The window kept claiming innocent creatures. The birds didn't have a chance against the lurking illusion. If Duane took away the window's reflective properties, he would save untold avian lives.

From there it was easy. Stepladder, paintbrush. A half hour of sloppily drawn swaths of Dover white. He'd been standing back from the vast snowy rectangle when his parents returned from the hardware store. They often left Duane and his older brothers alone while they ran errands, and though Duane's brothers were supposed to watch him, most of the time they ran around the neighbourhood with friends and left Duane to his own devices.

His parents hadn't been pleased.

His dad spanked the hell out of him when they saw what he'd done to the window. For months afterward the house had reeked of paint thinner, and for years afterward there'd remained a ghostly pale film on the glass that never completely washed away.

But the birds didn't crash into it quite as frequently, and Duane felt it had been worth it.

The thunking came again, and he remembered where he was. Not in his front room playing Legos.

In the front seat of his truck, sleeping in Savannah's driveway.

He opened his eyes and saw Savannah watching him through the driver's window. Duane stared blearily up at her pinched face.

"What are you doing out here?" she asked, her pretty mouth forming each syllable with either annoyance or concern. With the sunlight punishing his eyeballs, it was difficult to tell.

Savannah rapped the window, squinted at him.

Opening and shutting his lips, Duane reached over, turned the ignition key halfway, and thumbed down the automatic window.

"The front seat of your truck more comfortable than your bed?" Savannah asked.

Duane leaned away from her so she wouldn't scent his sewer breath. "I was worried about you."

The furrows in her brow deepened. "Why would you be worried about me?"

Duane sighed. "I'll tell you. On two conditions."

"I don't like conditions, Short Pump."

"One, you don't have me committed. I'm having trouble believing it myself."

"And the other?"

"Loan me a toothbrush. I feel like I gargled with cat litter."

★   ★   ★

Savannah was waiting for him at the kitchen table when he emerged from the bathroom. Thankful she had a spare toothbrush on hand, he took a chair across from her. He was about to tell her about the werewolf CPA when she sat forward and said, "Duane?"

"Yeah?"

"I need to say something."

"Is Jake still asleep?"

"Are you nuts? He's up at six thirty every morning."

"Then where—"

"My bedroom," she said. "Watching Thomas the Tank Engine."

"Ah."

"Now shut up and let me say this before my thoughts get out of order. I didn't sleep at all last night, and I'm having trouble putting together a coherent sentence."

Join the club, Duane thought. He'd remained awake and watchful until four in the morning.

"Savannah," he said. "I'm not devaluing what you're going to say, but I'm pretty sure what I have to tell you is more important."

"'Devaluing'? Where'd you get that, Short Pump? Daytime talk shows?"

Duane spread his palms. "I merely wanted you to know that I respected your—"

"Oh, shut up for a second, would you? You're either staring at my tits or treating me like I'm the queen of England. Just pretend I'm a person for once."

He fell silent.

Savannah squeezed her eyes shut, sat forward and massaged her forehead. "I thought about you all night, Short Pump, and I finally figured everything out. And not just you, either. I figured out every guy I've ever known."

"Great," Duane said. "Time to trot out the negative male stereotypes."

"Duane?"

"What?"

"Shut your goddamned mouth."

"What if I don't want to?"

"I'll rip off your nut sack and drop it down the garbage disposal."

He brought his legs together. "Jesus."

"You ready to listen?"

"I guess I have to be, huh?"

"I'm not a type."

He stared at her.

She went on. "Guys don't understand women. I mean, that's nothing new. It's been that way since we were walking hunched over in caves, and it'll be that way when we're all flying around with jet packs."

"Like Iron Man?"

She pointed to the garbage disposal. "You testing me?"

Duane shut up.

"But it isn't just the lack of understanding that causes problems, Duane. It's the misinformation that fills the void."

Duane opened his mouth, but before he could speak, Savannah held up a hand. "And I know women don't understand men either. You made your points about that issue last night, and a couple of them even made sense. But at the moment I'm the one talking, and you're the one keeping your trap shut. I've heard enough of the men's liberation movement for one weekend."

Duane leaned back in his chair.

"So last night I'm lying there," Savannah went on, "and I'm thinking of all the stuff you said to me. I'm thinking of Mike, Glenn—" She saw his face twist into a jealous scowl and said, "Get over it, all right? Be an adult. That's part of the problem here."

Duane tried to conceal his hurt by glancing at the refrigerator, where a number of Jake's drawings were displayed. To Duane they all looked like arrhythmic EKG lines, but hey, the kid was five, right?

"Anyway," Savannah said, "I went over all the relationships I've had with boys since elementary school, both the romantic ones and the platonic ones, and I looked for patterns."

Duane eyed her, trying not to look too interested.

"The outlier, of course, was Mike, but that was because of how he changed when he went pro."

"Actually," Duane said with a nasty grin, "he never made it to the pros."

"He became a professional baseball player the moment the Cubs paid him a signing bonus. And you just demonstrated one of the primary problems."

"Would you speak English?"

"Jealousy," Savannah said.

"Why would I be jealous of a dead man?" Duane said and immediately regretted it.

But if Savannah was hurt, she didn't show it. "Jealousy and insecurity. Plus the universal human need to compartmentalise."

Duane rubbed a hand over his mouth. "Hey, I'm sorry for what I said. I didn't mean—"

"Forget your regret for a moment, okay?"

Duane paused.

"Are you doing that?"

"I guess," he said.

"Focus on what I'm saying."

When she didn't go on, he said, "I'm focusing."

She narrowed her eyes, searching his. "I'm not convinced, but at least you're trying. So what I realised at some point between five and six a.m. is this: you and every other guy – with the exception of the postdraft Mike – see me as some elusive, unreachable goddess."

When he started to shake his head, she waved him off. "Or princess or queen or whatever terminology you want to use. You don't really see a *person*, Short Pump. You see these eyes, this hair. You see my freckles. Don't tell me you don't find them attractive."

Duane tried not to blush.

"You see the dimples in my cheeks. You notice my breasts, my ass. You see my complexion, my outer self. But neither you nor any other guy has seen what's inside."

He shook his head. "It's like we never even talked last night."

Savannah's eyes flared. "This isn't about you making me a sex object, Duane. This is a different discussion. It's about what you make of what's *inside* me."

"It's like I need a goddamned translator. Could you maybe furnish me with one? Provide subtitles or something?"

"It's simple," she said, enumerating her points on her fingers. "You take my appearance. My face, my body." She raised her eyebrows. "You with me so far?"

Duane shrugged.

"You have no idea what's inside me, but you know what's on the outside, and you know how that exterior makes you feel."

"This ought to be good."

"I provide a thrill. I make you wistful. I'm every rock ballad you've ever heard."

"You're not making sense." But he said it weakly, because what she was saying made too *much* sense.

"You know how I make you feel," she persisted. "Which is the way you felt back in elementary school and especially in junior high. I'm that unattainable goddess you pined for, that girl who starred in the personalised music videos you created for all those love songs."

Duane wouldn't even consider looking at her now. He felt hollowed out, shallow.

Exposed.

Savannah nodded. "The girl you created – and not just you, Duane, I'm talking about all the guys I've ever met – she's always riding shotgun in your convertible, her hair blowing all over the place, a small, inscrutable smile on her face. It's forever sunset, and I'm always there to look at you that way, to kiss you, to be languid and motherly yet always far away, except when you're making love to me. On blankets, under trees that are changing colours. Can you hear the music playing, Short Pump? Do you have the soundtrack in mind?"

There was a lump in his throat.

"But here's the problem, Short Pump. I'm not that girl. Whatever thoughts you're attributing to me. Whatever sphinxlike facial expressions, those aren't mine either."

Duane's voice was little more than a dry croak. "What are you then?"

She offered him a sad, wan smile. "I'm just me, Short Pump. Nothing special, nothing exciting."

When he started to protest, she leaned across the table, seized his hand. "Don't you *see*? That's all I *want* to be. That's all I *can* be. I'm not your ideal woman. I'm not anyone's. I'm just a person guys happen to think is attractive, which means I'm constantly starring in imaginary music videos. But I can never be the elusive pixie who confirms your false belief that the perfect girl is waiting for you. There *is* no perfect girl, Short Pump. Not for you, not for Glenn. Not even for Mike, had he lived."

Duane sat in smothered silence.

Tears shimmered in Savannah's eyes. "I could see Mike had gone back to thinking that way too. Making me into the Ideal Woman. He'd gone through so much misfortune, so much failure, he thought I was the one who'd make his life good again. Hell, maybe he even hoped I'd resurrect his baseball career."

Duane noticed she was still holding his hand.

She laughed at herself. "You want to know what's really inside me?"

He waited.

She wiped her eyes. "Other than gas?" When he chuckled, she said, "I mean it, Short Pump. I'm the gassiest person I know. Jake gets mad at me for farting so much."

Duane found himself smiling.

"But other than that," she said, "what's really inside is wondering what's wrong with me. Being mad at myself for being so difficult to please. Guys falling over themselves for me, it's spoiled me a little. But I don't feel worthy of all that, not deep down. I feel like I'm not very bright."

"You got good grades," Duane pointed out. "You got a college degree."

She grunted, dabbed at her eyes. "And I had to study my ass off to do that. Half the books I had to read, I still don't know what they were about." Seeing his look, she hurried on. "Oh, I'm not playing the dumb blond card or anything. I know I'm not feebleminded. But most of the time I feel like my intellect is...well, *average*."

"I feel that way sometimes too," he said.

Savannah said, "You're one of the smartest people I know."

He tried not to show how pleased he was. "Oh, I wouldn't say that. I'm fairly perceptive, but that doesn't get you all the way. You've got to be able to use what you know, right? Apply it?"

"I guess."

From the bedroom came the distant sound of a commercial, some electronic dance song, probably advertising a new toy Jake would want. The music was mindless, repetitive. Not unlike Dance Naked had sounded last night.

Duane jolted in his chair.

"What?" Savannah said, pulling her hand away.

"Are you done telling me how much I've misjudged you?"

She grinned a little. "For now."

"Good. Because I think I know who killed Mike."

Savannah's grin faded.

★   ★   ★

An hour later, after Duane washed the sleep grime off his face and after they'd dropped Jake off at the church stay-and-play, they motored over to Callahan's Collectibles to tell Barb everything they knew. Barb listened to the whole thing without saying a word. Or changing her expression. Duane let Savannah do most of the talking. Truth was, there was something about the six-foot-two woman standing behind the cash register that scared the crap out of him. Always had. The old saying was "She doesn't suffer fools", but to Duane it seemed like Barb wouldn't suffer *anybody*. At least, that was what her look suggested. Lines around her eyes, broad face beginning to sag into jowly old age. He figured Barb was only fifty-five or so, but there was enough mileage there to push her appearance closer to sixty-five.

When Savannah finished, Barb turned to Duane. "Anything else?"

Duane shook his head.

"You capable of speech?" Barb asked.

"I can talk."

"Then answer me a question. Who did the killer go after first?"

"Mike," Savannah said.

"And how many people were there?" Barb asked. Her voice was inflectionless, all business.

Savannah looked up at Duane. "I don't remember. What did the paper say? Fifty?"

"Around fifty," Duane agreed.

"And this guy, he went straight at Mike," Barb said.

"I told you it wasn't a man," Savannah said.

"I know what you told me," Barb said. "Forget semantics for now."

Savannah looked like she was about to protest, but Duane said, "He definitely went for Mike."

"Have you considered why?" Barb asked.

Duane and Savannah exchanged a glance. Savannah said, "I'm sure the police around here—"

"—have the cumulative intelligence of a rhubarb plant," Barb finished. "They don't know a thing. If the murders had happened in town, Pete Hoffman would've been in charge. But since it was outside city limits, it fell to Lane Cartwright, who's utterly incompetent. Now it's with the state police, who don't sound much better."

Duane grinned. "Lane Cartwright sounds like an Old West lawman."

Barb gave him a look. "So the killer goes for Mike, gets its appetite whetted, and goes on a blood frenzy. Everybody scatters. Then last night, someone who looks like the killer starts asking you about Mike."

Duane said, "He *might've* looked like the killer. I was drunk at the bonfire, so it could've been—"

Behind them, the bell over the front door tinkled. Duane spun, expecting the man from the Roof to be striding toward him, his face hairy and dripping with blood. But it was just a white-haired woman a few years younger than King Solomon. The woman shuffled over to a table populated by garishly painted gnomes.

"So we know who did it," Barb said. "The shape-shifting accountant."

Savannah's eyes widened. "You believe what we said about the werewolf?"

"I don't believe a bit of it," Barb said. "I was just trying to get into the spirit of the thing."

"Wait a second," Duane said. "I'm not saying the guy last night was *definitely* the same guy that...you know..."

"Transformed into a monster and disembowelled seven people?" Barb said. "For the moment, let's assume it was, all right? Where does that get us?"

"Nowhere," Savannah said.

"You're dumber than a titmouse."

"*Hey*," Savannah said, mouth agape.

"Well, use your goddamned brain then."

Savannah's nostrils flared. "Fine." She drew in a breath, let it out shudderingly. "The werewolf attacked Mike for a reason. So we need to establish a motive."

Duane glanced at Barb, but the woman's expression gave nothing away.

"Mike is the key," Savannah said. "So who has Mike hurt?"

"You," Duane said before he could stop himself.

Savannah gave him a thorny look. "I'm not the one who killed him."

"Who else?" Barb asked.

Savannah's expression grew pained, the vein in her forehead more pronounced. "I mean, he was arrogant...full of himself. He wasn't very nice to a lot of people, but it's not like he ever *wronged* them."

"Think harder," Barb said.

Savannah searched Barb's face. "You sound like you know."

Barb didn't answer right away, but she didn't have to. Because it had already slugged Duane in the gut, the obvious truth. Mike Freehafer had been a cocky, failed athlete, but he wasn't evil incarnate. His sin wouldn't have been deliberate or born of malice. It would have been an act of irresponsibility.

"The crash," Duane said. "He killed that girl on Highway 65. Which means the werewolf – whatever killed Mike was—"

"Someone close to the dead girl," Savannah finished.

Duane bit his lip. "Her boyfriend?"

Barb cocked an eyebrow at him. "How old did you say the man was?"

Savannah sucked in air. "The girl's father."

"Better," Barb said.

"So we look up the dead girl's name," Savannah said. "We get the information on her dad and we've got the killer."

"Seems too easy," Duane said. And it did. If that's all there was to it, he'd rue the fact that he hadn't put it together earlier.

Had the shape-shifting CPA killed the people at the drive-in?

As if she'd divined his thoughts, Barb said, "Why didn't you go to the cops right away?"

Duane scratched the back of his neck. "I don't know. I was at Savannah's."

"In her driveway," Barb said. "Protecting her."

"Well...yeah."

Barb's pitiless gaze burned into him. "What were you planning on doing if the killer showed up?"

Duane felt perspiration moistening his armpits. "You know, defend her."

"You got a gun?"

He hesitated. "No."

"What were you going to do, club him with an ice scraper?"

Savannah placed a hand on his shoulder. "Take it easy, Barb."

"You're just as bad," Barb said to her.

Savannah flinched. "Me?"

"You," Barb agreed. "Why'd you come here instead of the police?"

Savannah uttered a breathless laugh. "You said yourself how dumb the cops are. Why would we—"

"You two know the killer's probable identity. What if he's left town between last night and this morning?"

Savannah took out her cell phone. "Let's call the police and let them figure it out."

Duane shook his head. "This can't be all there is to it."

★   ★   ★

But that's all there was to it. They found Dave Garner – that was the name of the dead girl's father – staying at the Blue Bay Inn. He'd rented a cabin for the summer, evidently thinking he'd be able to kill for an entire season without detection.

According to Barb's sources, Dave Garner didn't act surprised at all. Didn't put up a fight. Just went peacefully with the armada of county police officers who descended on the Blue Bay Inn.

And what kind of a name, Duane wondered, was Dave Garner for a serial killer? The guy sounded like a former quarterback or a lawyer. Not a bloodthirsty berserker. That was the toughest part to swallow, the authorities had said: the notion that this guy, who seemed no more threatening than any other balding middle-aged man, could so thoroughly terrorise fifty people, not to mention slaughter seven of them in spectacularly bloody fashion.

So Garner was arrested.

Two hours later, Duane and Savannah were called in to confirm he was the Bonfire Killer.

CHAPTER TWENTY

Glenn was buried under a mound of blankets when he first heard the tap on the door.

Cops, he thought.

Then, *This is it.*

He'd done what he could to clean up the mess, but really, anyone could see that something terrible had happened here last night. The blood refused to disappear from the hallway carpet, and the tarp he'd stretched over the shattered front window screamed guilt.

The tapping came again, louder this time, and Glenn fleetingly wondered why the police were being so polite.

Glenn didn't know if there was a death sentence in Indiana, so when – not if – they got caught, he might find his miserable new existence swiftly ended. But whether he lived for six months or sixty years, he'd never be able to forget the way Weezer had treated him last night after the murders.

Put her body in the trunk of her car, Weezer had said.

At that point Glenn had been too horrified to move from the interior of the Ford Focus. So Weezer had seized him by the shirtfront, hauled him out bodily and heaved him into the yard. Just a few feet from where Rebecca's ravaged, glistening remains lay strewn in the grass.

Weezer's voice, though still guttural, was the most human thing about him. *Put her in the fucking car*, he repeated.

Glenn had glanced at the entrails. *She's...she's...*

All over the place, Weezer supplied. *Yeah, I can see that. Now get your ass moving before you end up the same way.*

And so chilling was Weezer's wolflike growl that Glenn had complied.

It was a hideous business. Glenn had vomited at least a half dozen times.

Then he was placed on carpet duty while Weezer drove the women's car to who knew where.

When Weezer returned, he looked pretty much human. It occurred to Glenn to ask how in the hell Weezer had gotten back to the house without the use of a car, but he decided it wasn't worth the trouble. Glenn was still on the floor, the carpet wet and sudsy and stained with what looked like red wine.

You listening? Weezer asked.

Glenn swallowed. Nodded.

That drive-in is old.

Glenn had not a clue what this had to do with anything, but he nodded. It seemed the prudent course of action.

Weezer went on. *They didn't even upgrade the projector until a couple years ago, so I'm reasonably certain they wouldn't have invested in a state-of-the-art security system.*

When Glenn didn't say anything, Weezer tilted his head. *You know what that means, right?*

Glenn frowned.

Moron, Weezer grunted. Glenn could see the dried blood foam crusted on Weezer's chin.

It means, Weezer said impatiently, *that there are no security cameras there, which means it's very likely no one saw us leave at the same time as the girls.*

Glenn listened.

Since we arrived separately, Weezer went on, *and our vehicles were in the far back of the lot, there's a good chance no one saw us with them at all. It was already pretty dark by the time I arrived.*

Glenn nodded, realising Weezer was right.

So there won't be any trouble, Weezer explained. He hunkered down next to Glenn — *over* Glenn.

The only way there'll be any trouble, Weezer said, *is if you fuck up. Are you going to fuck up, Glenn?*

Glenn shook his head. Weezer's breath smelled like spoiled hamburger.

That's not good enough, Weezer said, looming closer. Glenn outweighed him by at least thirty pounds, but overnight Weezer had transformed into something fearsome. *What I need,* Weezer said, enunciating each syllable savagely, *is for you to say you won't fuck this up.*

I won't, Glenn whispered.

Weezer glared at him. Blood flecks on his cheeks.

I won't fuck this up, Glenn said in a louder voice.

Weezer's lips curled. *That's good enough, I suppose. Now get this carpet clean. Anybody asks you about it, you got drunk, spilled some wine, and ended up throwing a baseball through your window.*

Glenn blinked at the absurdity of the story. *Baseball,* he repeated.

You were thinking about your old pal Mike. You got the ball and the mitt out and were throwing fastballs at that tree in your front yard. You were drunk and your aim was off. Weezer shrugged. *Shattered window.*

Glenn decided not to argue.

Weezer rose, strode through the living room. But before he disappeared into the kitchen and out the side door, he stopped and said, *Hey, Glenn?*

Glenn peered up at him.

You don't mention my name.

Weezer went out. Before he did, however, Glenn heard the fridge open, the clinking of bottles. Weezer grabbing some beers for the road.

After scrubbing, showering and crying some more, Glenn had crawled beneath the mountain of covers. Where he still quivered. And waited for the tapping on the door to cease.

It didn't.

He'd be damned if he'd answer it.

You're damned anyway, a voice whispered. *You're irredeemable.*

Glenn choked back a sob.

His body ached. The throb in his joints was nothing compared to the soul-racking guilt, but still, it hurt like nothing he'd ever experienced.

Tap tap tap.

Go away, Glenn pleaded.

Tap tap tap. Louder now.

Maybe it *was* the police.

Glenn's shivering grew more severe. His body was iced with sweat, the sheets as sodden as they'd been back when he'd discovered masturbation as a teen. Dimly, amid the roiling dread and the nausea, he realised he'd only experienced one erection since the bonfire.

The tapping wouldn't stop.

Tap tap tap.

Chest hitching, Glenn scrambled out of the tangled, wet sheets and staggered to the bedroom door. He sank against the wall, the laser blasts of pain searing his muscles, concussing his bones.

Tap tap tap.

Let's get this over with, he thought.

With an effort, he opened the door and tottered through the hallway, the carpet squishing under his bare feet. He realised his visitor was at the front door, which lent further credence to the notion it was the cops. No one used his front door. No one. A couple times there'd been breakdowns on the road, and folks had asked to use his phone, but other than that, he couldn't recall anyone coming to the front door.

Baseball, he reminded himself. *I was playing baseball.*

Glenn shuffled through the living room.

And dropped a bottle of wine, he thought. *That's why the carpet looks like a massacre site.*

Glenn winced. He was screwed.

He opened the door and gaped at the librarian.

She didn't smile. Only took in his appearance with a comprehensive glance.

He knew he should've been elated it wasn't the cops, but somehow he couldn't muster any gratefulness. Only desolation.

"What do you want?" he muttered.

She was wearing a black top that showed her arms. A black tennis skirt. Quite attractive, actually. Good muscle tone. Some curves.

Glenn felt not the slightest stirring of sexual desire.

The librarian had her purse slung over her shoulder and a book clutched to her chest. Like she was protecting the book. Or concealing it.

The sunlight was burning Glenn's eyes. "I'm not in the mood to talk," he said. "It's too early—"

"It's ten fifteen," she said.

Glenn dug his thumb and forefinger into his brow and rubbed. "Now isn't a good time."

"Did you hear about the murders?" she said.

Glenn studied her benign expression. No accusation there, he decided. Just interest.

"I don't know anything about it."

"Two murders and two missing women," the librarian explained. "They have someone in custody."

Oh Christ. Weezer.

"They think it's the same person who killed everyone at the bonfire."

Glenn's mind was a drunken carousel.

"Anyway," she hurried on, "I think we can help each other."

Glenn almost laughed at the notion.

"I know," she said, "that you think I'm some desiccated prude. But I'm not the person you think I am."

Despite the anxiety choking him, despite the weariness and the guilt and the miasmal hopelessness, Glenn found a wry smile forming.

The librarian smiled too. Joyce, he remembered. Her name was Joyce.

"May I come in?" she asked.

Glenn glanced at the book she grasped. He couldn't read the title, but it was an oversize paperback.

"Okay," he said. He hesitated, his gaze falling on the many wine-coloured stains in the carpet. "But come around to the side door."

★   ★   ★

Joyce sat across from him at the kitchen table. He'd positioned her near the side door and made a point of letting her know the bathroom was behind her. In the opposite direction of the living room. The room with the grey tarp for a window.

"I can't offer you any food," he said. The semicircles under his eyes were the colour of Concord grapes, and he looked like he hadn't shaved in days.

"I didn't come here for breakfast, Glenn," she said. She'd placed her purse on the table between them, the book between her and the purse. She didn't know if Glenn would understand the title, but if he did, he might ask her to leave. Or worse.

If, that was, he'd become what she suspected he'd become.

"Do you want to hear about the murders?" she asked.

The colour drained from his face. She went on. "What about the man they caught?"

Glenn stared at her. "They think he killed the other ones?"

"Other ones?"

Glenn made a pained face. "You know...the people at the bonfire. Was the murderer from the bonfire the one who killed the people..."

"At the drive-in," Joyce supplied.

When Glenn looked at her in anguish, she said, "The bodies were found in the men's restroom. The women who disappeared had been at the drive-in too. At least that's what they told some people from the campground. That they were going to the drive-in to meet a couple guys."

The naked terror in Glenn's face was too much for her. She looked down at the book to spare him further embarrassment. "The authorities have someone in custody, but he might not be the one responsible for the murders last night."

Glenn's eyes flitted down to his left forearm. The wounds, she saw, had healed completely.

Just like hers.

Joyce drew in a steadying breath, drummed her fingertips on the book. "I've learned some things that might help us."

Glenn sat back in his chair, which creaked, and covered his mouth with a hand. He said in a small voice, "I don't see how this can be helped."

It was as close to an admission as she was likely to get. She stroked the spine of *Lycanthropology*. "I've been trying to wrap my brain around what happened last weekend. And what's been happening since. My appetite is different. I'm having urges I've never had before."

He didn't talk. Just watched.

She leaned forward. "I'm changing, Glenn."

He turned in his chair, looking ready to bolt at any moment.

"And I want you to know," she hurried on, "that this isn't your fault."

"I don't know what you're talking about."

"You don't have to hide it from me, Glenn."

He pushed to his feet, shambled toward the back hallway. She followed. He got to the bathroom first, but she got her foot wedged in the door before he could close it. He turned away from her, braced himself on the sink. She noticed he wouldn't meet his own reflection.

Joyce waited for him to collect himself, and while she did she let her gaze wander. There was a towel balled in the corner. It looked damp. The ivory tub was ringed with a coral-coloured penumbra. She imagined blood was difficult to wash out.

She knew the longer the silence drew out, the tougher it would be to talk. Before she could lose her nerve, she said, "I want you to understand something."

"Please leave," he said. Despite the broadness of his back, the way his triceps bulged like flesh-toned hatchets, he seemed very weak stooped over the sink. Very frail.

"I'm not leaving. Not until you listen to what I have to say."

He hung his head.

"You need to know," she said, taking a step forward, "that I'm not going to hurt you. I won't go to the police."

He glanced at her in the mirror.

"As long as you promise to listen," she finished.

He didn't speak, but he didn't look away either.

"I know what you are," she said.

His eyes widened, panic flooding them.

"Because I'm becoming the same thing," she said.

His lips trembled.

"We were attacked, Glenn. It wasn't our fault. *We didn't choose this.*"

He shivered.

She stepped closer, riveted him with her gaze. "But we *can* make the most of it."

She placed a hand on his lower back, felt the hardness of the muscles there. "It's happened to you, hasn't it?"

His pleading look, the way his face crumpled, was almost too much to take. But she forced herself to stare into his tear-filled eyes. "I'm going to keep you safe. I want to make sure you can…manage the situation."

He laughed without humour, a harsh, barking sound that set her flesh to crawling. "It's beyond that now," he said. "It's not something…" He shook his head. "…it can't be managed."

She caressed his back. Slowly. Soothingly. "Yes, it can. But we have to be smart. We have to realise that this is what we are now."

He said, "Have you…you know?"

She shook her head.

"Then how do you know—"

"That's one of the things I need from you," she said, unable to keep the need from her voice.

"What?"

"The werewolf—"

"Don't say that word," he said and twisted on the cold water.

She reached out, twisted the water off, her body crowding his. "The werewolf is the most misunderstood of all creatures. Even those who believe in lycanthropy don't understand the physiology, the psychology…" She let her hand cover his on the sink edge. "…the *glory* of the werewolf."

His tone was guarded, but she could hear his interest now, his hunger to know more. "But if you haven't transformed, how do you know—"

"I said I haven't *changed*, but that doesn't mean I haven't changed."

She massaged his lower back, his hand. He didn't resist.

She said, "I drank my own menstruation."

He grimaced.

"I'm telling you this," she said, half-smiling, "because you need to know you're not crazy. You're not a monster."

He was quiet for so long that she worried he had shut down the conversation. Then he said, "I wasn't in control."

She paused for a moment. "The drive-in."

He nodded.

"That wasn't you," she said.

He buried his hands in his hair, looked like he'd tear it out in clumps. "How can you say that?"

"Would you have killed them in your normal state?"

"Of course not!"

"It was the change that did it. The other side of you. The shadow side."

"They won't care about that."

"What brought it on?"

He shook his head, pushed past her through the door. "I don't know. The guy in the bathroom, he wouldn't shut up. He was talking and talking and I wanted him to stop."

"Did he offend you?"

His bedroom smelled like an animal den. "He didn't deserve what happened," Glenn muttered.

"I need to hear about it," she said. "I need you to tell me every detail."

"I can't."

Noting the deplorable state of the covers, she said, "It's okay to be scared, Glenn."

He turned away, but she was not to be put off. "If you can understand it, you can control it."

"Why are you here?" he snapped.

"To save you."

He swayed a little. She reached out, steadied him with a hand.

He broke her hold and plopped down on the bed. Joyce stepped closer so that his downcast head was at a level with her thighs. She reached out, threaded her fingers through his hair.

"Please go," he said in a nearly inaudible voice.

"We need to put our minds together." She massaged his scalp. His body temperature must be at least a hundred. Maybe a hundred and two.

He thrust her hand away. "Just stop. I can't do this."

She peered down at his bloodshot eyes. He looked like hell.

She nodded. "I'm here to save both of us."

"You haven't transformed?"

"Not yet," she said. "Not so you could see it."

His eyes narrowed. "But—"

"It's happening, yes." She strode over to his dresser, leaned on it. "I need help getting all the way there."

She heard him laugh. A hollow, wooden sound. "You want this? You're *courting* this horrible thing?"

She turned and folded her arms. "It's what I am now. There's no changing it."

His eyes darted toward the wall, in the direction of the kitchen. "Is that what that book is about? Changing?"

She nodded. "But it's just like life," she said. "Books can only tell you so much." She laughed bitterly. "I've read everything under the sun. History, fantasy, erotica, everything. But I've never lived any of it. And now this…" She made a fist, knocked it against her hip. "This can't be another case of imagining. Of living vicariously through words. I need to *experience* it."

His voice was soft, marvelling. "That's why you came to me."

"I believe things happen for a reason."

"Then you're a fool."

"And I intend to make this experience all it can be."

He looked away. "Believe me, this isn't something you want to experience."

"Which part?" she asked. "The changing or the killing?"

"I don't know what you're talking about."

"You do," she said. "And you'll tell me about it."

He clenched his jaw. "What the hell is wrong with you?"

"I'm blocked," she said. "But you're going to help me fix that."

He squinted up at her. "You're deranged."

She touched his chin lightly, found herself smiling a little. "We're going to spend some time together. I'm going to make sure you're safe, and in return, you're going to help me change all the way. Why should you get to have all the fun?"

★　★　★

Melody spent an hour hiding in the thicket beyond the bean field. From her perspective she could see the pole barn, the farmhouse beyond it. Their cars were there, but that didn't mean they were all home. There were two working trucks inside the pole barn, another pickup in the garage. Not to mention the junkers they occasionally got running. If they were out looking for her, they probably wouldn't take one of their vehicles. It would arouse suspicion, creeping around at ten miles per hour, gazing into every copse of trees, cornfield and ditch in the vicinity of their property. No, her dad and brothers didn't want to be discovered any more than she wanted to be discovered.

But they *would* want her back. Oh, how they'd want her back.

And not just for their titillation either. They'd want to make sure she hadn't talked to anyone. And they'd want to punish her.

The couple times she had escaped, they'd brought her back and treated her like a POW.

She couldn't take it.

Even now, crouched down amid the thorn bushes and the bugs and the slanting, searing sunlight that punished her naked flesh, she preferred this existence to one in bondage.

And in a way, she'd be sparing them too. She knew what she was becoming. Last night had been a revelation. She'd been so worked up after they attacked her that she'd launched herself into the fastest sprint she could muster.

She was impossibly agile.

And she could run forever. Moving on all fours, she estimated she could reach forty miles per hour, maybe even fifty. Several times last night, on a whim, she'd find herself loping beside cars on Rangeline Road, running abreast of them for maybe a quarter mile before succumbing to fatigue.

Then there'd been the horse.

Melody had always liked horses. Growing up, some of the kids at school had raised horses, shown them in 4-H, but the closest Melody ever came to one was at a birthday party when she was nine. There'd been free pony rides, and my, how she'd enjoyed herself. Jostling along at a slow canter, laughing and clutching the reins in exhilaration and fear. When her dad arrived to pick her up, she'd cried and made sort of a scene, so of course he'd smacked her when he got her back in the truck. But the whole ride home, that night in bed, for months after the birthday party, all she could think about was sitting astride that horse, his beautiful chestnut hair catching and holding the sun glow, the comforting smell of him wrapping her, warm and full, as they moved back and forth along the edge of her friend's yard. It was a cherished memory, one she returned to often during the evenings in the pole barn, the nights spent under her father and brothers.

But last night she hadn't seen the horse as a companion.

It had looked different, for one thing. Rather than medium-sized and chestnut-hued, this one had been massive, a grey-and-white horse, the leprous blotches of colour showing on the great beast's neck like something unfinished or something diseased.

She'd come upon it suddenly, a good five or six miles from their house, and it happened quite by accident. She'd only intended to peer inside the bluish windows, to glimpse the people in the house watching television. She hadn't been particularly hungry at the time, so she didn't think she'd have bothered the people in the house regardless of what went on in the horse pen.

But when she did stumble upon the horse pen and spied the single horse standing inside, she found herself growing agitated. She hadn't been cognisant of it because it was all instinct. She'd been moving upright, and the glimpse she'd caught of herself in the people's window had revealed a being not unlike a woman. True, it had been an alarmingly wild-looking woman, one with yellowish eyes and a beastlike maw, but her figure, her shape, had been pretty much the same as it had always been.

But the horse knew.

Or sensed, rather. It saw her before she saw it, and perhaps the reason why it was so frightened of her was because it was a male horse. Melody didn't know much about horses. Knew, in fact, very little. Because her dad would never pay for lessons, and her brothers made fun of her whenever she'd bring a horse book home from the school library.

But she could see the big, hanging dick well enough, which explained the phrase "hung like a horse". The shock of the meaty black cylinder had scarcely registered when her eyes flicked up to the horse's white gaze, the expression she first mistook for terror. Or rather, for *only* terror. Because there was more there than fright. There was *loathing*.

The horse despised her and felt sullied by her presence. And mingling with this was an appalling species of bigotry. To the horse, she was *the other*, and though she'd only eked out a B-minus in Mrs. Culross's English class her senior year, she'd understood what Stevenson meant in *Dr. Jekyll and Mr. Hyde*, understood the revulsion people felt for what was different from them.

Because she had *always* been the other. Because of her clothes, which were first unstylish because her dad bought them, and were later skimpy because she picked them out. Because of her family. Because she'd never had a single female friend. And because she only ever had boyfriends for a short time because they tired of her or because her father and brothers threatened to kill the boy if she persisted in dating him.

The horse hated her not just because of what she was
(*shivering*)
but because of what she *wasn't*.
(*breath going ragged*)
It hated her and whinnied and stamped and its eyes and teeth showed and Melody climbed into the pen, forcing her way between the slats just before the change made
(*prowling forward on spreading paws*)
such a contortion impossible, and she followed the horse with preternatural patience as it galloped to the other end of the pen
(*shoulder muscles bunching, bones spiking*)
and she could tell it was freaked out, would leap over the top slat if she let it get too spooked, so she trotted along at a parallel, but not directly toward it because that would send it into a panic, and she took her yellow eyes off it and tried to feign indifference, but it was still bucking and staring at her as though it beheld all the demons of hell, and she timed it so the horse's underbelly was exposed, darted under its lethal front hooves and wrapped her sinuous arms around it, drove it back, and landed atop it in a whir of kicking legs and thrashing mane. Melody clambered over its great mottled torso before it could writhe onto its hooves again, but rather than gutting the animal as she could have easily done, she went for its eyes, its huge, staring eyes, her hooked nails piercing the white orbs and tearing trenches down them, and when the milky sclera gushed over her knuckles, the horse did shriek, and moments later the lights went on outside the house.

She knew the owners would have a gun – everyone out here did – so she removed the throat, let it gush over her snarling mouth, and the hot metallic liquid fired her throat, made her ravenous and sickened, and only later did she realise she'd also experienced a body-clenching orgasm, one so powerful and sustained that the owners were halfway to the horse pen before she realised the peril she was in. Keeping low, she scampered on all fours – it was easiest to move that way once the change was entire – and because she was too large in her new form, she simply lowered her head and shattered the bottom slat. The gate swung open as she rushed into the forest, and by the time she heard the wails, she was already a hundred yards away.

Melody jolted back to her senses when an orange truck barreled into the driveway of her house, the sunlight catching all the dents and the rust spots as it jangled toward the pole barn. It was one of Donny's projects, an International dump truck from the eighties. A diesel. She could smell its stale black fumes from here. Like corruption.

Like her brothers.

The truck stopped short of the pole barn and her brothers piled out. So did Father Bridwell. Donny had been driving, so he came last. He growled something at Robbie—"Call that bitch Adriana, see if she's heard from Melody"—and stepped toward the bean field.

Melody tensed. Though she was more than eighty yards from where Donny stood, she could see him perfectly well. Even more, she could smell him. He hadn't showered since the incident in the pole barn, and as a result she could smell the frustrated sex on him.

Unease trickled through her, whipped up a fine sheen of sweat. She passed a hand over her brow and felt the scrape of congealed blood.

She wiped her hand on some tall grass, remembering the horse. She must look a mess. Hair tangled. Crusted with blood. Sweaty and stinky and crawling with bugs. She needed a bath in the worst way, but she couldn't face her family. Not yet.

Donny moved several yards into the bean field, trying to retrace her steps. Melody remained hunkered down, confident in the inability of his puny eyesight to pick her out from this distance. If he came any closer, well, she'd just have to—

No. She wouldn't think about that, not yet.

She knew her days of being raped and beaten and tortured with splintery broom handles were over. No more ropes, no more cigarette burns. She had something that would protect her now. A deterrent. She didn't relish the idea of going home, but her stuff was there, and she refused to sneak in and out like some kind of thief. Besides, there were matters to be worked out. Money. And the understanding that she was not to be followed or harmed in any way.

She knew they would not accept that, not at first, but she was through with being terrorised.

Robbie came out of the house and moved up beside Donny, who asked him a question. Melody was amazed at her ability to pick up their words despite the great distance between them.

"Adriana know anything?" Donny asked.

"Hasn't heard from her. They're not really that close, you know."

Damn right we're not, Melody thought. *I'm only nice to her because she's your girlfriend, Robbie. When you're not around, she treats me like trash.*

"Did you lean on her?" Donny asked.

"*Lean* on her? This isn't the freakin' mob. Besides, I don't think Adriana and Mel ever talk."

"They're girls," Donny said. "All girls talk."

"That's dumb, Donny."

Quicker than she could have imagined, Donny backhanded Robbie, sent him spinning balletically into the bean plants. If she hadn't just witnessed it, she would've guessed Robbie's fall was choreographed. For one thing, there'd been no sound when Donny's hand had met Robbie's face. For another, Robbie had been launched backward several feet, like he'd been struck by a cannonball rather than a set of bony fingers. But Donny's face looked genuinely furious as he barked expletives at his supine brother.

She was so transfixed by the sight of Donny bullying their youngest sibling that she didn't hear the figure sneak up behind her, didn't even smell him because he was downwind of her. And the worst part was that even before she turned and gazed up at John's remorseless face and discovered the shotgun levelled at her forehead, she realised she'd been duped. Because Donny and Robbie were both staring this way, hands visoring their eyes as they stood, shoulder to shoulder, partners in deception.

"You know where to go," John said.

She watched him for a long moment, considered talking to him, but saw it would do no good. He was emotionless, like always. If there was a flicker of anything in his muddy brown eyes, it was sadism. The suppressed gleam you saw in the kid holding the magnifying glass as the ants crackled and burst in the white-hot pinprick of heat.

"Get going," he said. "Dad's already sore enough." John smiled, an expression so hideously out of place on his blank mask of a face that Melody wanted to scream. "Plus, you owe me one from last night."

Melody let the door in her mind crash shut. Like twisting valves, she closed off her emotions. This wouldn't be the end of things, she knew, but if she didn't go with John he'd make good on his threat. He really would shoot her. That's why they'd sent him. Because he felt so little, and what he did feel was black and slithery.

The gun like a living presence behind her, Melody emerged from the thicket and started across the bean field.

CHAPTER TWENTY-ONE

The waiting room at the sheriff's office fell silent. Duane stared at Savannah, certain he'd heard her wrong. "Come again?" he said.

But she only repeated herself. "It's not him."

Duane remained gape-mouthed for a moment. Then something clicked in his head. "You're just falling for the disguise, remembering the whole tough-guy image he had going. Look beyond that. At the actual face."

She tongued the inside of her cheek, her eyebrows raised. "I'm not an idiot, Short Pump. I looked at his face."

"Then you must see—"

"A different person," she said. "A completely different person."

Duane strode over to the sheriff. "Can I go in?"

Sheriff Lane Cartwright was on the short side, but well-built for a guy who had to be nearing sixty. He looked up at Duane. "Regardless of what you say in there, we've got to let him walk."

Duane made a show of examining the fifteen-by-fifteen room they were in. "Must be something wrong with the acoustics in here. It sounded to me like you're about to let Garner go free."

Cartwright sighed, but his tone was unruffled. "Six survivors from the bonfire incident have been in to see Mr. Garner, including Miss Summers here. Not a single one has ID'd Garner as the killer. Hell, this isn't even supposed to be my investigation. The state guys will have a fit if they found out I brought Garner in."

Duane opened his mouth to protest, but before he could, Cartwright went on. "You're aware of the killings at the drive-in last night?"

Duane motioned toward the holding room in which Garner was being questioned, but again Cartwright headed him off. "We've got witnesses saying Mr. Garner was at the Roof all evening—"

"But—"

"—including *you*, Mr. McKidd." Cartwright's look went icier. "Or have you forgotten the statement you gave us not thirty minutes ago?"

Duane resisted an urge to smack the look off the sheriff's face.

He could see Cartwright was about to dismiss him, and when that happened, it wouldn't be long before Dave Garner was dismissed too. Out of jail and into Lakeview, where he could stalk anyone he wanted, could threaten and menace and generally scare the shit out of them.

Or kill them.

"I'll talk to Garner," Duane said.

Cartwright's eyes widened in disbelief. "I hope you're talking about apologising to the man. Poor guy's been through the wringer. All he wanted was a quiet summer to forget what happened to his girl."

Duane nodded. "And how about that? He just happened to choose the town in which his daughter's killer was living?"

Savannah smacked him on the shoulder. "Show some respect for Mike."

He gestured feebly. "I'm not saying Mike deserved to die."

"You called him a killer."

"You know what I meant." His lips worked mutely. "Okay, how about accidental death-inducer?"

"That's not funny!"

"I'm not trying to be funny!"

Cartwright moved toward the door leading out. "I'll leave you two to sort out your differences."

"No," Duane said, rushing over to him. "Please. Just let me talk to Garner."

His hand on the door handle, Cartwright said, "Give me a good reason why."

"You can hear what we say in there, right?"

Cartwright eyeballed him. "Of course. It's an interrogation room."

"Then let me get what I can out of him."

Cartwright was shaking his head, but Duane backed off, gave the sheriff his most disarming look. "I swear I won't get anybody in trouble, least of all you."

"I'm not worried about *me*, I'm worried about a man who's been accused of mass murder, who's probably gonna sue the pants off us."

"They'll blame me," Duane said. "I'm the one who—"

"The *hell* they will," Cartwright snapped. "In this day and age people are just dying to bash the police. Every asshole with an iPhone wants to catch a cop doing something wrong. What do you think Garner will do? A guy with money and an honest-to-goodness reason to be mad at the police?"

"Look, I know you don't owe me anything."

"You're goddamned right I don't."

"But I'm begging you – please let me have five minutes with him. I'm sure he'll talk to me."

"I'm sure he will too," Cartwright answered. "He'll probably kick your teeth in."

"Then let him do it. You'll have a reason to lock him up."

"If I was him," Cartwright said, "I'd want to beat your ass too."

Duane didn't have an answer for that.

Duane was sure Cartwright would tell them to get the hell out of his jail, but the sheriff exhaled wearily, rubbed a hand over his whiskered cheeks and said, "Five minutes. He comes after you for telling lies, I'm not putting a stop to it."

★　　★　　★

Both Cartwright and one of his deputies, a younger guy with ginger hair and long, lanky limbs, leaned against the walls on either side of the room. Duane sat across the table from Dave Garner, who wore the same clothes he'd had on last night.

Garner was grinning at him. Or at least Duane assumed it was Garner.

Because the man's face was different.

A half-muffled voice in the back of Duane's mind cried out, *He's a shape-shifter! That's what they do. They shift shapes!*

Nonsense, he thought. There had to be some other rational reason for Garner's apparent alteration in facial structure.

Makeup?

Are you kidding me?

Or maybe it was the lighting in here.

The lighting is unremarkable, the voice argued. *Overhead fluorescents that haven't been cleaned since the Reagan era.*

Duane squirmed in his chair, willed himself to concentrate, to ignore the sweltering heat in the room, the baleful stares of the policemen flanking them. He examined Garner's narrow cheekbones, his grizzled jaw, which was recessed more than it had been last night at the Roof.

Then Duane had it.

Garner was sick. He had some type of condition that caused wild fluctuations in his weight, his skin colour. He was having a bad spell right now. A thyroid problem maybe.

Or maybe you have a problem facing reality, the voice answered. *Maybe you just don't want to admit you made a mistake, that you've caused an already grieving man a great deal of embarrassment and heartache.*

Duane asked, "Why did you come to Lakeview, Mr. Garner?"

Garner's smile never wavered. "I told you last night, Mr. McKidd."

"Tell the others what you told me," Duane said with a nod each at Cartwright and the deputy. "Tell them what you said about Savannah and Mike."

Garner's face remained impassive. "I wanted to know more about Savannah Summers. She's as much a victim as everybody else."

"Come again?"

"Well, Mike's death, of course," Garner said. His pale blue eyes didn't blink. "It's all a tragic business. Mike Freehafer kills my Cynthia. Then he too dies. Like me, Savannah lost the one who matters most to her."

Savannah was done with Mike, Duane nearly snapped, but he bit down on the words before they could escape. But Garner...yes, Garner could see how he'd nettled Duane.

"Savannah was such a pleasant girl," Garner said in a musing voice. "She didn't deserve to be put through the trauma of talking to me." Garner gave Duane a reproachful frown. "You really shouldn't have done that, Short Pump. Made her talk to me. It could prove harmful to her."

A chill gripped him. Duane glanced over at Cartwright, but it was as though Garner had merely commented on the weather. Couldn't the sheriff see what Garner was saying? Couldn't he make out the threat implicit in Garner's words?

Duane was sweating. He had to remain in command of his emotions. He cleared his throat with difficulty, shifted in his chair.

"Mr. Garner," he said. "Last night you told me you'd be seeing Savannah soon." He paused, letting that sink in. Letting Cartwright think about it. That was, if Cartwright was actually listening.

Duane went on. "Can you explain how you knew about Savannah? Her name? How you knew about me? For that matter, can you explain what you meant when you said you'd be 'seeing Savannah soon'?"

Duane glanced at the sheriff, who for the first time seemed interested. Interested, Duane thought, and a trifle suspicious.

Just don't push it.

Garner sighed, leaned back in his chair. "What you say is true, Short Pump. I did ask—"

"My name is Duane."

Garner smiled. "Of course. As I was explaining, I did mention Savannah last night. And I certainly won't deny having inquired about Mike's acquaintances."

Cartwright's voice had an edge. "And why would you do that, Mr. Garner?"

But Garner merely shrugged one shoulder, picked at a scar in the tabletop. "I suppose I should have left it alone. But Cynthia—" He glanced at Cartwright. "You know about my daughter, Sheriff?"

Cartwright didn't answer.

"She was all I had," Garner said. "My wife died years ago. Breast cancer. Cynthia and I developed a powerful bond." He smiled sadly. "I still find myself thinking she'll come skipping through my front door, even though she hasn't skipped anywhere since she was a little girl."

Duane shot a look at Cartwright to see if he was buying it, and dammit, it appeared that he was. Were the sheriff's eyes a little misty? Hell, Duane thought, even the skinny ginger-haired deputy looked like he might break down bawling.

Duane glared at Garner. The con artist.

Garner resumed. "Being home was unbearable, so I couldn't remain there, not this soon after Cynthia's death. Too many memories…"

Academy Award, Duane thought. *Fucking Oscar winner.*

"I don't have any family to speak of," Garner continued. "Just my late wife's parents, and they're both in a nursing home in Peoria. So," he said, leaning forward and interlacing his fingers, "I booked a cabin in Lakeview. It's only two hours south of Chicago. And I won't deny the place has been on my mind a great deal since my daughter's death." Garner paused. "Do you have children, Sheriff Cartwright?"

Cartwright's expression was unreadable. "Three."

"Any daughters?"

A nod. "Two of them."

"Cherish them, Sheriff Cartwright."

Good Lord, Duane thought. *What a load of shit.*

But Cartwright was gazing steadily at Garner. "I will."

"Oh for Christ's *sake*," Duane half-shouted.

Cartwright looked like he might gun Duane down. "Mr. McKidd, your five minutes are over."

"I can't believe this," Duane said. "He tells you some sob story about his daughter, and you guys start bonding over how much you love your kids—"

From across the table there came a trio of low popping sounds, Garner's knuckles cracking as he clenched his fists.

Go on, Duane told himself. *Make him mad.*

"Mr. McKidd," Cartwright was saying, "I'm going to say this one more time—"

"—but what he's really doing, Sheriff," Duane interrupted, "is diverting your attention from the truth."

"And that is?" Garner asked, through teeth that Duane saw were now gnashing together. And weren't the cheekbones widening, the chin jutting out farther than before?

Cartwright started toward Duane, but it was Garner he addressed. "You don't need to answer. This individual's about to get himself jailed for disorderly conduct."

"Disorderly conduct?" Duane laughed. "How about murdering seven people, ripping their—"

"That's enough, Mr. McKidd!"

"—guts out and chewing them up and wounding four more—"

Cartwright's hand clamped his shoulder, squeezed.

But Garner's face was definitely changing, the left cheekbone quivering now, the blue eyes tinged with yellow.

"—and if you let him out now, Sheriff Cartwright, he'll go after Savannah, and her blood—"

"Goddammit, McKidd!" Hauling him out of the chair.

"—will be on you. Hers and her little boy's."

Muscling him toward the door, Cartwright shouted, "Get out of my jail, McKidd. Right the hell now."

Duane turned, gestured toward Garner. "Would you *look* at him, for God's sake? His face is..."

Cartwright turned, but now Garner looked just as he'd been before. A little sweatier perhaps, his skin slightly darker, though that could have been a trick of the light.

It wasn't *possible*!

Jaw set, Cartwright seized Duane's collar, opened the door and thrust him through. But before Duane righted himself, he heard Garner say, "Don't worry, Short Pump. Savannah and Jake are safe."

"No guarantees about me, huh?" Duane called as he was hustled toward the exit.

It wasn't until Cartwright had practically thrown Duane through the front door that it occurred to him to wonder how Garner had learned the name of Savannah's boy.

★   ★   ★

Barb listened to their story, and when she spoke it was usually to clarify a point. Oftentimes she brought up things that neither of them had considered.

Duane tightened as he realised he hadn't seen Jake for several minutes. Barb noticed him looking around and nodded over her shoulder. "Jake's in the back. Playing games on his mom's phone."

Duane's muscles untensed.

"Is that all?" Barb asked when Savannah had finished.

"Isn't it enough?" Duane said.

Savannah frowned. "Let me guess. You're going to tell us we're imagining everything and that we've made a grieving father's life more difficult by harassing him."

"I believe you," Barb said.

Duane stared at her. He glanced at Savannah, who'd apparently been rendered as speechless as he was.

Savannah shook her head. "But how can you when it's so crazy?"

"Would you rather I didn't?"

Savannah ventured an incredulous smile. "I know how I'd feel if someone told me a story like that."

Duane scratched his neck uneasily. "We're happy you believe us, but I think what Savannah's trying to say—"

"I know what she's trying to say," Barb said, "because she said it. We don't need you to interpret for us."

Duane felt his balls shrink.

Barb looked at Savannah, said, "Let me tell you a story." She said to Duane, "You want to grab a couple stools?"

Duane strode briskly over to the corner, where several rustic-looking wooden stools surrounded a matching table. He snagged a couple stools, and almost dropped them when he realised how heavy they were. The kind of object you needed two hands to carry. But he'd already committed to toting one in each hand and wouldn't relent now. Not with Savannah watching, and certainly not with Barb watching. As he often did when he was with Barb, Duane felt his manhood threatened.

Barely keeping down a groan of effort, Duane made it to the counter and set the stools down. Savannah took hers with a muttered thank-you, but Barb was watching him impishly. Or as impishly as a six-foot-two woman could watch someone.

"Well," he said, sitting. "You were saying something about a story?"

"Damn near threw your back out, didn't you?" Barb said.

"I managed."

He glanced at Savannah, who looked like she was trying not to smile. "What?" he said.

"Nothing," she said lightly.

"You guys ever been to Shadeland?" Barb asked.

"Spent four years at Western Indiana University," Duane said. He shrugged. "Okay, four and a half."

Barb said, "You know the little town to the south of it?"

"Burnettsville?" he said. "Sure I do. There's a nice little restaurant there. Roberts's. Great prime rib."

"That's about all there is in Burnettsville," Barb said. "That, a post office and a gas station."

"Don't forget the flashing yellow light," Duane added.

"I haven't been there," Savannah said.

"You're not missing much," Barb said. "But there's an interesting legend about the place. It involves the ancient Iroquois."

"Hold on," Duane said. "You're not talking about that thing at Peaceful Valley, are you?"

God, he hoped not. A year ago there had been accounts of a massacre at the Peaceful Valley Nature Preserve, a new state park. Talk of deaths in the hundreds, whispers of bizarre creatures, and rumours about a government cover-up had surrounded Shadeland like a poisonous cloud.

But Barb was shaking her head. "Not that. But the Peaceful Valley incident only serves as further evidence of my point."

"What is your point?" Savannah asked.

"Not everything's explainable," Barb said.

Savannah made to get off her stool. "Maybe I should check on Jake."

"Sit," Barb said. "Your boy's fine and you know it. But you came here hoping I'd alleviate your fears, and instead you're about to have them confirmed. My advice is to suck it up and listen. Ignoring what's in front of you won't make a bad situation any better."

Chastened, Savannah sank onto her stool.

Barb resumed, leaning forward on the glass counter. "This doesn't relate to your wolf story – at least not directly. But it does get filed in the same general area: the Great Unknown.

"The town of Burnettsville is nothing more than a scattering of country houses that share the same zip code. At the last census there were six hundred people there, give or take, and I suspect the population was much the same back in the time of the Iroquois. A dwelling here, a dwelling there. Plenty of room for everybody." Barb's eyes widened meaningfully. "Except, plenty of room isn't always good. Not when things go bad."

Duane shifted uncomfortably. His jeans were pulled too far down on his ass. He was pretty sure his crack was showing. There weren't any other people in Callahan's Collectibles at the moment, but if anyone did stop in, they'd glimpse a hell of a plumber's butt. He resisted the urge to stand and tug his jeans up. But something told him Barb would be annoyed at having her story interrupted.

She resumed. "One winter – this was half a millennium ago, long before the area was settled by the white man – the temperatures sank to unbearable lows."

"How unbearable?" Savannah asked.

"I wasn't there, dear, but according to the folks at the university, the temperature dipped as low as seventy below zero."

Duane whistled.

"It was so cold," Barb continued, "that many Iroquois froze to death before they could return to their dwellings."

Savannah looked appalled. "It got cold that quickly?"

Barb nodded. "That's how the professors at WIU could measure it. A drastic change like that leaves its mark on the landscape."

Duane had no idea how a cold snap could affect the terrain in a way that could be measured half a millennium later, but opted to say nothing about his doubts. Barb didn't seem in the mood to debate the minutiae of the ancient Indiana climate.

Barb drummed her fingers on the counter. Her nails were cut short, Duane noticed. "It got cold in the surrounding areas too. Shadeland, Ravanna. Even here in Lakeview. Lots of folks died because they couldn't keep warm enough. Especially the elderly and the very young."

Savannah's face clouded.

Barb said, "The food ran out in lots of places – most scientists believe the cold spell lasted nearly three weeks – and there were casualties all over. Roughly forty percent of the Iroquois living in what's now known as Lakeview expired from exposure or malnourishment. There were even rumours of cannibalism."

Savannah raised her hand like a kid in elementary school. "Can I check on Jake?"

"Your attention span always this short?" Barb said. "Put your hand down."

Duane wished he could escape to the back office as well. He didn't like to think of weather that frigid. He hated the winter as it was. But negative seventy? That was *obscene*. The only time he recalled hearing numbers like that bandied about were in a novel about the failed Shackleton Expedition.

"You still with me?" Barb asked him.

Duane said, "Why wouldn't I be?"

"You had that slack expression on your face," Barb said. "Slacker than usual, I mean."

Duane crossed his arms, scowling.

"As I was saying," Barb went on, "there were losses all over the area.

Losses all over the Midwest. But nowhere was the death toll more severe than in Burnettsville."

"Worse than forty percent?" Savannah said.

"Everybody died," Barb said. "For a fifteen-mile radius, not a single soul survived."

Duane said, "That's easily explained. The whole community got together in one spot, and the food ran out."

"Most never left their dwellings," Barb said.

"How could anybody possibly—"

"The Iroquois were a highly advanced people. They kept records. It's not like we're talking about ancient Mesopotamia here."

Not having any opinions on ancient Mesopotamia, Duane remained silent.

"The tribes from the surrounding areas sent out scouting parties. The Algonquins. The Cherokee. The other Iroquois tribes." Barb paused. "You two eat lunch yet?"

"I think we can take it," Duane said.

Barb nodded. "In some of the dwellings, the dead were missing their skins."

Savannah's nose wrinkled. "They were *skinned*?"

"I didn't say they were skinned," Barb corrected. "I said they were missing their skins."

"What's the difference?" Duane asked.

"The difference is that something ate their skin off. Like a parasite or maybe a microorganism."

"Gross," Savannah said.

"Other corpses were found in many pieces, as if scattered by an explosion of some sort."

"Natural gas?" Duane said.

"You're not getting it," Barb said. "These bodies were found in various places. They looked like they'd been destroyed from the inside out."

"Hold on," Duane said. "Are you implying it was werewolves that did those things to the Iroquois people?"

Barb arched an eyebrow. "Did anybody's flesh rot off at the bonfire?"

"No, but—"

"Anybody burst apart like he'd just swallowed a grenade?"

Duane fell silent.

"What I'm doing is drawing a parallel. No one could explain what happened during the deep freeze. But it did happen. Everyone who's studied it independently has come to the same conclusion."

"They couldn't have embellished it?" Savannah asked.

Barb turned her pitiless gaze on her. "Are you embellishing what happened at the bonfire?"

"Why would we—"

"Why would the Iroquois make up a story about a desolated settlement?"

"Barb's got a point," Duane said.

"I don't need your support," Barb said. "What I need is for you two dolts to shut up and listen so we can come up with a plan."

Savannah folded her arms. "God, Barb. Do you have to be so mean?"

"Yes," Barb said. "That's the only way you'll appreciate the severity of the situation." Barb looked at Savannah. "You and Jake are moving in with me, effective immediately."

Savannah grunted. "Excuse me?"

Barb glanced at Duane. "You can move in too, as long as you promise not to skulk around trying to catch glimpses of Savannah in her birthday suit."

Savannah was shaking her head. "Barb, this is crazy."

"And I don't skulk," Duane said.

"Jake and I can stay where we are," Savannah said. "And Short Pump can take care of himself."

"Short Pump is about as imposing as a neutered wiener dog."

Duane cleared his throat. "Listen, Miss Callahan, we appreciate your help, but we—"

"—would rather get killed than listen to good advice," Barb finished. She directed her gaze at Savannah. "If it were just the two of you, I'd say piss off and let you get ripped apart like the rest of the town." She jerked a thumb over her shoulder. "But there's a child back there who needs protecting, and if his mother and the guy who wants to get in her pants—"

"Hey!" Duane said.

"—aren't intelligent enough to take precautions, I'm going to have to pull rank."

Savannah gawked at her. "'Pull rank'?"

"That's right," Barb said. "A person with brain cells can pull rank on two people without them." She nodded to her left, in the direction of the lake. "My house is down that lane, Short Pump. I suggest you pack what you need and get there before sundown."

Duane forced a smile. "Why before sundown? Are you worried about the full moon?"

"This is Thursday, and the full moon's not until next week," Barb answered. "But it's easier to kill someone and get away with it at night." She gave them a wry look. "In case you two haven't noticed."

Duane glanced at Savannah, who regarded him with large eyes.

"I guess we're staying with you," Duane said.

Barb said, "Go get Jake. It's almost suppertime."

Savannah went around the counter and disappeared through the office door. Duane made to rise, but Barb reached across the counter, shoved him back down.

"What I said about seeing her in her birthday suit."

Duane held up his hands. "Hey, I don't know why you think—"

"I think you're a man," Barb said. "You might be better than the average wolf, but you're still a man, and you still think with your pecker."

"Why do you care so much about Savannah?" he challenged. "Are you as smitten with her as I am?"

Duane immediately regretted it. For the first time since he'd met her, Barb appeared hurt. She looked like she might fire back at him, but then seemed to collect herself. "After a comment like that, you don't deserve an explanation, but since you're going to be staying with me until this shit storm has passed, I'm going to give you one anyway. Savannah came to work for me when she was thirteen."

Duane shrugged. "Sure, I remember. She needed a job, so she applied—"

"Are you biologically capable of shutting your piehole?"

Duane did.

"Savannah worked for me for nine summers, including the ones when she was home from college. And in all that time, she was hardworking and sincere." Barb nodded. "You know what a rare trait that is? Sincerity?"

Duane gave a small, grudging nod. "Savannah's a great person. I could've told you that."

"She might be a trifle naïve sometimes," Barb said, "but she's got a wonderful heart. She's a good mother to Jake, and if things go well, he'll be a good person too. Better than most men, at the very least."

Duane peered closely at her. "What makes you so sour on men? We're not all bad."

What emotion had shown in Barb's face died out. "Don't worry about it."

A moment later, Savannah came through the office door, leading Jake by the hand. His mouth was wet with slobber and streaks of blue, yellow and orange.

"He found your stash of saltwater taffy," Savannah explained. "I'll reimburse you."

Barb ignored her, bent toward Jake. "Was it tasty?"

Jake smiled at her. "Uh-huh."

"Good," she said. "I'll bring you some more tonight."

Savannah and Jake made their way toward the exit. Duane did too, but before he went out, he glanced back at Barb.

"Something on your mind?" Barb asked.

Duane picked up a ceramic toad, studied it. "What I wondered," Duane said, frowning. "Not that it's any of my business, but...do you like guys?"

Barb glared at him. "You're right, it isn't any of your business. Dumbass."

Duane cringed.

At length, Barb said, "Yes, I like men."

"So why didn't you ever get married?"

"I was married."

"What happened?" Duane asked.

"Six miscarriages," Barb answered. "Then he married someone who could carry a baby to term."

Duane's stomach sank.

"You're only the second person I've told that to, and the first was Savannah."

Duane caressed the ceramic toad. "I won't tell anybody."

"You're right, you won't. And if you do, I'll cram that toad so far up your ass, you'll gag on it."

Duane placed the toad on the shelf and exited the shop as briskly as he could.

CHAPTER TWENTY-TWO

It was just after nine o'clock on Thursday night. Glenn slumped forward in one of the aged cedar chairs, his head hanging nearly on a level with his spread knees. Joyce sat on the back deck with him, a couple feet away. The backyard spread out before them, reminding her of a state park gone to seed. There were tall trees back here, aspens and willows, oaks and sycamores. The grass and weeds weren't dense, but she could tell he hadn't mown for a couple of weeks. Behind them, a couple of Glenn's windows spilled a dull orange glow, but the night was almost suffocatingly dark, the patches of sky stitching the trees moonless and black.

"There has to be more," she said.

He sighed. "We've been through it."

"Again," Joyce said.

Without looking up, he said, "Give me one good reason why."

"Because our lives depend on it."

He rocked back in his chair like a surly adolescent. "You're attempting to attach meaning to something that makes no earthly sense. We're talking about werewolves here. Why treat it like it's natural science? It's like trying to study the mating habits of unicorns."

"Except unicorns," she pointed out, "don't exist."

Glenn looked away.

"And werewolves do," she added. "I'm looking at one right now."

He shoved to his feet, the chairback banging against the white siding of the house.

"Two days," he muttered, stalking down the steps. "Two days of what? Interrogation. Cross-examination. Studying that fucking book?

"*Lycanthropology* has been right about a lot of things."

"Sure, like those crazy Russian sisters?" He shook his head. "I should be at work anyway."

She followed him. "This is more important."

He whirled on her. "More important than not looking guilty? Than not looking like I've got something to hide? What if people start asking questions? You think the guys at the machine shop are going to cover for me? 'No, Officer, we haven't seen him at all. But he sounded strange on the phone.' The cops will be here in five minutes."

"They haven't come yet."

He stepped closer. "You don't know how it *feels*. You don't know what's it's like to kill someone. The guilt—" He cut off, sounding like he was about to lose it.

She grasped his arm before he could turn away. His bicep was hard, thrumming with energy. Was the change upon him? And if it was, would that support or refute her theory?

"I don't know what's it's like to change," she said. "But it's only a matter of time. Four of us were bitten, and we know that you and Weezer both transformed."

He glanced at her. "No word from—"

"Nobody answers at Melody's house, not the phone or the front door. I might try to break in later."

"That's a clever idea," he said. "Those hillbillies will shoot you for sport."

"What we need to do is draw a parallel between your change and Weezer's."

"There is no parallel."

"Not yet," she said. "But there has to be a connection."

He sighed, his muscles relaxing beneath her touch. "It was night during both attacks."

"Night is one commonality, though the moon wasn't full."

"That's just superstition."

She smiled. "You aren't allergic to silver."

"How do you—"

"We ate supper with silver utensils. My grandma's."

"Thanks a lot," he said. "Why the hell didn't you tell me?"

"I didn't want there to be any psychosomatic bias."

He studied her in silence. "Do you ever date?" he asked.

"Rarely," she answered. She thought about it. "Rarely to never."

"Why do you suppose that is?"

"We're going to analyse me now?"

His gaze didn't waver. "Change of pace."

"I last had a date in February."

"This February?"

"No, February of 1987. Of course this February." She gave him a little shove.

Laughing, he said, "Just the one date?"

"With that gentleman, yes."

"Why only one?"

She drew herself up. "We weren't compatible."

Glenn's grin darkened. "He wanted sex on the first date."

Joyce opened her mouth to tell him how accurate his guess was. Maybe even share the whole story, how the man – who later proved to be married – had tried to force himself on her, how his bad breath had nearly made her vomit. How she'd begun to fear for her safety before he finally relented and drove her back to her house in silence.

But something in Glenn's eyes made her stop. It was the darkness in them, the perverse hunger. Shadowed by the night and the trees, his eyes reminded her very much of a shark's.

She stepped past him and moved closer to the overhanging boughs of a maple tree so he wouldn't see her face. She'd always been an abysmal liar. "I was the aggressor."

Glenn snorted. "You?"

"Is that so difficult to imagine?" She became aware of the movements of her limbs, how lithe her body felt. God, the night air was crisp and warm. Joyce could smell pinesap and jasmine. She looked at him, her voice descending into a sultry purr. "I was aroused by him. What's wrong with that?"

Glenn's smile went away like dust motes whipped by a gale. He advanced toward her. She could see his broad chest heaving. "Who was it?"

But Joyce sidestepped a narrow birch tree, reached out, let her fingertips rove over the ghostly curls of bark. She imagined herself from his perspective. Bare shoulder blades in the crimson top. Decent enough rear end under the white tennis skirt. Nice legs, browner than usual. Whatever imperfections he might find in her figure would be concealed by the caul of darkness surrounding them.

"He was very handsome," she said. "I wanted him. He drove me out to some land he owned. He claimed he used it for hunting."

"Give me his name, Joyce."

To her left, some small animal scampered away, as if affrighted by Glenn's bridled rage.

"You don't get his name," she said, "but I'll tell you what happened between us."

What's wrong with you? a voice in her head screamed. *Don't tease him!*

But that wasn't what she was doing, was it? She was *experimenting*. And if she planted the seed that a man had found her attractive, what harm was there in that? It was time for Glenn to see her for what she was. A young, fairly attractive woman. No Savannah, of course, but it was time he let go of that obsession.

A firefly flashed a warning from several feet away.

She progressed through the yard, let the tip of a forefinger whisper over the prickling needles of a spruce. "He parked in the woods. We didn't get out because it was so cold. There was a chill under the torrid air blowing from his vents, but that only made it more exciting." She paused, the bite of the spruce needles poking her flesh. "My nipples were hard."

"Joyce, I don't want to—"

"He reached over and cupped one of my breasts." That much was true. The man had groped her first thing after parking, and though she'd warned him she had no interest in a one-night fling, his hand hadn't moved until she'd slapped his leering face.

But Glenn didn't need to know that.

"I reciprocated," she said. "I placed a hand on the crotch of his jeans. He was already erect."

"Joyce—"

"I longed to feel him inside of me." She closed her eyes, abandoning herself to the fantasy. "I lunged across the console and put my mouth on his. I slung a leg over, straddled him—"

"You need to—"

"—and began grinding. The heat between my legs was unbearable, and when the friction between us increased, I thought I was going to—"

"*NO!*" Glenn roared.

Gasping, she spun and saw him staggering back. Despite the gloom of the backyard, she could already see the hair sprouting in tufts from his cheeks, his throat, and now the fact of what was happening was driven home to her like a spike through her brain. She'd suspected what Glenn's trigger was. Perhaps it was her pride at taking Clark Lombardo Coulter PhD's research and applying it that had made her so careless, but she was here now. Alone in the forest with a man transforming into a monster.

Glenn flailed a hand at her – a clawed, pulsing hand – and stumbled away, the last vestiges of humanity fleeing before the change. She knew she had only moments before her fate was sealed as surely as those men at the drive-in restroom, before her skin flew in ribbons and the grass and weeds around her were doused with the wine of her veins. She had to go. Yet the house was at least thirty yards away, her car twenty more.

Glenn roared in agony. Joyce watched, transfixed.

He was not only getting hairier, but his facial bones were shifting, widening, his legs were cracking, the heels notching upward, the clothes splitting on his expanding frame. His eyes were squeezed shut, and it was the idea of them, the glaring wolflike eyes, that got her moving. If those eyes riveted on hers, she'd be unable to look away. She'd be rooted to the spot, a slab of hot meat, and the thing that was no longer Glenn would revel in her evisceration. She wove toward a stand of pines, hearing behind her a different sort of roar. There was agony in it, but she heard confusion there too.

And rage.

Joyce bolted away, hoping she'd judged the direction of her car correctly.

A howl rent the night. Joyce nearly stumbled in terror.

She skirted a vast oak tree, crested a small rise, and spotted the detached garage ahead of her.

The howling ceased, but the silence that replaced it frightened her even more.

Joyce sprinted for her car.

Had she left the keys in the console? She couldn't remember. She sometimes did and sometimes didn't, and what a fool she'd been to bring on the transformation, what a simpering, stupid fool. She fled past the garage, slapping at her hip pockets until she remembered she didn't keep her keys in her pockets. They were in her purse or in the car, and the difference, God help her, could mean the difference between life or death.

From behind her came a bloodcurdling roar, the voice containing no semblance of humanity.

Glenn was fully transformed.

Moaning, she scampered around the front of the Corolla and lunged toward the driver's door. She'd been so stupid. Treating this as if it were an academic exercise rather than a situation that could end in death.

She ripped open the door, plunged her hand inside the console for the keys, but her fingers only encountered lip gloss containers, crumpled receipts. She bent over the compartment, peered into the darkness within, but all she could make out were more papers, a napkin or two. Something that looked like a ruptured pack of breath mints. Dammit! Where were the—

A banging noise whipped her head up. She stared wide-eyed at the open garage doors.

No one there. She glanced to her right and detected no movement from the house.

Which meant Glenn was out here. Prowling, lurking. Glenn would find her any moment and rip her—

She'd left her car door open! With a hissing sound, she jerked her shoes inside the Corolla, snagged the door handle, and yanked the door shut.

Movement near the garage brought her eyes up. To the left of the garage, where the yard gave way to the cornfield. Was Glenn there? Or was he about to pounce on her hood, punch through the windshield, slash her throat open? Or maybe he was—

With a gasp she turned and stared through the driver's side window.

Nothing.

But at any moment he could appear, snarling, yellow eyes glowing like sinister lanterns, and…

She remembered where the keys were.

Under the seat. Her hand darted, plucked them from the floor, and then she was guiding the key toward the ignition, though her hand shook so much she kept stabbing the hard plastic sheath around the steering column. It occurred to her she hadn't locked the doors, but all her will was currently focused on fitting the key in the ignition. And locking the door really wouldn't do much anyway. Did werewolves know how to operate a door handle? With that kind of strength, did they need to?

An earsplitting howl rent the night. Joyce squirted urine into her underwear.

The howl dwindled to a low, mournful bay, but the sound still sent chills scurrying up and down her bare arms. It came from the cornfield.

Somehow, though she wasn't even looking at what she was doing, the key found its way into the ignition. Joyce twisted it, willing the engine to turn over. It had never failed to work before, yet a peculiar species of fatedness had descended on her. It was like watching herself in a movie. The hapless woman, a minor character really, about to be killed off by the bestial antagonist.

The Corolla's engine started.

Joyce moved the gearshift into reverse and began to back the Corolla down the long gravel lane. If the werewolf hadn't heard the engine start, he'd no doubt notice the red brake lights flashing on and off as she eased toward the road. But Joyce refused to act rashly. She remembered how once, during the onset of a violent storm, she'd been driving on a country road and the winds had begun to rocket at her. The trees had bent and thrashed, and for a dreadful instant Joyce had been certain a tornado would appear and send her spinning to her death. She'd panicked. Meaning to perform a U-turn, Joyce had stiff-armed the manoeuvre, veered wildly across the road at a drunken diagonal, and crashed into a telephone pole. Since she'd only been going fifteen miles an hour before the impact, the damage to the Corolla had been in the hundreds rather than the thousands, but it had still taught her how dangerous a thing fear could be.

If she crashed now, it would mean death. Not the actual accident, of course – she wasn't reversing the car that rapidly – but the aftermath. The werewolf discovering her crippled car and flensing her like an animal.

No. Her arm draped over the seat back, Joyce peered out the back window and guided the Corolla toward the road. There were pine trees on either side of Glenn's lane, but she would easily clear these.

Joyce passed unmolested through the pines, hooked her back end onto the country road. With a glance in the rearview mirror – no one coming – Joyce shifted into drive and motored through the loose gravel.

She exhaled shuddering breath. She'd made it. Other than the brief, uncontrolled urination, she'd kept her composure. That was no easy task, considering the danger that had threatened her. Glenn was a werewolf. An honest-to-goodness werewolf. She couldn't believe it. Even though she'd known what he was, the reality was still difficult to wrap her mind around. Even more perplexing was how he'd let her slip away. Was it possible there was enough of Glenn even in his transformed state to show compassion toward Joyce? Was this a sign that he really had feelings for her? The notion she was starring in some cut-rate horror film began to dissipate. In a horror film, she'd already be dead. Or prey to some jump-scare reveal. The werewolf crashing through the windshield.

Or the werewolf staring at her from the backseat.

Holy Mother of God!

She whirled, expecting to find the Glenn-creature, but the seat was vacant. Glenn was nowhere to be found.

She blew out harried breath, stared out the windshield. She needed to get back to town. Maybe use the library to decompress. She could read, get some ordering done. Anything to take her mind off the creature prowling the night.

She was thinking this when she became aware of a shape in the cornfield, a figure keeping pace with the car, off to her right and perhaps fifty feet from the road.

She wouldn't have believed it if she weren't seeing it.

Glenn – or what Glenn had become – was racing through the night, moving with a weird combination of human strides and wolflike bounds.

Joyce depressed the accelerator. A glance at the speedometer told her she was doing forty already, but she nudged it up to forty-five, careful to keep a steady handle on the wheel. She'd add ten or fifteen miles to her speed if not for the loose gravel of the country road; she had enough experience to know it only took a millisecond of negligence to end up in a ditch or worse. Flipped upside down and awaiting death in a smoking car.

The Glenn-thing ran apace with her. Thirty feet away now.

A T-road was approaching. This both chilled and heartened her. On one hand, the last thing she wanted to do was to slow down, but slow down she must unless she wanted to barrel right into the forest awaiting her at the end of the road. But if she could navigate the turn, manage to manoeuvre the Corolla onto the paved asphalt, she'd stand a good chance of escaping the Glenn-thing.

Though it made her teeth chatter to do it, Joyce eased the Corolla down to thirty, the T-road perhaps fifty yards ahead. The Glenn-thing raced along very near the car now, its clawed hands harrowing the strip of grass dividing the shallow ditch from the field. She didn't linger on the sight of Glenn's new body – she didn't want to crash the car out of simple distraction – but what she glimpsed both awed and horrified her.

His arms were rippling mounds of muscle, the hair thicker but not so thick you couldn't make out the striated muscles beneath. His legs were narrow, but they gave off an aura of tensile strength, of metal coils about to spring. But what finally made her turn away was his facial profile. Still more human than animal, but enough intimation of a wolf's muzzle to make her want to scream. And, of course, there were the eyes.

Fingers white on the wheel, Joyce slowed as much as she dared, prepared herself to swerve. Twenty yards away now. Ten.

Joyce began to turn the wheel.

The Glenn-thing catapulted over the ditch and crashed into the passenger's side window.

Chunks of glass pelted her right side. The jagged shards nicked her cheek, snagged in her hair. The Glenn-thing had an arm hooked over the inside of the door. The back end of the Corolla fishtailed, slewed wildly toward the woods. Joyce fought the spin, twisted the wheel to the right, though that meant skidding them precariously closer to the waiting forest. The Glenn-thing was snarling, growling, his immense body mowing down fence posts, the wiring between the posts snapping with a series of rusty twangs. Joyce got control of the Corolla, swung back toward the middle of the road, but the Glenn-thing remained fastened to the door. She made the mistake of glancing over at it, and in that moment she forgot all about who this was, forgot all about her feelings for Glenn.

The face glaring back at her was an abomination. Yellow-eyed, almost human, but with no humanity at all in its fiendish gaze, the long teeth tapered to vicious, sabrelike points. It grinned at her with diabolical anticipation.

With both feet she stood on the brake. The Glenn-thing tore loose of the door, tumbled down the road, the creature blurring in a flurry of somersaults. The car came to rest before the creature did.

Joyce didn't hesitate. She floored it. The creature had ended up perhaps ten feet beyond the car, but it was dazed, bloodied. So when the Corolla burst past, the Glenn-thing only made a foggy, halfhearted grab for it. Joyce pushed the Corolla up to fifty before she glanced in the rearview mirror, and by that time the Glenn-thing was merely a tall shape growing out of the sable ribbon of road.

She didn't slow down until the figure disappeared from view entirely.

★   ★   ★

Joyce drove around for a couple hours, relishing the mist that had descended on the countryside. Her terror gradually waned, and in its place came wonder. She'd proven her theory. Whether Glenn would accept her findings was another matter.

She crunched back up his drive at a quarter past eleven. She didn't think he'd have returned yet, not because the change would still be upon him, but rather because the change, having exhausted itself, would have rendered him strengthless and far from home. He would have to slog back through fields and forests, his body a snarl of aches from his transformations.

So Joyce sat and gazed out at the swirling mist. Her thoughts drifted to tomorrow night. The night of her friends' class reunion.

Savannah hadn't asked her to go, nor had Glenn. But Joyce would find a way to join them. She was beginning to trust her gut feelings, and she had a strong feeling that momentous things were afoot this Friday night. She wanted to be there to witness them.

When Glenn finally staggered up his driveway at midnight, she was waiting for him on his side porch. He was naked and winded. His hair was askew, and his hands were crusted with mud. But he didn't look bloody.

"What's..." he said, panting. "What the hell's wrong with you?"

"Jealousy," she said.

He stood there, arms akimbo, his shrivelled penis dangling before her like a flesh-toned jalapeño. "You put us both in danger."

"Clark Lombardo Coulter says—"

"I don't give a shit what he says," Glenn snapped. "I've heard enough of that pretentious fuckstick over the past twenty-four hours to last me a lifetime. Just tell me what *you* think."

She stood up, as much to get Glenn's penis out of her face as to have a normal conversation. "Why did Weezer change?"

Glenn looked away. "I don't want to talk about Weezer."

"You have to."

"You want to know what he was doing? He was ripping that poor girl's chest open."

"Not *during* the murders," she said. "Before."

Glenn shrugged. "I don't know. Dancing?"

She stepped closer. "But not just dancing, Glenn. You said they were grinding together. The three of them. The two women thrusting against him—"

"I got it," he said, glowering at her. "Jesus."

"Lust."

"What about it?"

"Weezer's trigger is lust. Yours is jealousy."

"That's your theory? The seven deadly sins? Is yours vanity?"

"Glenn, listen—"

"Don't look in the mirror," he said, a look of mock fright on his face. "You stare at yourself, you might transform."

"I didn't say anything about the seven—"

"Or is it gluttony, Joyce? Let's head over to the Chinese buffet, fill you full of chicken lo mein. I bet you'll be howling within minutes."

She seized his bare shoulders. "*Powerful negative emotions*," she said, punching each syllable. "For Weezer, it's animal lust. For you, it's envy. For others, it might be rage or sorrow or...I don't know. Fear?"

Some of the sarcasm left his face. "You were scared earlier, weren't you? When I was changing?"

"I was scared to death," she admitted.

"Well, there you go. You didn't change."

"I didn't say fear was *my* trigger."

He rolled his eyes, started toward the house. "Could you use a different word? Trigger sounds so...I don't know, political or something."

"How about 'catalyst'?"

"You're full of shit." He made his way up the steps.

She watched his back muscles flexing, the curve of his strong buttocks. The scent of his exertion wafted down to her, tingling her nostrils and setting her imagination racing. *Her* catalyst definitely wasn't lust, she decided. Otherwise, she'd have transformed two dozen times today. She resisted an urge to hurry after him and mash her body against his.

"Where are you going?" she asked.

He opened the screen door. "What's it look like?"

"Like you're avoiding me."

"I'm going to sleep," he muttered, the screen door banging shut behind him. "I'm tired, Joyce. Down to my bones. I want some rest. Plus, I think I ate a muskrat."

★　　★　　★

Six rings and she wasn't picking up. Weezer knew he could wait for the voicemail to kick on, but what was the point? He knew Jessica was awake. She'd always been a night owl. He supposed she could've changed in the years since he'd gone to school with her, but people were typically wired a certain way, and that was how they stayed.

Take Jessica Clinton, for example. Once a night owl, always a night owl.

Once a bitch, always a bitch.

Weezer chucked his cell aside, the old, cracked phone thunking off the armrest on the passenger's door. Had the two bitches he killed last night carried with them more than forty bucks and change, Weezer might have used the money to splurge on a new cell phone, but of course they didn't have any money between them because between them they barely had enough brain cells to survive.

Rely on men, that was their way. You don't need money when there are always poor, stupid saps around to buy dinner for you.

Weezer had a brief vision of Jessica that night back in high school, but he shunted that aside as rapidly as it arose, not wanting the change to overtake him. Not yet.

He flung open his door, hopped out. Maybe Jessica would be alerted to his presence by the slamming truck door. If not, he'd just have to ring her doorbell. Either way, she was letting him in.

She'd had four days to mourn her husband, and that was more than enough.

On the way up her walk – fancy lake house, two storeys, built sometime in the late eighties probably, white with black shutters – Weezer recalled the way the beast had hurled Jessica's husband, the ill-fated Dan, right into the raging bonfire, the way Dan had breakdanced atop the inferno. Weezer could still recall the scent of the man's scorched flesh. Like bacon sizzling, but more piquant.

Weezer's mouth flooded with saliva.

Not yet, he reminded himself.

Reaching out, he depressed the glowing doorbell. Through the long, rectangular window bordering the door, he could see through the house all the way to the great room in back, the big picture window leading to the lake. There was a TV going in the great room. He could see its reflection in the window. It looked like some kind of reality show about dancing or singing.

He resisted the urge to shatter the window with his fists.

Instead, he beat on the door, a steady, rhythmic concussion, and right away he saw a shadow scurry across the picture window, a dark shape hurrying toward him.

Weezer kept pounding.

The porch light spilled over him, a urine-coloured glow that showed plainly all the dead bugs on the porch. Some live ones too. In the brief instant before Jessica ripped the door open, Weezer reached out and smeared a giant moth into gloppy, powdery nothingness. The brown streak on the white aluminium siding looked like some really tall dude had run out of toilet paper and wiped his ass on the façade. Actually, that's what he felt like doing right now.

Jessica jerked open the interior door, squinted at him through the screen. "Weezer? What in God's name are you doing? It's almost one."

Weezer smiled, unabashed. "I knew you'd be up."

She was wearing a fluffy pink bathrobe, but what was beneath it? She must've noticed him ogling because she cinched it tighter at the throat. "Were you the one calling me?"

"I figured it would be polite to call first."

"*Weezer*. Nothing's polite at one in the morning." She brought her face right up to the screen, scrutinising him. "Are you shitfaced?"

"I'm utterly sober, Jessica. I just thought it would be nice to visit."

Looking troubled, she opened the screen door, moved aside so he could enter. In the dark foyer, she continued to scrutinise him. "You sure you're not drunk?"

Moving toward the great room, he said, "What makes you think that, Jessica?"

"I don't know," she muttered. "For one, you never call me by my name."

Nice room, he thought. Other than the shitty singing show on the television, the room was sort of impressive. A wood-burning fireplace on the south wall. Nice furniture, pretty stylish. The picture window was the real attraction, though. A breathtaking view of the lake, the water like polished obsidian.

"You want something?" she asked.

He looked at her, eyebrows raised.

"Like a drink," she hastened to add.

"I'm okay, Jessica. I really just came to talk."

"So talk," she said.

He fixed her with his profoundest gaze. "I thought it might do you good to open up about Dan."

That did it. Right away her eyes got red, and she sniffed back a trickle of snot.

"You're hurting," he said.

One of her hands covered her mouth, the other cupping her elbow. She was looking toward the window, but not really seeing, he could tell. Poor Jessica, he thought. Poor, twenty-eight-year-old widow. Six kids. No husband.

A real shame.

She wiped her nose, rubbed it on her robe, made a vague gesture toward the couch that backed up to the picture window. "You can have a seat if you like."

Weezer frowned. That wasn't where he'd imagined sitting. The one and only time he'd been here – he and Glenn had stopped by a couple years ago, though Glenn had been the one Dan Clinton had invited – there had been a nice, cosy leather La-Z-Boy recliner along the north wall. But now the leather chair was gone, and in its place there was a stiff-looking ivory chair, the kind you'd see in sitting rooms in movies set back in the 1800s. Thoroughly uncomfortable. Girly.

Still, he would've rather sat there than the couch because the view would've been better from the chair. But she was already sitting in the chair, next to which he noticed an end table with half a dozen empty beer bottles. Coors Light, which was like drinking cat piss.

Grudgingly, he eased himself onto the couch, which was comfortable enough. Even if it did face him away from the picture window and the lake.

Keeping his voice light, he said, "How are you coping, Jessica?"

She'd drawn her legs up beneath her, had her eyes on the TV, which was blessedly on mute. "I'm not."

"I know it must be very difficult."

Jessica said nothing, and Weezer thought, *You're good at that, aren't you? Saying nothing? You've practiced it for years, and when you want to, you just shut it down. Just ignore the other person, make like he doesn't exist.*

"How are your kids taking it? It must be hard not having Daddy around."

Her face squinched up at this, and that was good. That was part of it. Purging her of the salty tears and the quiet, quaking sobs. It was harder maybe for a strong woman like Jessica to mourn a loss because she was unaccustomed to tears.

"Which one's your oldest? Reggie?"

"Rory," she said, wiping away a tear. "He acts like it's his job to be strong." A smile flashed briefly. "You know, to be the man of the house? But he's just a kid."

"What is he?" Weezer asked, hands folded in his lap. "Ten years old?"

"Nine," she said. "I got pregnant the summer after we graduated."

"And were married that fall."

She glanced at him. "I loved Dan. We didn't marry because of Rory."

"I never suspected otherwise."

She made a harsh scoffing sound. "His parents did. They figured I was loose. Didn't want their precious Danny marrying me." Her expression went steely. "But we showed 'em. Danny got a good job. And now he's—" She paused, swallowed thickly. "—*was* vice president of his company. Six healthy children and a house on the lake."

"It's a nice house," Weezer agreed.

"Damn right," she said. "We showed 'em what we were made of."

Yes, you did, he thought. *You showed them, all right. You showed me too, showed me how little you thought of me. On a breakup with Dan, drunk at a graduation party, you let old Weezer have a quick lay, let me have my bright, gleaming moment in your parents' bedroom, and you never talked to me again, never looked at me again, and when you did it was like you were looking at an insect, or something worse, something vile and grotesque and unmentionable, a dark thing from your past, a revolting mistake, and a week later you were back with Dan. A week of unreturned phone calls and unanswered emails. Of dodging me like I had the fucking plague. And you didn't care how I ached. How I longed for you. You didn't care that it had meant something to me. That it—*

"Weezer?"

He jolted. She was watching him, wide-eyed.

"Sorry," he said. "I was thinking of something else."

"Well, whatever it was, it must not have been good."

Nice guess, he thought.

"I'm okay, Jessica. And I think I will have a drink."

The sound of a baby crying startled him. The noise was coming from his left. He glanced at her for an explanation.

"We converted Dan's office to a nursery. I better go," she said. "Stephanie's always fussing." Rising, she nodded toward the front of the house. "Beer's in the fridge."

She went out to quiet the baby, and Weezer moved down the hallway. When he reached the foyer, he ignored the kitchen, curled left, and ambled up the staircase. The first door he reached was ajar, and by screwing up his eyes a little he could see the child within, a small girl of maybe seven who took after her father. Her dead father.

Next up was a room on the right, this one housing bunk beds. The twins, Weezer recollected. They'd be about five. And feisty, like their mom. Weezer moved on.

Next up was a closed door on the lakeside of the house. That would be Rory, the oldest. He was old enough to want privacy, Weezer supposed.

Beyond that on the right was a bathroom.

He doubled back, listening for Jessica and the baby below. Little Stephanie was still crying, but not wailing anymore.

Weezer passed the staircase and saw there were two more rooms at this end of the hall. The first was a small room that evidently belonged to her two-year-old son. It was dark in there, and the kid's curly hair was long, but Weezer was pretty sure it was a boy.

At the end of the hall was the master suite. He could figure that much out by the layout of the house.

Weezer ran through it all in his head on the way down the stairs. He was so lost in his thoughts that he almost ran over Jessica.

She was standing at the foot of the stairs, staring at him. "What were you doing up there?"

He put on a smile. "Bathroom," he said.

"There's one on the main floor."

He reached the bottom step. "I didn't want to disturb you and Stephanie."

She continued to watch him a moment. Then she nodded absently.

They came back into the great room, but before she could make it to the stiff-backed ivory chair, he put an arm around her waist, directed her toward the couch. "Sit here, Jessica. It's more comfortable."

"But I don't wanna sit here," she said, sitting anyway. "There's a glare on the TV."

Weezer held his patient smile, crossed the room. "We're not going to worry about the television," he said, and pushed the Off button. He bent and lifted the stupid, uncomfortable chair and placed it directly across from Jessica, so that their knees would only be a foot or so apart, and he could face the window.

She eyed him warily, crossed her legs so that her robe folded open a little, the dark skin glimmering in the lamplight, about six inches of flesh above the knees. The black crease where her legs met.

"Weezer?" she asked.

His reverie broke and he was instantly in control again, instantly smooth. "We need to talk about your situation."

"My situation."

"You and your children, and what sort of future you're going to have."

She cocked an eyebrow. "You sure you're okay? You sound like a different person."

He smiled with good humour. "Do I? How so?"

"I don't know," she said, hugging herself and shivering a little. "You sound more mature. Smarter, I guess."

Thanks a lot, he thought. *Cunt.*

He forced a smile. "I guess what happened at the bonfire changed all of us."

It acted on her like a good hard fist to the jaw. She was about to cry again.

He reached out, took her hand, which had evidently been holding the robe closed because now it peeled open another couple inches, a good deal of her thighs visible now. The skin dark and shaved despite the ordeal she'd been through, despite the six kids and their needs.

A fighter, he thought. *Good.*

"Now listen," he said, in what he hoped was a rallying tone. "You've been through hell. You don't have to tell me that. Any fool could see how hard it's been on you."

She looked away, but he thought he'd seen a grateful smile ghost across her lips.

He pushed on. "I know I'm just an old high school acquaintance—"

"Friend," she amended.

He smiled, but it cost an effort. "Thanks, Jessica. But what I mean is that even though you're a strong girl, you shouldn't have to be. Not all the time."

She watched him, interested.

"What I'm proposing," he said, "is that you let me help you out. Make this transition a little easier."

"Transition?"

"You know, your life after Dan. Don't tell me you haven't thought about it."

Something darkened her face. Guilt? Anger maybe? Spiritual resentment over losing her life partner?

"Like I said, I know I'm not anyone's concept of the ideal man. But I could step in with your children, give them a good role model. Someone to roughhouse with. Someone to change diapers, to help them with their homework."

And God help him, he meant it. At that moment, he really meant it. On the way over here he'd been thinking only of how to punish her for the mortifying shunning that had taken place a decade ago, the broken heart she didn't give two shits about. Yet now, those old feelings of affection for her were getting dredged up. She was still a pretty girl, just about as pretty as she'd been that drunken night in her parents' bedroom. And he'd always had a soft spot for kids. Okay, not all kids. Maybe not even most of them. Most kids were royal pains in the ass, burdens who did nothing but take and whine and shit and make you sick with their Dorito breath. But there had been moments over the past few years when he'd toyed with the idea of being a dad. Hell, he'd found himself envying Dan Clinton at times, even imagining himself taking old Dan's place. And this was before Dan had gotten tossed onto that bonfire like a lively hunk of kindling.

And now, as he spoke, Weezer realised that this could be the realisation of a dream. He could be a father to all these urchins. He could be a husband to Jessica. Go down on her all he wanted and make up for that embarrassingly brief rut, the one where he'd gotten to pump maybe three or four times before squirting and wilting and climbing off with an apology that she hadn't listened to anyway because she was already half-dressed again.

But now Jessica was watching him with an expression that bordered on tragedy.

"Oh God, Weezer," she said, a horrible look of pity crumpling her face. She wiped her cheeks, glanced up at the ceiling.

"Go on," he said, knowing what was coming. Inviting it. "You can be honest with good old Weezer."

She gave him a grateful smile and the robe slid open another couple inches. If the pink material spread any wider, if the furry pink tie loosened any more, he'd see what was between her legs. Would she have even bothered with underwear? She hadn't planned on guests. The kids were in bed. It was just her and her beer and her stupid reality show.

Was she naked beneath the pink robe?

"Okay," she said, relaxing a trifle. "I mean, it's really nice of you to stop by, Weezer, and I want you to know how flattered I am by your offer..."

Go on, he urged. *Make it easier. Tell me how you think it's sweet of me, but how you don't feel ready for another relationship at the moment. How you care about me and all, but as a friend. A good, loyal friend.*

And that was pretty much what she said, though he was only half listening. Because the robe had split open a mite farther, and he realised she wasn't wearing any underwear, and though her legs were pressed together, he could just see the upper rim of her pubic hair, the same hair he'd luxuriated in that night ten years ago, the cleft she'd allowed him to lick, and he'd loved it, and so had she, writhing and squirming and moaning and calling out his name, and if he had to choose the greatest moment of his life it would have been then, then and the eight or ten seconds he'd been able to hold back from ejaculating while they had sex, but she didn't mind it, he could tell, because that part was for him, she'd already had her orgasm, and now she wouldn't have to go down on him to reciprocate, because maybe that was beneath her. Because *he* was beneath her, so far beneath her that she'd never acknowledged they'd been together. And because he could feel the pulse in his temples, the throb in his biceps, the twitch coming everywhere now, he decided to say it, to try her out so he'd know what her reaction would be.

"...and getting into another relationship this soon would confuse the kids," she was saying. "Not to mention making me look bad. And you wouldn't look too good either, going after a woman so soon after her husband's murder. She leaned forward. "You understand, don't you, Weezer?"

"But Jessica," he said, "we already had sex once."

She looked away immediately, shifting herself back on the couch. Covering her crotch with the robe in what might or might not have been a conscious gesture.

"Jessica?" he said. Beyond her head, the spangled water rippled and undulated, a breeze kicking up. The moon wasn't full, but it was waxing. And the moon was a halogen spotlight.

"That was a long time ago, Weezer," she said. "And I was drunk."

"I was drunk too," he pointed out.

Jessica shifted on the couch, looking everywhere but at him.

"Jessica?"

"What?" she snapped.

"Look at me."

She didn't. "It's late, Weezer."

He gripped both her legs, just above the knees. "Look at me."

But she was pawing at his hands. "*Weezer.*"

"*Fucking look at me, you bitch!*"

He could hear it in his voice, and apparently so could she, because she was seizing his forearms, toiling to prise them off her legs. But he sank the fingers in, his talons protracting. She began to cry out but he was too quick, thrusting a hand up and clamping a palm over her mouth, driving her backward into the voluminous green couch, and her eyes were bugging out. He repositioned his grip so he wouldn't cover her nose, suffocate her, hell no. She needed to see this. *Would* see this.

Was witnessing this as the coarse, dark hair slithered out of his knuckles, over his wrists, the muscles tautening under the cuffs of his black shirt, the thread straining, the material groaning like a live thing. And she gave up slapping at him and started fluttering her hands like a helpless damsel in a movie, and he wanted to laugh at her, a strong, liberated woman cowering like that, but he couldn't laugh because of the pain. It was exquisite, rapturous in its promise, but on a literal level it was fucking awful, a red-black agony, but he held his position, kept her pinned to the couch. She would witness the whole process, the entire goddamned show, and as his facial bones began to rearrange themselves she began to hammer at his arm, and he actually liked that, though to hold on to her face he had to squeeze a little, and apparently he didn't know his own strength because the skin at one of her ears split from being stretched so hard. But that wouldn't kill her, hell no, it wouldn't. Cast her into a state of anguish, maybe, scare the living shit out of her for sure, but not kill her. She drummed her bare feet against the front of the couch, sobbed into his hand, and from the nursery he heard the baby wailing, but that was fine. He'd be in there eventually. But first Jessica, then Rory. Then the seven-year-old, the twins, and the curly-haired boy.

The baby he would save for last.

CHAPTER TWENTY-THREE

From behind the pole barn, the dogs barked incessantly. Melody assumed her father and brothers had been too preoccupied to feed the dogs, which meant they'd grown scrawnier than they already were.

The images tore at her, so she pushed them away.

Melody did her best to collect her thoughts. She was fairly certain it was Friday evening. If that was correct, that meant they'd had her locked up in the basement for two days.

Keeping her prisoner.

Melody wished she were surprised by this, but the fact was, she'd idly wondered from time to time why they didn't just strip away the patina of normalcy with which they'd concealed their atrocities and treat her like what she was – a serially abused sex slave.

In the two days since Melody had been ambushed by John back in that thicket, Father Bridwell and her brothers had unleashed a torrent of physical and psychological abuse so horrific that, by the end of the first night, she'd found herself simply shutting down. Gone was the fury that had gripped her in the pole barn, gone was the indignation at their ill treatment. Her limbs were crosshatched with a gruesome network of scratches and slits, her genitalia and breasts crusted with dried blood and pus, her anus so swollen and painful she couldn't shit even if there'd been anything in her digestive system to expel. Melody lay on the dank concrete floor, her filth and the cobwebbed grime her only bedding. The sun would go down soon, and the degradations would begin anew. Eyeing the sombre bloodred rectangle of light from the basement's lone window, Melody realised the truth.

Her father and brothers had decided to kill her.

They would inflict violence on her until her body succumbed.

She was never going to breathe fresh air again.

She was never going to leave the basement.

She opened and closed her cracked, crusted lips and endeavoured to run her swollen tongue over them, but the pain made her stop, the feeble movement enough to clog her airway and set off an excruciating, body-racking coughing fit. She wheezed for breath, her nostrils too crammed with blood and mucus to be of any use. Her body juddered with the coughs, and her eyes burned from the gummy tears that oozed from their corners. A coppery heat sizzled in the back of her throat, and she realised that from somewhere, somehow, she was bleeding internally. She might not make it past sundown, might just expire before Father Bridwell and his sons got to work on her.

Melody's airway was needle-thin, the breaths of musty air she stole insufficient to keep her conscious. She wavered into a nebulous slate-coloured fog, her limbs going numb, her ears filling with the roar of sea tide.

Some time later – it might have been ten minutes, it might have been an hour – she blinked slowly awake to discover a shape hovering over her. She thought at first it was Father Bridwell, but when her vision swirled into focus, she realised it was her oldest brother.

Donny was leering at her, his knobby, grubby fingers kneading the bulge in his blue jeans.

My God, she marvelled. *How can you still view me as a sex object?* She imagined how she must look and shuddered. For the millionth time she was struck by the depravity of her family members, by their capacity for evil.

Donny reached for her, but just as his fingertips brushed her cheek, Father Bridwell's voice echoed from the basement steps. "Not yet, Donny."

Donny froze, an anguished look in his glittery eyes. He stood there a moment, perhaps debating whether or not he could disobey Father Bridwell this once. She thought she heard him moan in vexation. He glanced pleadingly up at his father, who was coming down the steps with Robbie and John in tow. All of them carried bulky white objects under their arms. She noticed the same self-satisfied grin on each of their faces. And as Donny watched them file in and take positions near her, his pained, horny expression morphed into one of smug anticipation.

Bemusedly, Melody surveyed their faces. Then, despite the pain blurring her vision, she understood what they were all grasping.

Her paintings.

They'd found out about the attic.

Melody began to whimper.

Father Bridwell's hatchet face split into a grin. "Figured that'd have an effect. And here I was beginning to think you were too far gone to care."

Melody opened her mouth, but the broken-glass anguish of her throat precluded speech.

"Donny," Father Bridwell said, "Head over to the workbench and bring me those shears. No, not those. The metal-cutting ones. Uh-huh, the black handles." Father Bridwell accepted them. "Thank you, son. Now," he said, turning toward Melody. "You need to explain something."

He turned one of the oil paintings so she could see it, and her heart sank. It was one of her favourites.

"Just what the hell is the gal in this picture doin'? Father Bridwell asked. "Flickin' her bean?"

Donny giggled. So did John. Robbie only watched her, stone-faced.

Melody said nothing.

Father Bridwell's grin grew fierce. "What makes you think you can bring this kinda garbage into my home?"

"Not garbage," Melody croaked.

Father Bridwell nodded sadly. "I feared you'd say that. It's the kind of relaxed morals that led you to perpetrate this filth in the first place."

Melody didn't even try to justify the painting. The woman in it was from a movie she'd once seen on the late show. Catherine Deneuve, the actress's name had been. In Melody's painting, Deneuve wasn't masturbating, precisely, but her hands were positioned on her abdomen and the middle of her chest as though she were in the thrall of some unquenchable passion. Though the movie had been old and in Italian, Melody had liked it and had especially liked Deneuve's acting. Vulnerable yet commanding. Sensual but at the same time enigmatic and full of dignity. Melody had wanted to be like that, but she didn't know how to be.

Yet she wouldn't dare say any of this to Father Bridwell or her brothers. They'd never understand, and more importantly, they'd use it against her. Use it as an excuse to inflict more pain, more humiliation. She tried to swallow, but her throat was an arid field of cracked tissue, a throbbing, itching horror. How long had she been without water?

Outside, the dogs barked louder.

Father Bridwell made a soft clucking sound. "Mel, Mel, Mel." He opened the shears, positioned them under the painting.

"Please," she croaked.

"Too late for that, Missy," he said. And began squeezing the shears, the sharp blades and his strong, grubby fingers more than able to crunch through the soft wooden frame and then to carve their way from Catherine Deneuve's bare feet, up her legs, into the shadow of her cleft, slicing through her tummy, the canvas dividing easily, the image divided in two.

Father Bridwell finished by snapping the top of the frame apart with his rough hands. He tossed the halves onto Melody's bare torso. "Here you go. Boys, why don't you pitch in too?"

As one, her brothers hurried over to the workbench to fetch various implements. Donny seized a chisel, thrust it through the centre of a painting, one she'd done years ago and to which she wasn't particularly attached. It didn't bother her, except the violation that she felt, the meanness of the act.

The one John was desecrating – he'd taken a carpet cutter and was sawing it vertically – was important to her, mainly because it was newer and represented some of her best work. She'd drawn Glenn Kershaw in that one, shirtless. And though Glenn had stopped calling her, like all guys eventually did, Glenn had treated her nicely when they were together. He'd touched her, used his mouth on her. Kissed her in a way that suggested she was more than a slab of meat. But now the likeness of Glenn was shredded, his face a disarranged parody, some amateurish attempt at a Picasso.

Her chest heaving, her teeth grinding, she blinked away the thick, Plasticine tears and turned to her youngest brother. Her ally. Her one hope in this unending descent.

Robbie was staring at her, but his eyes were unseeing. He clutched a painting in his right hand and a lighter in his left. The painting was turned away from her, but she knew what it was already, knew it even before he flipped it around and moved the flame below it. The yellow cone of fire licked at it, blackening a spot on the bottom left and making a black Christmas tree shape. And that was fitting, Melody decided, because she'd gotten this first canvas at Christmas, way back when she was in middle school. Robbie had bought it for her, and it occurred to her that Robbie was the only one who knew about the attic. He'd never ventured up there with her, but once or twice she'd confided in him about it, and on one occasion he'd asked her what she'd been working on.

The truth clanged home.

Robbie had led them to the attic.

Robbie, who clutched the painting she'd made of him and her, the pair of them holding hands. It wasn't the incineration of her artwork that wounded her – she'd been a shitty artist back then, with nary a clue how to draw faces – but the fact that Robbie had started this. Her protector. Her one friend.

Her betrayer.

"Look at her!" Donny hooted. He was stabbing at his painting, the chisel popping through the canvas like exit wounds in a pale man's back. "She's gettin' riled at us, I can tell!"

John eyed her over his ribboned canvas. "Good. Maybe she'll show some life when I take me a piece."

Father Bridwell discarded the mutilated image of Catherine Deneuve and began shearing a canvas of a man and woman making love, this one also inspired by a film, a dirty one her father had left in the VHS player. It was how she'd learned about sex. Well, that and having her father and brothers fuck her.

Her brothers were laughing now, sharing the joke. But not Robbie. He was staring at her over the flickering oil painting of them holding hands, and he was really staring at her now, seeing her. She appealed to him with her eyes, raised her head as far as she could so he'd see her face and understand the agony she was in, but the more he stared back at her the less he appeared to care.

No, that wasn't right. He did care, but not in the way she'd hoped he would. He hated her, was glaring at her with steely contempt. And it wasn't just her behaviour, her sleeping around. He hated what she *was*. Hated her all the way to her soul. And she thought, *How could you, Robbie? How could you be so unfeeling and selfish? How could you not care about what's happening to me? How could you—*

Her thoughts snapped off as she realised how he could let this happen.

He didn't care.

He'd *never* cared.

He'd only been nice to her so she'd sleep with him, so she wouldn't make him rape her the way the others did. Robbie liked her to be willing.

Robbie liked her to be tractable. Robbie wanted her to spread herself for him and French kiss him and pretend it was okay, it was perfectly natural. And the memory of those warm nights with him, those nights swaddled in the illusion of their shared regard, those nights when he'd stayed with her after using her and allowed her to bask in his warmth and his gentleness, the thought of it made her tendons creak, her muscles bunch. Donny was still laughing, but not Father Bridwell. He'd always been smarter than his sons, if no less diseased. Father Bridwell understood that something profound was taking place between her and Robbie, and it could have been that understanding that made him shift uneasily in his work boots.

Or maybe it was something else, she decided. For his eyes had swung to her left arm, which she realised was straining against the rope. This made Donny and John laugh harder, but not Father Bridwell. Father Bridwell was frowning – and sweating, she saw – but Robbie was merely drinking in her expression as the painting of them burned and burned. The flames were licking up the canvas now, the oils scorched and smelly. And the odour of it, the corrosive, unhealthy reek that clogged the room was making her angry, was making her *furious*, though not as furious as the look on Robbie's face was making her.

Forsaker.

Melody jerked on the rope. It strained taut. From behind the pole barn, the dogs were going absolutely berserk now, their barks so fast and fierce they merged into an unceasing buzz.

Deceiver.

Melody convulsed. She was dimly aware that John and Donny had ceased laughing. She glowered at Robbie, whose dead-faced mask was finally altering into something that might have been alarm.

Betrayer.

She growled at him.

Father Bridwell held up a hand. "Now, don't you go getting bent out of—"

"*BETRAYER!*" she bellowed.

With a roar, Melody tore in half the rope binding her left arm.

Donny shrilled out his terror. John backpedalled and tripped over one of the unspoiled canvases.

Father Bridwell was edging toward the stairs.

But it was at Robbie she was staring. Robbie who'd dropped the flaming canvas, the image there long since having scorched to a brown-black smudge. She strained to her left, heaved, and the rope around her right wrist snapped free. The pulsing, strobing pain in her back, her rib cage, her entire body, it doubled, tripled, skyrocketed. Yet as she flopped over onto all fours, her elbows hyperextending with twin blood splats on the grungy cement floor, she kept her eyes trained on Robbie, on the Forsaker, on the one who'd brought her to this place. Her paintings were the only things she had left, the only things they hadn't taken from her, and now they were gone

gone gone gone gone, and the laughing brother, she couldn't remember his name, was scrambling over the work bench toward the window. The unsmiling one

(*John? Was it John?*)

was still spread-eagle on the cement, watching in numb shock, but the oldest one

(*Father, it was her father*)

was making for the stairs and she knew she didn't have much time so instead of spilling Robbie's guts she went for the oldest one.

(*Father Bridwell, Father Bridwell*)

Melody launched herself onto the side of the staircase, clambered under the single rail, and rose, hulking over Father Bridwell, and in the swirling shadows of the naked bulb she reached toward him, lifted him higher, higher, and he was saying "Daughter, my Daughter, please don't do this, please don't hurt me", and she smelled his tobacco-stained teeth and his unwashed body, like a heap of rotten mushrooms, the stink washing over her as it did when he rutted his foulness into her this week, last month, last year, a decade ago, back when she was twelve, and sex was nausea, sex was *shame*, sex was holding down the vomit and avoiding punishment by not crying because of the bleeding and the depression and the horror and the shame.

"Don't, daughter," he pleaded. "Don't—"

And she reached down and tore through his jeans and scooped the hot mess of flesh and scrotum and blood and withered penis and shoved them all into his quivering face. Something hit her down around the ankle, and she dropped Father Bridwell and stared past her slashed ankle and beheld...

...John, the stoic one, with a hacksaw, the rusty-toothed implement that had opened her skin, made her bleed, and the growl was deep in her throat and good and growing and John realised how he'd angered her and backpedalled, and the smell rising from him into the stairwell was fear mixed with hot, tarry shit. She lunged under the stair rail, more lithe than any creature on earth, revelling in the fear stink and the soiled pants. With a bound he was under her, like a mewling, squealing baby, and all of his toughness was gone, all of his meanness. He'd raped her with a broom handle the night before, raped her and lubed her with her own blood and then taken her and pounded her while she wailed and blacked out and swam into consciousness again, and thinking of this she reached down, jerked his legs apart so hard that his pelvis cracked, and then she thrust her claws under the hot, squelching stinkpit of his ass and began steam-shovelling at the seat of his jeans, striping the tough fabric, ribboning the jeans and the underwear and the buttocks beneath, and he squalled and kicked and writhed to be free, and with the shit and the blood smeared up to her wire-haired forearms she made a fist and drove it up his rectum. His scream became a braying siren and though it hurt her sensitive ears she grinned, her slaver dripping into his thrashing, wild-eyed face, and then she was thrusting the fist, savaging his bowels, his small intestine, and the harder he screamed the wider her smile grew. She heard the window over the workbench hinge open and knew she'd have to finish before Donny got away, so she flicked open her hand, her razor nails shredding John's intestines, and his screams pleased her, so hoarse, so frail, so she opened her fist, closed it, scythed through his internal organs until the cement floor was a scarlet pool and John was a jittering shit-stained rag doll.

She shot a look at Donny, who'd gotten lodged in the rectangular window, the disused metal rusted and unyielding. Donny was wailing out a garbled combination of prayers and obscenities and entreaties for help, and Melody, rising to her new, full height of seven feet, two inches, strode right past her youngest brother, past...past...

...past Robbie, who was cowering on the floor not far from where John lay thrashing in his death spasms. And behind her on the stairwell landing lay her father. He was still alive, she realised, and was sobbing quietly to himself, maybe mourning his missing genitals. And...

...and not needing to climb onto the workbench to take hold of Donny's kicking legs, Melody reached up, made to grab one of his boots, and was promptly kicked in the face. She snarled, seized the foot, and wrenched it in a fierce one-eighty. Donny howled at the gruesome spiral fracture of his tibia, but his body was wedged so tightly in the rusty aperture of the stuck window that he could only buck and strain. Loving the sound of his wails, Melody twisted his other foot, but this time kept going, winding it counter-clockwise until the ankle skin split open and the bones snapped and she came away holding the foot and the haemorrhaging stub of ankle and the scent of the marrow was too enticing to resist. And then she was licking it, scooping the delicious lifesauce out of the bone shards and laughing at Donny's caterwauling screams.

"*Unnatural!*" someone was screaming from behind her. "*That's unnatural!*"

She climbed on the workbench, used her talons to spread the meat of Donny's calf, to gnaw at the muscle tissue, the gristle beneath, and she smelled more piss, more shit, and knew Donny had voided his bladder and bowels. That bothered her because the acrid yellow liquid dribbled down his leg onto her writhing lips, and in a fury she slammed his lower body down, breaking Donny's back, the blood and spinal fluid spurting out of his distressed flesh. She'd let him dangle there, she decided, while she tended to the other one, the Betrayer.

She strode over to Robbie and sprayed piss all over his face. The ammoniac odour was eye-watering, but it was hers and beneath it she caught a whiff of burned oil, of charred canvas. She was about to rip his head off when she heard herself asking, in a voice like none she'd ever heard before, "*Why?*"

The Betrayer sobbed out an answer, while from her right the voice kept shouting, "*Unnatural! It's not natural!*" and she knew it to be true, at least with regard to her life. None of it had been natural, none of it, and she saw

Robbie gaping up at her with hope in his eyes and it was too much and she jammed her sharp-nailed thumbs into his eyeballs, the ocular fluid splurting over her knuckles, and she dug and dug, and soon her nails were splintering through the back of his skull, scraping on concrete.

John had long since bled out. Donny was scarcely quivering too, the workbench and old tools lapped over with blood, and her father, the fool, was still clutching his nonexistent private parts and calling her unnatural, and she marched over and seized him by the hair, towed him up the stairs after her, dragged his flailing body into the kitchen, slammed it onto the table, and plunged her maw into the gory hole she'd made in his abdomen. She moaned with pleasure while he shrieked, and she feasted on his entrails for many minutes after he expired. She became aware that the dogs had ceased barking.

At some point she found herself weakening. She realised the change had ended. Maybe the intensity of it had been too much for her to sustain. She didn't know. What she did was head down to the basement, where the rope was stored. It didn't take her long to make what she needed, for she had practiced it before. And she soon found herself climbing the pull-down ladder into the attic, where only a handful of her canvases remained. She didn't take time to glance at these. What was the point? She had a chair up here, of course, because it got tiring to paint while she stood, and before long she'd tied the rope off, looped it under her chin. Without pause she stepped off the chair and felt the rope go snug around her neck. And then her vision darkened and she remembered the horse, the way it had hated her. Like everything she loved. It had hated her. Hated her. Hated...

PART FOUR
REUNION

CHAPTER TWENTY-FOUR

Glenn stared at the whiteboard Joyce had wheeled out of the library office. They were in the rear of the main floor, the board facing the tall casement windows that looked out on the twilit trees. Joyce had arranged it so they could spot anybody entering the library in time to erase what was written on the whiteboard:

CATALYSTS
GLENN: JEALOUSY.
WEEZER: LUST.
GARNER: RAGE/REVENGE.
JOYCE?
MELODY?

VARIABLES
SEVERITY OF BITE
DEPTH OF WOUND
TOTALITY OF CHANGE
SPEED AT WHICH MEDICAL AID WAS ADMINISTERED
BLOOD LOSS
LUNAR CYCLE?

But all Glenn could think about was the drive-in. The big oaf he'd disembowelled on the sink. The poor biker bastard who'd stumbled upon them and gotten killed for his bad timing.

Glenn knew he wasn't going to live much longer. Cosmic justice forbade it. Even if he was a different person than he'd been only last weekend, there was still a taint on him, an indelible stain that marked him as a monster, a defiler, a creature who deserved to be hunted, deserved to be killed.

It was a matter of time.

"We're missing something," Joyce said. She chewed her bottom lip, frowned. She jerked, her eyes opening wide. "Of course!" she said, and proceeded to add MANNER OF DEATH to the whiteboard.

Glenn eyed the big letters. "Isn't this a little morbid?"

"It's necessary," she answered. "When we get to the reunion, we'll need to be ready for what might happen."

"Like what?"

Joyce shrugged. "Anything. If Weezer's there, he'll be horny, and that makes him dangerous. If Garner comes, we're all in danger, especially Savannah."

Glenn tightened. "He won't get near Savannah."

"No need to get worked up."

"I'm not worked up, I'm..." He shook his head. "What does that book of yours say about killing a werewolf?"

"There are only two ways," she said. "I mean, only two agreed-upon methods, ones that are practical. So we'll exclude blowing them up with grenade launchers or dissolving them in acid."

Glenn waited, not bothering to conceal his impatience.

"Cremation or decapitation," she said.

That's a big help, he thought. Now they only needed to invest in some samurai swords and a truckload of napalm.

"The efficacy of burning is obvious," she said, as though he'd asked the question. "You reduce the body to ashes, but more importantly, you sever the link between the brain and the heart that supplies blood flow."

"Listen," he began. "I think we need to take a step back—"

"In all stories," she went on, "decapitation is effective. With zombies, vampires... You don't often hear about decapitation with werewolves – most fictional accounts end with a silver bullet, don't they? – but I'm certain it's the most expedient way. *Nothing* can live without a brain."

"Weezer did pretty well most of his life."

She dragged one of the soft leather chairs in front of him and sat. "Glenn," she said, "why did you become a machinist?"

He tensed. "I make a hell of a lot more money than you do. What do they pay you here, Joyce?"

She continued to search his face, unabashed. "I hardly make anything. You know that. Librarians never do."

"Then stop criticising."

"I'm not cri—" She broke off, took in a shuddering breath. "Look, I'm just asking a question, okay? There's nothing wrong with manual labour—"

"Damn straight."

"—but a person with your mind...a man who loves books and *thinks* about things...I just wonder why you didn't pursue something else."

And gazing at her in the shadows cast by the pines and maples outside, the violet glints of twilight forming glimmering columns on her face, he almost told her everything. But when he opened his mouth, the words refused to come. Because how did you explain all the trivialities of your past, the formative events that sound ludicrous now but were so painful back then? How when you moved from a not-very-good junior high to a good middle school in the seventh grade, you went from one of the best students in your class to a kid whose skills were below average? How you shut down emotionally because you didn't have friends and your grades were bad and you got to believing what the grades told you, that you were stupid. That everyone else understood books because they were smarter than you, so you found a friend in Weezer, who hated books and who laughed at your jokes because he was just as lonely as you were. And Short Pump was always around too, and though Short Pump did read books, he inevitably did it on the sly because he knew Weezer would mock him for it. And in the tenth grade when your class read *Lord of the Flies*, you liked the title and hoped you'd like the book. But on the first page they talked about walking out of a scar, and you wondered *How the hell can you walk out of a scar? A scar's on someone's face, and a person couldn't walk out of a face could he?* So you pretended to read the book and didn't read a damned page and failed the quizzes and barely passed English, and that was how it went in most of your classes. You had a C average, and what the hell could you do with that? Certainly not get into a good college. So you went to technical school like the other retreads and got a degree that amounted to absolutely nothing because you could have gotten that machinist's job anyway without college. But you were good at it and after eight years you're in the same job in the same town, and if that were all it wouldn't be so bad. But what makes it worse is that somewhere along the line Short Pump began rubbing off on you, and you began to borrow his books, and then you bought them on your own and read them and realised you weren't dumb after all. Just a quitter. On yourself. But life is unforgiving, especially to those who choose the wrong path when they're thirteen years old.

So yes, Joyce, he wanted to say. *I know I could have done better. Could maybe still do better. But it's so hard to change, you know? Even if I know I can do more, there's still that residual doubt, that insecurity. And there's the matter of how to do it. It's not like I could just not work for four years in order to get a bachelor's degree, and why would they accept me anyway? My sterling record as a machinist? And let's say I do get in, Joyce, what then? I become the creepy older guy sitting with a roomful of nineteen- and twenty-year-olds. My clothes are different, my face is different. Hell, I probably* smell *different.*

She reached out, touched his knee. Glenn jerked it away.

"Glenn?" she said. God, the sympathy in her liquid brown eyes. "Please tell me what's wrong. Please talk to me."

Sure, he thought. *It's that easy, isn't it? Just tell you everything I feel and admit how much I hate myself. Because beneath the insecurity and the embarrassment and all the other mental baggage, there's something worse. There's guilt, Joyce. Guilt, so thick and stultifying I can hardly stand it. Guilt over what I let myself become, but even more than that, guilt for the way I've treated women.*

I once dated a girl who was nice and caring but not quite cute enough for me to want to show her off around town. So I used her for a while and told myself it was okay, she was having a good time too. And one night after I'd decided it was time to let her fade from my life but hadn't informed her of this phasing out, she asked me, via a cell phone message, to go to the bars with her. I didn't want to, so I said I had plans. She was cool about it like she always was, but she said she'd left her ID at my house and needed to pick it up before she went out with her friends. I knew she and her friends would be going to the same bar I wanted to go to — I wanted to hook up with someone new, of course — and I didn't want her spoiling it. So I pretended I'd never gotten her message, and she stayed home while I went out, got drunk and picked up some girl I never saw again. Really funny, right? But you know the worst part? The part that makes me want to break things and cry out to my younger self, "What the hell is wrong with you?"

The worst part is when I told my dad about what I'd done — good old Fred Kershaw, longtime city councilman and a pillar of this community — do you know what he said? After I told him of how shittily I'd treated that poor girl, he asked me if I'd gotten lucky that night. I told him I had, told him about the woman I'd picked up. He clapped me on the back and said, "Well, I guess it worked out, huh, pal?"

"Will you talk to me?" Joyce asked.

No, I won't talk to you, and I won't tell you the truth. That the only reason I'm well regarded around here is that I've had sex with a lot of women. Some accomplishment, huh? And the quicker I disposed of them, the more people idolised me. No one would admit it, of course, but that's the honest truth. It's embarrassing and shallow and sad. I've capitalised on the twisted values of this twisted little town. And now that I'm a murderer, I finally see how horrible I've been. But I'm afraid I can't escape what I've become.

"Say something," Joyce urged.

Glenn stared at her, knowing he couldn't tell her these things.

What he did say was, "I just realised."

Joyce leaned forward a little, her hand on his knee. "Yes?"

He nodded. "I don't have a date for the reunion tonight."

She watched him, waiting. The vulnerability in her eyes broke his heart.

He went on. "But if you wouldn't mind being seen with a blue-collar worker..."

She coloured. "*Glenn.*"

"Would you go with me?"

"I accept," she said, removing her hand primly. "It's a good thing you asked."

He smiled. "And why is that?"

"You need me to protect you."

He laughed, but when she returned to the whiteboard his smile quickly faded. "From who?"

She eyed him steadily. "Yourself."

★ ★ ★

"This feels frivolous," Savannah said. She knew she was repeating herself, but she couldn't help it. She wanted to be with Jake, who was currently in the bedroom examining Barb's collection of Golden Classics and Little Critters books. For a woman who'd never had children, Barb sure had amassed a sizable array of children's books.

Short Pump leaned over the kitchen island – pearlescent quartz; stylish, like the rest of Barb's house – and fixed her with what she thought of as his earnest, pragmatic gaze. "It's not frivolous, Savannah, it's strategic. Jake's better off here than anywhere else. Garner won't know he's here, so there's nothing to worry about. But even if he did somehow trace us, Jake's got his own armed guard. Where else could he have that?"

Maybe I don't like the idea of Jake needing an armed guard, she thought but didn't say. Because she knew what Short Pump's answer would be, and furthermore, that he'd be right: *It might not be a pleasant concept, Savannah, but it's the reality.*

Still...the reality sucked.

It sucked that she had to attend her tenth reunion with a bunch of people she hardly knew anymore, sucked that she had to carry on the fiction of enjoying herself despite the fact that Lane Cartwright and his men would be monitoring the Roof while the celebrants pretended seven of their number hadn't been slaughtered last weekend.

"You think Weezer will show?" she heard herself asking.

Short Pump shrugged. "Still haven't heard from him."

"He's been too busy at the drive-in."

A shadow seemed to pass over Short Pump's face. "Just because he hasn't called me back doesn't mean he's a killer."

Savannah turned, spoke to Barb, who was moving into the kitchen, a white feather duster clutched in one big hand. "Do you know Weezer?"

Barb nodded. "Well enough."

"And?" Savannah said. "What do you think of him?"

Barb laid the feather duster on the counter. "Not much," she answered.

Short Pump glared at Barb. "What do you have against him? You ever talked to him?"

"Very little," Barb allowed.

"Then how can you—"

"He's a lackey, and lackeys are prone to secret cravings. He follows Glenn Kershaw around, yipping at his heels like a cartoon puppy."

"So?" Short Pump said. "Glenn's better with the ladies than Weezer is. Weezer idolises him for it. So what?"

"There's nothing more dangerous than a bottom feeder," Barb said. "Weezer wants what Glenn has, but hasn't the skill or the looks to get it."

Short Pump hid his hands in his pockets. "Lots of people struggle with confidence."

Barb chuckled without the slightest trace of warmth. "He doesn't lack confidence. The little worm will hit on any woman with a pulse, and the pulse part might be optional."

Short Pump started to protest, but Savannah cut in. "It's true, Short Pump. Weezer's always been sort of creepy."

"That's underselling it," Barb said. "Guy might as well have his hand down his trousers, stroking his pecker while he talks to a woman."

Short Pump glared at Barb. "You act like he's a sex offender."

"I've no doubt he is," Barb answered. "Or wants to be. Now if we're buying the notion that Dave Garner really is a shape-shifter, and we're really buying the theory of what Garner can spread to others, and if Garner truly was at the Roof when the drive-in murders took place, that leaves a handful of suspects: Joyce, who wouldn't hurt a mosquito if it landed on her nose and started to suck; Glenn, who's got a couple redeeming traits even though he chooses to behave like a sex-addicted imbecile—"

"Can't argue with that," Savannah said.

"—and Weezer, the guy no one's heard a peep from in days. That factory where he works? They fired him this morning."

"How do you know that?" Short Pump said.

"I know his boss," Barb said. "Weezer won't answer his phone or his door. Only reason they know he's not dead is his truck's been seen around town a couple times."

Short Pump gestured feebly. "I know it was Garner at the bonfire."

"Maybe it was," Barb said. "But we know it wasn't him at the drive-in. It's got to be Weezer."

"What about Melody Bridwell?" Savannah asked.

"I didn't forget Melody," Barb said. "But I'm not sure what to make of her. Never have. There's something off about that situation." She looked like she'd tasted something sour.

"What's wrong?" Savannah asked.

"You heard from her lately?" Barb asked.

Savannah gave her a dour look. "We don't exactly run in the same circles."

"Don't be a snob."

"I'm not—"

"And stop stalling," Barb said. She glanced at her watch. "It's after nine already. You two are the ones Garner wants. If you're not there soon, he might come looking for you."

Savannah shifted from foot to foot. "What about Weezer?"

Barb said, "He'll be at the reunion."

"Not necessarily," Savannah asked.

Barb tilted her head. "Will there be women at the Roof?"

"Of course."

"He'll be there."

Short Pump said, "She's right, Savannah. We better get over there."

Savannah's gut was a tight, tingling ball. She moved toward the living room. "At least let me say goodnight to Jakers."

Short Pump said something, but Savannah ignored it. She hated this, dammit, hated being forced into a situation she hadn't created. It wasn't her fault Mike had been so careless, wasn't her fault Garner's daughter was dead. She considered just taking Jake and getting the hell out of Lakeview.

To collect herself, she slipped into the half bath off the living room and shut the door. She didn't want to cry, but she didn't want to hold it in either. But the way she was feeling now was eerily similar to the way she'd felt six years ago when she'd learned she was pregnant.

Her parents had been emotionally distant in the first place, her mom addicted to prescription drugs, her dad forever disappointed she wasn't a boy. The only time he'd shown any interest in her was when she'd dated Mike, and though she hadn't recognised it at the time, looking back it was clear that her father had viewed Mike as the son he'd never had. When Mike had dumped Savannah and fizzled out as a baseball player, what little interest her dad had shown in her dwindled to nothing. In contrast, her mom didn't change appreciably when Mike dumped Savannah, instead remained sequestered inside her medicated cocoon, free of human emotions and entanglements.

But her mother and father both changed when they learned of Savannah's pregnancy. Oh, how they changed.

Her mom was a secretary, her father a sometimes-usher at the Apostolic Christian church in downtown Lakeview. Savannah had attended the church her whole life, had considered the old brick building a safe haven.

But when she'd announced to her parents she was pregnant, they forbade her from setting foot in the church again.

This was after a shitstorm of shouting and condemnation, a savage tirade by her father punctuated by wildly out-of-character declarations from her mother. Demands that she have an abortion, leave Lakeview, even that she have her last name changed so her parents wouldn't be associated with her bastard child.

That's what they called Jake. *The bastard.* Savannah had been so taken aback by the word that she'd simply gaped at them. She'd read old novels in which the children of unmarried women were referred to by that ugly term, but she'd never considered the possibility that people in the twenty-first century would employ it too, least of all her parents.

But use it they did, and even after Savannah began to show, they refused to associate with her. As she neared her due date, as she endured that terrible twenty-seven hours of labour, as she went through the emergency C-section...she went through all of it alone. Or mostly alone. Barb had done what she could during the ordeal. Short Pump had helped when she'd let him. A couple of her girlfriends had pitched in with meals after Jake was born. But mostly – emotionally, at least – she'd gone through it alone.

Her parents moved away when Jake was four months old.

They'd never met him.

Savannah gazed up into her reflection and was surprised to note the tears hadn't come. Maybe she was stronger than she thought.

Or maybe she was so tired of this shit that she was beyond tears.

Making sure the door was locked, she hitched up her blue sundress, eased down on the toilet and peed.

She refused to give up now. She'd survived the bonfire, survived her parents' callousness.

She'd survive this goddamned reunion too.

Savannah wiped, rucked up her panties and flushed. She washed her hands and went into Barb's bedroom to see her son.

The best thing in her life.

Jake didn't look up when she entered the room. He was sprawled out on top of the covers, a board book called *Hairy Maclary* propped open on his chest.

"How's my boy?" she asked, easing down to face him.

He didn't answer, only continued to examine the book.

She reached out, pushed his hair behind his ears. "Is that a good story?"

"It's about a dog," he said without looking up. He frowned, pointed. "What's this word?"

Savannah craned her head to see the book. "'Bumptious'," she said.

"What's that?"

She studied his smooth brow, his soft cheeks. "It means he's rowdy. He likes to bump into things and cause trouble."

Jake grinned.

She reached down, tickled his armpit. "Do we know anybody like that?"

Jake squirmed, grinning widely now. "Short Pump."

"Not Short Pump," she said, tickling with both hands now. "I'm talking about *you*."

Laughing, he wriggled to free himself. "I'm not bumptious!"

"Yes, you are," she said, laughing too.

It ended with her relenting and hugging him to her. He pretended not to be able to breathe, but his struggles were feigned. When she finally drew back, he was staring up at her, his hair mussed and his eyes shining happily. "How long will you be gone?"

"I don't know. Are you worried about staying with Aunt Barb?"

"She's nice. But when will you be back?"

"You'll be asleep by then," she said, finger-combing his hair. "But I'll be here when you wake up." She leaned over to kiss him.

"What if you aren't?"

Savannah tightened. She could see the incipient panic in his eyes. "Honey? What's wrong?"

He hesitated. "Is it true about the people dying?"

Be calm, she told herself, though her heart was galloping. *If you're calm, he will be too.*

"Yes, honey. At the bonfire, people died."

He frowned. "I thought it was at the movies."

She swallowed, chiding herself for divulging too much. "Well, yes. There were…" She exhaled shuddering breath. "Everything's fine now, honey, so we don't need to worry—"

"Then why aren't we staying at our house?"

Would you quit being so perceptive? she wanted to ask. She riffled through a half-dozen responses, but they each boiled down to two unhelpful options: either tell the truth and scare the hell out of him or lie to him and claim that nothing was wrong.

"Honey," she said, taking his hand. "You're safe. That's all you need to know."

Jake watched her with large eyes. She thought of his father, wondered for the thousandth time why she'd never told him he was Jake's dad.

"And you'll come back?" he asked.

"I promise."

She kissed his head and left the room.

Her tears didn't come until they were on the way to Beach Land.

★ ★ ★

Barb poured her coffee and wondered what kind of person Dave Garner was. Or rather, the kind of person he'd been. She'd never studied shape-shifting before – she'd always been more of a nonfiction, biography type of reader – but she wondered if he'd been a decent person before the change. He obviously loved his daughter, so there was that. And he was heartbroken enough to go on this vengeful rampage. Barb couldn't respect a cold-blooded killer, but she did understand how much a heart could hurt. Dave Garner had obviously known pain. Still did, or he'd have given up his mission by now.

Barb walked into the living room and there was Garner, sitting on the couch. She wasn't a person who startled easily, but she came very close to dropping her coffee mug. As it was, the mug joggled slightly in her grip, the steaming hot liquid searing her knuckles. But she didn't react. At least not much. Her lips formed a tight line and her fingers clenched the ceramic handle hard enough to crush it to powder, but she didn't cry out and she didn't show Garner how much the burn was hurting her.

He still seemed to pick up on her thoughts. He was leaning back on the couch, a knowing grin on his face. She didn't know what she expected from Garner, but what she didn't expect was this:

In almost every respect, he looked normal. Khaki pants, short-sleeved white button-down shirt, brown loafers with light tan socks and the merest bit of pale shin showing between the cuffs of his pants and his socks. Interestingly enough, Garner's legs appeared hairless.

But his face…that's what was bothering her. It appeared a bit formless. Hearing Duane tell it, she'd expected sharkish white teeth, protuberant cheekbones, a harsh, saturnine brow. But Garner featured none of those things. In fact, other than his pale blue eyes, Garner's face bore no distinguishing characteristics at all. He wasn't fat exactly – Barb was carrying as much weight as he was – but he was an imposing presence, even lounging there on the sofa.

To collect her thoughts and give her racing heartbeat a chance to decelerate, she placed the coffee on one of the bookcase shelves and took her time about it. *Breathe*, she told herself. *Remember to breathe. Assess the situation.*

Her back to him, Barb did.

The couch was about halfway between where she stood and her bedroom door. Which meant he could get to Jake faster than she could. He could also bar her route to the kitchen, where there were knives; her bedroom, where there were guns; or the driveway, where her Subaru Outback was parked.

In short, the situation looked bleak.

She knew she had to turn around, had to face him again, because not to do so was to admit that she was frightened of him, and that was tactical suicide. Garner's grin had communicated how accustomed he was to intimidating people, how much he revelled in their terror.

So turn around, she told herself. *Turn around and show him you're not afraid.*

She faced him and saw how he'd changed and she was very afraid indeed.

The alterations were subtle. So subtle she supposed that many observers would have missed them. But not Barb. There was hair on his legs now. Not a lot, just enough of it to suggest his bestial self. And his features were sharper. Almost aquiline.

She knew he was waiting for her to speak, but she had no idea what to say. He'd broken into her house. He'd surprised the hell out of her, and he knew it. She couldn't very well demand he leave because such a demand would be met with derision. Nor would threatening him help her situation. Or Jake's.

Garner finally spoke. "You're the one they chose."

There was no point pretending she didn't understand his meaning. "Savannah knows I care about her boy."

Garner spread his arms on the couch back, as though cuddling a pair of invisible concubines. "You'd know all about that? Having a child?"

"I won't let anything happen to Jake."

His eyebrows rose. "Oh, you won't?" He nodded, studying the darkened windows. "Well, sometimes we can't control what happens to our children, can we?"

"You won't get sympathy from me," she said.

He glanced at her, ran his tongue around his mouth. "Is that right? I suppose you don't think losing a child is much of a tragedy."

Barb felt the heat build at the base of her neck, forced herself to let it go. "You killed how many people at that bonfire, Garner? Seven? That's fourteen parents who'll never see their children again."

Garner looked away. "I didn't start this."

"No, a reckless driver started it. He was a screwup, and he took your daughter from you, and you killed him for it."

"That's right."

"And then you went about ten steps further and slaughtered innocent people." She noticed his forearms, which were hairier now. And the hue of his skin, which had darkened a tick. "You maybe even spread whatever the hell it is you have."

He chuckled, a jagged, deranged sound. "We are a highly developed species. You make it sound like a disease."

"Sadism is a disease."

He looked at her with renewed interest. "You think so?"

"You're a jackal."

"Why not appeal to my better nature? Maybe I'll spare you if I see the error of my ways."

"I don't need sparing."

Garner threw back his head and laughed. When he regarded her again, he was wiping a tear from his eye. "You really think you're going to survive the next five minutes? I crushed your cell phone and severed the landline. No one's coming to help you."

Barb didn't want to break eye contact, so she riffled through snapshots of this room in her mind. Behind her was the bookcase. If she were a packrat or maybe more kitschy, like her customers, there'd have been two dozen pieces of bric-a-brac on the shelves. Plates she could break into shards, pewter statues with which she could brain Garner. Ceramic sculptures of birds she could hurl at his grinning face. But Barb hated having the spines of her books covered up by useless junk and therefore kept the shelves clear. She could select one of her heaviest tomes – the family Bible she'd inherited from her grandma maybe; that thing weighed at least ten pounds – and try to bludgeon him with it, but that would mean getting close to him, and close to him was the last place she wanted to be.

Garner's smile grew triumphant. "It seems you've run out of words."

Barb said nothing, shifted her inner eye to what lay to her right. That was where the TV was. No hope there, unless she planned to hoist the flat screen off the wall, trudge over to where he sat and drop the damned thing on his head. There was a potted plant – a miniature palm tree – but that was too heavy. Maybe she could grasp the tree by the trunk and clobber him with the root ball. Or maybe she could grow antlers and gore him to death.

Shit.

"They're coming, you know."

Barb's attention snapped back to Garner. "Who's coming?"

"The Three," he said.

"That some sort of boy band?"

"I wouldn't joke about them."

"Why not?" she asked, glancing to her left. There were some old family pictures on the wall. The largest one, taken when she was an infant, featured her whole family.

"Because," he said, "the Three have been here longer than any of us. And they are vengeful beyond anyone's worst nightmares."

"So you guys kill," she said. "And you kill some more. Sounds like a highly developed species to me."

"I'd expect someone like you to scoff. Fallow and plagued with a masculine body. I'll bet the other kids made fun of you on the playground, didn't they?"

"They tried."

"We enjoy the taste of children," he said.

That stopped her. She didn't want to say it, but it came out anyway. "You're a vile excuse for a man."

"I'm not a man, Miss Callahan. Not anymore. And I do see the irony in it, my taste for young flesh. But there's something about its purity that appeals to the refined palate."

"How many kids have you killed?" she asked, her voice going hoarse. Anger was good, Barb decided. Anger might endow her with courage, and she needed courage right now. Anything to chip away at the mind-freezing fear. "How many children have suffered because of you, you ugly cocksucker?"

"Many," Garner answered. "Before my Cynthia was born, I killed indiscriminately. It necessitated more than one relocation for our little family. After Cynthia was taken from me, I killed her mother in a rage. It was her fault Cynthia was out driving that night. But that's because my wife was an idiot. You see, Cynthia and her mother weren't lycanthropes. My son was, though I haven't seen him in years."

"I don't give a shit about your family."

"Then why don't we bring this to a conclusion?"

"Fine with me."

Barb seized her hardback copy of *The Brothers Karamazov* and hurled it at the family picture. The spine nailed it dead centre, the glass splintered.

Garner launched himself off the couch.

If Barb hadn't moved when she did, Garner would've crushed her against the bookcase. But she was already halfway to the broken glass when Garner slammed into the bookcase and sent three dozen books tumbling to the floor. The whole case would've overturned on top of Garner if she hadn't bolted it to the wall as a safety measure in case any little kids tried to climb up onto it. That's what she got for being so safety conscious.

Barb reached the spill of glass shards. Behind her, she saw with a fleeting backward glance, Garner was snarling and scrambling around to face her. Bastard had disarranged half the books on her case. He had also altered appearance dramatically. She knew exactly what a shape-shifter was, had in theory accepted all Short Pump and Savannah had told her. But actually seeing Garner transform was a different matter entirely. As her fingers closed around a long, thin shard of glass, Barb realised she was more frightened than she'd ever been in her life.

No time to stall. Barb spun, crouched with the blade pointed up. Garner was coming at her. He was a good seven feet tall now, his eyes no longer pale blue but an incandescent yellow. His maw was wide open and crammed with teeth as sharp as rapiers. His claws were three inches long. Yellow, ancient-looking. They were reaching back to swipe at her.

Barb couldn't allow him to get close. He was only six feet away now, and if he got any nearer, he'd simply shred her like pulled pork. The shard of glass felt absurd in her hand, and she was dripping blood from grasping the sharp edge. She needed a gun, but the guns were in the bedroom with Jake, locked in a safe at the rear of her closet, and this wasn't how she'd imagined it. Garner had taken her by surprise in her own home, and she was going to die if something didn't change. She was going to—

"Aunt Barb?" a voice asked.

Barb turned and saw Jake in the doorway of her bedroom.

Four feet from her, the Garner-thing halted, glanced at Jake. Its canine features attenuated in a look of hideous longing.

Barb slashed at its eyes.

The shard was thick, so rather than snapping in half, the wickedly sharp edge split the leathery skin at the Garner-thing's temple, sheared right through his eyeball, and slit deeply into the bridge of his snout.

The Garner-thing bellowed.

"Get under the bed, Jake!" she shouted, and made to dash past the bellowing beast. But a hairy arm flashed out, its paw smashing into the side of her head and propelling her toward the tall casement window.

Barb was dazed, but not too dazed to notice how Jake was still standing there in his red Spiderman pyjamas, how Garner was recovering from the shock of being blinded in one eye. Though hidden from her view, she could tell by the Garner-thing's posture how fixated it was on Jake. In pain, yes, but still intent on tasting of the little boy's flesh.

Barb yelled, "Your daughter deserved to die!"

The werewolf turned slowly toward her, a look of fathomless loathing on its blood-drenched face.

"You failed!" she shouted. "It's your fault she's dead!"

The werewolf sprang at her. Barb stretched out her arms, as if accepting the beast in a lover's embrace, and as the creature's incredible weight crashed against her, she pivoted, heaving the beast over her massive hip and allowing herself to fly forward with its momentum. Its claws sank into her sides, its teeth into her shoulder. But then they hit the casement window together, their combined weight shattering the glass and casting them in a tangled mass toward the mulch bed outside her house. Barb felt glass nicking her face, her hands, but the werewolf absorbed the worst of it. It was squalling, the glass having no doubt lacerated its back in a dozen places. They hit the ground, and Barb immediately shoved away from the creature. She thought she'd break its death grip on her, and for a moment she did. Barb had just landed in the dewy grass and begun to gain her feet when a taloned hand lashed out, swiped at her lower leg. White-hot agony blazed in her calf muscle, and the leg threatened to buckle. Barb shifted her weight to her good leg and lurched forward. She wanted to either beat the werewolf to the Outback or return to the house, where she might be able to hide Jake and retrieve her guns. But a whir of movement behind her told her she'd never be able to outrun the beast, especially not with a bum leg. She glanced around frantically, realising she hadn't really improved their situation at all, had only made it easier for the beast to kill her.

She almost stumbled over the shepherd's hook. Four-and-a-half feet tall, the black steel rod ordinarily supported a hanging plant this time of year. But she'd been busy lately, and there was nothing hanging there now. Barb jerked up on the rod, heard the chuff of the werewolf's breath behind her. The steel hook jerked loose.

She pivoted and brought the shepherd's hook around as hard as she could. It was a desperate move – if the creature were too far away or right on top of her, the blow would accomplish nothing – but for the first time since Garner sullied her house with his presence, luck was with her. The curved bar bashed the creature on the side of the head with a dull, meaty crunch.

The werewolf went down.

Barb didn't hesitate. She straddled its muscled body and drove the double tines of the steel base straight into its chest. The tines only sank in about three inches, but werewolf or not, double stab wounds to the chest would have an effect.

The werewolf was flailing on the ground beneath her. Its clawed fingers encountered the shepherd's hook, but before it could dislodge it, Barb raised a foot and stood on the base's crossbar. The tines sank in another inch. The werewolf roared.

As she shoved the tines in deeper, she considered making a dash for her bedroom to fetch her shotgun. But that would draw the werewolf inside, and her overpowering instinct was to get the creature as far away from Jake as possible.

Barb sensed Jake watching her from the shattered living room window. "Get back in the bedroom," she shouted, "or I'll tell your mom you were a bad listener!"

Jake didn't move.

Smart kid, she decided as she set off toward her Outback. *He knows an empty threat when he hears it.*

Barb's keys weren't in the ignition, but she kept a spare under the floor mat. She climbed into the car, cringing at the pain in her flayed calf. She bent, worked her fingers under the rubber floor mat, which was not easy in the slightest since her feet were in the way, and more importantly, her bleeding calf was in the way, not to mention how violently her fingers were shaking.

A ghastly thought occurred to her.

What if the creature had already extricated the shepherd's hook?

What if Garner was going for Jake?

With a moan, Barb jammed her fingers under the mat, located the cold, hard shape of the key. She sat up, fitted the key into the ignition, and fired up the Outback. When she twisted on her headlamps and the spill of amber illuminated the side yard, she saw the werewolf had made it to one knee, was sliding the steel tines out of its chest.

Barb thrust the Outback into gear, stomped on the accelerator. The vehicle grabbed the driveway immediately. The werewolf rose, the shepherd's hook held aloft like a trident, but the Outback was rocketing forward, bearing down on the beast. Barb worried the werewolf might leap into the air, perform some otherworldly feat of gymnastics, but then her bumper was slamming the beast into the house, where the brick fireplace protruded from the white aluminium façade. She was doing maybe twenty-five when she slammed the beast, and when her front end blasted the siding and the brick, Barb was whipsawed straight into the steering column. The airbag didn't go off – fucking thing – so her forehead struck the windshield. The glass there spiderwebbed and the Outback rebounded a few feet.

Blood from her forehead dribbled into her eyes, but she could still make out the werewolf slumped against the house. The Outback had badly damaged the creature – its front was slicked with blood – but the slight shelter provided by the alcove where the chimney jutted from the siding had perhaps spared it from being crushed to death.

Barb's engine stalled, a curling ribbon of smoke oozing from beneath the hood. She reached down, twisted the key. Reluctantly, almost as though it were angry at her for treating it so roughly, the Outback grumbled to life.

The beast looked up at her. In the bloody, leathery countenance she detected no sign of Dave Garner.

Barb stood on the accelerator. The Outback lurched forward and crashed into the werewolf's bulging thighs. The impact brought its head whipping down at the hood, where it bowed the thin metal and shot a bright splatter of blood over the windshield. Barb kept the accelerator down, the Outback's tires grinding her lawn but grabbing enough purchase to keep the werewolf pinned. The beast writhed against her, growling and scoring the hood with its razor talons. An intermittent tap broke through the revving of the engine, and when Barb armed enough blood out of her eyes to see better she realised it was the shepherd's hook, still clutched in the werewolf's right hand. She had just noticed it when the beast reared back, face contorted in a rictus of rage, and thrust the shepherd's hook at her. The steel tines punctured the windshield easily, and before Barb could raise her arms to defend herself, the spikes stabbed her in the chest.

The pain was overwhelming. She didn't know precisely where the tines had pierced her flesh, but she had an idea the wounds were on the right side of her body rather than the left. Not fatal, hopefully, but damned painful.

She shot a look over the hood at the werewolf, which was baring its teeth in a taunt. The werewolf sank both sets of talons into the hood metal and began to hoist itself out. Grimacing, Barb slid the tines out of her chest. The spikes jerked free of her body, but the sound of blood slopping into her lap reminded her of someone who's knocked over a water bottle and allowed its contents to dribble all over the floor. With a last shove, Barb expelled the shepherd's hook from the mangled windshield. It clattered on the hood next to the werewolf.

The beast didn't appear to notice. With a convulsive lurch, it yanked itself up six or eight inches, bringing its killing hands closer to her windshield. The car continued to rev against the side of the house, but the beast was squirming out of its trap. It sank its talons into the hood just below the windshield wipers and dragged itself forward. Barb could see its bloodied midsection and thighs haemorrhaging over the savaged blue steel of the hood, but the creature didn't seem fazed at all. If anything, it seemed to be growing stronger. Barb, meanwhile, had a pair of goddamned holes in her chest and felt like screaming hell. If she didn't do something soon, the beast would climb right into the car with her, and then there'd be no one to protect Jake.

It was this prospect that galvanised her, demanded she take control of the situation. Wincing, Barb yanked back on the gearshift, reversed into the yard. The lawn seemed smooth whenever she walked on it, but her Outback bounced like a moon rover as she retreated from the beast. For a moment she was sure the werewolf would follow her into the yard. She even toyed with the notion of driving toward the main road in an attempt to draw it away from Jake. But after a moment's hesitation, the creature crawled toward the shattered living room window.

She wondered briefly if her neighbours were hearing any of this. Sure, she lived on ten acres down a dead-end lane, but it wasn't like this was Siberia. Surely someone had heard the Outback crashing into the house or the werewolf's roars. Barb reversed another twenty yards and brought the Outback to a halt. The distance between the chimney and the window was only about fifteen feet, but the werewolf's entire lower half had been torn and crushed by the Outback. Barb figured she had time. If she made her move now.

Barb slid the gearshift into drive, nudged the Outback forward, and rapidly picked up speed. The creature was maybe eight feet from where it had started. But not yet to the window. She wouldn't let it make it there. Though it hurt like hell to do so, Barb reached back, snagged the seatbelt. She clicked it into place and barreled straight at the beast, which had ceased crawling and was attempting to rise. Barb had a horrible vision of smashing right through the side of the house and injuring little Jake in the resulting spray of wood and sheetrock, but it was too late to worry about that now. She was doing more than thirty when the Outback crashed into the house, but even as she was catapulted forward, the seatbelt slicing into her flesh but the stupid airbag still not deploying, she knew something had gone wrong. The beast had gotten as low as it could before she crashed into it. As the Outback rebounded, Barb strained to see the base of the house. There was a great deal of dust. Chunks of masonry and several strips of mangled white siding. But no werewolf. *Oh my God*, she thought. *It's gone for Jake! It somehow made it to the broken window and pulled itself inside.* She was disengaging the seatbelt when she became aware of the scratching sound.

It came from beneath the car.

Barb swallowed, new fear dousing her like a cold March rain. The thing had managed to climb under the Outback and was clawing at the chassis to get at her.

She turned the key, but the Outback wouldn't start. The steam rising from the engine seeped through the ruined windshield. Barb's eyes watered, and she began to cough. She'd have to get out of the car, but she couldn't take any chances. She needed a weapon.

No, two weapons.

Like every driver in the western hemisphere with half a brain, she kept a crowbar in case of a flat. Additionally, she kept a hunting knife – her dad's hunting knife – in the glove box in case she got into a tight scrape.

Something told her that if this scrape got any tighter, a knife would be only marginally more useful than an overripe banana. Those claws were lethal.

The scratching got louder. Was the Garner-thing stuck?

If so, maybe she really could get her and Jake out of here alive. She had the four-wheeler.

As Barb retrieved the buck knife and the crowbar, the scratching grew more pronounced. Could the werewolf rip through the underbelly of the Outback?

Barb straightened in her seat, and a wave of dizziness drowsed over her. She jerked her head, heart hammering. Of all the options available to her, fainting was the least appealing. Fainting meant death for her and Jake.

Swallowing the sick lump of fear in her throat, Barb opened the door. She scooted over to the left edge of the seat, thinking she could avoid the creature's grasping talons if she stepped out far enough from the car, and that's when the hairy arm shot out and seized her ankle. Barb gasped, pawed at the steering wheel to anchor herself, but the beast simply yanked her straight out the door. Barb flopped down face-first, the crowbar pinned beneath her and the buck knife tumbling into the grass. She made a grab for the knife, got her fingers on the handle, but lost her grip as the werewolf dragged her under the car. Its talons sank deep into her ankle. Though the light beneath the car was poor, she could see well enough how the thing's right arm had gotten wedged between the muffler and the chassis, how if she'd gotten out on the passenger's side she might have avoided its grasp.

Most of all she noticed the hatred in the werewolf's eyes, the insatiable desire for revenge.

The werewolf dragged her nearer. The pain in her ankle was beyond anything she could have imagined. Mind-destroying pain.

Her twitching foot neared the werewolf's mouth.

Barb grasped the crowbar with both hands, bent at the waist, and jabbed its chiselled end at the beast's hand. The chisel point sank in, the werewolf roaring with pain. Straining, Barb worked the chisel point around, digging into the creature's tendons.

Its fingers came loose, and Barb jerked away. She clambered toward the moonlight, acutely aware of the werewolf behind her, sure at any moment it would seize her ankle again. It grabbed the cuff of her jeans, but she pulled free. She writhed forward on elbows and knees, her bloody leg trailing behind her. She shot a look back and saw the werewolf thrashing wildly, the ugly bastard's movements so vigorous that the muffler pipe was coming loose.

So was the werewolf's arm.

Barb had just cleared the underside of the Outback when she heard the beast thump down, detached from the car.

Barb pushed up on her good leg, dove forward, and seized the buck knife's handle. Before she could even roll over with it, the beast was hurtling from beneath the car, its hungry talons outstretched. Barb jerked the buck knife up, slashed at the wolf's hands, and felt the fine blade zip through two of the beast's fingers. Screeching in pain, it crashed down on her, but Barb immediately shot up a knee, nailed it in the testicles, and heaved it over her head with her hands and knees. The beast did a tilting somersault, spun and snarled at her on all fours, but Barb was already on her knees, the buck knife swinging in a tight strike at its mouth. The eight-inch blade ripped through each side of the creature's mouth, twin spurts of blood drenching the front of her body. The thing's eyes squeezed tight and it let loose with an almost human bray of agony. It was holding its mangled fingers to its mangled mouth, and that exposed its throat. Barb sank the knife there, driving the large blade to the hilt, and jerked down. The knife snicked all the way to the thing's breastbone, and blood gushed out like a scarlet spillway. The hot blood sprayed over Barb's knuckles. The beast sank its talons into her shoulders, made to push her away, but Barb dug in with the toes of her sneakers, twisted the buck knife, and started sawing with it in the direction of the creature's heart. She was astounded at how much blood was gushing from the creature's chest. Her arms were red to the shoulders, her shoulders bloody from the thing's claws. The beast's blood painted her face and coated the inside of her mouth. In the back of her mind, she wondered about infection. But that was assuming a lot, assuming most of all she would live, which was very much in doubt.

She had to end this.

The beast was still fighting her off. Its swipes were weak now, drastically less effective than they'd been a few minutes ago, but it was still digging at her flesh with its scythe-like talons, still striping her skin and allowing more avenues for her blood to leave her body. With a cry, Barb wrenched the knife out of the beast's torso, reared back, and jabbed the blade into its remaining eye. The buck knife didn't sink in to the hilt, but it came close. The beast forgot all about its other wounds and tumbled back, squalling. Barb clambered through the grass, scrabbled in the darkness for the crowbar. If werewolves really regenerated – and all the evidence pointed toward that very phenomenon – she might not have time to retrieve her .44 from the gun safe.

She heard Jake call out to her, but she gave no answer, didn't want him to think he could venture outside. Besides, it was all she could do to stay conscious. She didn't trust herself to form an intelligible response.

Her fingers happened on the cold, slick crowbar. She plucked it from the ground, rose, saw the werewolf had extricated the buck knife. But rather than coming for her, it had cast the knife aside, was attempting to crawl away.

Bastard, Barb thought.

She raised a knee and dropped onto the small of the creature's back. It went down, made to roll over, but before it could she drove the chisel point into its back, straight at its heart.

Her aim was true. The chisel point skewered the beast's heart and punctured the flesh of its chest. The thing's arms and legs splayed out, its torso convulsing, its head thrashing in the bloody grass as if it could escape death.

Barb felt her expression twitch into a savage smile. She stepped over, retrieved the buck knife, sat down on the creature's back, and fitted the blade under its larynx. With one hand she yanked back the beast's wiry black hair, and with the other she began sawing back and forth through the beast's skin and the tissue beneath. She heard the whistle of its breath now, the windpipe ruptured. Soon she was hacking through its spinal cord. The stench was awful, the yard drenched with gore. When the head came free, she staggered to her feet, lurched toward the garage. The main thing, she decided, was to remain conscious. If she could get Jake to safety, she'd be able to convince everybody. But to do that she had to finish this the right way.

She moved through the side garage door and shuffled through the darkness toward the workbench. What she needed was under there. Once she'd gotten what she was looking for, she moved to the front corner of the garage and activated the overhead door. Moonlight spilled through the gap, the whole front of the garage's interior now aglow. She moved to the four-wheeler, arranged her parcel on the back with the bungee cords she kept there. After a moment's debate, she snatched her machete from the workbench and eased it down the back of her waistband. She guided the four-wheeler out of the garage and over to the front porch, where Jake now stood. She let the front tires bump the bottom step and cut the engine.

"Is that you, Aunt Barb?"

She chuckled, but it hurt like hell. Drenched with blood and badly injured, she imagined she looked pretty wretched.

"Hold on a second," she said. She bent at the waist, hands on knees, and rode out another wave of lightheadedness.

Jake waited, his eyes huge, his red Spiderman pyjamas making him look even younger than his five years.

"You know where bedroom closet is?" she asked.

Jake shook his head.

"I need you to support me while I get some stuff out of there."

Jake didn't answer. She realised his eyes were fixed on something beyond her. She didn't need to turn around to know he was staring at the headless body.

"Look at me, honey," she said.

Jake continued to stare, his face whiter than her aluminium siding.

"*Look at me,*" she snapped, then felt a rush of guilt at the way he shrank from her.

She swallowed. Man, she was precariously close to passing out. "Jake, that thing I killed...the thing in the yard. There are more of them. They're going to—"

She stopped, debated how to phrase it, then decided bluntness was best, even if it scared the shit out of the child. Better for him to know how serious this was.

"They're going after your mom—" Jake began to whimper, but she pressed on, "—and we have to stop them."

Jake made to move down the steps.

"Hold it," she said. "I need you to do something first."

"Aunt Barb?" he asked.

"Help me up the steps."

"Where is its head?"

"Never mind that. Are you listening to me?"

He nodded.

"Here," she said. "Take my arm."

He did. They moved up the steps, through the house and into the bedroom. It took forever, and a couple times she snapped at him for getting distracted. She felt bad for being so brusque with him, but dammit, those creatures – the Three, Garner had called them – might already be at the Roof.

Eventually, she retrieved her .38 Smith & Wesson and her shotgun. Not trusting Jake to carry either, she instructed him to walk behind her while she hobbled her way back through the house and to the four-wheeler.

"Here," Barb said, hauling Jake up with one arm so he could sit in front of her. "We're getting you to a safe place."

"Are we getting help?" Jake asked.

She nodded. "The police."

"For Mommy?"

She nodded. "And Short Pump."

As Barb fired up the four-wheeler and they began to roll onto the lane, Jake said, "He likes to be called Duane."

"Is that right?" she said, picking up speed. "We'll call him Duane then."

CHAPTER TWENTY-FIVE

Duane had never felt more like getting drunk. He knew this was the worst possible time to do so, and of course he wasn't going to drink *too* much, but the need for something to relax him, the need for something to take the shake out of his hands...God, he could use a couple shots of whiskey and a good tall glass of beer.

Savannah was faring little better. Oh, she was smiling and chatting with their old classmates, and to them she probably looked the same as she always did. Amiable. Confident. Unhurried and graceful in every gesture. But Duane could tell by the tightness of her smile, the robotic way she nodded. Even the way she stood there was different. Like at any moment someone would seize her from behind.

A woman he hadn't seen in a while, Adriana Carlino, approached them. One of their classmates, the girlfriend of Robbie Bridwell, Adriana reminded Duane of that bald eagle on *The Muppet Show*. Known for getting into several fistfights in high school, her face a perpetual scowl, if Adriana had ever been in a good mood, Duane sure as hell had never witnessed it. But for reasons he couldn't at first identify, the sight of her this evening filled him with foreboding. Then she opened her mouth, and he understood why.

"Where the hell is Melody?" Adriana asked.

Adriana was a sullen bitch, but there was something in her expression he'd never seen before. Jealousy? Fear?

"You'd know better than we would," Savannah said.

Adriana's eyes narrowed to slits. "I haven't seen Robbie either. He hasn't answered my texts, and nobody answers the door even though their cars are in the driveway."

Duane's throat went dry.

It doesn't mean anything, he thought.

"When's the last time you heard from Melody?" he asked.

"Why do you think I'm asking you?" she shot back. "You know her better than I do. Melody's always talking about how nice you are."

Duane tried to hide how surprised he was.

"Easy, tiger," Savannah said.

Duane was amazed to see a trace of jealousy in her expression.

Adriana rolled her eyes. "Spare me. Anyway, I haven't seen her since the bonfire."

"I hope she's okay," Duane said.

Adriana yawned. "Whatever. You guys seen Jessica yet?"

"Jessica Clinton?" Savannah asked.

Adriana stared at her. "How many best friends named Jessica do I have?"

A numbness had started to seep through him. "What about her?"

"I texted her all afternoon, and she never responded. We were supposed to ride together."

"Did you go by her house?"

She snorted. "No thanks. She would've put me to work babysitting."

With that, Adriana walked away.

Duane and Savannah exchanged a look. Adriana went over and joined a trio of idiots – Billy Kramer, Colton Crane and Randy Murray – and began talking to them. Occasionally, Adriana or one of the guys would glance in Duane and Savannah's direction, baleful looks on their faces, but Duane wasn't in any mood to ask them why.

Duane looked toward the stage, where Dance Naked was struggling to cover Bon Jovi's "Dead or Alive". The lead singer kept cracking on the high notes, but the lead guitarist's harmonies were even weaker. He sounded like a dying tomcat. Duane was about to say something to get a laugh out of Savannah when someone tapped him on the shoulder. Duane turned and there was Weezer.

Or the person he used to think of as Weezer.

Because though this guy looked like Weezer, at least in the general details, it was like the difference between a living man and a wax sculpture. The new Weezer looked more at ease in his own skin. And it wasn't just the clothes – which were far more stylish than Weezer had ever worn before – it was his posture, his smile.

And the rest of his face, which looked totally unmarred.

Weezer looked around. "No Glenn yet?"

Duane glanced at Savannah, saw the dead way she was watching Weezer. To Savannah, at least, there was no doubt who was responsible for the drive-in killings and the disappearances of those two young women.

Weezer evidently noticed Savannah's scrutiny. "What's wrong, sweetie? Not feeling well?"

"Your face," she said.

His smile brightened. "Amazing what a little reconstructive surgery can accomplish, isn't it?"

"It was five days ago."

He shrugged. "Good doctors." His smile didn't waver.

Duane put a hand on Savannah's back. "Let's get a drink."

Weezer stepped sideways to block their way. "What kind of treatment is that? I nearly die, and after avoiding me all week, you two act like you don't know me?"

Duane studied Weezer's unscarred face. It was uncanny. If he needed any proof of their conjectures regarding lycanthropy, here it was. "I called you a dozen times, Weezer."

Weezer shook his head dolefully. "I never got any calls."

"And emailed you half as many."

Weezer turned away, favoured the crowd with a comprehensive glance. "Lots of faces missing tonight. Glenn. Jessica." His lips formed a ghastly grin.

Duane tensed. "What do you know about Jessica?"

"Pretty girl," Weezer said softly.

"What did you do?" Savannah demanded.

On stage, Dance Naked began to abuse Kiss's "Lick It Up".

"Good song," Weezer said. "Let me know when Glenn and that librarian bitch show up. I need to talk to them."

Weezer made to move through the crowd, but Savannah seized his arm. "Don't talk that way about Joyce."

Weezer eyed the hand clamped over his forearm. When his eyes flicked up to Savannah's, Duane felt his heart stutter.

Weezer's eyes were flecked with yellow.

"Let him go," Duane said.

Leering at Savannah, Weezer said, "I always did want to fuck you. I think I'll do it tonight."

Savannah released his arm. "You son of a bitch."

"Why don't you defend her honour, Duane?"

Duane tried to swallow, but he had no spit. "Say you're sorry."

"But I'm not," Weezer said. He stepped closer, his eyes roving up and down Savannah's body. Lingering on the cleavage showing above her royal-blue sundress. "I think I'll tear me off a piece of this ass right now."

"You're a filthy little coward," Savannah said.

Weezer's eyes lifted from Savannah's breasts, and Duane felt his breath congeal in his throat.

Weezer's eyes were glowing yellow ovals.

Duane's fist moved by itself. One moment it was clenched at his side. The next moment the fist was pistoning at Weezer's jaw. Duane was certain Weezer would deflect the blow, or maybe even intercept his fist before it reached its target. If their suspicions about what Weezer had become were accurate, he might possess superhuman reflexes.

But Weezer didn't do anything, and when Duane's knuckles collided with Weezer's underjaw, he heard his friend's teeth click together, saw the tip of Weezer's tongue sheared off neatly by his incisors.

Duane followed through, putting his considerable bulk behind the blow. Then Weezer was sprawling backward, upsetting a couple of people who'd been unlucky enough to position themselves behind him. A man dropped his glass and went stumbling away. A woman was driven to her knees by Weezer's flailing body, but she avoided spilling her drink.

Duane was certain that Weezer would spring to his feet to retaliate, but instead Weezer merely flopped over onto his belly, a pool of beer soaking his white shirt. Duane waited for the yellow eyes to batten onto his, waited for Weezer to change into something from a horror movie.

Yet when Weezer pushed up to his knees and looked up at him, all Duane saw was the same poor kid who used to get picked on in third grade. The only kid in Lakeview Elementary who was bullied more than Duane.

Weezer's eyes shone with tears.

This was no murderer, he realised. Whatever crazy shit had gone on during the past week, it wasn't because of Weezer. This was his friend. His friend who'd gone through a terrible ordeal. And even if Weezer had spoken offensively to Savannah, at heart he was the same tortured kid he'd always been.

Weezer got slowly to his feet. He peered down at his sodden clothes, his hands bloodied from the broken glass. Duane's mouth moved, but he couldn't speak. He took a step toward Weezer, but his friend was already ducking through the crowd, moving toward the bathroom.

Duane glanced at Savannah, whose eyes tracked Weezer's progress.

Duane indicated his fleeing friend with a thumb. "Maybe we should, you know..."

"Duane?" she said.

"Yeah?"

"Fuck him."

★   ★   ★

Barb spotted the security guard at the entrance to Beach Land. She couldn't place him right away but assumed he was one of the Martin boys. At least, he had the narrow face and recessed chin all the Martin boys had. When he climbed out of his cruiser and saw Barb and Jake, his weak chin began to bob.

"What happened to you?"

"Landscaping accident," she said.

The Martin boy gaped at her.

She climbed off the four-wheeler. "You're to do two things for me."

Other than gawking at her blood-slicked body, Martin's face remained unresponsive.

Barb slapped him.

Not hard enough to knock him down, but with enough force to kick-start his brain. He grasped his hand-marked cheek. "Why did you—"

"Two things," she said. "Can you handle two things?"

He gave her a noncommittal shrug.

"First," she said, "you will drive this little boy to the police chief's office. You know Pete Hoffman?"

He glared sullenly at her. "Course I know Pete Hoffman."

"That's the first thing. Take Jake here to Pete's office and tell him I need the boy protected. You got that?"

"Protected from what?"

"Second thing," she said, "is tell Pete to get ahold of every officer – city, county, the state police, *everyone* – and tell them all to come to Beach Land. Everyone, that is, except for whoever Pete assigns to take care of Jake."

The Martin boy broke into an incredulous grin. "Why you want everyone to come here? The splash park open tonight?"

"Three murderers are on the way to the Roof," she said. "If they're not here already."

"But Sheriff Cartwright's already up there," the Martin boy said.

"Lane won't make a difference," she said. "Now are you capable of executing two simple orders, or are people gonna die because of your incompetence?"

The Martin boy's eyes narrowed. "I don't take orders from you. What makes you think I'm gonna put up with your crap?"

Barb said, "Close your eyes, Jake."

She retrieved the burlap sack bungeed to the back of the four-wheeler.

"What you got there?" Martin said.

"Your eyes closed?" she asked, glancing at Jake. Hands over his eyes, he nodded.

She turned to the security guard. "Look at this." She shoved the sack into Martin's hands.

"It's heavy," he said, staring down at it. His nose wrinkled in distaste. "It's wet too. Hey, what the hell—"

"Open it."

He glared at her, but he followed orders this time, and when he did draw the werewolf's severed head from the burlap sack, his face immediately contorted into a look of such revulsion and horror that Barb feared he'd take off running. He didn't, though, merely bobbled the head for several moments before tripping over his own feet and landing on his ass. The head fell into his lap. Martin uttered a yodelling scream and scrambled backward, but for a moment Dave Garner's wolfish head merely rode along in Martin's lap like an adoring pet. Then Martin gave a convulsive lurch, and the head tumbled sideways.

"You believe me now?" Barb asked.

Martin's breath came in great, wheezing heaves.

"Can I open my eyes?" Jake said.

"Not yet," Barb said. She bent, retrieved the head, and stuffed it back inside the sack. "Okay, Jake."

Martin was on the verge of hyperventilating.

"Two things," she reminded him.

Martin staggered to his feet.

"What are the two things?" she demanded.

"Take him—" a nod at Jake, "—to Pete Hoffman."

"And?"

He opened his mouth, closed it. His eyes were fixed on the burlap sack.

"*And*?" Barb said.

"And—and tell Pete to get everyone down to Beach Land."

"To the Roof."

"To the Roof," he repeated.

"That's good enough," Barb said.

"Good en—"

"Get your ass in gear!" she shouted.

Martin jumped and made his way over to Jake. Soon they were buckled into Martin's Ford Taurus and pulling away. Barb mounted the four-wheeler, figuring she could drive it across the bridge. That would help, she decided. Her chest and calf were still bleeding, and she was closer to fainting than ever.

Her vision wavering, Barb guided the four-wheeler toward the Beach Land entrance.

CHAPTER TWENTY-SIX

When Glenn and Joyce walked in, Glenn had the strongest sense of déjà vu he'd ever experienced. Short Pump used to claim the existence of psychic phenomena, ghosts, all other kinds of weird stuff, but Glenn had never really bought in.

Then again, the last few days had changed his thinking on all sorts of things.

Glenn took a moment to scan the crowd. Beside him, he knew Joyce was doing the same. He'd already spotted Short Pump, Savannah and several other classmates among the dense crowd, yet of the nearly five hundred people packed into the Roof tonight, only a tenth or so were members of his graduating class.

Joyce squeezed his arm. He turned to look at her, surprised at the flush of warmth that tingled his skin, the hot spires of electricity that scurried up his back. She looked lovely, and he knew that was part of it. She smiled, and despite the fact that he'd never even hugged her before, Glenn was steamrolled by an overwhelming urge to throw his arms around her, dip her Rhett Butler-style, and kiss the living hell out of her, the rest of the bar be damned.

Joyce seemed to pick up on this, because her gaze became rawer, more vulnerable.

Kiss her, a voice demanded.

But Glenn couldn't, not yet.

From the corner of his eye, he saw a showy, scantily-clad woman saunter past, yet this diversion was easily ignored. As he gazed into Joyce's childlike, trusting eyes, two more perfect-ten types breezed past them, and though he was aware of the women, though his sharp, comprehensive eyesight registered their curves, their superficial beauty, his lack of interest in them confirmed it.

He only wanted Joyce.

He dared not tell her that, for she'd no doubt make some witty but too-incisive joke: *Congratulations, Glenn. At age twenty-eight and seven months, you've finally reached emotional maturity.*

Joyce's mouth was forming a smile now, and he had little doubt she knew exactly what he was thinking. For someone with so little experience with the opposite sex, she was pretty damned shrewd. Glenn smiled back at her, again toyed with the notion of kissing her. Then a figure detached itself from the crowd and placed its hands on Joyce's shoulders.

Savannah.

Joyce winked at Glenn and turned to embrace her friend. And what was astounding about it was that, despite the fact that Savannah looked ethereal tonight – the blue sundress bringing out the electrifying cobalt of her eyes, her hair looking like something from a shampoo commercial – Glenn still preferred to look at Joyce.

Because, gazing at Savannah, Glenn felt very little. He still liked her as a person and wanted her to avoid harm. But the worshipful frustration and hollowed-out bitterness seemed a memory now, which surprised him as much as his growing attachment to Joyce.

Savannah glanced at him. "Come on over and join us."

Joyce asked, "Is Weezer with you?"

Glenn tightened. He saw Savannah do the same. She shook her head, her brow knitting. "There was a... He went away, I think."

Joyce was searching Savannah's face. "What happened?"

Savannah glanced in Short Pump's direction, muttered something about not wanting to talk about it.

Glenn wanted Joyce to let it go, and she did. Savannah led them through the shifting crowd. Short Pump's head jutted up above most of the patrons, and when they got to where he stood – about fifteen feet from the bar – he extended his arms toward Glenn.

Glenn accepted the embrace, both surprised and touched by Short Pump's gesture. Short Pump often grew effusive after several drinks, but Glenn could see in his friend's eyes how sober he was, how genuinely happy he was to see him. *My God*, Glenn thought. Not since the night of the bonfire had they even spoken. Glenn had been too busy. Or too scared. But now, with Short Pump and Savannah smiling at him and Joyce at his side, he felt better than he had in a long time.

Then Billy Kramer appeared.

He was a good ways toward drunk already. Glenn could see that by the way he wove through the crowd. Billy was dancing to the discordant tunes of Dance Naked, a sure sign he was getting blitzed.

Billy leaned into Short Pump. "He locked himself in, man."

Short Pump frowned at Billy. "Who locked himself in?"

"Who the hell you think?" Billy said, his voice a bit slurry. "Weezer."

"In the bathroom?" Savannah asked.

Billy gave her an incredulous look. "Duh. Where else?"

Joyce's eyebrows drew inward in a frown. "Savannah? What happened with Weezer? We need to know."

"Hey, look," Billy Kramer said. Glenn followed Kramer's gaze to the bathroom, where one of the three hotties was knocking on the men's room door. She was startlingly blond and looked like she might burst out of her lemon-coloured halter top. The black miniskirt appeared painted on.

But why was she knocking on the men's room door? Was the women's restroom out of order?

Yet the blond knocking on the door seemed so...what? Purposeful?

Grim? A short way off, Glenn noticed the other two hotties; these two had black hair and red hair and were just as built as the blond.

His sphincter puckered like a sun-dried tomato.

They were staring at him.

They *knew*.

It was insane to think so, he realised, but he was certain of it. They knew what he'd done at the drive-in. More importantly, they knew what he was.

No!

Glenn turned away. He had to get away from the women, had to escape this overcrowded bar. If he didn't pass out soon he'd lose control.

"Look," Joyce said.

Snapped back to his senses, Glenn looked.

The bathroom door was opening, the blond going in.

"Now what the hell is that lady doing?" Billy asked. But rather than concern or wonderment in his tone, Glenn detected nothing but jealousy. "You don't suppose she likes Weezer, do you?"

★   ★   ★

Weezer opened the door not because he knew who was knocking but because he'd resolved to leave the Roof. He should have known it was too good to last. For the first time in his life he'd felt strong, in control.

So what if he'd taken a few lives? Were the lives taken really such catastrophic losses anyway? Mya and Rebecca were a couple of sluts no one outside their own families would mourn.

Jessica Clinton and her kids? Jessica deserved worse than she got, the stupid cunt. She'd had as much to do with Weezer's miserable adulthood as anybody, save Weezer's own folks. If Weezer could, he'd kill her again, only this time, he'd devour her children in front of her, see how she liked that.

He felt little compunction about killing the Clinton children. They were too young to know was happening anyway.

All these thoughts unfurled in his mind as he stood perched over the sink and staring at the mirrorless tile wall. It was odd that most men's rooms in bars didn't have mirrors. Short Pump had once explained how bar owners refrained from mounting them because of men's tendencies to punch mirrors when they were inebriated. According to Short Pump, severely drunk men were sometimes infuriated by the sight of their own reflections, so placing a mirror in a men's room was inviting trouble. Previously, Weezer had believed that theory to be one hundred percent bogus, but now…yeah, he could see it. He was thankful he couldn't gaze into his own lost eyes.

The knocking on the door persisted.

Weezer splashed some water on his face and didn't bother to towel off. He slid aside the bolt and pulled opened the door.

And was driven back by a tall, voluptuous blond in a yellow halter top. She thrust him backward like he was made of paper, and before his shoulders collided with the metal stall divider, she swung shut the door. He rebounded off the divider and fell against her, the entire room so small the two of them were practically connected already. She didn't seem fazed by the way his face mashed between her breasts, nor did she seem to exert any energy as she supported his weight. In the moments before he regained his balance, he heard the sliding door lock snick shut again, inhaled the exhilarating perfume of her skin. There was something maddeningly familiar about the scent, something that carved away at his self-possession. He recognised the stirrings within as the onset of the transformation, but before he could judge whether this was a good thing or a hideous thing, she righted him with an effortless nudge and said, "Down."

Weezer swayed on his feet, unable to process the word. He wasn't drunk, not really, and he'd considered himself capable of driving his truck home without incident. But now, in the presence of this goddess, he was not only struck mute and dizzy – he was so perplexed by the situation that his synapses refused to fire.

Down, she'd said.

Down. Now how, out of the million ways he could interpret that, could he possibly discern her meaning? He was opening his mouth to ask her when her arm blurred and her fingers flashed by and the tug on his cheek told him he'd been grazed. But the whole side of his face began to burn because she'd torn his cheek off, the entire flap of skin hinging open and the blood spraying everywhere.

"*Down*," the goddess repeated.

Through a glaze of shock and pain, Weezer tried to meet her unblinking stare, but one moment her eyes looked blue and another yellow and then a strobing mélange of colours, Jesus, like a psychedelic music video where the spiralling shapes made you feel like you were spinning down a bottomless vortex, and because he couldn't face those eyes anymore, would rather die than gaze into their vertiginous depths, he sank to his knees, his new khaki trousers instantly soaked in his own blood. And maybe it was instinct that guided him lower, his palms squelching on the bloody floor, but at some point she'd removed her sandal and proffered her left foot, and the toes were long and delectable, and though Weezer had never been a foot man, had only heard of such fetishes on porn sites, he *needed* to fit his mouth over her toes, *needed* to let his tongue slick over them. He licked the goddess's little toe, forced his tongue into the cleft beside it, and as he did he felt her hot flesh respond. He was responding too, God yes, and he began lapping at her middle toe, teasing it the same way he'd teased Jessica Clinton's clitoris those many years ago.

But he knew this wasn't a fleeting thrill. The goddess would not abandon him the way that bitch Jessica had. Jessica was dead, her kids were dead, her asshole husband was a pile of ashes. And the goddess was getting off on it as much as he was, and Weezer found the fourth toe, the longest, and he began sucking on it, not like an infant with its pacifier, but like a man – no, greater than that. An immortal! And as he graduated to her big toe, his tongue swirling and flicking over its broad, resilient surface, he understood what this was about, what this ceremony heralded. A new life. A new existence. He'd merely glimpsed the pleasures his recent gift promised. Desire and joy and lust and aggression like he'd never known coursed through his veins, brought forth the shimmering, transcendent being from within its pitiful human shell. Weezer growled and huffed as he cleaned the goddess's foot, his scrawny shoulders swelling, the matchstick arms becoming brawny. Weezer lapped at the goddess's heel, luxuriated in the removal of the grime. His hypersensitive tongue revelled in the dirt, the grains of sand. His frenetic, dripping tongue gave gladly to the goddess, purified her of man's taint.

As he neared his climax, he was seized by the goddess, who'd *become* while he was purifying her, who was taller and broader than he was, Christ, nearly nine feet tall and corded with muscles that jittered and pulsed with preternatural anticipation. And golden-haired too, almost as blond as she'd been in human form.

Weezer transformed.

"*Take me first,*" the goddess demanded, and Weezer moved forward knowing what the last word meant. This was merely prelude. This was but a foretaste.

He'd begun to enter her when she shoved him back. Despite his hulking body, she handled him like a child. He crashed into the divider, the whole thing caving backward, and as he scrambled to his feet, he became aware of the hammering from outside, a chorus of male voices beseeching him to open the door. Yet he allowed these to fade because the goddess was watching him sternly. He was her pupil now.

"*Not like that,*" she snarled.

It only took a moment to click. Weezer strode forward, grasped her broad, sinuous hips, and spun her around. Heat blazed through him. Saliva squirted from his mouth, glistened on her hairy back. Her ass, half human and half beast, was pushed out for him, offered up to him. Weezer squeezed her glorious hips. She lifted her ass, exposing her engorged sex, and he moved in, spreading her wide.

"*Good boy,*" she rumbled, and Weezer sank his burning spear inside her. He rutted wildly, feverishly, and the explosive heat of her sex made him clench in ecstasy. He roared his pleasure, howled into the mirrorless wall.

When he was spent, she turned and met his panting gaze. He saw madness in her eyes. The blood fever. Weezer saw she was ready and he knew he was ready.

When she tore open the door and the pitiful bar lock snapped, Weezer beheld the faces outside.

Saw them and celebrated their terror.

CHAPTER TWENTY-SEVEN

Glenn suppressed an urge to grab Joyce and run, but the same fatalistic aura had permeated the bar as had spread over the bonfire, and he knew he was bound in some way to remain here and see this through. He'd had a fleeting suspicion when he'd seen the tall, voluptuous blond approach the bathroom, and in the few minutes since she'd gone inside, that suspicion had morphed into a full-blown certainty.

The women were werewolves.

When Sheriff Cartwright – whom Glenn hadn't even noticed – began hammering at the bathroom door, Glenn understood how events were about to spiral out of control again, only this time would be much worse. Because there were, at minimum, four werewolves rather than one this time. And if the women were as ferocious as Glenn had been when in thrall to the change, every man and woman in the Roof – hell, everyone in the *park* – was in mortal danger.

"Glenn?" Joyce said. She stood very close to him.

Glenn looked down at her and wondered why she hadn't changed yet. Did that mean the beast inside her was simply waiting? A latent monster biding its time, or perhaps awaiting the right trigger to unleash its power?

He didn't know, and he didn't consider it any longer because at that moment the noises sounded from within the bathroom, the growls and roars and howls only half-diminished by the unceasing noise issuing from Dance Naked. The song they were eviscerating was, he thought, one of AC/DC's, but it was impossible to tell. If they'd only shut up for a couple minutes he might be able to figure out what was happening in the—

The door swung open.

Poor Billy Kramer. He'd sidled up next to Sheriff Cartwright, no doubt to get a better perspective on the action. But despite Cartwright's entreaties for Billy to stand the hell back, Billy had insisted on leaning against the door, ear cupped against the painted steel in an attempt to eavesdrop on Weezer and the blond woman.

When the door swung inward, revealing the two huge beasts looming in the doorway, Billy sprawled at the feet of the gigantic blond creature and lay staring upside-down at its hateful face. Billy opened his mouth, likely to beg for mercy, but before he could utter a single syllable, the blond werewolf stomped on his face.

Billy's head caved like an egg carton.

Sheriff Cartwright shouted something – in the commotion it was impossible to discern what – and opened fire on the creature. But the next moment an auburn shadow passed between Glenn and the sheriff, a powerful arm swept down and Lane Cartwright's wrist bones were snapped like twigs. Cartwright turned and looked up at the beast that had ruined his forearms, and Glenn realised the red-haired woman had transformed too.

So quick, he thought. *So appallingly quick.*

The auburn-haired werewolf grasped Cartwright by the temples, squeezed, and before Cartwright could scream, his eyes had exploded from his skull.

His head crushed, the sheriff slumped to the floor.

The bar descended into bedlam.

This is the moment, a voice declared in Glenn's mind, *that proves what you are. And just like Mike Freehafer, you're going to fail. You got bitten, sure, but the core of you never changed. You've been taking from people all your life and adding nothing to the world. Nothing but misery.*

Glenn swallowed, watched.

The blond werewolf tore down at a skinny younger guy and four deep stripes spread in the middle of his back, soaking his white muscle shirt, sending him yawing toward a table, where he cracked his head and lay without moving. The blond werewolf took two strides toward the skinny guy, reached down, and twisted his head off like a bottle cap.

No, Glenn thought weakly.

Yes, the cruel voice taunted. *You can look cool, you can seduce. But you can't fucking help people. And the worst part is, when the change comes upon you, it isn't a change at all, Glenn...*

No, he pleaded.

...it's a reveal. Because you're selfish to the marrow. And if you transform, you'll kill. Just like before, just like the drive-in. You can't escape what you are.

Please!

You've always been a monster.

Some instinct made the hackles on the back of his neck rise. One of the werewolves had—

Glenn turned and stared at the raven-haired beast, the one who'd snuck up behind him. Glenn started to throw up his arms to ward the raven creature off, but she swept up with a clawed hand, smacked his underjaw with such force that his teeth shattered. He was lifted into the air and hurled back, but the blow was so brutal his whole body had gone numb. Glenn landed near the bar, and beside him he saw two patrons beset by Weezer and the blond werewolf. Weezer had his maw buried in a man's neck and was ripping and tearing like a frenzied shark. The blond werewolf merely seized her victim – a black man in his thirties – extended the hooked talon of a forefinger and popped the man's jugular vein. Blood sprayed a fine mist over the blond beast's hairless face, and as the blood thickened into a fountain, the blond werewolf began guzzling it out of the air, sometimes actually moving the man's convulsing body left or right to improve her angle.

Glenn heard screaming, but it was as though someone had stuffed his ears with cotton. He couldn't see faces, just blurry, pale shapes. The raven wolf had cracked him so hard his nostrils were jetting scarlet. And the only thing he could hear now was Joyce, who'd splayed across him, who was sobbing and begging him not to die.

Well, he thought, *if it were up to me…*

A lump formed in his throat. He realised with horror he too was about to cry. Because finally, in the end, he understood what he wanted.

He wanted Joyce.

But he couldn't have her, would never have her. Because he was dying. The werewolf hadn't needed to tear him limb from limb. In his human form he was as vulnerable as a kitten. A single barbaric blow had done it. That was why he couldn't feel his limbs; he was paralysed. But he did feel the hot tears leaking over his temples. Did feel Joyce's tremoring body jostling his. Joyce was turned sideways now, hissing outraged words at the raven werewolf, and to his horror Joyce was remaining where she was, draped over him, and had he the strength he'd shove her off, tell the fucking monster to get it over with, to dine on his flesh and allow Joyce to live.

The raven wolf raised a taloned hand. The yellow, hateful eyes glowed with maniacal need.

And then everyone turned, even the raven werewolf.

Short Pump, Glenn thought. And smiling, he watched his friend swing the chair.

★   ★   ★

Duane's first thought on seeing Glenn sprawled out on the floor was that he couldn't possibly get to his friend in time. The massive black werewolf wasn't approaching Glenn swiftly, but the beast's progress was steady, inexorable, and Duane was a good twenty feet away. Duane grabbed the folding chair and hesitated. He was supposed to protect Savannah, he told himself.

But Glenn was about to die.

So Duane moved toward him, knocking over a pair of chairs and an entire table on his way. He even bowled over an older man he now recognised as his high school social studies teacher, Mr. Greene. But that was okay, Duane decided, because Mr. Greene had been a lazy, paycheck-collecting blowhard who'd bored the living shit out of him for an entire school year.

Several bar patrons scrambled across his vision as he approached, but he could see well enough to know that Joyce had fallen across Glenn, and the sight of her there, so small in comparison to the werewolves, gave Duane courage.

The black werewolf cocked an arm, ready to tear through both

Joyce's and Glenn's bodies, but before it could, Duane said, "Your halter top's ripping."

And so it was. It was amazing the garment could stretch so far, but the brown western-style top was holding on for dear life, the tassels mostly buried in a sea of wiry black hair. The werewolf's eyes widened imperceptibly, some flicker of human emotion registering on its face, and then Duane was swinging the chair with all his strength at the beast's head.

The werewolf got an arm up – its reflexes were unspeakably quick – but one of the chair legs jabbed it right in the eye. It roared, stumbled back, and for a moment, Duane was confident they could mount some sort of challenge against these monsters.

Then a giant figure sprang onto the bar, and Duane's hope fizzled like a defective bottle rocket.

Weezer crouched on all fours and leered at Duane with a look of infinite malice.

Duane froze, an icy gust of dread mooring him in place.

Weezer's leer broadened. He prepared to pounce.

And squalled as Savannah emerged from behind the bar and smashed a vodka bottle against the base of his skull.

Weezer tumbled forward, and Savannah clambered over the bar after him. Duane made to help Savannah, but before he could move two steps he was lifted and hurled into the air. He pinwheeled his arms, thrust out his hands in an attempt to catch himself, but he landed badly – right on top of a cluttered table – and went skidding over the top of it. He'd crushed maybe half a dozen beer bottles when he'd slammed the tabletop, and the front of his body was a shrieking agony. But before he could assess the damage, someone flew over him – or was *thrown* over him – and landed with a harsh thud against the side of a booth.

It was Joyce, he saw. He got to his knees, wincing at the multitudinous cuts on his torso, belly, and hands, but then Savannah was screaming, and Duane was sure Weezer had gotten her.

But that wasn't right, he saw. What Savannah was screaming at was the blond werewolf.

Who'd found Glenn.

Who was reaching toward Glenn's throat.

★   ★   ★

"Get away from him!" Savannah screamed at the blond werewolf.

The blond werewolf grinned at her, rose and stalked toward her.

Think of Jake, she told herself.

Savannah set her jaw, moved toward the blond werewolf.

You're being a fool! a voice in her head declared. *You're no good to your son if you're dead.*

And I'm no good to him if I'm a coward either, she thought. She brandished the broken bottle neck, stood her ground. The blond werewolf's eyes shifted to Savannah's left, in the direction of the bar. Savannah resisted turning that way for a moment, but she realised this wasn't a gambit of some sort. The blond beast was transfixed by something.

Savannah turned and saw Weezer rising from the floor.

Weezer's whole body trembled with rage.

I'm dead, she thought.

Something exploded behind her, and the side of Weezer's left shoulder evaporated. Whirling, she discovered Barb Callahan striding forward, a shotgun held out before her. The shotgun roared again, and Weezer, who had somehow not gone down from the first shot, did fall this time.

A hundred or so bar patrons who had swarmed toward the exit now dropped to the floor to take cover.

Barb turned her weapon on the blond werewolf. Behind the beast, Adriana Carlino stood frozen, a look of mute terror on her sullen face.

"Get down, dammit!" Barb shouted. From Barb's position, Savannah could see, there was no way to fire at the huge werewolf without endangering Adriana.

It didn't matter. The blond beast whirled, swung and tore off Adriana Carlino's head. Then it was loping away through the crowd. In moments the blond beast neared the railing that overlooked the boardwalk, but before it leaped over, it seized the lead singer of Dance Naked and dashed his brains out on the dance floor.

With the discarded singer's body lying broken under the strobing disco ball, the blond werewolf vaulted over the rail. Moments later, two more shapes followed: the auburn-haired beast, whose body was slathered in blood and viscera, and the black-haired werewolf, which still clutched a severed arm in its immense jaws.

"Look out!" Barb screamed, and Savannah spun just in time to avoid Weezer's clipping jaws. In spite of the shoulder wound, the Weezer-thing moved with appalling grace. From the corner of her eye, Savannah saw Barb tracking him with her shotgun. A moment before Weezer hit the dance floor, Barb squeezed the trigger. The blast caught Weezer in the side, but despite the breathless growl he emitted, he kept chugging toward the railing. Moments later, he leaped over too.

Some childish, irrational hope arose in Savannah that the horror had ended. After all, she saw with a quick glance around the bar, the beasts had already murdered more than ten people. Wasn't that enough?

But when the screams started below, she realised the atrocities had only begun.

Savannah moved over to Short Pump, who was leaning against a booth and looking like he might be sick. Several bar patrons had risen to their feet.

Savannah hovered over Short Pump, placed a hand on his back. "Did you get bitten?"

He shook his head. "Is Glenn dead?"

Savannah frowned. "I..." She turned and gazed over at Glenn's body, which was utterly motionless. Joyce was hunched over him, sobbing.

Savannah realised her eyes were welling too. She drifted over to Joyce, knelt beside her.

"I know you're hurting," Savannah whispered, then realised how inadequate that was. "Is he...you know..."

Though Joyce's shadow kept Glenn's face in semidarkness, the stillness of his body, the glassy look in his eyes...Savannah already knew. She was surprised at the way her throat began to clench, the way her chest had started to burn.

Savannah stroked Joyce's back, fought off a selfish surge of anguish. "He really liked you," she said. "I could tell. I wish I'd introduced you two earlier."

"*But you didn't,*" a voice that was nothing like Joyce's rumbled.

Savannah jerked her hand away and gazed in horror at the savage face that stared at her from atop Joyce's body, which was twitching, each limb and sinew a hopping bed of spasms, the satiny skin threading with black hair, the muscles stretching, bulging, the face becoming less and less like Joyce's as this new being rose to its feet. Savannah scuttled away on her elbows and heels, and then Short Pump was at her side, his arms around her. Joyce quaked, her back popping, ropes of bloody slaver drooling from her lips.

"Come on," Short Pump said at her ear. "We have to go..."

Savannah nodded, but on some level she thought his words preposterous. Go? Go where? The four beasts were rampaging below – even now she could hear the shrieks of terror and the sustained caterwauling of someone in extreme pain – so leaving the bar and entering the warzone below made little sense to her.

Then Joyce loomed over her, and all thoughts of safety fled Savannah's mind.

Joyce's face was like the others, only infinitely more horrible because Savannah could still see her friend in there. In the shape of the eyes. The lips. And of course the shredded clothes. Joyce was still inside this creature somewhere.

Movement from her periphery drew her attention.

Barb raised the shotgun, levelled it at Joyce's face.

"Stop!" Savannah shouted.

She thought she was too late, actually saw Barb's trigger finger whitening as it squeezed.

The shot sounded.

Another.

But they were too muffled, too remote.

Savannah realised Barb hadn't fired at all. The shots had come from below, from the boardwalk.

"Guess a couple of tourists came armed tonight," Barb said.

Savannah started to respond, but before she could, Joyce had bounded toward the railing, taking roughly the same path the other four werewolves had taken.

Was it self-preservation, Savannah wondered, or a desire for revenge that had fueled Joyce's flight? Or maybe it was neither of those things. Maybe the region of her brain that still registered human emotion knew if she didn't escape now, she might kill Savannah or other innocent people.

Savannah watched the thing her friend had become leap over the railing.

Savannah turned to Short Pump, whose face was fish-white.

"I thought Barb was gonna kill her," he said.

"I did too," Barb answered.

"They don't like guns," Short Pump said.

Barb set the shotgun on a table, pulled out a handgun. "Who does?"

Savannah swallowed. "What now?"

But Barb was moving toward the bathrooms. Duane watched her, confused, but then she returned carrying two handguns. They looked identical. "Smith & Wessons," she said, handing them to Savannah and Short Pump. "At least Cartwright had good taste in guns." Barb chambered more shells in the shotgun and started toward the exit. "I hope you two are ready to use those things."

"Not on Joyce?" Savannah asked, her pulse quickening.

"Uh-uh," Barb said. "The other four."

They'd gotten almost to the stairs when Barb stopped. "But if your friend comes anywhere near me, I'm not going to spare her just because she waived a couple of my late book fees."

And with that, they all three headed down to the boardwalk.

CHAPTER TWENTY-EIGHT

Melody gasped, her eyes fluttering wide. There were implacable fingers locked around her throat. Her windpipe creased on itself like a slice of ham. She was aware of a tremendous pressure on her jaws, the base of her skull, but it wasn't until her vision clarified that she noticed the rope tethered to the attic rafter. She began to kick, the joist from which she hung groaning, and though she still couldn't breathe, she realised something was different now, something had changed.

Her temples tightened. *Of course*, she thought.

She had changed.

Growling with determination, she worked her powerful fingers under the noose, contracted her throat muscles until she could grip the rope. But once she'd gotten hold of it, she couldn't gain the necessary leverage to rip the noose apart. Her fault for choosing such a sturdy rope. There was blood in her throat from the compression of the noose; she could taste it. But she was confident of her escape.

The change had saved her.

With one clawed hand between the noose and her skin, Melody began sawing at the rope with her fingernails, and though the individual strands were snapping and curling, she was still choking. Angry now, she began to hack at the rope, the strands twanging and giving way several at a time. Soon she was halfway through the rope. But even this wasn't fast enough. The blood in her throat enraged her, the raw, scored feeling of the soft tissue. Like the world's worst case of laryngitis.

Savagely, Melody gripped the rope and began to climb upward, hand over hand. When she reached the joist to which the rope was attached, she assumed the pressure on her throat would slacken, and to an extent it did.

But not enough. Her throat still burned. Her breath still came in fugitive gasps. And goddammit, she wanted to *live*. For the first time in her life, her father and brothers would not be around to plague her, to terrorise her, to haunt her every moment and make her hate herself. Fuck their everlasting souls. She wished she could rip their throats again, indeed might do that very thing. Desecrate their bodies or drag them into the road, where they'd be run over, feasted on by carrion crows, publicly humiliated as the maggots squirmed in their putrefying eye sockets.

Melody lunged and snapped at the gnarled rope. She clipped through most of it with her formidable new jaws. The rage was building inside her, boiling over, fulminating. She lashed out again, this time shearing through the pitiful fibres, and then she was dropping, landing on her footpads, the claws piercing the dusty plywood floor. Melody clambered over to the open trapdoor, dropped through.

Racing toward the stairs, she thought of the reunion, of her old classmates, the ones who'd jeered at her. They would know terror tonight. They would know suffering.

They would never mock her again.

★   ★   ★

Never did he think it could be this way. His heart full of joy, the very air like cool, slaking water, Weezer marauded through Beach Land, ripping and tearing and spilling blood wherever he went. At times one of the others was beside him, and though he frequently glanced at the red one's glorious muzzle or the black one's rippling leg muscles, there was no need for him to. Because their mental communion was something more intimate, something felt so deeply he could predict each wolf's movements seconds in advance.

The ride operators didn't understand what was happening. None of the humans did, with the exception of the very young, perhaps because they were willing to surrender to their atavistic reactions, to be ruled by terror. Or maybe they simply lacked the sophistication to rationalise the creatures bounding down the boardwalk toward the rides. The yellow wolf – their leader – moved on two feet, as did the red and the black, but Weezer preferred to race along on all fours because of how childlike it made him feel.

Perhaps this was why the child flesh tasted so delicious to him.

Last night at the Clintons' he had saved the infant for last because he knew it could not escape him. Yet what a wondrous surprise it had been when the succulent pink flesh had filled his maw. He could *feel* the child's vitality suffusing him with its potency, its pure, glowing energy. He *was* power. He *was* force. He was bristling, ineffable perfection, a highly evolved machine with all the toxic accouterments of man stripped away from him, leaving only strength, sinew, fang and claw.

And hunger.

My God, the *hunger*.

Weezer bounded toward the rides. He spied a pregnant mother. She was watching a man who might have been her husband, and a boy of perhaps four years as they were whipped about by the Scrambler. The man probably saw Weezer take down his pregnant wife, but because the ride was jerking him and the boy so frenetically, he might not have believed his senses.

But the woman believed. Oh, did she believe.

The pimple-faced boy operating the ride had begun to panic, and to silence his ululating scream, Weezer longed to tear his throat out. But the meat of the pregnant woman – and the delicacy within her womb – was so ethereal that he couldn't be burdened with other matters.

In moments the scream stopped anyway, as his sleek pack mate, the red wolf, separated the pimple-faced boy's head from his body and, embracing the headless corpse like a lover, guzzled the vermilion spray that issued from the neck stump.

The Scrambler was still spinning its mindless convolutions, but it had begun to decelerate. All the rides, the human part of Weezer remembered, were on timers. This meant that soon every ride in Beach Land would grind to a halt. There would be no merriment along the boardwalk, no moving attractions in which the lambs might take quarter. He imagined Turtle Cove – oh, how he longed to run wild among the bleating, defenceless children! He thought of the water park. The lambs would take refuge there, no doubt because the water park was closed at night, and they would think themselves safe in the darkness.

But the darkness was where his kind ruled.

The Scrambler had nearly stopped, but the man who'd come here with the pregnant woman was out of his seat and leaping onto the wooden platform. The man had left his boy behind, and wasn't that like human beings? To act thoughtlessly? To forsake logic on some frantic whim?

The man vaulted over the rail and landed a few feet from where Weezer feasted. The man was reaching for Weezer, and despite Weezer's position – kneeling like a penitent beside the twitching corpse, her half-eaten heart in his hand – he could sense the man's sneakered foot swinging toward his head.

Weezer shot out a hand, caught the foot and yanked. The man's other foot skidded on the blood-soaked boardwalk, and the back of the man's skull cracked on the weathered wood. His movements so quick they were nearly a blur, Weezer placed what remained of the heart on top of the corpse – he didn't want the meat sullied by the grime of the unwashed wood – lifted the man's leg with one hand and sank his talons into the meat of the man's hamstring, just below the buttock. With an effortless tug he peeled the hamstring off the leg, the thick muscle curling like a bloody snail shell. The man gaped down at his mangled leg, but then his eyes shifted up to the Scrambler platform, where a round, shocked face was gaping down at the scene. It was the man's son, Weezer knew, and for a fleeting moment Weezer was gripped by indecision – finish the man or go for the child? Weezer's pride demanded the former; this pitiful man had dared to challenge him and deserved to suffer for his hubris. But the child's flesh called to him...the savoury young meat...

In the end the red wolf decided matters for him. One moment the child was staring down at them from above, his pale face stretched wide in horror; the next moment a red blur took the child out of Weezer's view. Runnels of blood poured down the side of the platform.

Around them, the slaughter continued. In less than five minutes there were scores of corpses scattered along the boardwalk.

CHAPTER TWENTY-NINE

They jogged hunched over, the gun in Duane's hand feeling way too heavy. Of course, it was nothing compared to the heavy feeling in the pit of his stomach. Taking care not to fall too far behind, he fingered the deep trench in his shoulder, told himself it could've been a shard of glass that had gored him so deeply.

Sure, a wheedling voice whispered. *Glass*.

They were getting nearer to the gunshots, which seemed to be gathered near the centre of Beach Land: the big open area by the fountain, the haunted house and the Viking ship.

"Careful," Barb muttered.

Savannah started to speak, but Barb slowed, brought a hand up and quieted them both with a stern look. Duane glanced down at Barb's bloody shirt and wondered how the woman wasn't dead yet. Hunkering down behind a giant fake palm tree, Barb surveyed the boardwalk area ahead.

"Barb?" Savannah said.

"Dammit," Barb growled, "you're just like having a little kid around. You ask more questions than Jake."

"You're sure he's okay?"

"Sure as I can be without actually seeing him locked inside the police station."

They all three peered through the deep green fronds of the palm tree. There seemed to be no movement, though Duane could discern several ominous-looking shapes on the concrete.

"Something's up there," Barb said.

He followed Barb's gaze to the roof of the Devil's Lair, where a colossal pale figure stood gazing down at the boardwalk. It was the blond werewolf, Duane realised, assessing the situation, or perhaps revelling in the carnage it had inflicted. He became aware of the silence, the total absence of gunshots. The childish, delusive part of him wanted to believe everyone had gotten away, or that the battle had moved outside the borders of Beach Land. But a closer study of the blond werewolf's body language revealed a darker story.

It turned toward the southern border of the park, the suspension bridge entryway. It pivoted and faced the northern border, the entrance he and Savannah had used. There was a maze of cottages over there, but only one way into the park: through the tall, gated entrance that had always reminded him of some medieval keep.

The blond wolf turned toward the lake, its all-encompassing gaze taking in the boardwalk, the murky brown waters that sloshed gently at the seawall beneath.

"They've blocked all the exits," Duane said.

Savannah stared at him. "You don't know that."

"He's right," Barb said.

It was the first time Duane could remember the woman agreeing with him. He wished fervently she'd contradicted him instead.

He noticed something poking from her lower back. "What's under your shirt?"

"Machete," Barb said. "You want it?"

"Not particularly," he said.

She eyed him. "Since we're probably going to die, why the hell do they call you Short Pump? Is it because—"

"*No*," Duane snapped.

"Shhh," Savannah cautioned.

"Well," he said, "you'd get pretty sick of it too, if you were me. Everybody making jokes—"

"So stand up for yourself," Savannah said.

Duane opened his mouth to respond, but Barb cut him off by saying, "There he is."

Duane spotted the werewolf that had once been his close friend. Weezer was patrolling an outcropping wharf, one that offered a panoramic view of the lengthy boardwalk.

"What do we do?" Savannah asked.

"Depends," Barb answered.

Duane and Savannah exchanged a look. "On what?" he said.

Barb nodded, the shotgun pointed in the general direction of the blond werewolf on the Devil's Lair roof. "Do we want to be heroes, or do we want to live?"

"Option B," Duane said immediately.

"B," Savannah agreed.

"Thank God," Barb said. "I figured you two would be too dumb to choose B." Barb turned and moved back the way they'd come. "I don't want anything to do with that blond bitch. We'll take our chances with one of the others."

★   ★   ★

It took Joyce very little time to adjust to her new body. She'd been awkward at first, but the sense of manipulating limbs, of operating some new machine to which she wasn't accustomed had faded swiftly and was replaced by a breath-stealing exuberance, a sense of invulnerability. She knew she could still be killed. Superhuman regenerative powers aside, she understood how mortal she was. After all, she had felt pain every day over the past week in one form or another. She even felt pain now, the aftereffects of the gruesome transformation still reverberating through her body.

Yet she was beginning to grasp how incredible her abilities were, how vast her capacity for extraordinary feats. As she rushed through the warm, moonlit air, her footpads moving lightly over the western shore of Beach Land, back where only the technicians and mechanics ventured when a ride needed maintenance, she listened for gunshots, for screams, but very few drifted to her. She could hear very little at all, save for the faraway sound of the merry-go-round, the one ride apparently left running when the werewolves had begun their attack.

Though Joyce had craved this new state of being and was awed by it, there were unforeseen elements at work in her that dampened her excitement considerably. For one, she was gripped by bloodlust. Not just hunger, but an ungovernable need to wash her muzzle with blood, to chew with her new mandibles, to rend with her tapered talons.

To kill.

But she mustn't do that, mustn't give in. It was hard to resist. She hadn't counted on this, hadn't counted on the imperious demands of her new body.

Nor had she foreseen the fear.

True, she was no longer self-conscious. This new frame was too magnificent for such mundane concerns. Beauty was hers. Measureless strength was hers.

But control?

Back at the Roof, Joyce had come very close to killing Savannah. And in those terrible moments when she was stalking toward her best friend, there had been another, deeper layer of desire in her, a nascent yet very real urge that made every vestige of her humanity quail.

She had *wanted* to murder Savannah.

Worse, she had wanted to hear Savannah's screams, to revel in her anguish. Images of Savannah's nude body, her skin splashed with blood, her eyes wild with terror, her supple belly split open to reveal the treasures within…these images had flashed through Joyce's mind as she'd approached her friend.

Shivering, Joyce dashed along the shore in the direction of the suspension bridge. She must not give in to that sinister urge. She must not kill an innocent person.

Least of all her best friend.

Joyce neared the Devil's Lair, veered behind it. She needed to keep to the shadows, avoid the blond werewolf.

Joyce was upon the man before she realised it.

Bedecked in a thick brown Carhartt coat despite the sultriness of the night, the man had apparently taken refuge behind the towering haunted house, had been concealed in the bunched shadows, which was why Joyce hadn't noticed him. But now he was bellowing in terror and swinging a hammer at her. So unexpected was the attack that the hammer caught her in the side of the face, and though the blow hurt, what took Joyce unawares was the fireball of rage that bloomed in her mind. Unthinkingly, she lashed out, and then the man was slumping against the cinderblock wall, his head crooked and the gash in his neck spurting arterial blood all over the ground. The sight of the blood enflamed Joyce's desire, and she took a step toward the dying worker, thinking to guzzle the glorious red liquid.

Then she froze, horrified, and shambled away.

God, it had been so easy! She hadn't meant to kill the man, but he'd struck first, and—

And there was no rationalising it. Not even in her transformed state. She wasn't herself now, but she wasn't so removed from her humanity that she could justify what she'd done.

Joyce was shocked to find a sob welling in her throat. It sounded like a growl.

She had to put this behind her, had to focus her energy on saving as many people as she could. It wouldn't make up for the worker, but it would demonstrate that she wasn't entirely evil.

Ahead, the shore curved inward, the misshapen peninsula on which Beach Land was constructed thinning to a flat spur of land people traversed when completing the long walk along the sprawling suspension bridge. Joyce moved behind a taco stand, a strip of shops and restrooms, and as she crept out from between a pair of outbuildings, she heard a chorus of sounds from within. Everywhere, she felt the stir of breath, heard the sibilant rasp of frightened whispers. There were hundreds of people hidden inside these buildings.

Then Joyce became aware of another presence.

Yes, she decided as she stole closer to the dark suspension bridge exit. It was as she'd suspected – one of the werewolves had taken a post here. If they barred both exits, the other two would have free rein to hunt and kill. How long would it be before a force large enough and brave enough to oppose them appeared at Beach Land? The first wave of policemen who'd ventured into the park had been unceremoniously slaughtered. Why should the second wave or the third be any different? Who would believe the nature of what they were fighting until they actually beheld it? And who, beholding it, would be courageous and cunning enough to battle the creatures and survive?

Joyce was thinking these thoughts as she hurried into the darkness of the overhang, the sheltered ramp that spanned perhaps twenty yards before the open-air suspension bridge began.

Directly in front of her, no more than ten feet away, a shape rose from the ramp and opened its yellow eyes.

Joyce cursed her clumsiness. She wasn't ready for this, had no clue how to fight such a creature. In contrast, her opponent – she saw it was the auburn-haired werewolf – looked eager, *maniacally* eager to do battle. The auburn werewolf was taller than Joyce was, was broader through the shoulders. She could see the strands of ruddy hair stir on its magnificent arms, could hear the deep, gravelly chortle of its laughter as it prepared to strike. The leer on its face gave it the look of a towering, misshapen clown.

Without thinking, Joyce flew at it.

Her teeth sank into its belly. Driven back, it squalled, began digging at Joyce's back, her shoulders, but Joyce's teeth sank deeper into its hairy flesh, and when she reared back, a hole the size of a grapefruit opened in the auburn werewolf's stomach. Immediately, the opening was filled with a bulge of purple entrails, but rather than marvelling at the wound she'd inflicted, Joyce darted in again, this time going for the beast's throat.

Mistake, she realised as the werewolf jerked aside. Not only did she miss the beast's throat, but she'd exposed her own torso to the auburn werewolf's claws, which raked down and tore through one of her breasts.

Joyce bellowed in pain, but it came out a ferocious roar, and the sound of it galvanised her, caused her to hammer down at the werewolf's ankle. The Achilles tendon snapped with a juicy twang, and the beast went down. Joyce scrambled closer to finish the werewolf, sank a claw into one of its eyes. She tore down, ruining the eye, but again she underestimated the creature's slyness. Its claws flashed, this time tearing off a patch of skin near her hip, and unthinkingly, Joyce turned her back in an effort to escape.

Another mistake, she immediately realised. The flesh between her shoulder blades erupted with searing pain.

Joyce spun, snarling.

But it lashed out at her again. Joyce went stumbling back. The creature struck her in the stomach, its movements too fast to resist. Even in its diminished state, even with its entrails dangling from its belly and one eye sluicing some pinkish-yellow fluid, it was eager for battle.

Joyce swayed on her feet. Blood dripped from her wounds. She shook her head, screwed up her eyes in an effort to remember all she'd read about lycanthropy. She recalled her session with Glenn in the library. The memory was painful, so painful it stole her breath and filled her with a desolation that was worse than her wounds. She should have kissed Glenn, should have made love to him. If she'd only known...

A snatch of reading flickered across her mind. *Decapitation*, she remembered. Decapitation was the only way to kill a werewolf. That or burning, and burning accomplished the same thing – the separation of the head from the body, the dividing of mind and heart. The end of the terror.

There was a renewed vitality in the auburn werewolf's expression, a heightened awareness in the yellow eyes. If Joyce allowed the creature, mutilated as it was, to escape without further injury, would it regenerate to its former glory? She believed it would.

As Joyce watched, the auburn werewolf's pupils dilated, then contracted. The werewolf tensed, preparing for a spring.

Teeth bared, Joyce feinted low, hoping the werewolf would react defensively.

It did.

Joyce swung with all her might, plunged three claws into the soft shelf of flesh under the beast's chin. Joyce jerked down, opened a giant red smile in its throat. It tumbled back, choking on its own blood.

Joyce followed. She reached down, grasped the long, matted mane and, using her wicked talons to scythe through cartilage and tissue, removed the head from the body. Panting, Joyce stepped over to the bridge railing and heaved the head over the side. There was a muted splash.

She became aware of eyes watching her.

Joyce turned, beheld the small group of onlookers clustered about sixty feet away, their wide-eyed faces half-shadowed by the sheltering roof.

Joyce opened her mouth to speak, but all that came out was a rumbling growl.

The onlookers retreated.

Dammit. Joyce cleared her throat, concentrated on forming the words.

"*Safe,*" she managed to rumble.

Most of the onlookers continued to backpedal, but a short woman in her late forties paused and squinted at her. The woman glanced around, took a couple steps forward. "Did you say 'safe'?"

Joyce nodded.

A man crept up next to the short woman. He had a black crew cut and wore a red-and-white Western Indiana T-shirt. "Why should we trust you? It's a massacre back there." He nodded toward the park.

Joyce stood irresolutely for a moment, doubting her ability to articulate her message. Instead, she turned and gestured toward the headless werewolf.

More of the onlookers crept forward.

Joyce brought up her hands – and they *were* hands now, she realised. Or at least partially. The change seemed to be reversing.

"Don't go near her!" someone from the rear of the group called. "Just look at her, for chrissakes!"

Joyce suppressed a surge of irritation. Not only did she not have time to reassure these people, she was also in an enormous amount of pain. While the transformation into a werewolf had been unspeakably painful, the reversal to her normal body wasn't much better. Joyce doubled over, her long, tapered teeth cutting their way back into her gums, her human jaws reforming.

"I don't trust it," someone muttered, and there were numerous murmurs of assent.

From the park a bellowing howl rent the night air, raising the hackles on the back of her neck, making the onlookers whimper in terror. She thought of the other ones, the still-living werewolves. Weezer. The black-haired beast. The blond werewolf.

The one who'd killed Glenn.

The memory of his broken body lying amid the dregs of beer and shattered glass did it to her, reversed the reversal.

Sorrow, she realised. *It's my sorrow that brings the change.*

The onlookers had begun to whisper and mutter again, and she knew in moments they'd flee. And then they'd be right back in harm's way – perhaps even in danger of being killed by Joyce – and the battle she'd fought against the auburn-haired werewolf would be for naught.

Mustering all her concentration, Joyce moved to the suspension bridge railing, pointed down the bridge's length toward the exit and roared, "*Go!*"

A couple people broke loose in terror and disappeared back into the park. The rest simply froze, gaping at her with a look of mute horror.

"*NOW!*" she thundered.

As one, the onlookers rushed forward, the entire mass of eighty or ninety people crowding the opposite railing from where she stood, the transformation seizing hold of her, bending her double, dropping her to her knees, which were popping, cracking, the vertebrae reforming. She felt the bridge beneath her yaw slightly and had a moment to wonder if the concentrated weight of the fleeing crowd might cause the whole bridge to snap free of its moorings. But as the change neared completion, and a new, even larger group of park patrons scurried past her, she realised the bridge would hold. She glanced at the departing mass and estimated she'd saved maybe two hundred lives.

But there were more of them, she knew, all over the park. Hidden in the many indoor rides. Taking refuge in the shops and arcades. Even cowering inside the Devil's Lair.

She had to save them.

Had to save Savannah most of all.

Her face a mask of grim determination, Joyce began to run toward the tunnel. By the time she reached the boardwalk, she was moving faster than she ever had.

PART FIVE
THE DEVIL'S LAIR

CHAPTER THIRTY

"I've never heard you so quiet," Savannah said over her shoulder.

That's because I've never been scratched by a werewolf before, Duane thought.

He knew he'd been sliced by broken glass during the melee, knew he'd been contused by his bone-rattling collision with the table.

But the gouge in his shoulder...that wasn't from any broken bottle. It was deep and it was burning and it was...he couldn't escape the word.

Alive.

As they hurried through the maze of cottages and two-storey dormitories, the ones in which the summer employees lived, the flesh and tissue around the wound seemed to writhe and squirm and throb with life.

And what was more, Barb, who'd been limping badly when she'd first arrived at the Roof, now seemed to move with little trouble. He remembered the rapid way the others had healed after the bonfire attack and couldn't help drawing a parallel.

"*Stop,*" Barb hissed.

Duane stopped, but not quickly enough to avoid ploughing into Savannah, who went sprawling forward. Duane had a moment of sheer terror when he realised she'd landed on her gun – what if it fired straight into her belly? – but the look she gave him when he went to help her up was more than enough to assure him she was perfectly fine, if a little pissed off at his clumsiness.

"Sorry," he muttered, helping her to her feet.

"What were you thinking about?" she asked him under her breath.

Lon Chaney in The Wolfman? he wanted to answer. *David Naughton in* An American Werewolf in London?

"One of them is nearby," Barb whispered. She'd taken a knee at the corner of a cottage and was gazing in the direction of the main entrance.

Savannah hunkered down next to her. "How do you know?"

Barb nodded. "Because nobody's guarding the way out."

Savannah exchanged a bemused glance with him, but there was no need to verbalise what he was thinking. Wouldn't the absence of a werewolf suggest they might actually escape rather than the contrary?

Savannah whispered, "Let's make a run for it."

Barb glared back at her. "I think all that peroxide has pickled your brain."

Duane crowded closer, and as he and Savannah peered through the darkness at the gaudy blue-and-yellow archway, the five turnstiles that admitted people into the park, and the quartet of ticket booths, he saw only barren space and the glittering sea of cars beyond. The way looked clear.

Savannah must have come to the same conclusion because she started to rise and move forward. Then Barb was seizing her by the back of the shirt and hauling her down.

"Jesus, Barb," Savannah said. "What's your—"

"The ground," Barb said through clenched teeth. "Look at the ground."

Duane did.

And nearly tossed his cookies.

The grassy areas around the sidewalk were landscaped with body parts.

Duane uttered a choked whimper. He looked away, his eyes wet, but he couldn't expunge the images stamped on his brain:

A small arm, severed at the shoulder, the orange plastic pay-one-price band still adorning its wrist. Some woman's entire lower body decorating the rim of a flowerbed. Five heads, most of them belonging to men, tilted against a trashcan, almost as if they'd been charged with encouraging people not to litter in Beach Land. Most horrible of all, a spill of mangled carcasses to their immediate left, a ghastly sight they hadn't taken in at first because the edge of the cottage had screened their view. Duane closed his eyes to ward off the images, but they remained in his head.

"Let's run for it," Savannah said.

"That's what it does." Barb's voice was low and tight. "It leaves the entrance clear so you'll think you can make it. Then it pounces."

Which one is it though? Duane wondered. The blond beast had been on the Devil's Lair roof a short while ago, and Weezer was monitoring the boardwalk and the water. Which left the black one or the red one.

He gasped, suddenly sure one of them had snuck up behind them. He whirled, Lane Cartwright's Smith & Wesson pointed at—

—nothing.

Duane exhaled raggedly. He'd damn near fired the gun. And then where would they have been? The noise would have drawn the werewolf right to them. Duane turned toward Savannah, and the cottage window above him exploded in a hail of glass. The huge black shape came down between Barb and Savannah, and though Barb was quick – the shotgun barrels were rising even as the black werewolf landed – the beast was quicker. It knocked the shotgun aside, both barrels detonating into the sky, and swept down at Barb with its other hand. Barb's throat was latticed with deep slits, and as the blood began to pour from the slits in bright red rills, the beast lunged forward and fastened its enormous jaws over Barb's face. Something large and shiny tumbled from beneath Barb's shirt – the machete. Even in the act of dying, Barb fought valiantly. She gripped the creature in a bear hug and tumbled backward, a movement Duane was certain was meant to give them time to escape.

Unthinkingly, he snatched up the machete and followed Savannah, who was a step ahead of him, was leading him away from the horrible snarling and squelching noises.

There were, he saw as he pelted down the sidewalk, dozens of corpses littering the grass. How many people could one werewolf eat? Or was it the bloodletting they enjoyed?

Duane and Savannah sprinted side by side, were nearing the turnstiles. Only twenty more yards and they'd be out.

A shape bounded toward them, and Duane knew it was the black werewolf even before it leaped onto the sidewalk before them and skidded in the congealing lake of blood. Duane pushed Savannah behind him and raised the Smith & Wesson. As he aimed he got a good look at the black werewolf, distinguished in its animalistic features the sultry raven-haired goddess from the Roof.

Duane squeezed the trigger. At the same instant, the werewolf struck at the gun. Duane felt a tug, thought he'd nailed the monster dead in the face, but then he beheld the look of triumph, the maw open in a leer, and realised the werewolf had moved too swiftly for him, the shot gone astray. Pain flooded his hand. He glanced down and saw that his trigger finger had been broken so utterly that it pointed sideways.

An explosion at his right ear made him cry out, land prostrate at the beast's feet. But the beast was backpedalling, he saw, getting tangled up, landing against a turnstile. It was grasping the meat joining its neck and shoulder, a spurt of blood jetting between its fingers. Duane looked up and saw Savannah striding forward, gun outstretched. She fired again and the werewolf jolted, the slug popping the creature in the chest. Savannah stopped ten feet from the beast and took aim.

Spun around as a howl split the night.

Duane felt his stomach plummet.

The blond beast was barreling toward them, head low, moving like the world's hairiest freight train. If it hadn't been so bone-chilling, it would have been beautiful.

Savannah cried out. Duane glanced back and realised the black werewolf had kicked Savannah's legs out from under her. Duane lurched toward Savannah, grabbed her wrists and jerked her away from the black werewolf just before it pounced. Then they were backing into the grass, throwing glances at the black werewolf, which was rising to its feet, and at the blond werewolf, which had slowed, apparently no longer fearful of their escape.

Duane shot glances right and left, gnashed his teeth at sight of the ludicrously tall security fence, and dammit, was that really necessary? This was an amusement park, not the fucking Kremlin. Was the epidemic of kids sneaking into the arcade so severe that Beach Land needed to take such extreme measures to keep them out?

Duane took Savannah's hand, felt something bump his ankle. He glanced down, saw he'd gotten his foot wedged under a mutilated leg. He was getting his balance again when he glimpsed something dark and shiny between the severed leg and what looked like a pile of intestines.

Lane Cartwright's gun.

With a surge of relief, he snatched it off the ground, then yelped when his broken index finger protested. Grimacing, he switched the gun to his left hand and felt what little excitement he'd experienced ebb. He'd never been ambidextrous, couldn't even hold a spoon comfortably in his left hand. How the hell could he operate a gun with it?

The blond wolf closed in, but instead of attacking on their flank as he assumed it would, the blond beast chose to join the black wolf on the sidewalk.

Both of them blocking the exit.

"Duane," Savannah said.

He couldn't respond. Could only stare at the huge beasts as they began to step toward them.

But Savannah was tugging on his arm. "*Look*," she demanded.

He turned, followed her gaze, and saw, through the grating of the tall fence, a shape bounding down the hill and entering the parking lot.

"It's another one," Savannah said in a thin voice.

He nodded, but he didn't speak. Because as crazy as it sounded, there was something familiar about the figure. Duane leaned forward, squinted.

"It looks angry," Savannah whispered. He glanced at her, then at the werewolves, which had also taken note of the new arrival.

Savannah seized his arm. "Run," she said.

They ran.

★　　★　　★

Melody neared the front gate.

These were the ones, she knew. The wolves watching her from the other side of the fence were two of the creatures she'd seen in her dreams. Where the third one was she didn't know, but she knew with an unshakable certitude that the unseen wolf would be red, because these two were yellow and black.

It was the yellow one Melody wanted to kill most. It was the yellow one who had started all this.

The first werewolf.

So when the yellow wolf wheeled around and set off after Savannah and Short Pump, Melody growled deep in her glorious throat. She knew it would be better for her to face one wolf rather than two, but still she lusted for the gush of the yellow wolf's blood, longed to make the queen wolf pay for all she had started, for the horror she had brought to Lakeview.

Melody slowed as she neared the turnstiles.

On a level she didn't care to examine, Melody understood how it had been. The yellow one had been the first; the black and red were her sisters. The yellow one had dabbled in the unholy arts, had eaten of the dead wolf flesh and had become bestial. The yellow one had converted her sisters, and the Three had been born. The Three had lived for centuries. Perhaps millennia. They craved new adventures, new conquests.

New victims.

And when one of their unholy progeny had spilled blood at the bonfire and had made new wolves, the Three had arrived to control the population, to ensure their kind didn't multiply.

They'd come here to kill.

To kill Glenn.

To kill Joyce.

To kill Weezer, which wouldn't be such a loss.

But they'd come to kill Melody too.

She reached the turnstile and leaped over it just as the yellow wolf disappeared between a pair of cottages. The black wolf hadn't moved, was perhaps curious about Melody owing to the scarcity of werewolves in the world.

How many were there?

Not many, she was sure. The queen wouldn't want competition, wouldn't want to threaten her supremacy, her total control.

The black wolf eyed her from the grass.

Grass that was littered with entrails.

Melody thought of Father Bridwell, of her brothers. She recalled their screams, their sobs, their anguished pleas.

In a way, it was all due to the Three, the beasts who had started this.

That wasn't true, she realised, pulling up short. On all fours, she gazed up at the black wolf, discerned a great many emotions in the bestial features. But whatever this creature was, however abhorrent the black wolf and her two companions were, they were not responsible for her family's depravity.

The black wolf stepped nearer, the humanoid nose scenting the air. What would the black wolf smell on her? Melody wondered. Blood? Faecal matter? Her coat was slathered in every body fluid imaginable. The slaughter of her family had been a blood orgy.

The black wolf seemed unbothered by the stink emanating from Melody's matted coat. The black wolf stepped closer, its yellow eyes battened on Melody.

Melody retreated, her lips writhing into a warning snarl.

But the black wolf kept on, her graceful gait and upright posture making Melody feel more like a pet than a peer, and this troubled her because it brought back her customary confusion, her perpetual fog of doubt. The black wolf uttered a deep, purring growl that bore no resemblance to human speech, yet Melody understood its meaning clearly: *Be still. You have nothing to fear from me.*

Melody retreated, but with not quite the same alarm.

Again sounded the peculiar growl from deep in the black wolf's throat, and again it worked a mysterious alchemy on Melody's nerves. She was still wary, but she no longer believed the black wolf's friendliness was a ruse to lull her into complacency. No, the teeth were sheathed in the speckled red-and-black lips; the retracted claws resembled mere fishing hooks curving from the flesh pads of the black wolf's fingers. As Melody watched, a growl trembling in her throat, the black wolf loomed over her, reached out and trailed the fishhook nails through Melody's wiry mane. Melody twitched but did not pull away. The soothing growl came again, another gentle caress. Melody felt herself relax, her granite-hard muscles unbunching by degrees. The black wolf moved closer, the beast's midsection on a level with Melody's face, and though Melody knew the Three were all female, the hair here was so thick that Melody could not make out even a hint of the creature's sex.

Both long-fingered hands were on Melody's head now, gently stroking. The fishhook nails teased the flesh of her forehead, her temples, then combed delicately over the base of her neck. They lingered on her shoulders, moving in smooth, luxuriant curlicues, the effect somewhere between a mother's nurturing touch and the caress of a patient lover. Melody's snarl began to slacken, her growl to abate. She felt the wet grass beneath her palms, smelled the damp earth struggling to overcome the reek of death surrounding her. The black wolf was rubbing her back now, the fingers strong but surprisingly delicate. Melody could imagine how the creature looked when she wasn't a wolf.

Or perhaps she didn't have to imagine. Melody craned her head slowly up to gaze into the eyes of the black wolf, and as she did she caught a glimpse of her own face reflected in the amber eyes of the creature. What she saw didn't surprise her on a physical level; she'd caught too many reflections of her wolflike visage to be surprised by the change anymore. No, what caught her off guard was the expression on her own face, the naked longing in her eyes. She saw how very small and hopeful she appeared.

The black wolf was grinning. Not the soulless, sadistic grin Melody had glimpsed on her own face while she was eviscerating her father and her brothers, but something far more alarming than that.

The black wolf's eyes were gloating.

Melody went rigid under the kneading fingertips.

Because the black wolf wasn't reassuring her, wasn't trying to give her pleasure. The black wolf was *subjugating* her.

My God, Melody thought, *just look at me. On all fours with my face by the black wolf's musky cunt. She's massaging me, yes, but she's also holding me down. Holding. Me. Down. And she's doing it because she can, because the pecking order is already established. It's the queen and then the black and the red. And after that, it's everyone else. There is no question about supremacy, no possibility of sharing the leadership.*

And by God, Melody thought, she wasn't escaping from one prison to willfully enter another. Fuck. That.

And fuck this cozening creature.

With a roar, Melody sprang upright and whipped her protracted claws in a vicious, backhanded *V*. Her talons opened four deep troughs on either side of the black wolf's chest, and as the black wolf's face stretched in a look of stupefied astonishment, Melody realised with unreasoning delight that they were the same size.

As the blood sluiced down the black wolf's sides and the shock of what had happened gave way to a scalding fury, Melody sank her claws in just over the widening yellow eyes and raked down with all her strength. The keen eyes popped like overheated eggs, the roar that exploded from the creature's mouth so loud it made Melody's eardrums rattle. Melody made a fist and drove it into the black wolf's unhinged lower jaw. The teeth clicked together and promptly sheared off the beast's tongue, which tumbled at Melody's feet and lay squirming like a lively wad of chewing gum.

The black wolf was staggering back and emitting an eerily human wail. It looked a thousand years old, a broken, misshapen thing, its gory blindness a fitting counterpart to its haemorrhaging sides and the clipped stump of its tongue. Melody stalked forward, knowing she'd learned the secret of the Three, the root enforcement of their terrorism.

Servants walked on all fours; masters trod on two.

To pound home her point, she spun the black wolf around, seized her around the neck and drove her to the bloodmoist grass. The creature drummed her limbs and thrashed her head in a frenzy of anguish, but Melody straddled her back, pinned her down, the hairy backbone exposed and waiting. Melody fitted her teeth around the back of the black wolf's neck and bit down. The jerking body in her grip became a live wire, and Melody was nearly bucked off. But instead she bit deeper, chewing the vertebrae, relishing the spinal fluid. With a merciless wrench she twisted the head off the body, spun away with it.

She flirted with the idea of presenting it to the queen, but Melody knew she'd travel lighter and fight better unencumbered. A howl of triumph trembled in her throat, and she let loose with it, her back arching, her blood-smeared face kissing the sky, her full-throated song loud enough to shatter glass, to puncture eardrums.

To announce to the blond bitch Melody would be serving no one. Not anymore.

And never again.

CHAPTER THIRTY-ONE

Savannah sprinted beside Short Pump and didn't even try to suppress the tears that spilled down her cheeks.

Barb was dead.

Barb was gone forever.

And there was no way out. She and Short Pump were trapped. She'd never see Jake again. And Glenn...

She couldn't think of that, couldn't linger on things that could no longer be helped. That monstrous blond wolf was on their tails now and would soon run them down if they didn't come up with some plan, some strategy to—

"This way," Short Pump said and nearly yanked her off her feet as he veered toward the game area.

"Wait," she said in a ragged whisper. "There's nothing over here. There's nowhere to hide."

"The bathhouse," Short Pump said.

They wove into the tunnel leading to the bathhouse stairs. They curled around a white wooden divider and hurried up the ramp, turned a corner, then hustled up the next level until they were on the second floor. For a moment they were sprinting through a tenebrous overhang that simultaneously terrified and comforted her. She hated having no idea what was around them, but she also clung to the notion that they were better off concealed by the darkness than outside and exposed.

She wished Barb were still with them.

"Got to get you somewhere safe," he muttered.

The door to the men's bathhouse was on the left, the women's on the right. Up ahead, there was an opening through which they could see the water park and the lake beyond. Savannah was about to push through the door to their right – she'd selected the women's bathhouse by habit, maybe – but Short Pump paused.

"What are you doing?" she demanded.

His face clouded. "Savannah, there's something you need to know."

"Whatever it is, it can wait. Now come on before they—"

"*Short Pump*," a voice rumbled down the tunnel.

They spun and beheld a figure silhouetted against the roller coaster lights beyond. It was wolflike, it was brawny and it was taller than it had been in human form.

But it was undoubtedly Weezer.

Weezer moved leisurely forward, strolling like he was on the way to the water park for some nighttime aquatic fun.

Short Pump stepped in front of Savannah. "You don't want to hurt us, Weezer."

Savannah could see the way Short Pump's hands were trembling at his sides, but his voice was steady enough. She felt a desperate wave of affection for him.

"*I don't want to* hurt *you*," the gravelly voice rumbled. "*I want to* kill *you, Short Pump. And I want to rape Savannah hard enough to split her open.*"

Short Pump took a step forward. "I won't let you."

Weezer bellowed laughter.

"This way," Duane said over his shoulder in a voice so low Savannah could barely hear it. He nodded toward the women's dressing room.

Weezer was shaking with laughter, but he recovered enough to say, "*You won't be safe from me in the ladies' room, Savannah. Do you think I couldn't hear him?*" Weezer stepped closer, his eyes glinting maniacally. "*I hear everything. I hear your blood beating in your veins, you fucking bitch.*"

"Don't call her that," Short Pump said. About twenty yards separated them.

Weezer drew closer. "*My God, Savannah,*" he rumbled, jutting out his pelvis in a way she associated with catcalling construction workers. "*I can smell your pussy from here.*" He twitched his head. "*I can't wait to taste it.*"

"You're not tasting anything," Short Pump said and set off in a grim march.

Weezer nodded. "*Then I'll kill you first, Short Pump.*"

Duane clenched his fists. "My name's Duane!" he shouted, and barreled straight at Weezer.

Just before the impact of Duane's body against Weezer's, she heard Duane shout, "Now, Savannah!" and knew she had only moments before her escape route was closed off. So she raced for the dressing room door. Just before she darted inside, she saw Duane leap into the air. Then she heard a muffled *oomph* and lunged inside the door.

And immediately sprawled onto a sea of corpses.

Savannah landed facedown, her mouth unfortunately open, so the pooled blood on the floor squirted over her teeth, triggered her gag reflex. The blood was fresh — Jesus — the bodies still warm. Whatever had happened in here had happened very recently, and she had to get out, had to escape this squishy, nightmarish abattoir, but every time she planted her hands on the floor, they slipped in gore, her feet scrambling about as though attempting to scale an icy incline. Outside the door she heard the sounds of a struggle, a cry of pain that belonged to Duane.

Dammit, why had she hidden in here? Why had she taken refuge like a coward?

Wanting to live isn't cowardly.

Yes, it is, she thought. And with tears in her eyes she crawled over the mangled bodies, one of which twitched and coughed when she trailed over it. The blood slime and reek of shit was everywhere.

Savannah was most of the way through the dressing room and nearing the exit leading to the water park when she heard the sounds emanating from the shower area. She froze, not wanting to give away her whereabouts, then realised if the thing in the shower hadn't heard her by now, it wouldn't hear her if she kept her ass moving. She clambered over more bodies and had almost reached the door when she heard a blood-freezing growl from the shower.

"Oh no," she whispered. But she couldn't make her body move.

The growl echoed off the shower tiles, deep and guttural.

With a whimper, Savannah lunged forward and landed right on top of a corpse.

Chugging breath from the shower, the thing coming for her.

Savannah lurched ahead, reached up, snagged the hooked bar that opened the door. But even when she hauled herself to standing, she couldn't yank the door open. A corpse was blocking the way, as if to spite her for still living. Behind her, heavy footsteps clumped through the dressing room, very close now. Savannah reared back on the door with both hands and the corpse slid reproachfully aside. The door opened a foot, sixteen inches. Savannah turned sideways and knifed through.

Made it through, her shoulders breaking into the night air. She hopped sideways through the aperture, all but one leg now.

Something seized her foot.

Savannah screamed, went down. She wriggled in the thing's grip, but its hold was unbreakable. She was hauled backward, her sundress riding up to her hips. The leather belt prevented it from rising even higher, but her crotch was exposed. Ridiculously, she covered herself with a bit of blood-wet fabric, but then the creature poked its head through the column of darkness in the doorway, and she felt her scream coagulate in her throat.

Glenn leered down at her, his grin maniacal.

As horrible as Weezer had been, as ghastly as the little worm had looked in his new form, the sight of Weezer as a werewolf had been nothing compared to the horror of seeing Glenn this way. Glenn was even larger than Weezer was. Even more disturbingly, Glenn's features appeared to have been altered to a greater degree by the transformation. Where before Glenn had appeared brooding, almost taciturn, his face now blazed with unholy need, his eyes alight with the desire to rend and kill.

With a sense of doom, Savannah finally connected the beast leering down at her with the horror in the dressing room.

That had been Glenn's doing, she now realised. Glenn, whom she'd known since junior high. Glenn, who'd always carried a torch for her. Glenn, who...who...

He jerked her toward him, his leer hinging wider, the hot saliva dripping like acid from his scimitar teeth.

"*Don't,*" she begged.

Glenn's yellow eyes blazed. He bent at the waist to take a bite out of her foot.

"Please, Glenn! You don't want to kill me."

He paused and met her eyes. A deep chortle sounded in his throat. The pressure on her ankle increased, his filthy fingers compressing her ankle like it was made of Styrofoam. Glenn's yellow eyes crawled up her body. He grinned.

"*Meat,*" he said.

She opened her mouth, but the sadism in his gaze prohibited speech. Her ankle compacted in his grip, lightning bolts of pain sizzling up her calf.

"You're Jake's father," she said.

Glenn froze. His head was tilted sideways, his mouth open. But his eyes were riveted on hers, the yellow ovals narrowing with either suspicion or anger or something else. Savannah couldn't tell. She was crying, though that hardly mattered.

She said, "That night...when I got back from visiting Mike...you stayed with me." Her face twisted, but she fought it off, knowing this would be her only chance at reaching him. "And the next year Jake was born."

Glenn began to growl, the whites of his canines showing.

"Do the math!" she cried, then realised how foolish that was. This... this *thing* could no more employ reason than a mongrel could reject a fresh morsel. Even now...his lips were trembling, the growl reverberating in a fiendish vibrato.

A howl split the night.

It came from below, on the other side of the dressing areas.

Where Duane and Weezer had been.

At the noise, Glenn whipped his head around and released her foot. His posture was wary. For the first time he was unsure of himself.

Savannah began to retreat, scuttling backward as noiselessly as she could on her elbows and heels. When Glenn's heaving chest and leonine head remained fixed in the opposite direction, she ventured to gain her feet, to backpedal away.

A strident bellow sounded from the same direction as before.

The voice sounded like Duane's.

Too late now, she thought. If Duane was dead, Weezer would soon be coming for her. And there was Glenn to deal with, Glenn who at any moment might—

Glenn turned to face her.

Savannah sucked in breath, bolted down the stone stairs to the water park. She was halfway down the steps when she heard the clatter of toenails behind her. Gripping the central handrail, she swivelled her head in time to see a huge black shape rocket out of the dark and swoop toward her. Savannah took the stairs three at a time, nearly sprained her ankle, recovered and stumbled onto the sidewalk. A millisecond later the Glenn-thing landed behind her, the muscular limbs instantly in motion, bearing down on her. Savannah's legs screamed, her bare feet numb and heavy. There was nowhere to go, no chance to escape. Beside her, tall bushes loomed, before her the chest-high cement of the Lazy River. Jesus Christ, she was going to die.

She thought of Jake and compressed her lips. *No!*

With a last burst of speed she scampered toward the Lazy River, the breath of the beast right at her back. Fifteen feet away, ten...

Something snatched at her hair, tore away a clump at the roots. Two strides. Savannah leaped.

Her stomach hit the rounded cement barrier of the Lazy River, her momentum carrying her forward. Her feet swung up, and as they did something whickered through the air behind her. Savannah went under headfirst, the water fractionally cooler than the air. The swift current took her right away, propelled her around a curve. Savannah breached the water's surface, saw she'd entered a straightaway of perhaps a hundred feet. She heard a plopping sound, Glenn's burly form pounding the water. Savannah dove forward, stroked for her life. Her momentum slowed, the jets underwater here gentler than they'd been on the curve, and behind her she heard the churning tumult of Glenn's pursuit. She imagined his hulking body thrashing through the waist-high water and knew he'd overtake her. And even if she did make it to the end of the straightaway, then what? On the other side of the wall, there was a narrow catwalk and then the lake, and neither one provided shelter from the beast pursuing her. To her left was a lifeguard station, but there was no help there, only a folding chair, a life buoy and a long steel rod with a blotch of red paint halfway up, the tool the guards used to judge a child's height.

Savannah chanced a look behind her, saw whatever gains she'd made had been halved. Glenn was closing fast. He was so big, his legs so long and muscular that he seemed to traverse the shallow channel as though it were a mere puddle, while Savannah had to lurch and swim, shove with her legs as well as she could while her sodden dress trawled through the water like a heavy second skin. Glenn was nearing, nearing, and she was only halfway to the barrier. And it was pointless, futile, the beast would rend her to shreds. The father of her child. She never would have guessed—

Savannah swam forward, a fatalistic caul shadowing the night around her, sealing her fate, stealing the final, paltry vestiges of hope to which she'd clung. Behind her – *right behind her* – Glenn snarled in triumph.

In front of her, Joyce launched herself out of the water.

Savannah went under as Glenn's lethal claws tore through the air, and then the world was full of muffled roars and churning water, and when she came up she saw them tangled together, the claws ripping, the teeth clashing and tearing. Savannah was taken downstream another twenty feet before she stopped, her body trembling, and beheld the terrible battle. The wolf-Joyce was smaller than Glenn, but she fought with even greater ferocity. Glenn's throat was torn and bleeding, a swath of flesh gone from the side of his face, revealing the lethal molars, a large section of his jawbone. Glenn roared, caught Joyce a ferocious blow to the forehead, and her face was drenched in a glistening scrim of blood. Glenn advanced, sensing the kill now, and Savannah moved toward them unthinkingly, knowing she couldn't abandon another friend. Joyce stumbled back, nearly went down.

Savannah veered to her right, reached toward the lifeguard stand.

Grabbed the slender steel rod. Glenn had pinned Joyce under the surface, her limbs whirring, her blood roiling and blackening the water. Savannah whipped the rod at Glenn's head, caught him in the skull. Glenn stumbled sideways, roaring in pain, and relinquished his hold on Joyce, who came up spluttering and grasping her gushing throat. Glenn rounded on Savannah, his great chest heaving, his muscles shivering with rage.

"Come on!" she screamed and took a backward step. "Come on, you worthless bastard! Come on and fucking do it!"

Glenn leaped.

Savannah fell back, brought the rod up.

His entire weight came down on it, drove the base into the crook of her arm, *through* her arm, shattering the elbow, the fire burst of pain indescribable. But his weight immediately left her. The bar slurped free of her arm, the scrape of steel on bone so appalling she nearly lost consciousness.

Savannah got her legs under her, shoved herself toward the wall. Her arm dangled like a severed umbilicus, the blood coursing from the ragged hole in her elbow. Her vision going gauzy, she slumped against the wall, saw Glenn staggering forward, the steel rod having impaled him in the chest. Through the heart?

It couldn't have, she decided moments later. Because he still had the strength to seize hold of Joyce, lift her over the wall, beyond which was the lake and the framework of the adjacent roller coaster. Savannah took a step in that direction, but she needn't have. As Glenn hoisted Joyce over the edge, Joyce's talons sank into his biceps, and together they disappeared over the side of the Lazy River, into the lake below.

★　　★　　★

Joyce twisted as they fell, thinking to return the favour, to plunge Glenn's head underwater, to hold him there until he either died or came to his senses. But the place where they fell was too shallow, the water no more than a couple feet deep.

Joyce landed on Glenn, but she came down hard on the steel rod. Gasped when it punched a hole in her belly. The pain was terrible, but she'd been in a wasted state anyway, the red wolf having shredded a good deal of her flesh, her side a stringy crimson mess. Glenn, goddamn him, continued to attack her, to tear at her arms, to growl and champ and writhe. Doing her best to blot out the pain in her punctured belly, she reached out, seized hold of his wrists and spread them so the killing talons couldn't get at her. Still he snapped at her, his lethal teeth nipping her breasts, the son of a bitch doing his best impression of a monstrous, suckling infant.

Hissing, she slammed his arms down, the movement forcing his head under. He gave off biting her immediately, his body bucking her six inches in the air. But no more than that, she realised, because they were fused together by this cursed rod, the damned thing poking out her lower back. She wanted to reach back there to see how far it protruded from her body, to gauge her chances of freeing herself, but that would allow Glenn to slash at her again with those claws, and she knew she couldn't sustain many more wounds.

Beneath her, underwater, Glenn writhed and thrashed. Large, bloody bubbles rose to the surface.

But he wouldn't die, she knew. Even if he drowned, it wouldn't be permanent. She'd believed him dead before, up in the bar, his neck torn. But he hadn't been dead. That took decapitation.

She'd been such a fool.

The water around them was splashing as though alive. Joyce realised she was weeping. Because this was horror. This wretched new existence. And she had *invited* it. Such a fool. She had longed for something different and exciting and had fallen prey to the allure of a legend, the notion of power and control and extended life.

But what kind of life was this?

Joyce remembered that poor worker behind the Devil's Lair. She hadn't meant to kill him.

Something flopped against the side of her face, and she realised what all the splashing was from.

The carp had found them.

The legends about the fish were ridiculous, of course, because they weren't carnivorous. But damn, were they huge. Joyce wanted out of the water, wanted away from this shallow area, which reeked of oil and weeds and dead marine life.

She jolted as a hand fell on her shoulder. She half-twisted – as much as the steel bar impaling her would allow – and stared up into the face peering down at her.

Savannah.

Joyce reached for her.

And gasped when Glenn's face shot out of the water and snapped at her throat. Instinctively, she thrust up a forearm to obstruct his teeth. The awl-like points sank into the meat of her arm. She grimaced and shoved her arm against Glenn's face, but Glenn held on, the teeth lodged in her arm like immovable pitons.

Savannah was batting at Glenn's head, and Joyce knew if Glenn bit Savannah, she'd either die or be infected, and Joyce couldn't allow either of those things to happen. Joyce looked down at Glenn's exposed Adam's apple and knew what she had to do.

Moaning, Joyce plunged her fangs into his throat. Beneath her, Glenn bucked and growled, but it was too late, too late, there was no choice anymore. Joyce ripped and chewed until she'd eaten through the neck, while around her the carp darted and tore at the flaps of Glenn's skin, and then hands appeared at the top of her vision, Savannah's fingers grasping Glenn's jittering head. With a wrench, Savannah tore Glenn's head off and tossed it into the lake. Joyce was choking on the blood, sobbing, and she only managed two words.

"*Kill me,*" she croaked. "*Kill me.*"

CHAPTER THIRTY-TWO

Duane needed to coax Weezer into letting his guard down.

Weezer wasn't used to being the dominant combatant, so Duane figured on some extra arrogance from his former friend. He wouldn't be surprised if Weezer monologued a little, recounted all the times Duane and others had done him wrong.

What Duane hadn't counted on was what Weezer actually did, which was strike him so hard he momentarily lost consciousness.

One moment Duane was striding forward, feeling for all the world like Clint Eastwood. The next he was blinking up at the wolflike visage, the face like something from a childhood nightmare.

For a time, he lay there in a heap against the second-storey railing and listened to the sound of music tinkling as though nothing much were happening in the park tonight.

Duane moaned weakly, pawed his hip pocket for the gun. The Weezer-thing's eyes shifted to Duane's probing hand, and then Weezer's fingers closed over the bulge of the gun, squeezed, and the pocket and gun and a couple scraps of Duane's flesh came off in Weezer's hand. Laughing demonically, Weezer chucked the gun aside and seized Duane by the shirt. He lifted Duane into the air, the lethal jaws opening wide.

Duane realised he couldn't reach back for the machete in time to stab Weezer, so he did the only thing he could do, which was to thrust out a hand toward Weezer's face.

So quickly he barely saw it, Weezer's teeth clicked together, and the middle three fingers of Duane's right hand disappeared. His index finger had been broken already, but he'd still been pretty fond of it. To discover the middle and ring fingers also severed at the second knuckle was a nasty shock.

Slowly, luxuriantly, Weezer chewed Duane's fingers. The sight of it wasn't pleasant, but the sounds Weezer made…man, it made Duane sick. Perhaps Weezer detected some of Duane's revulsion, for he lifted him closer, made a show of gulping down the meat.

Duane jabbed his left thumb into one of Weezer's eyes.

Roaring, Weezer hurled Duane toward the rail overlooking the parking lot. Duane sailed through the air a good five feet before colliding shoulder-first with the steel rails. Had his finger stumps not been shrieking so loudly, the shoulder trauma would no doubt have felt awful. But all he could feel were the ragged stumps and the searing pain, and dammit, he was going grey. He reached down for the gun, then remembered Weezer had taken it. He still had the machete, or at least he hoped he had it, but Weezer was on him again, lifting him, and just as Duane turned to see Weezer's virulent face, he felt himself floating into space, realised that Weezer had cast him over the railing toward the parking lot below. At that moment, as sure as he was that he was about to die, Duane realised where the music was coming from: the merry-go-round.

Duane's body tilted, his feet swinging over and his eyes coming up to face the sky. He landed on something that gave a little despite the sharp pain it caused.

With an effort, he swivelled his head left and right and realised he'd landed on a car roof. Duane had no idea of the car's make or model, but he knew he weighed over two hundred and seventy pounds, and he doubted the driver would be taking the car out for a spin anytime soon.

He also doubted he'd be walking anytime soon.

Unless you're becoming one of them.

The thought jolted him, made the pain momentarily dim. How long did it take? He couldn't imagine his fingers regenerating, but the agony in his back, all the other bruises and cuts he'd sustained...what if those simply went away after a few hours?

What if you don't live for a few more hours?

Surprisingly, the prospect didn't scare him much. Maybe because he was distracted by the other side of this, the notion that he was stronger than he realised. Was it possible the change happened so rapidly?

He swallowed. No time to worry about that now. Weezer was coming. Duane pushed up on an elbow, turned and saw Weezer leaping over the railing, his gigantic, agile frame landing as lightly as a tomcat on the pavement below.

Could Duane move like that?

He started to sit up and froze when a lightning bolt of pain sizzled through the middle of his back.

Okay, he thought. Maybe he hadn't been bitten after all.

Or maybe you're a pussy and you need to fight through this.

He heard Weezer's almost-silent footfalls approach the car. Grimacing, Duane tried to sit up again, and though yes, it did hurt like a son of a bitch, it was maybe a trifle more bearable than he'd at first thought. He saw Weezer stalking toward him in his left periphery, and Duane threw all his weight to the right. He tumbled off the pulverised car roof – he saw it was a Buick LeSabre when he hit the ground – and pushed onto all fours. From above him came a thump, and he knew Weezer had leaped onto the crushed roof.

Show-off, he thought.

Duane started to rise, and though he did feel healthier than he had any right to feel, he knew he'd never be quick enough to stop Weezer from attacking him again. And this time, he doubted there'd be a respite from death. In his new wolf form, Weezer was either smarter than he used to be, or he was simply more cunning. Either way...

Duane froze at the sound of a guttural snarl.

Oh hell, he thought. He knew what he'd see even before he turned and beheld the blond werewolf's hulking form only ten yards behind him. But she wasn't looking at Duane or Weezer. She was looking at something behind Weezer, something in the direction of Turtle Cove. Weezer turned and looked that way too.

Duane rubbed his eyes, his vision adjusting, and discovered what they were staring at.

Oh no, he thought. *Oh God.*

There was a shelter between the merry-go-round and a ride featuring flying fish – Duane always assumed they were salmon, but what the hell did he know? Out of that shelter were emerging several tiny bodies, which were apparently being shepherded to safety by an adult. Only the adult was a moron because the werewolves had spotted the exodus, were even now bristling and panting at the sight of all the fresh young meat. Duane felt a desolation gust through his belly, recalled the many times he'd caught Weezer leering at a girl far too young to warrant that kind of attention. And just like everybody else, Duane had dismissed it, had convinced himself there was really no problem there at all. It had been his imagination. His friend certainly wasn't a latent paedophile.

Enabler. The word imprinted itself in his mind's eye. *You're an enabler. You're part of the problem, one of the reasons why scum like Weezer end up victimising innocent kids.*

Gunshots in the distance. The werewolves turned that way, as did Duane. They came from the direction of the parking lot, back where Barb had been killed. Which meant the cops had finally shown up, or at least more of them had. And thinking of the park entrance reminded him of Savannah. Where was she? The last he'd seen of her, she'd been slipping through the doors of the dressing room. Was she still in there? Would Weezer simply head back upstairs and murder her when he was done with Duane?

Focus! he told himself. *Deal with this situation!*

Sure, he thought. *It's a simple matter of besting two foes more ferocious than you'd find in a horror movie. I'll get right on that.*

The blond wolf and Weezer exchanged a glance, and some sort of communication seemed to pass between them. The blond werewolf abruptly turned and dashed past Duane, the immense body moving with a grace so fluid and effortless that Duane would have been captivated were it not for the fact that the body in question belonged to a monster.

Was the blond werewolf going after Savannah?

Weezer turned to Duane. Weezer's bestial mouth writhed into a grin. Then he spun and leaped, clearing a car next to the one Duane had landed on. Duane watched with dawning horror as Weezer loped on all fours toward Turtle Cove.

Toward the tiny figures emerging from the shelter.

No, Duane thought. *Please, God, no.*

You have to do something, a voice demanded. *Now. You have to do something now.*

Duane took a deep breath, reached back and slid out the machete.

Grasping it, he set off after Weezer.

★　　★　　★

Melody heard the sirens long before their irritating red-and-blue lights began to strobe over the inns and hotels lining the entrance road. Melody had been gorging on the black wolf – the meat wasn't as succulent as her brothers' flesh had been – but perhaps that was owing to the black wolf's age, which Melody estimated at several hundred years.

And how many innocents had the black wolf preyed on in that lifespan? How many good men and women, how many little kids had she and her sisters slaughtered?

The police cars neared, their wailing like scalpels on Melody's sensitive eardrums.

The growl started deep in the base of her throat. She had prowled forward several paces before she regained her senses, realised how she must look to them. She was also crouched on all fours, and goddammit, no more of that. Melody rose up on her hind legs, watched the police cars approach.

A shot sounded before the first cop emerged from his car.

It missed her, but not by much. Then another shot sounded from a different gun, and this one did not miss. The slug tore through the meat above her knee, grazing her but hurting her all the same. The cops were racing to the fence, the cowards lining up behind the sheltering metal wire, but didn't they see how easily she could kill them, how effortlessly she could rend the chain link fencing and turn their throats to hot red slush?

Two more slugs tore into her in rapid succession, the first one merely skimming the top of her foot, but the second catching her flush in the side, right where she believed her kidney was located. Damn, the pain was bad.

And the rage. As they opened fire on her – eight different shooters at least – Melody's vision was tinged with a blazing orange light, a shuddery, electrifying rage. She knew she had to move. Had to move *now*. As the guns erupted in a fusillade of crashing thunder, she launched herself into the air, rising, rising, surprising even herself with the agility of her leap. She caught a glimpse of the cops below, their faces shocked moons, and their shooting had left off, all but one of them. This one, she saw, was grim-faced, younger than the rest. He had a crew cut and a square jaw, and as she neared the ground, she saw in his eyes the cold sadism of her brother John, the same unfeeling emptiness in his eyes, the absence of empathy, the only urge to inflict pain, to oppress.

Melody hit the ground, roared, and the son of a bitch fired again, and though he missed again – he was neither intelligent nor skillful – his raw hatred of her enflamed her, sent her catapulting forward, bouncing off her tensile toes and crashing against the fence, punching through the pitiful wires, grasping his bicep. As her powerful new body rebounded from the fence, she tore his arm off at the shoulder. His eyes went vast and horrorstruck and he staggered backward, the pumping jet of blood splashing over one of his fellow officers. Then the rest of the policemen were awash with terror, some of them standing mutely, others turning and dashing back to their cruisers.

One, though, was licking his lips as if to gather himself, and in his face she detected neither sadism nor greed. No, this one had just witnessed a murder and probably knew that his dying comrade was a piece of trash, but that it was still his duty to bring down his comrade's killer.

Melody decided she would not murder this policeman.

She vaulted sideways as the policeman fired, and she scrambled away toward the cottages, making sure to jag unpredictably as she did so. Other guns joined in the booming chorus, but none of the bullets found their mark. She was wounded, she knew. The slug that had pierced her kidney plagued her most of all. But she was alive and mostly unfettered by pain. A bullet whizzed by her face as she hurried toward the cottages. When she drew even with a porch, a slug slammed into a wooden pillar, and then she was safely hidden and racing toward the amusement park.

Racing toward the yellow wolf.

*　　*　　*

"Hold still, dammit," Savannah grunted. She understood why Joyce was moving around so much – the carp were making her antsy too – but it was rendering an already difficult job well-nigh impossible. The change had mostly reversed itself, which made Savannah even more frantic to save her friend's life.

"Just kill me," Joyce moaned.

Savannah grasped the pole jutting out of Joyce's back, but her fingers kept slipping off, the damned thing so wedged into Joyce's and Glenn's bodies that it wouldn't even budge. To make matters worse, there was the fact that Savannah only had one good hand – her right arm was shattered, the bones of her elbow a shrieking horror – and there was blood and lake water and perspiration slicking the steel.

"Kill me," Joyce repeated.

"I can't," she said.

"You have to!" Joyce snapped back.

Around them, the carp rolled over, flopped.

Savannah wrapped her sodden, torn sundress around the rod, grasped it, and strained to yank it free, but it was no good. The thing stayed firmly embedded in Joyce's stomach.

Savannah was straining to remove the bar when Joyce's eyes shot up to something behind Savannah. She whirled in time to see the blond beast leap at them, the giant werewolf's eyes gleaming a hellish amber. Savannah did the only thing instinct would allow – she dove sideways. The blond werewolf came down on Joyce.

Savannah glanced around, casting about for anything that would deter the blond werewolf. Her gaze landed on a clump of concrete just under the water's surface. She hefted it – the object had to weigh ten pounds – but she managed to carry it. She strode over to the trio, the blond werewolf reaching down to grasp Joyce's head. Savannah raised the concrete rock.

And brayed in horror as the werewolf ripped Joyce's head from her body.

Joyce's headless body slithered down the rod on top of Glenn.

Savannah continued to scream, but she brought the rock down as hard as she could on the base of the blond wolf's skull. The giant werewolf crumpled, landed beside Joyce's corpse.

Weeping, Savannah turned and sloshed through the water toward the boardwalk. She pushed off as hard as she could, her bare feet squelching as they left the sucking, muddy lake bottom, and swung her lower body up under the railing. She rolled over onto her stomach, her shattered right elbow protesting horribly as her weight shifted over it, and chanced a look back toward the shallow water.

Where the blond werewolf was already rising.

Savannah gained her feet, began running as fast as her weary body would allow in the direction of the southern exit, the suspension bridge. Technically, it was farther away than the main exit, but the last time she'd glimpsed the main exit, there were werewolves in its vicinity. There were no guarantees the suspension bridge was clear, but she could think of nowhere else to go.

"Hey!" a voice shouted.

Savannah gasped, jerked her head to the right, and spotted a trio of cops with their weapons drawn. They were moving toward her from the wide walkway that divided the Viking ship from the Devil's Lair.

She ran toward them.

The one on the left took aim at her.

Savannah realised how she must look to him. Bloody, bedraggled. But did he actually think she was one of the monsters?

"Jesus, Mick!" an officer gasped and slapped his partner's gun down. "What the hell is wrong with you?"

Mick's eyes seemed to clear, and he gave a quick shake of his head. "Sorry. It's just..." He shrugged lamely.

The cop who had prevented Mick from shooting her stepped forward, his free hand extended. "Come on," he said. "Let's get you somewhere safe."

Tears brimming in her eyes, she jogged toward him.

"Uh…Brant?" Mick said. "Here it comes."

The helpful cop – Brant, apparently – glanced beyond her, and his eyes widened. "Shit," he muttered.

When Savannah drew even with the three cops – Brant appeared to be the leader, though they all looked like they were in their late thirties or early forties – she turned and saw the blond wolf moving toward them up the boardwalk.

The giant werewolf carried a head in each hand, grasping them by the hair.

Joyce and Glenn.

"Get behind us," Brant said, raising his weapon.

"Let's get out of here," said the one to their left, a heavyset man with a brown mustache.

"Shoot it, Brant," Mick said.

"We all shoot," Brant said, and though his voice was steady, Savannah could see how his hands were trembling.

"When?" the mustachioed cop asked, but he needn't have. Because at that moment, Brant opened fire.

The first slug opened a red oval on the side of the blond werewolf's neck. Mick and Mustache began to fire too, though their aim wasn't as accurate as Brant's. Brant fired again, and this one nailed the werewolf in the centre of the chest. Fifty feet from them now, the werewolf roared, half-turned, then pivoted and heaved Glenn's head at them. It drizzled blood as it tumbled through the air and hit the pavement between Mick and Brant, bounced a few times, and came to rest about ten feet behind Savannah. She turned away from Glenn's staring, dead eyes.

And saw Joyce's head hurtling through the air, this one blazing straight at them. It smashed into Mustache's face, propelling him backward. Brant fired, caught the blond werewolf again, but the monster appeared unfazed, began chugging forward, its face grim, its ferocious teeth bared.

"Brant?" Mick asked in a choked whisper.

"Come on," Brant muttered. He took Savannah by the arm and led her toward the Devil's Lair.

Mick remained fixed in place, a cardboard cutout come to life.

"Mick!" Brant yelled.

But Mick didn't budge, only squeezed the trigger, once, twice, three times, a couple of the bullets finding their mark, but doing little to slow the beast down. It overtook him as Savannah and Brant reached the Devil's Lair. As they disappeared under the overhanging archway, Savannah saw the blond werewolf take Mick down, its claws whirring the cop's chest into bloody hamburger. *Holy God*, Savannah thought as the darkness swallowed them. How many people had the beasts slaughtered tonight? Fifty? A hundred? And how many more would they kill?

She was certain Duane was dead. And it was only a matter of time before she and this brave cop joined the ranks of corpses littering Beach Land.

"This way," Brant said, shuttling her past the barred ticket booth into the holding area. As they moved into the holding area, Savannah distinguished movement within the booth, someone no doubt having taken refuge in there from the werewolves.

Still grasping her arm, Brant led her past the closed elevator doors and toward a door marked with an illuminated red EXIT sign.

He reached out, grasped the doorknob. As he did, she noticed a pool of some sludgy substance leaking out from under the exit door. Brant opened the door and a tide of body parts spilled out.

Gagging, he stumbled back. He'd shoved a forearm against his mouth, was coughing and swaying toward the elevator doors. Savannah pushed the button, and the elevator wheezed open. She lurched inside. Brant made to follow, then froze, his eyes going huge in the dimness.

The blond werewolf took him down. The holding area filled with his strident screams. Savannah jammed her index finger against the button that would close the doors, but the doors remained open. Brant's screams cut off, the sounds becoming pulpy and wet. The fresh coppery scent of blood drifted into the elevator.

The werewolf snarled, champed, and Savannah jabbed the button again and again, and as the beast rose, its front a slick red horror, the doors began to close. It stared at her, its wicked lips curving into a grin, as the doors cinched shut.

As the elevator started to rise, she realised the blond werewolf had allowed her this momentary respite.

It was enjoying itself too much to kill her now.

It wanted her to cower. It wanted her to suffer.

It wanted to hunt.

Savannah choked back a sob as the elevator continued to rise.

CHAPTER THIRTY-THREE

Duane was maybe fifty feet behind Weezer, both of them moving stealthily, Weezer no doubt to make sure he could take his young quarry by surprise, Duane because he knew he'd only get one chance to ambush Weezer.

The adult leading the children out of the shelter turned out to be a short middle-aged woman with a tight ball of curly brown hair and a butt like two globes crammed inside a pair of khaki pants. She looked vaguely familiar.

But she was completely unaware of the werewolf approaching her. So were the twenty or so children congregated around the merry-go-round. The sight of one little girl, who couldn't have been more than five years old, watching the revolving horses and unicorns longingly made Duane's heart ache.

He hustled forward, doing his best to make as little sound as possible. Duane reduced the distance between him and Weezer. Thirty feet now. Twenty.

Without warning, Weezer broke into a loping sprint, straight at the woman and the pair of kids she was ushering out of the shelter.

Knowing he couldn't wait, Duane yelled, "Weezer!"

Weezer skidded to a stop, the woman and the children whirling to stare at the werewolf that had halted only fifteen feet from them. Duane continued to rush forward, and as he neared Weezer — whose eyes were slitted in rage — he realised who the woman was.

His second grade teacher, Miss Hayward. She'd just been starting out when she'd had Duane in class, but now, two decades later, she looked like a different person.

Or maybe she was just scared shitless.

But God love her, she was being as brave as anyone could be, extending her stubby arms and pushing as many kids as she could behind her. But her mouth was frozen in a terrified O, and the crotch of her khakis had gone a much darker shade.

On all fours, Weezer roared at Duane.

Who barreled forward, aware that he'd done this before. But the first time he'd been rash. He'd left the gun in his pocket instead of emptying it into Weezer's accursed face, and now the gun was lost and there was nothing he could do about it.

But he did have the machete, and if luck was on his side, maybe the weapon still contained a trace of Barb Callahan's courage. Twenty feet from

Weezer, Duane stumbled, nearly landed on the machete, and wouldn't that have been something? Committing hari-kari in front of these screeching children and removing all hope they might have of surviving?

Gunshots sounded from the direction of the Viking ship and the Devil's Lair, and Duane had a moment to wonder about Savannah. Was she dead already? Or cornered by one of the remaining werewolves?

No time to think about it now. He was bearing down on Weezer.

Weezer vaulted at him, his teeth bared and his claws extended.

Instinctively, Duane went into a double-kneed slide, the pavement chewing up his knees. As Weezer hurtled toward him, then over him, Duane slashed out with the machete, and was stunned when the blade unzipped a gash from Weezer's chest to his abdomen. The machete was nearly torn from Duane's grip as Weezer's body sailed past, but he held on, and then he was scrambling around to face Weezer.

Who landed awkwardly and stood on two feet. In profile, Duane watched Weezer take a long glance down his cleaved torso, Weezer's face going slack with surprise.

Without taking his eyes off Weezer, Duane hissed over his shoulder, "Get them back inside the shelter."

Miss Hayward – or maybe it was Mrs. Something now – didn't say anything, but she began to usher the shrieking kids back into the shelter. This close to the building, Duane realised it wasn't really meant to house people – it looked like little more than an oversize white garden shed – and the kids must've been jammed in there like cigarettes in a pack. But at least there'd be something between them and Weezer, even if it was only a wall of aged plywood.

With a start, Duane realised Weezer was eyeballing the children. His chest was heaving, there was an unwholesome look in his eyes. And... holy shit.

Weezer had an erection.

"You son of a bitch," Duane muttered. He strode toward Weezer. Raised the machete.

He was certain Weezer would counterattack, but instead of lashing out like Duane expected, the Weezer-thing rolled sideways and came up loping toward the merry-go-round. Duane spun and discovered with a sinking feeling that the little blond girl who'd been watching the carousel earlier hadn't moved at all, except to mine for a booger in her right nostril. Her index finger was buried almost to the hilt, and she didn't seem aware of the monster about to devour her.

Duane took off toward them, but he knew it was fruitless. He'd never get there in—

A figure darted in from the right, and Weezer roared as he was flung off course. He missed the nose-picking girl by mere inches and crashed into the underside of the revolving merry-go-round. As Duane reached the girl, he beheld Miss Hayward grasping the chain with which she'd belted Weezer, as well as the huge padlock that dangled from the end of the chain. It wasn't a lethal weapon, not against a werewolf, but she'd nailed Weezer right in the head with it, and that proved enough to give the blond girl time to exhume her finger from her nose and scamper back inside the shelter with the others.

"Stay with them," Duane said to Miss Hayward, who seemed eager to comply.

It's just the two of us now, Duane thought.

Then realised he was wrong as the carousel revealed a little red-haired boy sitting atop a white unicorn. Weezer spotted the boy at the same time, the kid only six or seven but old enough to know how to follow directions. *The little shit*, Duane thought. He was wearing an Angry Birds T-shirt and gaping at Weezer, whose look of consternation transformed into one of vilest hunger. Without pause, Weezer sprang onto the side of the carousel. To his credit, the little red-haired boy reacted quickly as well. He pushed off the unicorn and promptly landed on a sleigh, one of those bench seats grandparents or unadventurous kids sat on during the ride.

Weezer went after him. Duane was moving too, and though Weezer had gotten a half-second head start, Duane covered the distance between them faster than he would've believed possible. The implications of this flashed through his head – was he changing? – but the thought was gone in an instant. Because Weezer had ahold of the waistband of the kid's shorts, was dragging the kid toward him.

Leaving Weezer's back exposed.

Duane chopped down at it with the machete.

At least three inches of steel disappeared into Weezer's lower back. Weezer bellowed, whirled and caught Duane with a vicious backhand. Duane flew backward and landed on the carousel's silver platform. Duane shook his head as the horses rising and falling on either side of him danced into vague equine blurs.

The red-haired boy's shrill scream brought Duane back to his senses, or at least most of the way there, and he forced himself to sit up, to grab hold of one of the horse's stirrups. It lifted him up, allowed him to gather himself, to see if he still had time to save the little boy.

He did, he realised. But not much. Weezer had the poor kid suspended in the air by one ankle, the boy's upside-down face on a level with Weezer's open jaws. Duane wished he had the machete, but he had no idea where it had gone.

So he reared back and aimed a sideways kick at Weezer's knee.

Weezer crumpled against the bench seat, the boy dropping to the platform and landing right on his red-haired skull. Duane was pretty sure the kid was knocked unconscious, and he was pretty sure that was a good thing. Because Weezer was whirling toward Duane with his claws out and his yellow eyes alight with fury, and Duane had not the slightest idea how to protect himself. Weezer plunged his talons into Duane's shoulders, the razor-sharp tips sinking into Duane's flesh as easily as meat thermometers into a holiday ham. Duane sucked in breath, his fingers acting on their own accord, seizing the flaps of the machete wound he'd made in Weezer's chest, jerking wider the incision, the pale muscle tissue of Weezer's pectorals exposed and pulsing blood. Weezer gasped. His claws came loose of Duane's shoulders, slapped at Duane's hands as though Duane were some purse-snatching hooligan and Weezer his elderly mark. When Weezer's hands came free, Duane balled a fist, reared back, and clobbered Weezer's snarling face dead in the nose. Weezer's head snapped back, came darting at Duane's throat, but Duane leapedhopped nimbly aside, evading Weezer and taking refuge behind a pistoning black horse.

He was abruptly aware of how screwed he was. As if to confirm this notion, Weezer swiped at him over the pumping black horse and tore a ragged groove across Duane's forehead. A sheet of blood poured over Duane's brow, dripped in his eyes, and though he flicked his head from side to side and mopped his brow as well as he could, he knew he was toast. Moaning, Duane armed away the blood, kept hold of a carousel bar so he wouldn't tumble off the ride, but it was no use. Any second now, Weezer would open his belly, remove his entrails in a gruesome string, and—

Duane froze.

Weezer was going for the little boy.

*　　*　　*

Though it made no earthly sense, though she needed to be thinking about survival right now and though her very life depended on what she did in the next two minutes, the only thing Savannah could think about on the long ride up the elevator was Short Pump.

No, her mind corrected. *Duane. His name is Duane.*

But he didn't think of himself as Duane before, she argued. *He saw himself as Short Pump, as the butt of the joke.*

You should have helped him see more. You should have believed in him.

Okay, she thought, *but why the hell am I worrying about this now?*

Because you wish Duane were here with you.

Savannah sank against the back wall of the elevator, realising this was true. She hadn't appreciated Duane when they'd been here earlier this week. But now that he was gone – now that she was nearing her own death – she wished she could go back.

The elevator crawled higher, higher.

She remembered the way Duane had charged at Weezer. Giving her time to get away. Creating a diversion. Showing more bravery than she would have guessed he had in him.

That's a theme with you, isn't it, Savannah? Underestimating people. Taking them for granted—

The elevator climbed higher.

—letting your looks carry you through life, and see where they've carried you?

Right to the top of this death house. And you know what the cruelest irony is, Savannah? You little fucking princess?

The elevator jarred to a stop.

You're not going to be pretty for much longer.

The elevator doors slid open. The eerie soundtrack lapped over her. Deep chords played by a tuneless organ. Industrial thuds and creaks. Maniacal laughter from some deep, distorting cave.

Savannah quaked with terror.

The blond werewolf is going to rend that face of yours to ribbons.

She drew even with the double doors.

And eat what's left of you.

Savannah emerged from the elevator but paused, listening. She couldn't hear anything, but what did that prove? The blond werewolf was preternaturally cunning. Savannah peered into the gloom and saw, about fifteen yards ahead, the place where the corridor turned, the only illumination the infernal orange glow that shone between intermittent cracks in the walls.

She swallowed, her whole body trembling. What if she simply stepped back inside the elevator, rode it down to the holding area? What if she outfoxed the beast, managed to escape the Devil's Lair and ran like hell for the suspension bridge? It was doubtful, but it seemed a lot more appealing than tiptoeing around these labyrinthine corridors and waiting for the blond wolf to leap out at her and rip her apart.

What if it doesn't rip you apart? the teasing voice asked. *What if it disfigures you instead? What if it leaves you so blighted that your own son won't be able to look at you without screaming in horror?*

The ghastly Devil's Lair soundtrack seemed to taunt her. The thudding. The organ. The hateful laughter. It filled the corridor, swelling, until she felt she'd happened into some terrible nineteenth century mental ward. Inhabited by the damned. Their shrieking voices plagued her.

She barely heard the elevator doors slide shut.

Savannah whirled, thinking to jab the illuminated button, but that was madness too. If she rode the elevator back down, the werewolf would have plenty of time to catch up to her, to slaughter her the moment the doors opened.

So she was basically out of options. She could either stand here until the werewolf came or take her chances navigating the murky corridors in the feeble hope she could evade the creature.

Her heart thudding painfully, her right arm dangling uselessly at her side, Savannah stepped forward.

Halfway to the *T* in the hallway, she froze, listening.

Furtive footsteps echoed down the corridor. Coming nearer? Savannah grimaced, concentrating on the sounds, struggling to trace them to a specific place.

The footsteps paused. Or maybe the speaker noise drowned them out.

Dammit, couldn't the old woman in the ticket booth have killed the grisly soundtrack once things started to go to hell? How many more people had died because the piped-in sound had masked the approach of the werewolves?

Footfalls again. Faster this time. They sounded like they were emanating from the walls.

Maybe they were, she realised with a jolt. Maybe the blond werewolf was still climbing up the many flights of stairs on the way to the fifth floor. Savannah began to move a bit faster. As she did, she listened as hard as she could and racked her brain to recall where the nearest exit sign had been when she and Duane had come this week.

She crept forward, wishing someone, anyone were here with her now.

Well, she amended, *anyone but the blond werewolf.*

She listened for the rabid breath of the beast, the clitter of toenails on wood. If she could—

"*Oh my God!*" she yelled as something battered her from the right, something hard and fast, and then she was sprawled against the wall, staring in shock at the grasping hands that had emerged, the same fucking ones that had scared the shit out of her and Duane the last time they'd been here, only this time they'd bumped against her ruined right arm, and if she got out of here alive she'd sue the assholes who'd designed this attraction.

Savannah pushed away from the wall with her good elbow, told herself to get a freaking grip. She threw one last hateful look at the groping green hands, which had begun their slow recession into the wall, and she moved around the corner. The glow shifted from orange to red. Savannah pivoted slowly to her right, in the direction of a small, recessed alcove.

Above which a red sign said EXIT.

Savannah bit her lip and wondered how she should play this. The blond werewolf could hurtle out of this door at any moment.

Unless there was another stairwell, another exit sign. She rummaged through the scrap heap of her memory for images of other exit signs, but she drew a blank. She knew it should be a fairly straightforward process determining whether or not this was the same stairwell that she'd glimpsed in the holding area, the one choked with half-eaten body parts.

But she wasn't sure.

She took a hesitant step forward. If this wasn't the exit that connected to the holding area, she might very well use it to make her escape.

Then again, if it *was* the same stairwell, the werewolf was likely in there right now.

"Damn," she whispered. She punched her thighs, considering. Maybe she should, after all, scamper back to the elevator and ride it down to the holding area. Maybe the werewolf wouldn't expect her to retrace her steps. Maybe the werewolf believed she'd disembarked on another floor.

Or perhaps the werewolf was on the other side of *this* door.

Her body frozen with dread, she stared at the black door and waited for it to wheeze inward, the monstrous blond werewolf to explode out at her.

The cackle of demented witches sounded on the Devil's Lair soundtrack. Savannah fancied she could hear breathing right behind her.

She whirled, arms thrown up to fend off the werewolf.

The hallway was empty.

Then go! a voice somewhere within her cried out.

Nodding to herself, she set off down the hallway. She had to do *something*, that was what mattered. Waiting meant certain death. If she acted now, she might live, she might die, but at least—

She heard a creaking sound behind her.

Savannah turned, saw the black door open.

Bathed in lurid red light, the blond werewolf emerged.

Savannah was appalled by its height, its rippling muscles.

Its mouth writhed into a grin.

Savannah whirled and sprinted away. She heard the clattering of the werewolf's pursuit.

And as she ran, it was as though the act of moving somehow unstuck the machinery of her mind. She remembered how Duane, in an attempt to soothe her jangling nerves, had narrated the layout of the Devil's Lair to her, had explained how each floor had a theme. This one, Duane had said, was merely a warm-up of sorts, an illumined skull here, a pair of groping hands there. In fact, she thought as she raced around a corner, the attraction hadn't actually gotten scary until they'd descended to the third floor, the one with the zombie theme.

Of course, she hadn't had a werewolf chasing her last time. That tended to make the experience a little more harrowing.

She neared a corner, this one washed in a spectral green light, and risked a look behind her.

The werewolf was only twenty feet away. And closing.

Whimpering, Savannah veered around the corner and encountered a straight stretch of hall. She remembered walking it with Duane. She remembered...

The werewolf snarled as it leaped at her.

Savannah hit the floor. Another set of groping hands shot out of the wall, collided with the werewolf. The mechanical arms snapped off as the werewolf crashed into them, tumbled over Savannah, its body skidding on the floor. With a bellow of outrage, the werewolf rolled over in a whir of hairy limbs. Savannah was already on her feet, racing back the way she'd come. She swerved around the corner, heard the werewolf roar behind her, the sound a thunderous booming in the tight corridor. Savannah moved faster now, glad to have a plan, even if it was a poor one. If she could make it back to the elevator, if she could get the doors shut in time...

She heard the steam engine huff of the werewolf behind her. The goddamned thing moved as fast as a train too. She flirted briefly with the idea of continuing to the staircase, then realised that was folly. The stairwell was a slaughterhouse. How many victims had taken refuge there in the hope that they'd escape the monsters? True, she'd only glimpsed the base of the stairwell earlier, but the bodies had looked like they were piled five high. And very few of them appeared to be in one piece.

Behind her, the werewolf growled.

Savannah sprinted for her life. She rounded a corner and the exit sign appeared ahead. She waited until the last possible second, then lunged for the corridor that would take her to the elevator doors. But she lost her footing as she tried to navigate the turn, and the werewolf merely leaped at the hallway in midstride, caught itself on the wall and landed right behind her. She took a floundering step but felt something shove against her lower back. She landed on her chest. It knocked the wind out of her, but that didn't matter. The beast was bearing down on her, looming over her. She crawled forward, grimacing. She was going to die. No one was coming to her rescue. Not the police, not Duane.

Something tugged at the belt of her sundress, the thin leather strap she'd used to give the dress some shape. The werewolf was lifting her by the belt, toying with her, she realised. Savannah reached down with her good left hand, jerked the belt free of its buckle. Then she was tumbling to the ground, the wolf having lost hold of her. The beast snarled, discarded the belt. In a frenzy of terror, she rolled over, grabbed for the belt, which lay to her left. Her fingers closed on it just as the werewolf reached down, grasped her by the throat. She was lifted off the floor, her feet kicking, the breath being slowly strangled out of her. The odours of blood and shit blanketed her. Savannah's eyes watered, her revulsion only outfaced by her terror. The werewolf raised her toward its amber eyes, and through her pain-fueled tears she saw the hellfire banked within those eyes, the insane hunger and ceaseless need to dominate. The bear-trap jaws hinged open. Slaver dripped from the tapered fangs.

Savannah swung the belt, watched the silver buckle carve a deep slit in the werewolf's temple.

The werewolf roared, threw her backward. Savannah sailed through the air with the belt still clutched in her hand. She hit the floor, her head snapping back. In the dim orange light she saw the wolf stalking forward, the gash in its temple dribbling blood. It was nodding, leering, its mouth opening wide. Savannah adjusted her grip on the belt, slid the single prong through the gap between her index and middle fingers.

Growling triumphantly, the werewolf leapedvaulted at her, landed on her. At the last second, Savannah jabbed at its right eye with the steel prong.

And then the werewolf was squalling, stumbling back, clutching its punctured eye. Dazed, Savannah gained her feet, stumbled toward the elevator. She'd dropped the belt, she realised. But that no longer mattered. The only thing that mattered was opening the door and closing it again, putting something between her and the werewolf, no matter what it was. She thumbed the button, praying the elevator hadn't descended after delivering her to the top floor.

The doors slid open. Moaning, Savannah lurched forward. The lights inside the elevator flickered.

Savannah jabbed at the button to close the doors.

The doors began to close.

A blur of movement swam toward her, the blond werewolf racing toward the dwindling gap. Savannah pushed against the back wall, certain the wolf would beat the closing doors. The gap was six inches wide when the wolf leaped.

It closed at the exact moment the wolf crashed against the doors.

The elevator began to descend.

An unearthly bellow of fury sounded from just above her. She heard scratching, a guttural grunting. The sounds of maniacal effort.

Oh God, she thought. *It's prying the doors open.*

A moment later the elevator rocked as something enormous landed on top of it.

She wished the elevator car would travel faster than it was, but she knew she was at its torpid mercy. Savannah moved to the corner of the elevator, her eyes on the ceiling.

The elevator slowly descended. Savannah trembled, waited for the sounds of scratching, of rending metal.

But she heard something else instead. The elevator began to rock, to shudder.

It ground to a halt.

The werewolf had managed to stop its downward progress.

Savannah sank down to the rubber-stripped floor, bit a knuckle to stifle her scream. She listened for the werewolf.

A thud sounded, low and leaden.

In the centre of the ceiling, the metal twitched downward.

The werewolf was trying to punch a hole through the elevator roof.

★   ★   ★

Melody decided she'd have to scour the park for the yellow werewolf, not because the bitch would be hiding from her, but because the queen, having exhausted her supply of easy victims, would have resorted to prowling through the buildings to frighten them out of hiding.

The thought of the yellow bitch hunting innocent victims was fuel enough to sustain Melody's wolf form. Melody welcomed the rage, welcomed the killing urge. Several times during her flight through the housing area of the park, she'd torn open cottage windows, ripped doors off hinges, to find terrified tourists huddling in the shadows, none of them foolhardy enough to attack her.

But their warm flesh was difficult to resist.

As yet she hadn't killed wantonly, but God, it was getting harder. The flesh of her father and brothers still lay in her belly, but the taste of their blood, the glorious gush over her lips, her teeth…oh, how she longed for the sensation again, longed to bathe in the molten spray.

But each time she found them – in the shops, in the main office, in closets and under beds – she was able to ward off the hunger, was able to resist taking more lives.

But the police kept hunting her.

Twice now she'd been surprised by the thunder of their guns. Several times she'd been caught by their bullets. On two occasions the hateful slugs had simply grazed her and travelled on. Once, when she'd been caught in the hip, she'd been able to simply scoop out the bullet with the flick of a fingernail, the wound shallow. But two of the slugs still burned in her flesh, and those white-hot points of agony also served to enflame her rage. She believed she could resist the urge to open the throats of the lambs who hid in the shadows, the parents shielding their children, the harmless elderly men and women who'd come to Beach Land to eat saltwater taffy and to reminisce about their younger days.

But the gunmen…the trigger-happy tormentors…

Melody was inside a clothing shop when she heard the crunch of glass under sneakers.

One of the maverick cops had followed her inside.

Melody was in the back corner of the capacious shop, examining the dressing stalls for signs of the yellow beast. She knew if she could pick up the bitch's scent, she'd be able to follow it until their final confrontation. But there was nothing in the stalls save a young mother and her infant son.

When Melody first yanked the yellow curtain aside, the mother yelped and pressed her infant against her shoulder. The baby immediately began fussing, and the mother rocked the child, her teary eyes never leaving Melody's.

"Who's there?" the cop called. His voice sounded shaky, Melody judged, but not the cautious kind of shaky. It was the fear of one who'll do anything to save himself, the terror of the drowning man.

The young mother's eyes flitted from Melody to the direction from which the cop's voice emanated.

"I hear you in there," the cop said, and Melody knew there was no avoiding it.

She glanced at mother and child, and when Melody's eyes took in the infant, the mother must've seen something in Melody's expression that horrified her. Because she began screaming for help, and that brought the clumsy footsteps closer, the cop and his stinging weapon poised and ready to unleash its mindless wrath on Melody.

She knew she had to kill him, but she glanced in all directions in an attempt to avoid murder. The dressing stalls were floor-to-ceiling, and there appeared no other way out.

The cop was approaching the edge of the first dressing room. Another moment and he'd spot Melody.

With a gasp, Melody lunged into the stall next to the young mother's. The curtain swung up, a couple rings twanging free of their fabric, but the curtain remaining intact. Melody reached up, jerked the curtain sideways to close the gap, but it was no use, and anyway, the cop was only feet away now.

He appeared in the sliver of pellucid light slanting in from a transom window. He peered into the gap, screwing up his eyes to make out what lay within. Something flickered in his eyes – Fear? Recognition? – but as he raised his weapon, the infant in the dressing room beside Melody's cried out, and the cop twitched forward. He sucked in surprised breath. The mother said something to him. But before he could react, Melody was rocketing out of the stall and diving to her right, away from the cop. He fired just as Melody bounded around the dressing stalls, and then she was leaping through the shattered picture window and moving rapidly through the night.

She hadn't travelled fifty feet before another barrage of bullets tore the air around her, one of them embedding painfully in her heel. The wound was severe enough to slow her progress. Melody had made the mistake of passing through the parking lot, where the police were thicker. Had she chosen the boardwalk, she might have had better luck, but that didn't matter now. They were firing at her from behind parked cars, from the shelter of a Slushie stand. Reckless. Blazing away. Another bullet passed within an inch of her nose, and growling, Melody fell to all fours to present a more difficult target. She heard a commotion to her right, something happening near the merry-go-round. But the policemen were right behind her now, their efforts concentrated on bringing her down.

Melody loped toward the Devil's Lair.

Maybe she could take refuge behind it. Or in the bay water beyond.

This notion held some allure for her. She wanted to live, after all.

But even stronger was the desire to end the queen's life.

The bullets whizzing past her, Melody raced toward the Devil's Lair.

★　　★　　★

Weezer stooped over the little red-haired boy, who was indeed unconscious. Duane's vision was blurry and his eyes stung from his own blood, but he could see well enough to know he had to act now. If only he had the damned machete!

Duane threaded between a horse and a unicorn and aimed a kick at Weezer's hairy ass. He regretted it when one of Weezer's knees landed on the red-haired boy's prone body. The kid scarcely moved, and Duane had a momentary worry that Weezer had already killed him.

But Duane had to proceed as though the boy were alive. And at any rate, the kids in the shed were definitely still alive, as was Miss Hayward. If Duane couldn't save the little red-haired shit, he could save the rest of them.

Weezer sprang at Duane, who barely had time to fling up an arm to protect his throat. Weezer's jaws clamped down on Duane's forearm, squeezed. Duane bellowed in pain as the dull crunch of compressed bone sounded beneath the carousel's merry organ. Weezer was attached to Duane's flesh like a furry armband, the teeth grinding now, shredding, and in desperation Duane thrust a thumb at the dark hollow of Weezer's ear. The thumbnail punctured Weezer's eardrum, burrowed its way in, and Weezer's mouth opened in a bellow, Duane's forearm released. He stumbled away, alive and still in one piece.

But in monumental pain, pain unlike anything he would have believed possible. The one blessing, he thought ruefully, was that most of the damage was limited to the right side of his body. His missing fingers. His mutilated forearm.

Weezer was stalking toward him.

Duane backpedalled, glancing right and left for the machete. It wasn't embedded in Weezer's back, and it damn sure wasn't lying out in the open. Had Weezer thrown it clear of the merry-go-round?

Duane swallowed, decided he needed to get off this freaking ride. At the very least that would lead Weezer away from the unconscious boy. There'd been gunshots from the central boardwalk area only a minute ago; maybe Duane would get lucky and encounter some cops.

Or maybe they'd shoot Duane dead in a fit of dreadful irony.

Duane was just turning to step off the platform when Weezer launched himself toward him. So sudden was the leap and so unprepared was Duane that he reacted instinctively, simply falling backward and hoping that Weezer went somersaulting over him.

But Weezer didn't. He landed on Duane's chest, his knees pinning Duane's arms, and for a crazy moment, Duane was reminded of elementary school, of all the times smaller, scrappier kids had picked fights with him in order to prove themselves, the kind of bullying no one talked about. Because you didn't feel bad for the big kid who got bullied. Only the little ones. When the big ones got treated worse because everyone thought they could take it.

Weezer was grinning at him now, his deep chortling and jeering yellow eyes like the mean-spirited little bastards who had made Duane's grade school days such a living hell.

Duane thrust his arms up and bucked with his midsection as hard as he could. The movement was forceful enough to compel Weezer forward, his hairy genitalia passing an inch over Duane's face. Duane made to rise, but his right arm failed him. He collapsed on his side. Weezer reached for him, and Duane made to crawl underneath one of the moving horses when something bumped his shoulder. He figured it was one of the unconscious kid's feet, but no, the kid was ten feet away at least. As Weezer's talons closed on Duane's ankle, Duane swivelled his head and saw it was the machete he'd bumped. He threw out his left hand to grab the machete, but

Weezer jerked his leg back, yanked Duane's body away from the weapon.

Weezer fell on him, opened his stinking, slavering maw wide, and lowered to within inches of Duane's face.

"*Taste death, Short Pump,*" Weezer croaked.

"Not yet, asshole," Duane answered and bit down on Weezer's bottom lip.

Weezer gasped, jerked away, but Duane refused to relinquish his hold. The smell was rancid, eye-watering, but Duane held on, clenched his teeth harder. Weezer screamed, a high-pitched, keening scream, and the lip began to tear free of his face. Duane shoved him away. Weezer tumbled off, garbling in some anguished, alien language. Duane clambered toward the machete, grasped its handle, pushed to his feet.

Weezer was on his feet too, and he was clutching his spraying lip, the blood wet and red and everywhere, and his eyes shot up to fasten on Duane's. But Duane was already letting loose with a backhanded stroke, the machete slicing through Weezer's throat, freezing him, opening a sluice gate of scarlet, the rills lapping over Weezer's chest, Weezer's eyes goggling down at himself.

Duane swung the machete at the side of Weezer's neck, the blade chunking in diagonally, but before Weezer could grab the machete, Duane yanked it away, circled his stunned opponent. Weezer was choking on his own blood, coughing and spattering the carousel horses with happy red paint. Duane cut loose with another swing, this one so powerful the machete sank completely into the back of Weezer's neck. Weezer staggered forward, the machete lodged in his neck, his blood gushing all over the metal platform. Duane followed him, intent on ending this right fucking now. Weezer's knees clunked down on the soupy metal surface, but Duane caught him before he tumbled forward.

"Like to hurt little kids now?" Duane heard himself shouting. "Like to eat them, you motherfucking cretin? Well, how about *this*?" He planted a foot on Weezer's shoulder, got hold of the slick machete handle and pushed Weezer forward until the blade slurped loose. Weezer's face gonged against the bloody metal platform. Duane realised he was getting a little sick from the constant revolving motion of the carousel, but he made himself shuffle up beside Weezer's sprawled body, raise the machete again and tear down at Weezer's gore-streaked neck. The blow separated most of the remaining tissue, but he wanted to be sure, so he hacked down three more times until there could be no doubt, until the head lay four inches away from the rest of Weezer's neck. Out of breath, Duane reared back and punted the head, which careened off one of the outer bars and went skittering into the grass. A moment later, Duane staggered off the carousel and just missed falling forward onto his face. He stood there for a moment, eyes closed, chest heaving, the machete clutched at his side. Then he opened his eyes and saw the children and his second-grade teacher clustered around him, their eyes wide and staring.

Duane swallowed. "Hey, Miss Hayward," he said, panting and bending over with his hands on his knees. When she only gaped at him, he said, "Are you still Miss Hayward? Or did you get married? I never asked."

She didn't answer. Duane decided that was okay.

He didn't really give a shit anyway.

CHAPTER THIRTY-FOUR

The blond werewolf punched through the metal on the fourth attempt.

On the floor, Savannah had a good five feet of clearance from its grasp, but the flimsy metal of the elevator car wouldn't hold the werewolf off for long. And the car itself was not moving. How the werewolf had managed to brook its progress she had no idea, but the stark truth now staring her in the face was that she'd die if she didn't escape the car soon. She had thirty seconds, probably less, before the werewolf dropped down into the car with her.

She scuttled over to the control board and jabbed the 1 button, thinking she'd activate the elevator's downward motion again. But though the button lit up, the action accomplished nothing; the car didn't even tremor.

Savannah jammed the button to open the doors and cried out with relief as they began to move. But her first glimpse of what lay on the other side caused her excitement to curdle, and what was more, the doors ceased opening after revealing a ten-inch aperture.

There was open black space at her feet, the gap there up to her ankles. From her ankles to her tummy there appeared multiple strata of building materials: drywall, plywood, a thick gunmetal-coloured layer that might have been the cooling duct, then the sub-floor and floor of what she assumed was the fourth level of the Devil's Lair.

Savannah stared at the narrow gap and felt her heartbeat slamming harder and harder. She took hold of the elevator doors, attempted to prise them apart, but they didn't budge at all.

Then she'd just have to squirm through the opening as it was. Savannah slid her arms through the gap at chest level, turned her head sideways to make it through the narrow aperture, then pushed off as hard as she could to lift herself through.

Her breasts wedged painfully against the door; she cursed how much nursing Jake for the first two years of his life had enlarged them. Who gave a damn if men found her boobs attractive? Practically speaking, they were a pain in the ass, two leaden volleyballs she had to lug around constantly. And now it appeared they might get her killed.

Baring her teeth, she pushed up harder, but the moment her nipples scraped beyond the rubber edges of the door, the elevator car gave a violent lurch, and she found herself lifted off her feet, tossed upward, then caught again. The car was descending.

She was about to be chopped in half.

With a gagging scream, she thrust backward into the car, and a split second later the car jerked downward another three feet. The upper passage through the elevator doors – the one leading to the fourth floor of the Devil's Lair – was completely gone.

Rough fingers seized her hair, yanked her upward.

Savannah shrieked, but the sound was cut off when her head collided with the jagged split metal of the ceiling. She felt icy fire spread through her scalp, the hair tearing free, the sharp metal digging grooves in her skin. She grasped the werewolf's hand, which felt as large as a baseball glove, and sank her nails into the tough, leathery flesh. Rather than relinquishing its hold on her hair, the werewolf jerked up again, the concussion even more severe this time, a glancing blow against the vicious metal flaps that ploughed trenches through her scalp, sent smouldering rivulets of blood streaming down her forehead. Savannah battered at the werewolf's hand, but it did no good, the creature's grip as implacable as it was cruel. Savannah began scissoring her legs, screaming, flailing like a berserker against the monstrous grip, and as it yanked her up a third time, she felt vast clumps of her hair tearing out by the roots. As her bloodied scalp rammed the metal flaps for the third time, her weight finally separated her from the werewolf's grip, and though the pain in her torn scalp was exquisite, she cried aloud with joy when she thumped down on the elevator car floor.

The roar from above her made her teeth chatter.

Another hole appeared in the ceiling, this one horribly close to the first one, and as Savannah watched, a miasmal dread spreading through her, the werewolf set to smashing the tendril of metal between the two punctures.

Savannah clambered toward the slim gap in the doors. The car seemed to have stabilised, but even if it did lurch down again, remaining in the car was madness. As she shoved herself through the ten-inch aperture, she saw, peripherally, the metal tendril split open, the oval hole in the ceiling now a foot long.

It was still too narrow to accommodate the beast's girth, but the werewolf would widen the gap. She had to escape.

Savannah gritted her teeth, drove with all her leg strength and moaned as her breasts cleared the doors. Then her tummy was scraping through.

A shriek of rending metal above her. Savannah didn't need to turn to know the werewolf had widened the hole.

She'd reached the place where her hips were the main concern, and before Savannah could get wedged within the gap again, she braced her hands on the smooth outer surface of the doors and thrust against them, her neck and head straining into the third floor corridor to free her hips from the doors' embrace.

The werewolf snarled, and she knew from the sound it had spotted her below, that it knew she was making progress in her escape.

Or perhaps, she amended, *reprieve* was the more appropriate word.

No. She *would* get away, would get through this gap, dammit, because she *had* to, had to escape this nightmare alive, had to live to see Jake grow into a man.

She wouldn't leave him without a mother.

It was this prospect that galvanised her, that compelled her forward. She thrust against the grip of the doors, and then her hips were squeezing through, her sundress tearing. Her pelvis scraped against the doors, her upper thighs. She was making it out!

Behind her, the werewolf thumped down into the car.

Savannah's eyes shot wide, her breath freezing in her throat. Frantically, she wriggled away from the doors, her movements increasingly unfettered, the reality of her exposed calves, her vulnerable bare feet too ghastly to consider. Any moment she'd feel the searing talons rake down the length of her ankles, feel the agony of razor teeth shredding her toes.

Savannah's calves scraped through. She jerked her feet toward her just as something grabbed for her right foot. Gasping, Savannah scrambled to her feet and pelted down the corridor.

This was the zombie floor, she remembered, the level during which the Devil's Lair became downright scary. But she could deal with anything as long as the werewolf was stuck in the—

The werewolf let loose with a deafening roar. She chanced a look over her shoulder, saw the beast's hateful face shoved through the elevator doors. Its claws were grasping the doors, grinding them slowly but inexorably apart, and in moments the beast would be through.

Savannah pounded around the corner and almost smashed into the black door beneath yet another red exit sign. She put a hand on the knob and had started to turn it before she realised something was terribly amiss. For one thing, it wouldn't budge. For another...

The crimson light was faint, but her eyes had pretty well adjusted to the near darkness of the corridor. She noticed how the door was bowed in the middle, had been bent out of shape near the knob. She took a step back to examine the damage, and her bare foot squelched in some viscous substance she knew was blood despite how black it appeared in the gloom. Goddammit! The blond werewolf – or one of the others – had twisted the door out of shape, almost certainly to prevent its victims from escaping. There was no getting through this way.

Savannah spun and sprinted back the way she'd come, for a moment darting past the corridor leading to the elevator. The brief glimpse she caught of the blond werewolf showed her it had almost made it through the double doors, would soon be running her down like a defenceless animal.

No! She dashed past the corridor, followed the curving walkway to the left, and though her bloody feet slipped a few times on the smooth wood of the floor, she felt as though she'd never sprinted so fast, was beginning to believe she might outrun the beast.

A growling figure lunged from between red curtains and nearly landed on her. Savannah squealed, ducked and skidded on her knees before she realised it was a fake zombie, just some fucking mannequin cooked up by the Devil's Lair designers to scare the bejesus out of people.

"*Fuck you!*" she screamed at it, and then she was on her feet again, racing around a tight corner, only jumping a little as another zombie flopped out. Ahead, the hallway forked, and Savannah took a left, thinking it would lead to a down-trending ramp, the path that would eventually deliver her to the second floor. Then, if she could reach the stairwell, or even follow the corridors to the first floor, she might—

Pitch blackness ahead. *Oh shit*, she thought. A dead end. She was about to turn when a group of zombies flailed out at her, a half-dozen screaming mannequins, and despite herself she shrieked again, then balled her fists and shook them at the stupid fucking zombies, who'd not only succeeded in making her piss herself in terror, but who'd likely coerced her into announcing her exact position to her pursuer.

Cringing, she wheeled back the way she'd come, scampered toward the fork in the hallway, and glimpsed the werewolf only thirty feet to her right.

It spotted her, the yellow eyes flashing in triumph.

But as it surged ahead, one of the zombies who'd scared the crap out of her came screaming out of the darkness at the blond werewolf. And though Savannah wouldn't have believed it possible, the werewolf recoiled, startled. It straightened, roared, and as Savannah took off again through the nearly lightless tunnel, she saw it swipe ferociously at the zombie mannequin, the undead rubber head tumbling off as neatly as a snipped rose.

Savannah heard the clatter of the werewolf's toenails as it rumbled toward the forked corridor, but she was already rounding another corner, this time realising with a surge of hope that she'd chosen correctly, that she only needed one more turn to make it to the ramp leading downward to the second floor. There, she could either continue her dire flight through hallways fraught with vampires, werewolves and other fake beasts, or risk taking the more direct route, the stairwell leading straight down to the ground floor.

The werewolf raced on behind her, but Savannah was flying now, her legs pumping as though she engaged in this sort of activity all the time, moving faster than she had since high school. She rounded a corner and pelted down a long ramp, and within moments she was hustling through the archway of the second level.

There was an exit sign ahead.

Savannah darted toward it, felt her stomach clench in dread at the prospect of this door also being mangled beyond functionality, then twisted the knob and felt its weight swing freely open, a flood of surprise surging through her.

Savannah paused under the exit sign and debated whether to take the carnage-strewn stairwell or brave the monster-filled second floor.

Savannah lurched through the door and pulled it shut behind her.

She'd had enough of werewolves for one night.

★   ★   ★

Two more shooters materialised to Melody's right, and though she heard children's voices and was momentarily heartened that they'd survived, the shooters opened fire anyway, spraying the air with bullets, risking not only her life but the lives of the survivors who were now emerging from their hiding places all over Beach Land. Hot torrents of rage washed over her at sight of the shooters, these men not cops and therefore even less cautious than the cops had been. These men were her classmates, Colton Crane and Randy Murray, and they were firing at her so wildly they might as well have been drunkards playing a video game.

Melody hustled past the Turtle Cove rides, hurdled the gate enclosing the Viking ship, and then the Devil's Lair loomed over her, shadowed her, and as the bullets pinged off its stone façade, Melody hurried into the darkness beside the building.

And promptly encountered a policeman.

There was no avoiding it this time, not unless the cop decided to give her the chance to—

But no, he was already levelling his gun, was pointing it at her face, and as it spat its yellow fire Melody lashed out, removing the gun and the hand that gripped it, the blood jetting over her face as the report of the pistol pummeled her sensitive eardrums. From behind her came a shout, and Melody knew the two classmates who'd chased her were about to open fire. She didn't want this one-handed, gape-mouthed cop to get caught in the crossfire, didn't want to end his life because, as foolhardy as he was, he'd only been trying to do his duty. She bounded to her left, toward the stone walls of the castle, and a huge white object filled her vision – a propane cylinder. She leaped away as the bullets whined, hoping she'd gotten away from it in time, but then the propane tank exploded, the flames billowing out in a rolling maelstrom, and the cop whose hand she'd torn off was incinerated, the classmates who'd fired at her were blasted back, and Melody herself was propelled high into the air, the flames blistering her back, scorching the hair and skin off her shoulders, her ass, and she continued outward, her arms and legs pinwheeling, the brown water of the bay racing toward her. Melody splashed under, the lake water instantly soothing her roasted flesh, and though her ears rang from the earth-rattling explosion, she hoped she would live through it.

As for her classmates, the two idiots who'd blown up the propane tank...

Underwater, Melody's lips curled into a snarl.

★   ★   ★

My God, Savannah realised. *I might actually make it out alive.*

As she'd expected, the stairwell was a nightmare reel of gore and mayhem, the body count in the dozens.

At least the stairs were better illuminated than the rest of the Devil's Lair. It was still dim here, but state safety codes likely prohibited the same stygian gloom that enshrouded the rest of the castle from enveloping this route. Savannah tried not to think about the bloody goulash through which her feet were sloshing, tried not to fixate on the staring eyes and the plum-coloured intestines strung across the steps like moist Christmas garland. Savannah navigated the landing without issue, but nearly plunged headlong down the stairs when she slipped on a puddle of blood that appeared to issue out of a young man's severed head.

Above her, the second-storey door banged open.

But she was well ahead of the werewolf and still making good progress. She heard the thudding clatter of the beast's feet above her, but she could see, below and to her left, the door that would lead to the holding area.

Savannah was halfway down the last flight of stairs when the Devil's Lair seemed to shift sideways and the body parts underfoot to reanimate.

A shrieking boom shook the world.

She experienced a weightless moment of shock, the vertiginous sensation of floating in bare space, and then she was bumping down the steps knees first, her bare flesh cracking against the merciless concrete edges, their impacts like hammerblows to her kneecaps. Savannah groped desperately for the railing, but it was slick with blood, and she was tilting sideways, nearly to the bottom now, her useless right arm choosing this inopportune moment to awaken, to reach out to pad her fall, and then her entire weight came down on her broken arm, the pain a titanic, soul-destroying burst of white light, and when she rolled onto her back she beheld the werewolf at the top of the stairs, the yellow eyes like hellfire, the satanic leer pronouncing her life over, her pitiful existence expunged.

"*No*," she moaned. She rolled over on her side. Above her she sensed the werewolf gathering for its leap down the stairs. But as she crawled toward the door, she smelled something new, something acrid and penetrating, something patently out of place in this corpse-choked stairwell.

Smoke. Curling in pale wisps under the door.

The werewolf sprang.

Savannah clambered forward, the smoke insinuating itself into her nostrils, making her eyes water, her throat itch.

The beast hit the wet concrete six feet behind her, its momentum carrying it forward into the cinderblock wall. Savannah made it to the door, scrambled over the heaped bodies, reached out, twisted the knob.

Scraping, clittering behind her. The werewolf was scrambling toward her.

Savannah dove through the doorway, the air at her feet whickering with the swipe of the werewolf's claws. She pushed to her feet, shambled into the holding area, past the elevator doors.

Behind her the stairwell door whooshed open. She heard the werewolf surge toward her.

Savannah limped ahead, straining against the pain, pleading with her legs to move, move, move. The bright lights of the broad thoroughfare blinded her, but she hobbled toward them, humming deep in her throat. She emerged from the castle.

Behind her the werewolf barreled closer.

★   ★   ★

A shockwave of sound and heat flattened Duane.

Blinking, the trees and lights overhead swimming, splitting, reforming, Duane strove to recover his senses. Something terrible had happened behind the Devil's Lair, some explosion that had almost certainly taken more lives. It had come from the exact place where the brown werewolf and the shooters – Colton Crane and Randy Murray? – had gathered. Duane didn't give a shit about Colton and Randy; they were thoughtless assholes who deserved little better. But the brown werewolf...there'd been something familiar about it. Something different from the others he'd encountered tonight.

And there was still the matter of Savannah's whereabouts.

It was this thought that got Duane moving. He opened his eyes, and though the world still swirled in a sickly, blurred kaleidoscope and his ears felt as though they'd been stuffed with gauze, he was able to roll over onto his stomach and push to his feet.

Where he swayed, yawed to the right, and promptly landed on his side.

His right side, of course, and his injured right hand. He didn't need to glance at the severed fingers to know the wounds had begun to leak again. Damn, it hurt. But there was no time for that now. Because something had happened...something near the bay...

Duane gained his feet again and this time took it easier, his arms extended as though he were treading on a balance beam rather than flat concrete.

He limped toward the luminous main thoroughfare, but he'd only advanced a few steps when he realised how surreal the area between the Viking ship and the Devil's Lair appeared. Smoke was skirling there and growing thicker, and he distinguished a shape shambling through the misty air, the person injured and wearing...

Jesus Christ, he thought. *Savannah*.

Duane broke into an awkward run. He reached down for the machete but realised he'd dropped it at some point, likely when he'd been levelled by the explosion. He opened his mouth to hail her, but the smoke he sucked down irritated his throat, sent him off on a ragged series of wet coughs. Goddammit, of all the times to be doubled over, to be incapacitated by something as simple as smoke. Though the coughing fit refused to loose its hold on him, he compelled his body forward, toward Savannah's lurching form.

Another figure emerged from the Devil's Lair. An enormous figure. Savannah went down. The blond beast surged out of the darkness and made straight for her. It would arrive there well before Duane would. He urged his legs to move faster, horribly aware of how fruitless it was. Savannah had survived until the end, but now the queen beast was looming over her, preparing to kill.

Then something drew its gaze. It remained hulking over Savannah, its great body heaving with exertion and what might have been frustration. Duane kept moving toward them, but he too saw what had arrested the blond beast's attention.

The brown werewolf.

It climbed out of the bay, its eyes like glittering amber diamonds. It was glaring not at the men who'd been trying to shoot it – Duane discovered that Colton Crane and Randy Murray had survived the blast, though both men were struggling to stand – but at the blond beast hunched over Savannah.

Duane realised he'd stopped, had been standing there like an idiot while Savannah's life hung in the balance. He pushed forward again, and though he felt worse than ever – had he sustained a concussion when he was hurled backward by the blast? – he knew this was it, this was the endgame. If he failed now, Savannah would die, and he would almost certainly be killed as well.

Limping toward the strange tableau, he made a cursory scan of the ground between him and the blond werewolf, but if there was anything of use there, it was shrouded by the veil of white smoke.

Only ten yards away now.

He had just about resolved to drop-kick the yellow werewolf in the face like some flabby Caucasian Bruce Lee when the beast suddenly bounded forward, abandoning Savannah and roaring loudly enough to turn Duane's blood to ice water.

He'd just reached Savannah when the brown wolf rocketed forward too.

"Duane?" a croaky voice said.

He looked down at Savannah, saw her sweaty, blood-streaked face peering up at him. He dropped to his knees, cradled her head, but had to stifle a gasp of horror at how ravaged her scalp was, how mangled her right elbow.

"Hey, just take it easy," he said, gathering her closer. "Don't worry about any—"

But the rest was cut off by a howl of agony.

*   *   *

When she emerged from the water and spotted the bitch towering over Savannah Summers, Melody's body was gripped with a pulsing black hatred.

This creature, Melody thought as she rose to her full height, was the cause of untold suffering, of bloodshed and heartbreak and families torn asunder. Babies had died because of the yellow menace. Sucklings ripped forcibly from the teat, the unborn savagely torn from their mothers' wombs. The young, the elderly. Writ on the yellow wolf's face were the epitaphs of a thousand innocent victims, the life-shattering laments of mothers and fathers.

It would end tonight.

The yellow wolf darted toward her, but Melody was ready for the charge. Melody lowered to all fours, but just before their heads came together like rival rams in some rural pasture, the yellow wolf veered to the side, back talons flashing.

Pain as cold as hoarfrost erupted along Melody's shoulder, and she made the mistake of turning her head to mark the yellow wolf's passing.

For the creature's preternatural agility had allowed it to plant, to reverse its progress even as Melody was registering the pain in her shoulder. The yellow wolf sprang upon Melody, its heavily muscled body crashing down on her back, and the killing fangs sank into her shoulders. The forepaws slashed down the length of her arms, ribboning the furry flesh, exposing tendon and sinew. Yelping, Melody flopped down to dislodge the snarling queen, but she realised her error immediately, understood that this was what the queen had wanted, to prostrate her so she could reach the tender throat. The queen lunged, but before the jaws could close on her neck, Melody thrust up an arm, felt the horrible teeth sink in. The fangs scraped bone, began to crunch through, and before Melody lost the use of her limb completely, she clawed at the queen with her free hand, exulted at the scarlet furrows she opened on the side of her face. The queen roared, relinquished her hold on Melody's forearm.

For an instant, their eyes met. One of the queen's eyes, Melody saw, was clotted with gore. It still glared at Melody, but the gaze was compromised, the yellow crusted by a dark maroon cataract.

The queen's good eye blazed down at Melody, hypnotising her.

You're mine, the eye said. *Like all the others, like the many wolves who have served and died, you belong to me.*

With a sickening jolt, Melody realised the queen was grinning.

In that grin she discerned traces of Father Bridwell, of Donny and John and Robbie. The black wolf, the one Melody had faced – and slain – at the entrance of the park…it had stared at her in the same mocking way. It was the way *everyone* looked at her. Her family. Her classmates. The men who leered at her around town.

The yellow face darted for her throat, but this time Melody brought her head up, smashed her forehead into the queen's nose. The queen's body jolted with shock, and in that brief instant Melody realised the queen's good eye had gone foggy with pain.

And in that moment Melody struck. Her long, scythelike teeth sank into the queen's throat, the queen's lifeblood flooding Melody's mouth, spraying her tongue and pooling in the back of her mouth. Melody swallowed, tore, and as the huge gobbet of neck meat slapped down on the concrete beside them, Melody plunged her maw deeper into the gaping red cavity in the queen's throat. Melody burrowed inside the queen, her four limbs wrapped tightly around her prey, their bodies mashed together like passionate lovers, and around Melody the queen's ancient limbs danced in a mindless paroxysm of horror, the unthinkable occurring, this newborn progeny ending her reign and claiming her throne.

Melody champed and tore until only a few strands of skin and gristle connected the great head to the giant body. And then she heaved the body over, keeping hold of the head, and when the head came free, she flung it aside disdainfully.

Melody's chest burned with fury and exaltation. She stood on her hind legs and bayed into the night.

And squalled as the bullets pierced her body.

★ ★ ★

"NO!" Duane bellowed.

But the idiots were already opening up again, Colton Crane firing a big black handgun and Randy Murray squeezing the trigger of a revolver that looked like something out of a Clint Eastwood western. The first barrage had cut off the victorious werewolf's howl and spun it around to face its new attackers; the second flurry of shots had knocked the werewolf down and sent it into a series of shrill, doglike wails.

Duane started forward, but Savannah seized him by the shirt.

"*What are you doing?*" she demanded.

He shook his head. "Don't know."

But he did know. Because even before the two werewolves had slammed together like snarling tides, he'd glimpsed the person behind the brown wolf's feral countenance.

Melody Bridwell. He knew it was Melody.

Despite the corona of wiry hair reefing its face, despite the fact that this beast was far taller than Melody and weighed easily twice as much, despite the yellow jack-o'-lantern eyes and the oversize white rapiers gleaming from its mouth...

Beneath all of it he detected the suffering.

The werewolf writhed on the pavement, its wounds spurting blood.

Melody.

Colton Crane and Randy Murray were advancing, Colton with his black gun still extended, Randy fumbling in his pockets for more bullets.

In the distance, Duane heard voices. The wail of sirens.

Though Duane and Savannah were equidistant from the shooters and the werewolf, it was toward the werewolf that Duane sprinted. Behind him Savannah shouted his name, but all Duane could see was the spreading pool of blood, the glaze of manic glee in the shooters' eyes. Randy was reloading now, Colton lowering his weapon toward the werewolf's head, apparently meaning to shoot it at close range.

"Stop!" Duane shouted. He was almost there, but Colton's gaze was fixed on the werewolf's face.

"Don't shoot her," Duane yelled, nearing them. "It's Melody."

The words must have broken through the shell of bloodlust encasing the two men. Randy blinked at Duane.

But Colton raised his eyebrows and said, "What in the blue fuck are you talking about?"

The chorus of sirens drew nearer. Several voices called out.

"Melody Bridwell," Duane panted as he moved up next to the prone figure.

Colton shook his head dismissively. "You're a moron, Duane." He aimed the gun.

"Wait a second," Randy said.

"Wait for what?" Colton answered. His finger on the trigger.

"Please don't shoot," Duane said.

Melody's eyes were closed, her movements weakening. Duane felt a dull throb at his temples, a sick roiling in his gut.

"It *is* her," Randy said in a hushed voice.

"Is who?"

"Melody."

Colton glared at Randy, then shifted his gaze to Duane.

"Look at her face," Duane said.

Colton did.

Randy nodded slowly. "Uh-huh. I'd recognise that whore anywhere."

Melody's eyes shot open.

"Holy sh—" Colton began, but her hand shot out, snagged his pant leg. She yanked him off his feet, and the gun went off. Sparks flew off the pavement to Duane's immediate left, and he backpedalled instinctively.

Randy raised his gun, but it trembled, and then Melody was launching herself toward him, removing his face with a well-aimed swipe. Her talons flashed again, again, and then Randy's head was skidding across the smoky walkway.

Colton got up, took a couple ungainly strides toward Turtle Cove, but Melody hurtled toward him, rode him down, attacked the back of his neck, her face a blurring snarl, and then he too lay in pieces, his body on its stomach, his head facing Duane.

Melody rose, faced Duane.

"Oh shit," he whispered.

He heard Savannah shout something, the slaps of her footsteps approaching from behind. Her head down, her yellow eyes blazing, Melody charged at him, a nightmarish brown wraith cleaving through the cloud of smoke. Melody leaped, her dark form arcing gracefully.

Then Melody came down, pinning Duane with one hand and Savannah with the other.

Melody's lips writhed, her teeth flecked with blood. Slaver drooled out of her mouth, collected on Duane's trembling lips. *No,* he thought. Melody twitched her head toward Savannah, and more saliva pooled over Savannah's face. Duane heard a growl deep in Melody's throat.

He swallowed, waited for the end.

Melody's eyes fixed on his. She stared at him for a long time.

Then her eyes widened, the change almost undetectable.

But he'd seen it.

Duane stared up at her.

Voices sounded from behind them, demanding any survivors to show themselves. The warbling scream of sirens filled the night air.

Melody watched Duane, her yellow eyes unblinking.

Without warning, Melody wheeled and bounded away, her lithe form disappearing into the smoke. Duane gaped after her, listened for gunshots. He heard none, but a moment later there was a splashing sound, something large hitting the water of the bay.

Beside him, Savannah was coughing.

"Come on," he said. He helped her to her feet, led her toward the boardwalk. Here the smoke was only a faint haze, but his throat still burned with it. As they moved down the boardwalk, Savannah helped support him.

"Where are we going?"

He coughed, ground a palm into his watering eyes. "My truck."

Savannah glanced back toward the burning castle. "Shouldn't we—"

"Risk getting shot?" he said.

They continued on. When they neared the suspension bridge, she asked, "Won't there be police here too?"

"Police I'm not worried about," he said, limping up the ramp. "It's the assholes like Colton and Randy that scare me."

They reached the suspension bridge, distinguished six or seven shell-shocked faces staring out over the water. Farther away but coming toward them fast were firemen, paramedics. Another cop, this one a woman of maybe forty.

"Keep moving," he said. "They've got too much on their minds to worry about us."

"Maybe you're right," she said, eyeing the approaching figures. "If we get hung up here, it'll take longer to get to Jake."

The firemen and others dashed past them with hardly a glance. As they neared the end of the suspension bridge, Savannah said, "What if that... what if Melody is still around?"

Duane cast a glance at the bay, the water even darker than the inky night sky. He shook his head. "We've got nothing to fear from her."

Savannah grunted. "Tell that to Colton and Randy."

CHAPTER THIRTY-FIVE

Duane drove them toward town, acutely aware of how silent the countryside was. He was surprised they made it past all the ambulances and fire trucks, but then again, those weren't the same as police cars, were they? And most of the police force from Lakeview, from the county, from the nearby state police post had been slaughtered by the werewolves.

He frowned. What if he and Savannah weren't safe yet? What if they were making a mistake?

Duane thought of Melody, her bristling brown hair, her fierce expression. There'd been a moment when he was sure she'd kill him.

But she hadn't. And wouldn't. He didn't know why he was certain of this, but he was. They had nothing left to fear. At least, Savannah didn't.

As for Duane...

He shoved the thought away, concentrated on the road. They were maybe two minutes from town.

"So how did you get it?" Savannah asked.

Duane glanced at her.

"The nickname," she explained.

"Ah," he said. "That."

She watched him.

He shifted in his seat, made to put his right hand on the wheel, but winced when he remembered how it had been maimed. He caught a brief glimpse at the stumps where his middle three fingers had been severed and quickly looked away, his heart slamming.

With his left hand on the wheel, he said, "It'll be pretty anticlimactic."

She shrugged. "Most of life is."

He glanced out over the countryside, saw hints of Savannah's subdivision beyond the cornfield. He felt a pang of longing in his chest and forced himself to ignore it.

"We took a road trip one summer. Glenn, Weezer and I."

"The one to Virginia Beach?"

He grunted. "It was supposed to be. We planned on spending a week on the coast, but we only ended up getting as far as Williamsburg."

"Run out of money?"

"Weezer was broke halfway through Ohio. We were only eighteen, but we somehow got into a titty bar. Weezer emptied his checking account at the ATM and spent all his cash getting lap dances."

"Sounds like Weezer."

Duane scowled, feeling no fondness for his friend's memory. None at all. "On the way to Virginia, we came across a bunch of weird town names. Stubbville. Camp Slaughter. Roscoe—"

"And Short Pump."

Smiling ruefully, he nodded.

Savannah watched him. "But why did the name go to you? Why not Weezer or Glenn?"

"Well, Weezer already had a nickname, didn't he? And Glenn…well, Glenn wasn't really the type for a nickname."

"No," Savannah said. "He wasn't."

"You gonna tell Jake?" Duane heard himself asking.

Savannah looked away. "Tell him what? That his dad was a high school classmate with whom I had a one-night stand and that I didn't tell the guy about his son until he was a werewolf? That he might've died not knowing he was Jake's father?"

Duane stared moodily through the windshield. "I guess you're right."

The glow from Lakeview intensified. Thirty seconds from town now. Another minute to the police chief's office. Duane experienced a swelling in his throat.

"Duane?"

"What?" he answered, his eyes straight ahead.

They passed under the flashing yellow light, the Dairy Queen on the left. The one he and Savannah had often visited years ago. When she was struggling to get over Mike.

"You know what?" she said.

He went to rub his hand over his mouth, but when his finger stumps brushed his lips, he jerked his hand away, gritted his teeth. The turn onto Washington Street was coming up.

Gingerly, he slid his right hand into his pocket.

"You can move in with us," she said. "Tomorrow, if you want."

"Move in with you," he repeated tonelessly.

He could hear a quaver in her voice. "And we'll see how it goes."

He didn't speak. Instead activated his turn signal.

"Duane?"

He turned left, hearing approaching sirens in the distance. Coming from Highway 24. There was another state police post about thirty miles down the highway.

"Please answer me," she said.

His chest was burning, a sick lump clogging his throat. "What do you want me to say?"

"Yes? That you'd love to come live with us? That you'd be what Jake has never had before?"

"A plump, lovable nanny?"

She swatted him in the arm. "Goddammit, Duane, what do you want me to say? I'm sorry for the way I treated you, all right?"

"You've got nothing to be sorry about."

"Stop the passive-aggressive bullshit."

The turn onto Illinois Street neared. Two blocks to the police station.

"I mean it, Savannah," he said, his tone subdued. "You feel how you feel. It's not a bad thing or a good thing. It's just—"

"It is what it is," she said. "I hate that fucking saying."

"You're cussing a lot."

"So? It feels good to cuss."

"You don't think of me that way," he said, angling the Silverado onto the deserted street.

"It was different," she said, a trace of panic stitching her voice.

He looked at her.

"In the elevator tonight," she explained. "In the Devil's Lair. On the way up to the top, I kept thinking about you. About how we rode in it together. I...I missed you."

"No one ever said you don't care about me, Savannah."

He made a U-turn, pulled the pickup to a stop along the curb. Shifted the truck into park.

"I see what you're doing," she said, wiping her eyes. "You're getting even with me. You're getting revenge for all those years I never paid attention to you."

He cut the engine, turned in the seat. "Listen, Savannah."

"Go to hell," she said, looking out the passenger's window.

Duane looked too. Was Jake okay inside the station?

He thought so. When they'd made the U-turn, he'd caught a glimpse of two people inside the station, one of them a uniformed officer, the other a woman who looked like a receptionist.

Neither of them looked like werewolves.

Jake was safe inside.

Savannah had apparently come to the same conclusion. Tears dribbled down her cheeks, but she seemed in no hurry to get out of the car.

"Savannah, I don't know how to..." He sighed. "You ever watch romantic comedies?"

She glared at him. "Why? Because I'm a girl, and all girls love chick flicks?"

He waited.

She looked away. "Yes, I watch them."

"You like them?" he asked.

"And you don't, I suppose. Because you're a big, tough man, and men don't like that mushy crap."

He chuckled softly. "It doesn't have anything to do with that."

"Just get it over with, Duane. Stop trying to let me down easy."

He smiled sadly at her, scratched the back of his neck. "I sort of do like some of them. A couple of my favourite movies are romantic comedies."

She swivelled her head toward him, suspicion plain in her narrowed eyes.

"It's true," he said. "But most of them are really bad."

She rolled her eyes. "Of course."

"Not because they're not well made or because they're poorly acted… though now that I think about it, quite a few of them are poorly made and poorly acted."

"*Duane.*"

"But the point is, the reason I don't like most of them has nothing to do with the acting or the direction."

She studied his face. "So…what? You don't believe in love?"

"Quite the opposite," he said. "I believe in love more than anyone I know. But it has to be the right kind of love."

She continued to watch him, something dawning in her blue eyes.

"The problem with most of those films is the belief that there has to be a tidy, upbeat ending. That the two main characters have to wind up together."

"There are movies where they don't."

"But most of the time they do."

"What's your point?"

He leaned toward her. "That most of the time, they *shouldn't*. That being attractive or funny or whatever isn't a reasonable basis for spending the rest of their lives together."

"Duane—"

"You care about me, Savannah, I know that. And if I were somebody else, or you were somebody else, maybe we could end up together, and that would be the right thing."

"I'm not talking about getting married tomorrow, Duane."

"I know you're not, but there's a whole lot neither one of us is saying. That maybe, in time, you can learn to look past the fact that you're not attracted to me."

"You don't know how I feel."

"I know you've never looked at me the way you used to look at Mike. Or even Glenn."

"Low blow."

"Savannah, it's—"

"About sex, isn't it? That's what it comes down to. You're just like—"

"No one, Savannah. I'm like no one and you know it. Now stop steering the argument in that direction. I'm talking about romantic love, which, without the sex or not, is a part of marriage. Or should be. And while I've pined away for you like a lovelorn puppy for the better part of two decades—"

"Duane—"

"—you've never felt the same thing for me."

"That's not fair!"

"It's not a put-down, Savannah. It's the cold truth. And saying otherwise only delays the inevitable."

"And what's that?"

"That I'll be your friend for as long as I can."

She drew back from him, a hurt, frightened look on her face. "What are you saying?"

He opened his mouth, then thought, *No, don't be too nice. Hurting her now will be better than the alternative. Having been on the other end of this sort of thing your whole life, you should sure as hell know that.*

"Duane?" she asked, her eyes shining. "What are you telling me?"

He straightened in his seat, nodded toward the glass front doors, where the uniformed officer was now standing, watching them. "You need to get in there with your boy."

"But you're coming with me, right? You have to come in."

Duane stared out the windshield, unable to meet her gaze.

"Duane?"

"I'll see you soon, Savannah."

She made no move to leave. "Damn you, Duane, I need to know what's happening."

Duane couldn't look at her. "Go to your boy. He needs you."

She was watching him, but she wasn't speaking. Peripherally, Duane noticed that the cop at the glass doors had been joined by the receptionist.

"They're waiting," he said.

She reached up, took hold of the door handle and paused. "Will Jake and I be safe?"

And then Duane finally did look at her. Looked at her and smiled at her without guile or concern. "That's one thing I can promise you, Savannah. Nothing's going to happen to you or Jake."

She glanced down at her lap, the tears welling over, pattering on her bare, scraped-up knees. She took a deep breath, let it out and opened the door. She looked back at him once, but he'd withdrawn by then and only barely glimpsed her anguished expression. The door closed with a thud that Duane felt in his bones.

Savannah had hobbled halfway to the double doors before the cop and the receptionist apparently realised what a terrible state she was in. The cop came rushing out to throw an arm around her, and the receptionist appeared to call to someone over her shoulder.

Duane slid the truck into gear.

The cop was glaring at Duane through the windshield, as though Duane were the one who'd beaten Savannah up so badly, but Duane hardly noticed. He was watching the receptionist, who in turn seemed to track the approach of someone else, someone Duane fervently hoped was Jake.

It was, he saw a moment later, and that was his cue. Before the boy could spot him behind the wheel, and more importantly, before Duane could be persuaded to climb out and sweep mother and son into a joyful embrace, he eased the pickup away from the curb and was lucky enough to hit a green light when he came to Illinois Street.

He made it back to Washington, and by then, the tears had come, and he drove slowly to give them time to flow. He'd never been a big crier when he got sad – he was more the kind of guy who cried at the end of movies – but now he indulged himself a little. Goddammit, he *did* want to be Jake's stepfather, and though he'd meant what he'd said about Savannah not being attached to him in a romantic way, a part of him wondered if things had changed enough for those romantic feelings to start developing. He was a different man than he'd been a week ago, with a different outlook. He'd killed a werewolf, for chrissakes, and if that didn't show an increased sense of adventure, he didn't know what did.

But this, Duane knew, had nothing to do with self-esteem, had nothing to do with being more courageous. This was about…this was about…

The tingling in his wounds.

Ahead, sirens wailed on Beach Road. More state troopers, or maybe police from the surrounding towns. They'd soon join the fire trucks and the ambulances, and though Duane suspected the ambulances would be of little use – all the victims he'd spotted had been mutilated beyond recognition and in most cases beheaded – he hoped the fire trucks would be able to slow down the conflagration at the Devil's Lair.

A police cruiser whizzed by as he neared the turn onto Beach Road. Duane turned left to follow the cruiser, though it was going so fast it swiftly became a distant flicker of red-and-blue lights. Duane considered turning on the radio, but most of what would be on was shit. He could play his audiobook – Stephen King's fourth *Dark Tower* story – but damned if he felt like hearing about more death just now.

Instead, he thumbed down his window and leaned into the opening, the sultry summer air moistening his face. He kept it around thirty-five even after leaving the city limits because every now and then he had to pull over as another police car zoomed by. He passed the cornfield that hid Savannah's subdivision, and soon he was nearing Beach Land, which was lit up like a Parisian music festival. Above the sodium lights of the south entrance and the trees fringing the bay, he could see orange billows of smoke, the continuous strobe of multitudinous flashing lights.

But before he reached the south parking lot, he turned left.

In this direction everything was dark. The bean fields to his left, the humble cottages to his right. The forest that soon swallowed the road.

As the hellish orange sky behind him gave way to an endless navy-blue dome overhead, Duane became aware of a tingling at the base of his spine. It whispered up his vertebrae, thrummed in his shoulders. He caught his left foot drumming on the floor mat and forced it to remain still. He applied more pressure to the accelerator despite the approaching incline and the railroad tracks at the crest of the rise. The pickup was doing fifty when it launched over the tracks, and for a long moment Duane felt himself rising weightlessly toward the roof. When the truck jounced down, the front end began to yaw to his right, all four tires skidding deliriously on the lonesome strip of asphalt. Duane easily corrected the skid, motored on for another mile or so before taking his foot off the accelerator and allowing the Silverado to ease gradually to a stop.

The grassy shoulders on either side of the road were pretty much level with the asphalt, so Duane angled the pickup gently to the right until he'd completely vacated the road.

Duane slid the pickup into park and got out.

He crossed the road without checking for cars. There was no need. It was utterly deserted out here, the nearest farmhouse a half mile away.

Duane stepped into the grass and continued into the bean field.

He breathed deeply of the country air, which had never been so redolent of life, of good soil.

His shoes were drenched with sweat and blood, and besides their generally slimy feel, they felt restrictive. So he removed them, as well as his socks, and left them lying at the edge of the field. Savouring the soft earth under his feet, Duane strode slowly into the field. As he moved, he kept his eyes on the rows of beans ahead, though it was his sense of smell he primarily relied on. From the direction of Beach Land, he heard another siren shrill past, but it was so faint he didn't give it much thought. No one would be coming this way.

Duane ambled deeper into the field. He'd ventured about a hundred yards when he scented what he'd been searching for. He jogged purposefully forward, his body responding sharply to his commands. He accelerated to a sprint – a tight, efficient sprint – then he suddenly halted, his gaze avid and his flesh prickling.

He discerned footprints in the bean field.

They moved from the east – from Beach Land – to the field bordering Melody Bridwell's property.

Duane turned his back on the distant orange glow, cleared his head of the sirens. Upwind of the park, there drifted only the faintest tinge of smoke, but it still displeased him. Acrid, unwholesome.

He followed Melody's tracks.

They were spaced far apart, but they fell evenly, right foot, left foot. No palm prints, no fingerprints. She'd made her escape upright and proud. Duane recalled the look on her face just before she'd spared his life. Had it been recognition, as he suspected? Or just some residual trace of human compassion?

He didn't know.

But he knew he could never go back to Savannah and Jake, even if he wanted to.

Duane knew Melody wouldn't be in the house even before he neared the thick gravel driveway. Her scent led first to the pole barn, but a fresher trail led across the driveway to the house. He was glad to bypass the pole barn because the odour wafting out of its ugly yellow façade made him more than distrustful – it made him angry. But when he crossed to the house and caught a whiff of the death within, he was overcome with a dozen swirling emotions, almost all of them powerfully negative, though somewhere within that black, churning cloud there were glimmers of pain for Melody, a regret for the suffering she'd endured. Duane made it to the porch steps and almost went in, but before he allowed the stinking sarcophagus of the Bridwells' home to swallow him up, he was assailed by three incontrovertible certainties:

All the male Bridwells were dead.

Melody had stopped here after her escape from Beach Land.

She was gone now.

A quick sniff of the yard confirmed this. The trail was fresher here than any he'd yet scented, and it was fresher by a goodly margin. Which told him she'd lingered in the house for several minutes before moving on. Maybe he'd just missed her.

Why had she stopped here? Given the reputations of her father and her brothers, it hadn't been for sentimental reasons.

Duane opened the side door, peered in.

And gagged at what he saw. Two skeletal black dogs perched on the kitchen table, their faces buried in the remains of Melody's father. Not only did the sounds of snarling and smacking fill the kitchen, Duane thought he detected similar sounds from the basement as well.

So that's why she'd stopped here.

To feed the dogs.

Duane hurried outside and gazed hard into the distance for a large brown shape, but though his eyes worked exceptionally well given the late hour, the only things he could make out ahead were more fields, more thickets of trees.

Duane surged forward, his bare feet moulding to the grass, the road beyond, then the soft soil of the cornfield. The abrasive husks scraped his arms and face as he barreled along, but he soon learned that by ducking somewhat and charging forward in that position, he could avoid the worst of the assault.

Melody's scent grew stronger. Exhilarating, invigorating. He felt an almost sexual thrill at the idea of overtaking her.

Presently, Duane burst out of the cornfield, leapedvaulted an overgrown barbed-wire fence, and wove his way through a thicket of pine trees. Though the smell of the pines – verdant and rife with sap – made him grin with happiness and sent shivers of warm pleasure through his limbs, it was the undercurrent of Melody's passage that entranced him. He was close to her, by God. Close enough to spot her should he make his way out of this burr-ridden forest.

Soon, he did. He managed to locate a trail of sorts, and when a downed bough from one of the giant oak trees barred his way, Duane merely hurdled it, landed and sprang up again, his large girth easily clearing the barbed-wire fence separating the thicket from the next field, this one rolling and furred with knee-high wheat.

Duane advanced farther into the wheat field until he spotted the figure in the distance, the moonlight bathing its motionless form on a gentle rise between the wheat field and another forest.

Duane continued his approach, and though he didn't move cautiously, he took his time now.

The figure wasn't fleeing.

When he got within fifty yards of the figure, he realised it wasn't as large as he'd thought. Yes, there was a spray of wild brown hair surrounding the silvered moon of a face, but the figure was just a woman after all. Nude, her skin tawny and supple, Melody peered at Duane through the moonshot night, her expression betraying nothing, her posture proud, unafraid.

Duane stepped closer, closer, only twenty feet away now. He realised that Melody was very close to the forest. Only two or three strides and she could disappear within its enclosing shadows. Behind her, the wheat field seemed to stretch for miles.

Duane stopped ten feet from Melody and gazed up at her.

The silence drew out.

The verdant air around them seemed to crystallise, to bind them in its warmth, its fecundity. Duane found himself averting his eyes from her nude body, not out of embarrassment or desire, but in attempt to breathe again in the presence of her awe-inspiring beauty.

His gaze settled on his right hand.

The blood was crusted and nearly black in the moonlight, but the stumps of his missing fingers had altered. The change had been nearly imperceptible as he'd driven Savannah into town, but now there was no doubt about it at all.

The fingers had begun to regenerate. The skin there was pink, the infant nubs tender but undeniably longer than they'd been only a half hour earlier.

This surprised him, but what surprised him even more was how clear his feelings were, how powerful.

He looked up at Melody. Her eyes were riveted on his new fingers.

Something seemed to flit across her face, but it was gone before he could identify it.

Unable to stare into that ethereal face too long, Duane allowed himself to study her naked body. Unmarked, lovely. He shifted his gaze to her face so he wouldn't faint.

Her eyes were locked on his, and though her mouth didn't move at all, he was sure he could make out the ghost of a smile. She watched him unself-consciously, the wry gleam in her eyes perhaps excusing his obvious attraction to her. He opened his mouth to speak, then realised no words would be right. He would only taint their communion and the deep, moonlit night.

She raised her chin, her gaze perhaps teasing, perhaps inviting. She turned away from the forest and began walking away from him. She spared him a single backward glance, and this time the smile touched her lips as well as her eyes. She moved away through the wheat field, in no hurry at all. Duane blew out the breath he'd been holding, his eyes on the mane of brown hair, the curve of her lower back, her perfect buttocks. He began removing his shirt, his belt. He let his pants fall. He stripped off his underwear.

Then, the night air enlivening his naked body, Duane followed Melody into the pale moonlight.

ACKNOWLEDGMENTS

The first and most important individuals that helped this tale come to be are my family: my wife, my boy, and my two daughters. If you know me, you know how much they mean to me. Their love and laughter make me the happiest man alive.

Thank you also to my mom, my grandma, and my grandpa. You are amazing people who've never wavered in your support of me.

Someone else I'd like to thank is Don D'Auria, my wonderful editor at Flame Tree.

I wish I could thank all the readers and writers who have responded so positively to me and my work, but for now I'll limit it to just a few: Tim and Tod, the best pre-readers a guy could have, and who both made essential contributions to this book; Mark Sieber, for being a good friend; Kristopher Rufty, Brian Moreland, Hunter Shea, and Russell James, who have been with me from the beginning and have become cherished friends; the late and amazing Jack Ketchum/Dallas Mayr, whom I miss terribly; Tim Waggoner, another great friend; Bryan Smith, who always has time for me; Ronald Kelly, whose support has been extremely helpful to me; Jeff Strand, Paul Tremblay, and Mary SanGiovanni, who are always there to help; and Joe R. Lansdale, who is always kinder than he has to be. Lastly, I want to thank Brian Keene. I love his books and learn from them, but what I appreciate most of all is how he has treated me and my family. I can never repay all you've done for me, Brian, but I hope you know how much it has meant to me. Thank you.

FLAME TREE PRESS
FICTION WITHOUT FRONTIERS
Award-Winning Authors & Original Voices

Flame Tree Press is the trade fiction imprint of Flame Tree Publishing, focusing on excellent writing in horror and the supernatural, crime and mystery, science fiction and fantasy. Our aim is to explore beyond the boundaries of the everyday, with tales from both award-winning authors and original voices.

•

Other titles available include:
Junction by Daniel M. Bensen
Thirteen Days by Sunset Beach by Ramsey Campbell
Think Yourself Lucky by Ramsey Campbell
The Haunting of Henderson Close by Catherine Cavendish
The House by the Cemetery by John Everson
The Toy Thief by D.W. Gillespie
Black Wings by Megan Hart
The Playing Card Killer by Russell James
The Siren and the Spectre by Jonathan Janz
The Sorrows by Jonathan Janz
Savage Species by Jonathan Janz
The Nightmare Girl by Jonathan Janz
The Widening Gyre by Michael R. Johnston
Will Haunt You by Brian Kirk
Kosmos by Adrian Laing
The Sky Woman by J.D. Moyer
Creature by Hunter Shea
The Bad Neighbour by David Tallerman
Ten Thousand Thunders by Brian Trent
Night Shift by Robin Triggs
The Mouth of the Dark by Tim Waggoner

•

Join our mailing list for free short stories, new release details, news about our authors and special promotions:

flametreepress.com